first frost

Edith Darke pushes her hands deeper into her fleece against the cold, exhales a cloud of water vapour, and crunches her way down the snow-covered bank, stumbling onto the narrow path round the lake. A startled moorhen flaps its way across the ice and disappears into a dark thicket.

Edith smiles.

She's the first human to tread here this morning – not surprising given the hour – and her size-five Caterpillars leave patterned tracks behind her in the almost perfect snow. Almost perfect because, though she may be the first human being to pass this way, she's not the first creature. The sharp, pronged prints of birds crisscross the path ahead of her, lit by the glacial light of an almost full moon. And something larger. A fox, maybe? Or a small badger. Something with fat padded paws that have left deep imprints in the snow. She slips her phone from her pocket and snaps a quick pic so she can look it up later and add it to her diary. Maybe she'll ask Mrs Peters if she recognises it.

Her hands crackle in the biting cold, and the three metal studs in her right ear are aching. She's beginning to regret shaving her head quite so thoroughly yesterday. She prefers to keep it as short as possible, less hassle that way. Less chance Alice Clitherow can attach chewing gum to her in Economics and, of course, cheaper than going to a hairdresser. But maybe she should have settled for the number three guard this time, at least until the weather gets warmer. She tucks her hands back into her pockets. She could do with some gloves, and a hat maybe. But there's no way they can afford that at the moment. She moves on along the path.

When she walks, it's for the sake of walking, and she varies her route with her mood. She sets out early, sometimes 4 or 5am, and enjoys the way the landscape wakens with the dawn. Sometimes she heads west towards Bradfield. Or, if she feels like going the full distance, she'll follow the River Don as it winds its way north and west through Deepcar and towards Penistone. The river's a constant companion, stretching away towards its source deep in the Pennines. She never has the time to go all that far but one day she will, she promises herself. There's something about moving backward along the flow of a river that makes her feel as though she's travelling through time, walking into history, greeting the water as it barrels towards her on its endless journey.

This morning though, she settles for a quick circuit of Damflask Reservoir. She's been here a lot lately but given the snow will slow her down, it makes sense to pick a shorter route than some of the others she could choose. She can't afford to be late to school. Not again. And there's the dark to consider. The reservoir is better lit than the river, the silvery moonlight reflecting off the vast expanse of water and the cold blue blanket of snow.

This is *her* time. The small part of the day she carves out for herself, away from responsibility. For the rest of the day, people will want things from her. Her mother, her teachers, even Alice Clitherow. She has many roles to play and she knows them all well. But this short window of opportunity at the start of each day is just for her, a couple of hours before her mother wakes and calls out in pain – real or imagined, Edith isn't sure anymore.

Now she's off the main road though, she's beginning to rethink her choice. It's becoming a chore just to lift each foot and put it down again in front of her. She doesn't think she'll get much farther before she's forced to turn back.

The gunshot, when it comes, cracks loudly across the lake, startling a number of birds into flight. Edith stops still, the hair raised on the back of her neck and arms, her heart beating in her chest as she listens to the echo fade. Birdsong slowly returns to fill the empty space left behind. She knows what a gunshot sounds like. She has grown up around farms. It has a distinctive, deep crack, not at all like a car backfiring, like they're always saying on those old cop shows her mother watches all the time. Edith's not even sure what a car backfiring is. No, it was a gunshot, she's positive. She glances round, unsure which direction the sound came from. It could be a hunter, she supposes, but people don't hunt at the reservoir. Do they? Still, if it is a hunter, she doesn't want to be mistaken for a deer. She quickens her pace a little and decides to head back to the main road above, rather than finish circumnavigating the lake as was her original idea.

The path opens out before reaching the main road, and

there's an abandoned boatshed here, with a concrete slip leading down into the half-frozen water. In the summer, it's busy with canoeists and sailors, and all those people who seem to love messing around on the water. But this morning the area's empty. This particular place is the reason she comes here so often. It's where she feels closest to her father. She knows it's silly. After all, she's never met the man, doesn't know anything about him. Except that he was here once. A long time ago. And that tiny piece of information gives this place a special hold on her heart.

Edith's almost level with the boatshed when the man steps out and stops, staring straight at her. There's a bare bulb hanging above the door and her own pace slows as their eyes lock in the eerie orange light. There's something about the man, or perhaps it's the sound of the gun still echoing inside her mind that makes her instantly wary. It's early enough that there's no one else around, not so much as a lone car passing on the road above them. Still he stares and Edith's pace slows further. He's slightly ahead of her but the path to the road branches off here and the ground beneath her feet is already rising. A few more paces and she'll be properly ahead of him.

The man raises a hand in greeting and says something. She can't quite make it out and yet his intent seems clear. *Hey, can I trouble you for a moment?* Or, *Morning, you couldn't just give me a hand . . . ?* His body language is open, friendly. He just needs a moment of her time. Edith finds herself slowing further, unwilling to fully commit to stopping but too polite to ignore someone who's addressing her directly. But then she notices his eyes and they say something entirely different. She's seen that look before, or something like it. It raises her hackles, provokes some primal instinct that she has long been in tune with. She runs.

She's past him quickly as the path turns away from the boatshed and angles up to the road, but even from the corner of her eye she sees him break after her and this spurs her on even more. She's a fast runner, often in the top five at cross-country, and now she's running faster than she ever has before. She doesn't look back, just pushes on, her progress hampered by the thick snow. It occurs to her that he won't have that same problem, following in the tracks she's leaving for him.

Even as she thinks it she stumbles, her feet catching on something hidden but her body continuing forward with the momentum. She falls, pushing her hands out to brace herself and landing with a soft thump, her face dipping into the ice-cold snow. She pushes herself up, convinced she's about to feel his hands on her shoulders at any moment. She doesn't stop to look but stumbles on, ignoring the cold wet crystals encrusting her fingers, ploughing on up the hill.

A few more seconds and she breaks free of the trees, skidding out onto the tarmac. The snow's less deep here and she has a split second to choose a direction, left towards the village, the closest sanctuary, or right towards Sheffield. Either way leaves her dangerously exposed. She's younger than him. Fitter. But that gunshot still reverberates in her head. She'll be an easy target, the sole traveller in a pristine white landscape. All this goes through her mind in nanoseconds and her feet never slow. She leaps into the treeline on the far side of the road and careers down the bank, bare branches and twigs slapping and tearing at her face and clothes. Still she doesn't stop, hurling herself through undergrowth she hopes will hide her tracks. On through the trees and bushes.

Time passes. Minutes that feel like hours. The cold air burns in her lungs and throat. Still she hasn't looked back. He could be right on her heels or she could have lost him ages ago. The trees end suddenly and she bursts out into an empty field, changing direction without slowing, cutting diagonally across the corner towards the next copse. Her feet are betraying her, leaving their tell-tale marks in the snow.

And then, all at once she finds herself back in civilisation, emerging onto a housing estate she knows well. There's a man de-icing his car for the morning commute. He frowns as she passes him at full tilt. It only occurs to her afterwards that she might have stopped and asked for help. She's too intent on getting away, putting as much distance as possible between her and that man.

Finally, her lungs give out. She turns even as she slows and stops, but there's no sign of him. The road behind her is empty. She pants out the crisp morning air, her heart hammering in her chest, every part of her burning and freezing. Adrenaline, she thinks, or what's left of it. Her science teacher, Dr Erikson, would be pleased with her. The sticky sweat on her forehead and neck begins to chill and she starts to wonder if she imagined the whole thing.

And only now does she realise her mistake. She has led him

back to her home. Or near enough. He didn't need to chase her. He can simply follow her tracks. It has been snowing for days; why did it have to stop today?

Edith trots up some steps onto the walkway of the nearest block of flats. It isn't her own home but the paths that lead through the buildings are covered over and free of snow. She can pick her way from one to another until she's almost home. He might know the general direction she's taken but at least he won't be able to follow her to her door.

She tells herself she's being stupid. She imagined it all, surely? Why would this man want to do her harm? But there are people like that, aren't there? Her mother's always warning her about strange men. And Mrs Abassi, the newsagent; she's always telling her to be careful as well. But she always thought they were just worrying about her. It's never occurred to her before that there might actually be someone out there who would want to seriously hurt her. Not like Alice and her gang, throwing snowballs with rocks in, tripping her up in the street. No, that everyday cruelty she's used to. This was something else. Something . . . cold and dark and pitiless. Something she'd glimpsed for a moment in those eyes.

Edith lets herself in through the front door and closes it firmly behind her.

'Edith? Is that you?' The familiar voice travels down the stairs.

'Yeah, Mum. I'll be right there.'

'I *need* you.'

'Yes, I'm coming.'

Edith shrugs herself out of her fleece and unlaces her boots while sitting on the floor. Within minutes she's consumed with her mother and the daily routine. So much so that she pushes the thought of the man with the cold eyes to the back of her mind. She says nothing to her mother. After all, it would only worry her.

But it comes back to her later, no matter how hard she tries to forget. Long after she's bathed her mother and combed her hair, and made sure there's a sandwich prepared for her for lunch – *Not corned beef again, Edith, Jesus Christ!* – and remade it. After she gets a telling off from Mrs Khatri for being late, and a more serious rebuke from Dr Erikson for not having completed her science homework. When she's sitting in Miss Foster's class, trying to concentrate on the English Civil War while simultaneously trying to ignore Alice Clitherow making farting noises behind her and giggling with her gang. Edith feels something hit her in the back and there's another round of tittering from Alice and the girls.

Then someone whispers, 'Freak!' a bit too loudly, and Miss Foster stops mid-sentence, plainly aware something's got out of her control, if not entirely sure what. The chatter dissipates and Miss Foster goes on, but for some reason Edith's heart has started pounding again. It's not the threat of Alice Clitherow though, nor the objects and insults they throw at her. She can deal with all that.

No. It's the memory of that man's hateful eyes that sends a chill down her spine, and the thought of what he wanted to do to her.

day one

The ICER recordings #112

(Archivists' note: Voice analysis would indicate this is a voice not previously heard on any of the earlier recordings. As such it is labelled: Unidentified Caller 4. Investigations continue as to the identity of this caller [03/05/18])

Call received: 20:18 Friday 2nd Mar 2018
Duration: 2 minutes 49 seconds

Partial Transcript:
ICER   Go ahead.

Unidentified Caller 4 *(clearing of throat)* Is this … ? I … I was told to call this number.

(Recording is silent for 4 seconds, some audible sound of breathing)

We have a problem. I was told you … you could help with … unusual situations. *(pause 2 seconds)* This *is* the Emergency contact number?

ICER   This number is out of service. I'm retired.

UC4   Yes, I was told that too. But . . . under the circumstances, it was hoped you might . . . reconsider.

ICER   What circumstances?

UC4   Well . . . this problem, you see . . . it's potentially . . . that is to say . . . this might be a problem for you as well.

ICER   I don't respond well to threats.

UC4   No, no, no, no! I didn't mean to . . . that is . . . Shit! *(Inaudible speech 1 second)* What I mean is the . . . the *problem* that needs sorting is connected to a previous problem that you . . . sorted for us. A while ago. If you remember the name of the guy was—

ICER   No names. Give me the file number.

UC4   Oh . . . sorry . . . just a minute *(pause 3 seconds)* Case number zero zero zero one. Oh! I guess that was the first one?

(recording is silent for 4 seconds)

ICER   That *was* a while ago.

UC4   Anyway, someone's given a folder of information to the police – we think we know who, we've had our eye on him for a while now – but the bigger problem is that Stevens . . . *Shit!* Sorry, I mean, our man on the inside had to take . . . shall we say . . . precipitate action, and it's left us vulnerable. *(pause 1 second)* It's left us *all* vulnerable.

ICER   So you're asking me to clear up your man's mess *and* deal with the leak?

UC4 A sort of two birds, one stone approach, if you catch my drift. *(laughter)*

ICER Double the usual fee.

UC4 *Double?*

ICER There's no negotiation here. Take it or leave it.

UC4 Can you just hang on a minute? *(Recording is silent for 9 seconds. Sounds of mumbled conversation, content inaudible)* Yes, that ... that will be fine. So ... how do we finalise the details?

ICER I need full names and recent photographs. Use a messaging service that can't be traced. If I agree to the job you'll receive the bank details for transfer. Payment in full, in advance.

UC4 That's ... fine. Er ... there's a possibility we may need ... one other problem dealing with. We think the informant might have been talking to someone else as well. Someone with a familial connection to case zero zero zero one. We were wondering, would you be prepared to ... ?

ICER *(pause 3 seconds)* Yes, yes I would. In fact, I'd be delighted.

Call ends 20:21

The man with the scar on his cheek treads carefully up the steps built into the side of the hill, the biting wind forcing its way up and over his collar, sending a chill down his back. His shoes crunch through the deep snow, the noise louder than he might have expected. There's that dull flatness to the air that heavy snowfall creates. The white fields around him reflect every sound, every glare. It's dazzling.

Near the top of the hill he turns and looks back across the city below. Sheffield is blackened and dull, its usually distinctive sandstone buildings blanched of colour by the grey sky hanging heavy overhead and the impenetrable banks of white surrounding it. At least it's stopped snowing. For now.

He walks on, turning left and working his way towards the towering expanse of the Park Hill Flats. An elderly man totters towards him across the icy pavement, leaning heavily on a walking stick. A gang of kids, six – no, seven of them – are gathered at the top of the overgrown path that leads back down to the station. One of them spots an opportunity and points, and soon all seven are peeling away from the path, crossing the road, heading straight for the man with the stick. One or two fall behind the pack as they stoop to gather fistfuls of snow but the three in the lead stay on target, closing the distance until they are alongside the man. They walk with him, chatting amiably at first.

The man with the scar on his cheek quickens his pace.

The elderly man senses danger but can do no more than politely field their enquiries. His own pace quickens, and he starts to take risks with his footing. One of the stragglers lets loose a snowball that hits the man low on his overcoat, a shot across the bow, as it were. The boys snicker. They're *all* boys, the man with the scar notes, most of them barely into double figures. One of the ringleaders, the youngest-looking, perhaps only seven or eight, jostles the man slightly and he stumbles.

'Hey!' shouts the man with the scar, but the boys are still too far away and if they hear him they don't acknowledge it. They have the scent of blood now, the victim displays ever more vulnerability as he raises his stick in a useless but provocative gesture.

The man with the scar begins to run but he knows he's too late. One of the pack leaders pushes out a leg while another barks in the old man's face, causing him to flinch and step back. He trips on the outstretched leg and two more snow-balls make contact in quick succession, one to his abdomen, one glancing off his ear. The old man goes down.

The man with the scar shouts again as he closes the gap and the boys look up, aware perhaps they've gone too far but still revelling in the thrill of the attack. One of them, the youngster, shouts, 'Mind your own business, *fuck-tard!*' But they back off all the same.

He helps the elderly gentleman to his feet. 'You okay?'

The old man nods nervously but doesn't speak.

The boys close ranks and several begin scooping up more snow from the icy ground.

'You don't want to do that.'

The boys laugh as though he's said something ridiculous. Perhaps he has. If he's misjudged the situation and these are more than just school kids hyped up on jellied sweets, then he knows the odds are not good. Seven on one, and the old man to protect as well. As young as they are, they could still do some damage. But as long as they're still gathering snow and not reaching for knives he thinks he can manage.

The ringleader sneers. 'Who the fuck are you anyway?'

'Tyler!' says a voice from behind, and Tyler turns to see a familiar face crossing the road to join them. '*Detective Sergeant* Tyler. So unless you want to get hauled down the cop shop you best fuck off out of it, the lot of you.'

Tyler turns back to face the gang. They grumble and swear but several fists unclench and powdered snow falls back to the ground. There are a few more choice remarks from the ringleader but as some of the others break apart and melt back into the frozen landscape, he must realise the odds are shortening and decides on a tactical withdrawal. In one last stubborn act of defiance he throws the snowball in his hand. It falls short by a few feet and the boy and his lieutenants drift slowly back into the bushes.

Tyler helps the old man negotiate the kerb and watches until he reaches the relative safety of the main road.

'I had it under control,' he says as the newcomer arrives at his side. The high-pitched voices of the kids are fading into the distance behind them.

DI Jim Doggett smiles at him and pats him on the back. 'You're welcome,' he says.

Tyler sits opposite Doggett and watches him. The DI licks a speck of brown sauce from his finger, then uses the wet tip to pick up a few errant crumbs from the plate. He washes them down with a gulp of weak tea, smacks his lips, and leans back in the chair. 'So,' he says. 'Anything?'

Tyler picks up his own mug of black coffee and shakes his head. 'I searched her place again last night.'

Doggett tips the chair back onto its hind legs. 'What's that, the third time now?'

It's the fifth, but Tyler doesn't tell him that. In fact, he has nothing new to say. It makes him question the point of these daily briefings Doggett insists upon, when neither of them have anything new to report. But he knows the answer to that question really. Neither of them are ready to give up either.

Doggett blows out his cheeks and rocks back and forth like a school kid. He's a thin, wiry man – *all hair and creases*, as Tyler once heard Guy Daley describe him. He pushes the thought of Daley to the back of his mind. He's getting quite good at that.

Tyler can almost see Doggett thinking, hoping perhaps that the answers they've been looking for will strike him in a moment of inspiration. His face creases even further as he comes up empty once again.

It has been three weeks since DCI Diane Jordan disappeared. She drove out of town in her Subaru on the Friday evening and, as far as anyone can tell, she never came back. The alarm was raised almost immediately when she didn't turn up for work on Saturday morning. Tyler wasn't the only one who was concerned; the last time Jordan took time off without notice was for an emergency appendectomy three years ago, and even then she'd managed to text someone as they were wheeling her into surgery.

When there was still no news of her on the Sunday there wasn't a single member of the team who wasn't deeply concerned but Tyler more so than most. Because Jordan's more than a boss. She's his godmother, his maternal role model, his friend. She's the woman who saved him when he was at his lowest ebb.

He let himself into her house for the first time that evening and looked for anything that might explain her absence. But there was nothing. The house was a mess, clothes and belongings flung all over the place, but that in itself was not unusual. Diane isn't the most fastidious of housekeepers. But there was no sign she intended on being away for any length of time. He'd gone straight to Superintendent Stevens who, to his credit – and Tyler really didn't enjoy giving the man credit – had taken his concerns far more seriously than might have been expected.

The café doors slide open to let in some new patrons and

a blast of ice-cold air fights its way past the heat curtain and cools the back of Tyler's neck.

'She can't have just disappeared,' Doggett says. He's probably said it a dozen times by now and it's no more convincing this time than the last eleven. They both know people disappear all the time. They know that better than anyone.

'What are we missing?' Tyler asks.

The DI rocks on his chair. 'We've been through it a hundred times.'

'So we go through it a hundred more!' Tyler's voice is louder than he means it to be, and the couple sitting opposite look up. Doggett simply nods. Tyler takes another mouthful of coffee. It's already cold.

The chair settles back to the floor and Doggett puts his elbows on the table and steeples his fingers. 'Okay,' he says. 'She went south-west, towards the Peaks. So where was she headed? Whirlow? Dore?'

'Or Manchester.'

Doggett shakes his head. 'If she was Manchester-bound, she'd have taken the Snake Pass. It's quicker. And the cameras would have picked her up on the other side.'

'Only if she made it that far.'

The last CCTV footage they have is from a garage fore-court on Ecclesall Road. Over the past weeks they've all taken turns following the various roads Diane could have taken from there. Himself, Doggett, Rabbani ... half of South Yorkshire Police probably.

'There's no sign of an accident,' Doggett says. 'Let's hold on to that.'

But the snow had started not long after and they both know that if she'd gone off one of the passes and into any of the deep ravines that line the major routes through the Peaks, her car could easily still be covered. Tyler pushes the thought out of his mind. Doggett's right, there are no signs of anything like that. And both Derbyshire Police and the Peak District Mountain Rescue Organisation seem adamant she's not out there somewhere. He just wishes he believed them.

Doggett picks up what's left of his bacon sandwich. 'Someone's nobbled her,' he says, and sinks his teeth into soft white bread.

'We don't know that.'

'True enough,' Doggett says, chewing his words along with his mouthful. 'But ...' He pauses to swallow. '... we don't know I'm not gonna be on the Queen's Honours List this year either, but we can hazard a fair guess.'

Tyler turns away and looks out at the snow. Somewhere behind him a milk steamer is hissing. 'She's alive,' he says, and immediately feels guilty for voicing the thought, as though it implies the opposite.

'Maybe.' Doggett finishes his breakfast and drains the last of his tea. 'But if she is, someone's got her.'

'Who? Why?'

'That's exactly what we need to work out.'

Tyler pauses, unwilling to voice the thought that jumps

into his head. The same thought this conversation of theirs always leads to, the same thought *every* conversation with Doggett leads to, and has done for the past year or more – the death of his father, Richard Tyler.

'Do you think it's connected?' he says, finally. He doesn't need to say more, the shorthand he and Doggett have established is becoming increasingly effective.

'I don't see how,' Doggett says, just as he always does. 'Jordan didn't know anything about that.'

And Tyler replies, just as he always does. 'That we know of.'

His mobile vibrates in his pocket and he pulls it out and reads the name *Laura Franklin* on the screen. His chest tightens.

Doggett must read something in his expression. 'What?' he asks.

'Our new Assistant Chief Constable.'

'Well? Answer it then.'

He lifts the mobile to his ear. 'Any news, ma'am?'

There's a slight pause. 'I'm sorry, Tyler, no. Nothing.'

Doggett's watching him intently across the table so he shakes his head. The scruffy little man sighs and falls back in his chair.

'There's a case, Tyler. Body found this morning out at Damflask Reservoir.' And then, as though she's read his mind, she adds, '*Male* body.'

He can't help breathing a sigh of relief. 'Ma'am, I—'

'Before you start, Tyler, this is a cold case. I need your expertise on it.'

'You need me out of the way,' he tells her. She's trying

to distract him so that he doesn't involve himself with the investigation into Jordan's disappearance.

Doggett looks up and rolls his eyes. He mouths the word, *careful*, across the table. At least Tyler thinks that's what it was.

'Either way, DS Tyler, this isn't a request. I'll text you the location. Oh, I'm assuming DI Doggett's with you at the moment?'

Tyler hesitates. How could she possibly know that? 'He is.'

'Then you can save me a phone call and ask him to tag along as well. I want him as SIO on this.' She hangs up on him.

'We've got a case,' Tyler tells Doggett.

'We?'

'She wants us both on it.'

Doggett shrugs. 'Must be because we work so well together,' he says, grinning.

Detective Constable Amina Rabbani looks across the water at some little black birds with white heads that are flapping their way to the far bank. Ducks? She doesn't think so but she's always been a bit rubbish with birds. It's beautiful out here. The dam wall itself is effectively a long road bridge across the southern end of the water and that's where Mina stands now, her back to the road and nothing but a small stone wall between her and the vast expanse of water. It's a magnificent view, even more so with the wooded landscape to either side coated in snow. She shivers and clutches the arms of her faux leather jacket.

'Not exactly dressed for it, are you?'

She turns to see DI Doggett trudging towards her along the pavement.

'I didn't *exactly* expect to be freezing me arse off out here this morning.'

She'd dressed for the office which, due to a faulty thermostat, is experiencing an unseasonable heatwave. That, and the fact she'd been running late again, so she'd grabbed the first jacket that came to hand when she ran out of the house. For some reason there had been no sign of the fur-collared, fleece-lined puffer jacket she'd bought last week. No doubt it was just a coincidence that her cousin had been round last night, although Priti's inquiry – *Is that Michael Kors?* – cast some suspicion on the matter. Maybe her cousin didn't believe her when Mina told her it was just River Island. Or maybe she didn't care as much as the lip curl had suggested.

Despite his question, Doggett hasn't made any concessions to the weather either, dressed as he is in his usual uniform of un-ironed striped blue shirt and brown chinos. The crumpled three-quarter-length coat's the same one he always wears, as well. At least Mina has a scarf and gloves.

'Never mind,' says Doggett. 'Jill will have us all wrapped in polythene before you know it.' He gestures down to the reservoir below them and the old boatshed where Jill Harris is bossing about her SOCOs and making sure no one steps anywhere they shouldn't.

Jill is the main reason Mina's standing about waiting in the cold. The crime scene manager wouldn't let her in until the others arrived. 'No point contaminating everything twice. DS Vaughan's done enough damage already. I'd rather the rest of you went in together.'

Jenny Vaughan had scowled across at them at the sound of her own name. Having recently transferred from Doncaster to make up numbers, Vaughan had yet to win herself many fans. *The poor woman can't do right for doing wrong.* Mina wonders how much of that is Vaughan's fault though, or whether it has more to do with her filling a dead man's shoes.

'What's it like down there?' Doggett asks.

'I'm not sure,' Mina admits. 'But from what I've gathered so far, it's a bit ... unusual.'

Doggett looks as though he wants to ask more but he doesn't. He's always banging on at her about how important it is to make your own appraisal of a scene, to not let your perceptions be coloured by the opinions of others, so maybe he's trying to set a good example. More than likely he's just refusing to ask because he knows she wants him to. It's like he gets off on being an awkward bastard. She consoles herself with the thought that it'll be killing him she might know more than he does.

'Where's Tyler?' she asks.

Another shrug. 'He was right behind me but he drives like an old woman.'

She realises that's what Doggett's waiting for now, Tyler's arrival. She is too, of course, and once again she isn't looking forward to seeing him. He's taken to checking up on her lately, and asking if she's all right all the time. But it's as though he's doing it because he thinks he has to rather than out of genuine concern. It's infinitely more annoying than when he used to just ignore her. And – *Damn him!* – it makes her feel so much more guilty about what she's agreed to do.

He has been different recently. Certainly, since DCI Jordan went missing. But now she thinks about it, it's longer than that.

Ever since Daley.

Mina can't help herself, her mind flashes back to that night in the Botanical Gardens a few months ago looking down into the Bear Pit at Guy Daley's body slumped in a heap. She'd been the first to reach him, faster than the injured Tyler, and had gone straight into first-aid mode, tearing off her jumper and using it to try and plug the holes in Daley's chest. She'd never felt so useless, his warm blood soaking through in seconds, pumping its way over her hands and wrists, running in a thick itchy trail down to her elbow.

She shudders and rubs her arms again.

'You okay?' Doggett asks, displaying an uncharacteristic concern of his own. Perhaps they're all a bit different since that night in the Gardens.

'I'm fine,' she says, and he nods in a manner that somehow manages to convey the fact that he doesn't believe a word of it.

Tyler arrives and pulls up onto the kerb, risking his tyres getting stuck in the deep snow. Doggett heads across to meet him but Mina stays where she is. She watches the DS get out of the car and the two of them exchange a few words by the roadside. *Here we go again!* It's only a short conversation but given their history it's remarkably civil. A casual acquaintance might think this makes sense, they both care about Jordan enough to put their differences aside and work together to find her. But it's more than that. And whatever it is they're up to, it's her job to find out.

Doggett heads off towards the path that leads down to the reservoir but Tyler crosses the road to meet her. He looks out across the semi-frozen water.

'You okay?' he asks, and Mina resists the urge to sigh. 'What have we got?'

She points to the boatshed. 'Dog walker was coming round the lake this morning and the door to this boatshed thing was open. Apparently the place has been abandoned for a while and it's usually locked. The dog ran in and she went in after it. Found a body.'

Tyler nods, still looking out at the dark water. 'That's it?'

'That's all I've got so far. Jill's trying to limit any further contamination of evidence. The dog and its owner have already made enough of a mess down there apparently.' She leaves out DS Vaughan's involvement. No need to drop her in it any further.

'Right,' he says. He turns to look at her for the first time and frowns. 'Aren't you a bit cold in that?'

'Yes.'

'Right.' He seems to consider this for a moment but obviously decides not to pursue it. 'Come on, then. Let's see what she's got for us.'

*

Doggett whistles one long descending note. 'Well,' he says. 'That's a new one, all right!'

The boatshed is bigger than Tyler would have imagined, a good thirty or forty feet end to end and maybe fifteen feet across. Big enough to have held a lifeboat perhaps, although it seems unlikely the RNLI would have had a rescue boat on a reservoir. Unless it was for training, he supposes. But Doggett assures them the place has only ever been used to store equipment for the university sailing club. There are still a handful of items lying about, visible under the flickering light of the one remaining fluorescent strip – a couple of deflated life vests, a long oar held up on one wall by two large rusting iron brackets, a chalkboard with faint markings still visible even in the gloom of the shed – but the bulk of whatever equipment used to be stored here is now in a purpose-built facility a little ways around the lake. Doggett's inside knowledge comes courtesy of a dalliance he once had with a South African canoeist named Thelma, the details of which he was only too happy to share while they were suiting up outside.

The building has two entrances. The first is a regular, human-sized doorway at the end nearest the road. The three of them – Tyler, Doggett and Rabbani – had filed through in their matching white scene-of-crime outfits, with Jill shouting instructions at them to be careful. The wooden floor of the shed slopes downward away from them towards the second entrance, a pair of enormous wooden doors that take up most of the far wall and open onto the lake. At one time whatever boats were stored in the shed could be wheeled down the sloping wooden jetty directly into the water but, even if there were still boats here, that would no longer be possible, given that a substantial section of the floor at that end is missing.

They found Dr Emma Ridgeway squatting precariously close to the hole in the floor, looking down into the darkness beneath. She'd beckoned them forward. 'Appreciate yer coming slowly,' she'd said through her mask with her southern US twang. 'Don't y'all fall into my crime scene.' And with that the two SOCOs flanking her finished setting up the arc lamps and switched them on.

Cue Doggett's whistle.

Lying just beneath the wooden planks of the boatshed floor is the shallow edge of the reservoir. Resting in the half-frozen water is the body of an adult male. He's curled into a foetal position with his wrists and ankles bound together with what looks like rope. The details are remarkably clear. The flesh of the body appears to have shrunken slightly and there are dark mottled patches all over his skin but it's still easy enough to make out his features, even through the permafrost that covers him. He looks to be in his early to mid-twenties at most.

'Frozen solid,' Ridgeway informs them. 'But starting to thaw.'

'Bloody hell!' says Rabbani.

'I guess that about covers it.' Ridgeway straightens up and steps back so they can take turns peering into the hole.

'Adult male, dressed in some kind of work boots and overalls. There's a symbol on the arm, looks like a hammer. Or a tool of some kind, I guess.'

'It's a hammer,' Tyler says, his stomach turning in recognition. He glances at Doggett and the DI nods. 'This is why Franklin wanted us here?'

Ridgeway nods. 'She thought it could be related to a cold case and you'd wanna be involved.'

How the hell could Franklin know that?

'And me?' asks Doggett. 'Any particular reason I'm freezing m' knackers off as well?'

'You're here, Detective Inspector, because of this.' Ridgeway turns and treads carefully towards the side wall of the boatshed. She lifts the torch to illuminate what looks like a darker patch of wall about six feet from the ground. The blood has hit the wooden panels with some force and is splayed out in a rough circle. Gravity has pulled the thicker red at the centre downward in three distinctive streaks. Tyler always thinks of those Rorschach inkblot tests when he sees blood spatter patterns. This one looks like some obscene three-stemmed flower. A dandelion with its tiny red seeds flying away. He wonders what that says about him. If anything.

Ridgeway uses the torch beam like a pointer. 'Gunshot back spatter. From the height, I think it's safe to say it was a head wound. There're no visible fragments of bone or brain matter but we're most likely gonna find 'em.'

'Fatal?' Tyler asks.

Ridgeway hesitates and then nods. 'Yes, sir. I'd say so.'

Doggett tuts. 'If not, he's certainly got a headache.'

'He?' Tyler asks faintly. He's not sure anyone else heard but Doggett steps closer and lowers his voice.

'Diane's five foot nothing,' he says softly. 'Unless she was standing on a box, it's not her.'

Tyler nods. He's missing things. Obvious things. He needs to focus. 'Anything else?' he asks Ridgeway.

'There's more blood on the floor where the body likely fell but not a lot else so far. No body, no bullet, no signs of struggle. Jill's team are examining the local area, just in case the victim wandered off somewhere and collapsed but it looks very much like whoever killed the guy took the body with him. Cleanly too, apart from that.' She points at the blood spatter on the wall. 'I guess he either ran out of time or was disturbed in some way, or he wouldn't have left the mess that he did.'

Rabbani is crouched over the body in the hole. 'And it couldn't be this bloke?' she asks. 'I mean, I know we can't see a bullet hole but it doesn't mean there isn't one ... somewhere.'

Ridgeway gestures to the SOCO standing by and he steps forward to begin collecting samples from the wall. She inches her way carefully back over the busted planks towards them. 'The blood's fresh. It's been there a few hours at most. This guy's been frozen a lot longer than that.'

Doggett sucks air in through his teeth and sighs heavily.

'We have a body that could be connected to an old crime then and evidence connected to a new one.' He turns to Tyler. 'Looks like Franklin's got a team-up on her mind.'

'Good job we work so well together,' Tyler says, and Doggett grins again. Above her mask, Rabbani's eyes roll.

'So,' Doggett asks Ridgeway, 'how the fuck are you gonna get him out?'

Ridgeway turns to face him. 'That there, sir, is the sixty-four billion dollar question.'

They all stand there staring down at the body in silence for a few moments. The wind whistles through the slats in the slipway doors. Somewhere behind him, Tyler can hear water dripping. At least, he hopes it's water. Another scratching sound makes him turn and glance back at the SOCO, who is scraping some kind of metal tool across the blood-stained wooden planks.

It's not her, he tells himself. It can't be.

'How are we going to do this?' Tyler asks Doggett.

They're standing on the bridge again, looking down at the SOCOs securing the scene of the crime. There are white-clad figures crawling all over the equally white landscape. The glare of the winter sun reflecting off the ice is dazzling. Rabbani's a little further down the road re-interviewing the dog walker who found the body.

Doggett sucks some saliva through his teeth. 'We can't establish much until the evidence has been fully collected and fuck knows how long it's gonna take to get that body out! Why don't you head back and start things rolling there? No point all of us freezing our arses off.'

It makes sense but Tyler knows that Doggett often has an agenda he doesn't tell you about.

'You recognised the logo, didn't you?'

The DI stares out at the dark flat surface of the reservoir. 'Of course I did. Demeter Fabrications. I've looked at that case file a thousand times.'

A little over a year ago Jim Doggett had told Tyler something that had changed his life – that his father hadn't taken his own life, as he'd always been told, but that he had in fact been murdered. Doggett told him Richard Tyler had come to him the week before he died to tell him about a conspiracy he'd uncovered, something involving old cases he'd been looking into. And then, only a week later, he was dead.

For more than a year the two of them had gone over every case Richard had been looking into before he died, a large number of them cold cases from years before. But there was one case that was more recent. The death of a security guard killed during the robbery of a steel factory. It had happened only a month or so before Richard died, in 2002.

'We never found any link between Demeter and any of the other cases,' Tyler says.

'We didn't have a body then.'

'You think this body is from way back then? It was sixteen years ago.'

'I don't know, maybe the body's from back then or maybe just the uniform is. All I'm saying is I recognised that logo.'

'So did Franklin. How could she possibly know about that case?'

Doggett shrugs. It's his signature move and he's very good at it. 'She was around back then. It's possible she could have remembered it.'

'But she can't have been to the crime scene already this morning.'

'Nope. Which means someone who has been here, told her about it.'

Tyler finds himself looking around at the team of officers and SOCOs working the area. It was unnerving to think they had a colleague reporting things over their heads but the alternative was worse; that somehow Franklin could have known in advance what they were going to find.

Doggett sends a flurry of snow skittering over the edge to the frozen surface of the reservoir. 'I suggest you start by digging out that file.'

'What are you going to do?'

'I'll stick around here for now, in case the SOCOs turn up anything in the woods.'

'You hoping for a trail of footprints to lead you to the killer?' Tyler kicks at some ice himself. He's not good at sarcasm but he must have managed to convey some of his feeling because Doggett smiles.

'Something like that.' He reaches out suddenly and puts a hand on Tyler's arm. 'This doesn't change anything, right? We work this case, and we see where it leads us and whether it helps us with our . . . other little project.' Doggett makes bunny ear motions with his fingers around the last words. 'But our main focus is still finding Jordan. If we have to work twenty-four hours a day, we'll bloody well find her.'

Tyler wants to believe him but the truth is they both know they're running out of options. The first twenty-four hours are the most crucial in a missing person's case. If Diane hasn't been found by now it's either because she doesn't want to be or ... It *has* to be that.

Down the road, Rabbani has finished with the dog-walker and stands jogging on the spot, rubbing her arms. Doggett points her out. 'You'd best take that one with you as well before we end up with another frozen corpse on our hands.'

Tyler can't help smiling but then he remembers the crime scene and the frozen body staring up at them from the ice. 'Have you ever seen anything like that?' he asks. 'I mean, how does someone end up frozen in a lake?'

'It's a reservoir,' says Doggett. 'And no, I haven't.'

'It has to have been staged, surely?'

Doggett nods. 'That body hasn't been lying there since 2002. Which means someone put it there deliberately.'

'Before or after they shot someone else in the head and carried the body away?'

'Precisely. We've got too many questions and not enough answers.'

Tyler feels his mobile vibrate in his pocket and he hurries to dig it out. It could be news. It could be her. But it's not. He reads the message in silence, pauses for a moment and then slips the phone back into his jeans.

'Anything?' asks Doggett.

Tyler rubs his hands together against the cold. 'Our new ACC again. She wants to see Rabbani and me, as soon as we get back.'

'Cheer up, son.' Doggett grins. 'You never know, it might be good news.'

Tyler leaves him there chuckling to himself and goes to fetch Rabbani.

Mina stares out of the car window at the bank of snow piled next to her. The radio chatters away with some mid-morning talk show, the voice of the presenter almost as irritating as that of the caller, who has dialled in apoplectic about the number of homeless littering the city's streets.

'Do we have to listen to this?' She doesn't mean to sound so sharp and the fact she's given away her frustration annoys her even more.

Tyler ceases his drumming on the steering wheel and glances at her. He leans forward and switches off the radio.

'Thanks,' she says.

If he notices her prickly behaviour he says nothing about it, just continues to stare out of the windscreen at the endless line of stationary red lights visible ahead of them. The rush hour has spread long and dug in deep, the commuters starting later than usual after their morning ritual of de-icing the car. Mina shivers and flicks the air vent so that the blast of warm stale air hits her square in the face. The window next to her begins to fog up with condensation.

'You okay?' Tyler asks without looking at her, but not because he's actually noticed her mood. It's just another one of his annoying attempts to be human.

'I'm fine!' she says, and she can hear the petulance in her own voice. Her mother's voice echoes in response. *Ay, Mina, stop acting like a child!* She sighs heavily and closes her eyes for a moment, calming her frustration. After all, he isn't the sole reason she's out of sorts. *You should never have agreed to it*, says the voice in her head, and her arms break out in goosebumps. 'What were you and Doggett talking about?'

'Nothing really.'

'There,' she snaps before she can help herself. '*That's* what's wrong.'

He turns in his seat slightly so that he's facing her. He stares at her for a moment in that way that always makes her feel so uncomfortable. Not like he's eyeing her up – not in a sexual sense anyway – but as though he's analysing her, working out in his own very particular way who she is and what she's about. It's the same thing he does with suspects, she realises. But it's long past time they had this talk and she isn't a suspect. Even if she does feel guilty enough to be one. She turns in her own seat and forces herself to meet his eye. She knows this trick. He's trying to make her speak first. She isn't going to be the one to break. *So what if it's childish!* She crosses her arms.

He smiles. 'Talk to me, Mina.'

'That's my point,' she tells him. 'You *don't* talk to me. You never talk about anything. I have to drag every little bit of information out of you and even then I'm not sure if you're telling me everything.' She trails off, slightly embarrassed at her own tirade. *No, I'm not gonna back down.* 'We need to start communicating better or . . .' She stops.

'Or what?'

'I don't know,' she says, feeling her cheeks warm. 'We just do, that's all.'

Or someone else is gonna end up dead. That's what she had been about to say. But that isn't fair. She doesn't really blame him for Daley. Does she? *Is that why I agreed to do this?*

'Okay. Doggett was telling me that the logo on the arm of the uniform was from a company called Demeter Fabrications. He recognised it from an old case involving a murdered security guard back in 2002. He wants us to look into it.'

Liar. The thought brings her up short. She's never caught him in an outright lie before but she'd seen the look in his eyes back at the reservoir and he'd recognised that logo just as much as Doggett had. 'That's it? That's all he said?'

Tyler shrugs. 'I guess I'm not the only one who likes to keep secrets.'

For a moment she thinks he means her and she can't stop herself blushing. But he's referring to Doggett. He means it as a joke, but she knows he still isn't telling her everything. The pair of them think no one's noticed this new-found camaraderie that's sprung up between them but she has. On the surface they argue just as much as they used to and they're careful around the office to make it obvious that one can barely tolerate the presence of the other, but she's seen them when they don't think they're being watched. On smoke breaks at the end of the car park, fielding mysterious phone calls from each other. If it wasn't so laughable she might believe there was something romantic going on between them. But that is laughable. The DCI going missing might explain some of it but it's been going on longer than that. It's something else. Something they're doing their best to keep her out of, and the fact they might be doing that for her own good doesn't make it any less annoying.

But the impetus she'd felt a few moments ago has faded and she can no longer bring herself to pursue it. *Fine, let them have their secrets.* She's a detective now too. She'll find out what they're up to on her own.

As the traffic inches forward and Tyler turns his attention back to the road, Mina takes out her mobile and googles *Demeter Fabrications*. As she reads she becomes aware of Tyler glancing in her direction whenever the traffic allows. *Bollocks to him!* She's not going to volunteer any information until he asks.

Assistant Chief Constable Laura Franklin welcomes Tyler and Rabbani into the conference suite. It's a grand title for what is effectively just a meeting room cordoned off at one end of the office but titles are important. Like Assistant Chief Constable. Important enough that she's pretty much commandeered this room as her own since she arrived. She gestures that they should take a seat, using both hands to point to either side of the table. She's splitting them up, Tyler realises. Divide and conquer.

She's a small woman, in terms of both height and build, and yet there's nothing diminutive about her presence, not least because she comes with a mighty reputation for dealing with trouble.

She's tidy and precise in every way, with her cropped grey hair and her shiny pleated uniform. The opposite to Jordan, in fact. And even Superintendent Stevens has been known to loosen his tie once in a while. Tyler can't imagine this woman ever loosening anything. Certainly not the leash she has already effectively placed around his neck by forcing him to work this cold case. What is she up to?

To give her some credit, however, she doesn't wait for him to ask about Diane. 'There's still no more news, I'm afraid,' she tells him specifically, as the two of them file in and sit down at the conference table. 'We're doing everything we can, I promise you that, Adam.'

He baulks at the use of his name. No one at work calls him Adam. No one except Diane. But he appreciates the sentiment behind the update nevertheless. He nods an acknowledgment and she nods back.

'Right,' she says, 'down to business.' She tosses a manila folder to each of them and Rabbani meets his eye as they retrieve them. She seems worried about something. She often looks nervous around the ACC but he supposes that's understandable. Lately though she's begun to seem anxious around him as well. She'd seemed pissed off at him in the car but that's nothing new. It's more than that though. Unless he's misreading things again; normally he'd rely on Diane to tell him if it was that.

As Tyler leafs through the reports inside, he wonders how Franklin's found time to put this together, to get so involved in something that's so far beneath her purview. Assistant Chief Constables are there to attend press conferences and political parties where their sole purpose as far as he can see is to press the flesh, and try to wring more money out of the government. Why is she so involved in this case, so quickly?

'In the summer of 2002,' she goes on, 'there was a robbery at a steelworks in the Don Valley called—'

'Demeter Fabrications Limited.' It's a small win, intended to demonstrate that he knows stuff too. But he catches Rabbani shaking her head slightly and grimacing.

'Very good,' Franklin says, apparently unfazed. 'I see someone's done their homework. You must thank DI Doggett for me.' She meets his eye directly with an inscrutable expression she's very good at. 'As I was saying. In 2002 Demeter Fabrications were a struggling steel manufacturer specialising in parts for construction machinery and farm equipment. On the 23rd of August their factory was broken into and the safe robbed. The owner of the business was a little old school when it came to operating in cash, no doubt one of the reasons his business didn't make it through the financial crisis of '08. So there was a significant amount of money in the safe at the time, some fifty thousand pounds which was never recovered. Added to this, the security guard who was working that night received a blow to the head that killed him. It was a big news story at the time so if this body we've found does have some link to that case I would very much like to know about it before the media does.'

'I'm curious, ma'am,' Tyler asks. 'Do you have a personal interest in the case?'

Franklin blinks at him without speaking.

'It's just that you seem very well informed about a body that was only discovered a few hours ago. I wondered if you were involved in the original investigation.'

'I don't know what you've been used to in the past, DS Tyler, but it's my job to be very well informed. I make it my business to be aware of *everything* I'm in charge of. And *everyone*.' She stands up. 'Now, if there are no further questions, I'll leave you to familiarise yourself with the details.' She clearly has no intention of answering the question he didn't quite ask.

Rabbani stands up as well and Tyler reluctantly follows her, picking up the folder Franklin's prepared for them. How has she managed it so quickly? Unless ... she was already looking into this for some reason.

Rabbani makes it to the door first but as Tyler turns to follow Franklin speaks again. 'A moment, DS Tyler.'

Rabbani hesitates and then lets the door close behind her.

'Take a seat,' she says again.

She waits for him to comply and then sits down herself, putting her hands together and her elbows on the table, and staring over the top of her knitted fingers at him as though she's about to pass judgement. He wonders what he's done this time. He can't think of anything in particular.

'How are you?' she asks, eventually.

The question catches him on the back foot. 'Sorry?'

'I wanted to make sure you're okay.' She waits for him to respond but when he doesn't go on she evidently decides to explain further. 'Given everything you've been through in recent months.'

'Everything I've been through?' He knows what she's referring to, of course, but it doesn't pay to let them know you know too much, as Doggett never tires of reminding him.

'First, that unfortunate business with the fires and Gerald Cartwright. That case struck uncomfortably close to home for you, I believe.' This time she doesn't wait for him to respond. 'And then the tragic circumstances surrounding DC Daley's death last year—'

'That wasn't my fault.' He didn't mean to say that but now it's out he can't think of a way to retrieve it.

Franklin stares at him across the table. 'I'm not looking to apportion blame, Adam. I just want to make sure you're coping after what has been a very challenging time for all of us, but perhaps for you most of all.'

'Why me most of all?'

'I just know that under more normal circumstances you would have had the luxury of a shoulder to cry on, in the form of your godmother, DCI Jordan.' Her chumminess is beginning to irritate him. 'In light of Diane's disappearance ... well, it would be enough to upset even those with the most robust mental constitutions.'

'The implication being that I am *not* one of those.'

'Adam, I'm not the enemy here. I'm on your side.'

'I'd rather you were on Diane's side. What's happening with the investigation?'

'I appreciate this is hard for you, Adam, but I can assure you I will keep you informed of any new developments. As soon as I know anything, you'll know.'

She says all the right things but he's struggling to believe them.

'As you know,' she goes on, 'I've been brought in to this department to examine the way we operate. Not solely because of the events you've been involved in lately.' Again, the words say one thing on the surface but the implication is something else. 'My job here is to shift the paradigm,' she says, smiling.

'Do what?'

She smiles again. 'To see if we can't ... leverage a best practice into place. You've been doing impressive work with this CCRU unit of yours but we are long past the days when results counted more than procedure. I simply wanted to touch base with you and ensure you have everything you need to take CCRU forward in a more ... progressive, future-proof manner.'

He can't decide if she's messing with him. 'Leverage a best practice'? She's going to start running things up flag-poles in a minute. 'I was very much under the impression Superintendent Stevens wanted to *shift the paradigm* in a different direction. At our last meeting he made it clear CCRU *had* no future, progressive or otherwise.'

Franklin inclines her head. 'The Superintendent has his own ideas about restructuring but there's a bigger picture now.'

What bigger picture? 'So you *do* want to make changes to CCRU?

'I'm impressed with the work you've been doing. I want you to think of me as being here solely to empower. To ensure you have the resources you need to take your department to the next level. You can reach out to me, you know? If you need anything, want to talk to me about anything, all you have to do is ask.'

What does she think he wants to talk about? CCRU? Daley? Or something else? Maybe he and Doggett haven't been as careful in their investigations as they thought. Could she know what they've been doing? And if she does ... does that mean she's involved in some way? He realises he hasn't spoken for a while. 'I ... *We* certainly appreciate that CCRU has your full support,' he manages.

Franklin smiles again. 'Well, *if it ain't broke, don't fix it,* I always say.' And then the smile vanishes. 'It isn't broken, is it, Adam?'

'No. No, ma'am.'

She holds his eye for a second and is apparently satisfied by whatever she sees. 'Good,' she says, sitting back. 'Now, while we're on the subject of damage limitation, all those who worked directly with DS Daley have now undergone mandatory interviews in the wake of his death. All but you.'

'I'm fine, really.'

'Do you need me to define what the word mandatory means, DS Tyler?'

He could do with her defining some of the other words she used. 'No, ma'am.'

'This isn't a request. You have an appointment with Occupational Health the day after tomorrow at 8am. I hope that isn't a problem for you?'

'I'm not sure—'

'Ten am, then? Eleven? Mr Austin assures me he has cleared his diary for you.'

'Eight will be fine.'

'Good. You should know that I'll be following up with him to make sure you attend. Is that understood?'

He nods.

'Well, that's about it then. I'll allow you to liaise with DI Doggett regarding the details of how you work this case but I imagine he will want to focus on the blood spatter victim while you look into the cold case element. I've organised a room for you on the sixth floor.'

'A room?'

'I thought it was about time CCRU had its own space; the two of you are a bit cramped in the corner over there. The room's more than big enough for you and DC Rabbani, and there's space for a couple more should you need to co-opt anyone else from the department, or if we decide to expand you at some later date. I would suggest, as long as he's willing, DI Doggett joins you up there as well. For the duration of this investigation. I hope that's helpful?'

'Yes . . .' he says. For once he's properly at a loss for words. 'Is this—?'

'Good, good,' Franklin cuts him off. 'Well, I don't need all the details. Just let me know if you do need anyone else and I'll clear it with their superiors. In the meantime, I've every confidence in the three of you.' She smiles again and gestures with an open palm for him to leave. Tyler gets to his feet feeling dazed. What the hell just happened?

He turns and walks slowly out of the room, the conversation with its convoluted office-speak twisting and turning in his head.

Things hadn't always been so bad with Melanie. There was a time when it was just the three of them – Edith, Melanie and her grandfather. They didn't have much and even then, Melanie was prone to the occasional bout of melancholia, but for the most part they were happy. While her mother worked, Grandad looked after her and told her stories about the grandmother she'd never known, the woman who had passed on her old-fashioned name. And if her mum was a little bit sadder than her friends' mums, Edith didn't yet know quite how serious that sadness was nor exactly how it related to her father.

The first time she remembers asking about him, she was six. 'He's gone, sweetheart,' had been Melanie's perplexing but fixed response, and for many years after Edith had been unable to budge her on this nor elicit any further information. The responses varied in their exact wording but their overall sense was the same. *He's gone. He's not around anymore. You don't need to worry about that.* But Edith never entirely gave up.

It was after Grandad died and Melanie stopped working that things started to go downhill. Edith began to notice how easily her mum got tired. She began to rack up diagnoses of anxiety and depression, and eventually she exhausted the patience of her doctors entirely. Edith learned how she could use her mother's illness to her own advantage. Like a besieging army might strike in the early hours of morning (Edith had a love of the Greek and Roman myths and the siege of Troy was one of her favourites), she learned to coordinate her attacks with those moments when her mother seemed most vulnerable. She would wait until the afternoon slump, usually around 3pm, when Melanie would begin to inch down the sofa until almost horizontal, her eyes losing focus on her favourite TV shows. Edith would slip in from school and make a cup of tea as her opening salvo. Then she'd quiz her mother as far as she dared but with no great success.

It was on one such afternoon, the summer Edith turned thirteen, that she managed her most significant breakthrough. Melanie had been more awake than usual that day, and when Edith brought the tea, she'd patted the sofa cushion next to her in invitation.

'Come and have a snuggle,' she said, beaming at Edith, and for once the whole question of her father's identity flew out of her mind. They cuddled up under the blanket clutching their steaming cups and Melanie explained what had happened so far in *Taggart*. She didn't need to, Edith had seen the episode so many times she could recite the lines. Unusually, her mother was awake, sharp and switched on to the world – even if that world was only that of a 90s Glaswegian television detective. These moments were rare and they were precious.

It was a shock when Melanie, out of the blue, said, 'I used to watch this with your dad.'

Edith froze, all the questions she'd ever wanted to ask leaping into her head at once. She kept quiet, not wanting even to move in case she scared her prey. But she needn't have worried. It was as though something had loosened in her mother that day.

'Your grandad didn't like him coming round so we had to wait until he was at work and then he'd sneak over and we'd cuddle up together on the sofa, just like this.' Melanie shared a secretive wink with her daughter. 'Of course, that wasn't all we got up to.'

Edith waited patiently for more. She was sure it was coming now, and sure enough after a minute or two Melanie went on.

'When we couldn't meet here we'd go down to the reservoir. Your dad had the key to the boatshed and we'd slip inside and curl up on some old rugs.' Edith stayed quiet and listened, worrying that she might break the spell, even when her mother, perhaps forgetting who she was talking to altogether, began telling her details about the boatshed that turned Edith's cheeks red. It lasted a good few minutes and then a car alarm sounded somewhere right outside and whatever spell Melanie had been under was broken, just like that.

'Mum?' Edith tried. 'Mum. What else? Tell me about him.'

A tear slid down Melanie's cheek. 'I miss him, baby girl. I miss him so much.' And then she'd turned back to her programme, put down her mug and closed her eyes.

Edith tried something else, drawing Melanie back to the TV screen. 'Mum. What's Taggart doing now? Does he think that man's the killer?' But it was too late. The strange magic had dissipated and Melanie had that half-fluttering to her eyelids that indicated she was close to sleep.

This led to a period of renewed attack on Edith's part. Armed with the scant details she'd uncovered she set out to discover more. 'How come he had a key, Mum? Did he work at the boatshed? Why didn't Grandad like him? How old was he?' But this only caused her mother to shut down even more. Melanie would outright ignore her enquiries now, not even bothering with the grunts or the ne'er-you-minds. Her mother never opened up in the same way again and Edith began to believe that, if anything, that rare moment of candour had unsettled Melanie so badly it had somehow made her illness worse.

In the months that followed, Edith resigned herself to a different approach. Maybe her mother had given her enough to go on. Were the clues detailed enough? How would Taggart solve the mystery? She began brainstorming ideas about why her grandfather might not have liked her dad. She began looking into the history of the boatshed as best she could but there wasn't much information; it had been abandoned for years.

Her father must have had some sort of job or something that involved the place – how else would he have had the keys?

And finally she began visiting the boatshed as often as she could, getting up earlier and earlier to go out and explore. Not just the boatshed but the reservoir in general. Maybe her father was a park ranger. Did they have those? Maybe he worked for the water board. If he was something to do with sewage treatment would that have been enough for her grandad to disapprove? Her morning walks expanded out from this central location, exploring the village and the fields around the area. Until eventually, now, they had become something more than a fact-finding mission. They were walks for their own sake. But somewhere deep in the back of her mind she kept that knowledge of what she was really looking for. He was out there somewhere, she knew it.

Mrs Andrews coughs pointedly and Edith jumps. She puts her head back down to her reading book just as everyone else is doing but her eyes don't focus on the words. There's to be a quiz after this and she's barely got further than page two; she needs to focus.

She's never seen anyone at the boatshed before, though. Not until today. Finally, she'd had a chance to get inside and she'd missed her opportunity. What had it been about that man that had scared her so much? It was almost as though a voice in her head had told her to run before she'd even had a chance to properly think about it. She'd looked into those eyes and . . . She shivers. She had been so sure he was going to hurt her. So very sure. And there was the gunshot, she didn't imagine that. Did she? Now, in the relative safety of the classroom, looking out at the sun reflecting off the bright sheet of the school field, it seems so silly. Could she have been wrong? What if – and this is a thought she hasn't allowed herself to voice properly yet – what if that had actually been him? What if she'd run away from her own father?

'A-hem!' exclaims Mrs Andrews. 'Miss Darke, I don't know what you think is so fascinating about the playing field this afternoon but you should be aware that you will be getting the first question and you only have five minutes left.'

Alice Clitherow titters and someone whispers, 'Saddo bitch!' Edith knows it isn't aimed at the teacher.

'Eyes down!' shouts Mrs Andrews.

As the afternoon wears on and her fear begins to fade, Edith tries to convince herself she got it wrong. Maybe the man hadn't meant her any harm at all. He'd reached out, as though he'd wanted to talk to her. Maybe he recognised her or something. Not that she looks very much like her mother but it was possible, wasn't it? More likely in fact. She must have been wrong about the gunshot too. Wrong about everything. That sort of thing might happen in her mother's TV shows but it didn't happen in real life, did it?

Why, then, is that little voice in her head still telling her to run?

'Bloody hell!' Mina says, squinting into the sun.

The room Tyler's brought her to is bright and airy and looks out over the city rooftops. It's a corner office, a lot higher up in the building, hence the view, which will mean a lot more stairs to negotiate on a regular basis but she reckons that's more than worth the trade-off.

There are four brand new desks, still with the polythene wrapping visible where it's been torn off at the legs. There are whiteboards running the length of the right-hand wall, two filing cabinets in the corner and a separate desk with a laser printer on it. Everything smells of plastic and new paint. Someone has even thought to put a plant on top of one of the filing cabinets and a watercooler next to it.

'Have we won the lottery, or summat?'

'Looks that way,' Tyler tells her. 'Well, go on then, take your pick.'

Three of the desks have computers wired up on them, the fourth stands empty. Mina's tempted to take the one nearest the window but it's clearly been arranged for whoever runs the department so she sits down at the desk that backs onto it. At least it gives her the best view out of the window.

Tyler grins and walks round the desk to sit down. They spin in their ergonomic chairs like school kids, beaming at each other. But then the grin on Mina's face fades. *What is Franklin up to?*

'All right,' Tyler says finally, 'let's get to work.'

They begin collating information, passing it back and forth, building the outlines of a case which they take turns pinning to the noticeboard. Tyler prints out the photo of the frozen body and pins it to the whiteboard, then writes

'Demeter Fabrications' and a large curved arrow pointing towards the victim. That's how it starts and it grows from there. They fill in a few blanks but after a couple of hours they have little more to go on than the information Franklin provided them. Information that Franklin somehow had before they did. She'd like to hear Tyler's thoughts on that but that would take them a little too close to certain topics of conversation she'd rather avoid.

'Kevin Linville,' Tyler says from behind his desk.

Mina turns round from the whiteboard. 'Who?'

'That's the name of the security guard who was killed. He was thirty-one. He had a wife.'

Mina writes the relevant details on the board. 'Were there any suspects at the time?'

Tyler inclines his head. 'A few disgruntled ex-employees but no one the investigating team took very seriously. There was Gareth Whitehouse though, the director of the company. The fact that there was such a large sum of money in the safe might indicate an inside job, prior knowledge that the place was worth ripping off.'

'Is that in the original investigation?'

'No, not really. They interviewed Whitehouse a couple of times but there's nothing in the file to suggest they thought he was involved. In fact, there's a note from DI Johnson that says he thought the man seemed pretty genuine. He was sick at the thought of losing the cash, implied it was the end of the business.' He frowns.

'What?'

'Hm? Oh, nothing. It's just . . . Johnson seems a bit quick to move on from this. I might have dug a bit deeper. There's not much in the way of financial info here.'

'And it ended up taking the company another seven years to go under. Maybe it's worth looking into again?'

Tyler nods and Mina writes Whitehouse's name on the board as their first suspect. Then she stops, a thought occurring to her as she writes. 'Sarge?'

'Mina, you know you don't have to call me that, don't you? It was bad enough when you used to call me "sir".'

'I know . . . it's just . . . habit, I guess.' What else is she supposed to call him? *'Tyler'* makes it sound like she's trying to be one of the lads and *'Adam'* . . . well, no one calls him Adam.

'Go on.'

'I was just thinking. Are we assuming these cases are linked? Or do we treat them as two separate cases that need solving – the robbery that led to the murder of the security guard, and the body in the ice?'

Tyler nods. 'You're right. We should consider them separate for now and see where they overlap. It's possible the Demeter uniform on the body is a coincidence.' Which leads them to another half hour of rejigging the information on the wall so that they have two separate investigations and Demeter Fabrications pinning them together.

It's late by the time Doggett arrives and pokes his head through the doorway, and Mina has already made several very obvious gestures of looking at her watch, which Tyler has failed to notice. She'd been wondering how she was going to get away. She could just ask him, of course, but she can't think of a good reason to be running off so early when they've just started a new case. And it's not as though she can tell him the real reason. Once again the thought of what she's doing brings a flood of heat to her face, especially in the light of how well they've worked together this afternoon.

Doggett glances around the room and lets out a long whistle. 'Blimey, how the other half live, eh? Looks like someone's going up in the world.'

'I'm sure it's only temporary,' says Tyler. He gestures to one of the empty desks. 'Pull up a pew.'

Doggett shakes his head. 'I know my place,' he says, but there's a smile on his face. 'Just came to fill you in.'

He outlines what he has from the crime scene. The removal of the body from the water had been far from straightforward, they'd had to take a number of precautions to prevent any accidents. But the ice holding the body in place hadn't been as thick as they first thought, lending credence to the theory the body hadn't been in the reservoir very long. Between them, Doggett, acting as Senior Investigating Officer, Jill the crime scene manager and Emma Ridgeway as consulting forensic pathologist escorted the remains to the mortuary.

'Anything more in terms of the blood spatter?' Tyler asks.

Doggett shakes his head. 'Nothing. Less than nothing, in fact. Whoever removed the gunshot victim knew exactly what they were doing. There's no sign of the body being taken away so my guess is the killer, or killers, wrapped up the victim and carried the corpse up to the roadside. There were no vehicle tracks down by the lake. I've got forensics casting tracks but enough traffic went through before we closed the road that I think they'll struggle to come up with anything concrete.' Doggett folds his arm and leans against the filing cabinet. 'Did you ... er, look into that thing we were talking about?'

Tyler and Doggett exchange a look with each other.

'Why don't you get yourself off, Mina?' Tyler tells her. 'It's getting late.'

They're at it again. She tuts her annoyance loudly but realises this gives her exactly the excuse she needs. She grabs her bag and coat. 'Great. Okay. Well, I have got plans actually so ...' She trails off. 'I'll see you in the morning then,' she offers, but they're already huddled together by the window. She briefly considers lurking in the corridor to eavesdrop but another check of the time makes her realise she's way too late.

She *will* find out what they're up to though. She promises herself that.

As she steps out into the chill evening air Mina clutches the thin sleeves of her summer jacket and once again lets out a few choice words for her cousin, Priti. It's already dark as she makes her way through town, dodging the last of the afternoon shoppers and the office workers well on their way to being tanked up. The drinking fountain outside the Peace Gardens has sprung a leak and a group of teenagers are using the place as their own private skating rink. Mina skirts round them and heads gingerly down the road towards the Moor, hurrying now, as she's seriously late for her rendezvous.

Her destination is a Chinese restaurant. It's situated on the upper floor and entrance is by way of a small stairwell sandwiched between a fish and chip takeaway and a betting shop. She's just about to step through the doorway when a woman steps out and almost collides with her. DS Vaughan.

'Oh, hi!' Mina says, but Vaughan looks her up and down and hurries away without speaking. *Rude!*

At the top of the stairs the restaurant opens out across three or four units and she sees the person she's come to meet waving to her from a booth tucked in the back corner next to a window. Not that it would have been hard to find her, they appear to have the entire place to themselves.

Assistant Chief Constable Laura Franklin stands up as Mina walks towards her and signals for the waiter, who arrives almost instantly to take Mina's jacket. She wouldn't have minded hanging on to it a bit longer but she reluctantly lets the waiter disappear with it somewhere. She hopes that's not another one lost.

'Thanks for coming, Mina,' Franklin says as she sits back down, and the friendliness of the greeting makes Mina feel wretched. She's been meeting Franklin on a weekly basis since the ACC arrived but always before it's been within the safety of the station. This feels far more clandestine. *What am I doing here?* She should never have agreed to any of this.

Mina sits down and after a few moments of silence where

Franklin does nothing but stare at her, the waiter returns with two bowls of pale broth with lumps of some kind of pasta floating in them.

'I took the liberty of ordering,' Franklin says, perhaps reading Mina's trepidation about the food on her face. 'I hope you don't mind.' Mina hesitates but Franklin goes on. 'It's all vegetarian.'

Mina smiles and pushes the soggy noodles round the bowl without making any effort to bring the spoon to her lips. Now that she's here she finds she has very little appetite. She asks if there's any further news on DCI Jordan but Franklin tells her there isn't. Mina's not sure the woman would tell her anything even if there was. After that, the small talk dries up. The waiter brings several plates of crispy fried food and tops up their glasses with mineral water.

'So,' Franklin says, after he's out of hearing. 'What do you have for me?'

Mina sits back in her chair. 'I . . . I really haven't had the chance to find out anything yet.' She feels her face burning with shame.

Franklin encourages her with another smile. 'But you still believe DI Doggett and DS Tyler have an agenda they aren't sharing with you. Or with me, for that matter.'

Mina shakes her head. 'It's not like that exactly . . .' The woman is twisting her words.

When Franklin agreed to mentor her, Mina had been thrilled at the potential opportunity. Okay, maybe she'd laid it on a bit thick about how hard it was to be a young woman constantly battling the patriarchy but she hadn't expected the ACC to pick up on her insecurities about Tyler and Doggett and take them so seriously.

'Mina.' Franklin puts down her chopsticks and knits her hands together, resting her elbows on the table. 'I appreciate I'm putting you in a delicate position.'

'I feel like a spy!'

Franklin gestures as though dismissing the idea. 'You're doing your job. As *they* should be. If they really have information pertinent to DCI Jordan's disappearance don't you think they should be sharing it?'

Mina's horrified. 'I never meant to imply that. Whatever it is they're doing ... *if* they're doing anything, I can't believe it has anything to do with DCI Jordan. It's been going on longer than that anyway ...' She shouldn't have said that. She swallows another mouthful of water, trying to buy herself time to marshal her words. She doesn't want to say the wrong thing again. 'They've always been a bit, well ... closed off, I guess. That's all. I'm more junior to them though, they don't have to share everything with me.' Now she's just trying to downplay things and Franklin will see right through that.

The appearance of DS Vaughan has unsettled her. *How many other people is she mentoring?* Mina supposes it was pretty ridiculous of her to think she was special in some way. That might explain how Franklin knew about the crime scene before any of them. Vaughan had been the first one on the scene. That still left one question unanswered though – had

Vaughan recognised the uniform from Demeter Fabrications or had Franklin?

'They like to do things their own way,' Franklin says, and it takes Mina a moment to realise she's still talking about Tyler and Doggett. 'You'd be surprised how often I've been told that over the years. But times have changed, Mina. The days of rogue officers doing things *their* way is long past. It's part of the reason I was drafted in here in the first place and I intend to make sure that before I leave again this entire department knows it.'

Mina takes another sip of water and looks down at a stain on the tablecloth. She can feel Franklin's eyes on her.

'But I think,' Franklin tells her, 'that you know that already. I think that's why you first came to me with your suspicions regarding Superintendent Stevens.'

'I never said I knew anything concrete—'

'You can leave Stevens to me, Mina, don't worry. My point is that you represent what this organisation will be in twenty years' time. I'll be gone by then, retired on a fat pension if I'm lucky, but you . . . you'll be running the show. I can see a lot of potential in you. You're a rising star, Mina, and I want to help you get up there.'

The words are flattering and Mina can feel herself blushing, but a little voice inside warns her to stay quiet. *Be careful, Mina. You need to watch this one.* She can't decide whose voice it is – Doggett's, Tyler's, or her own? Maybe she doesn't know the difference anymore. But she has to. That's what Franklin is trying to tell her. She's known this for a while now.

They've taught her a lot but she's different to them. She's looking to the future while they're both stuck in the past.

Franklin must read her thoughts. 'You can't let them hold you back, Mina. Their time is waning while yours is just beginning.'

Mina turns the water glass in circles with her right hand. 'They do know something they're not telling me,' she says eventually, and Franklin nods over her interlaced fingers.

When Mina had spoken to DI Cooper last year the woman had implied . . . no, all but said outright that Superintendent Stevens was bent. But Tyler and Doggett hadn't wanted to know. They've been keeping her at arms' length ever since. At first she'd put it down to Daley's death and the fact that maybe they were trying to protect her, and she hopes . . . she's sure, that ultimately that's still their intention. But they're treating her like some fragile thing. She's a police officer – a detective! – just the same as they are.

'Can you find out what it is?' Franklin asks.

She'd tried in the car but in fairness not all that hard. She doesn't want to spy on these men she respects, for Franklin or for anyone. But she really doesn't owe them anything either, not when they're freezing her out like this. Maybe it's time she started making her own luck.

'Yes,' she says. 'Whatever it is they're up to, I can figure it out.'

Franklin nods, a small grin raising one side of her mouth. 'Well then, good. If you need to talk to me, text me. I'll reply with a date and time, and we'll meet back here. Best we keep this talk out of the office from now on.' She says it as though it's a matter of fact and yet it suddenly makes Mina wonder if she's making a mistake. She doesn't know this woman, none of them do. She still has no idea what's happening about Stevens, if anything. She hasn't seen him for a few days though, come to think of it. Does that mean Professional Standards are looking into what she's told them or not? Have they found out something? Something that implicated Doggett and Tyler?

And then a worse thought hits her. She'd assumed it was safe to talk to Franklin about her suspicions, given the woman had only just arrived in the department, but what if she was wrong about that? What if Franklin is working with Stevens as well?

As Mina forces down food that she can't taste she wonders if she can really trust the woman sitting opposite her. Whatever it is Doggett and Tyler are keeping from her, she hopes it isn't something that's going to get them into too much trouble.

The house sits in darkness, a veil of quiet hanging over it. It was never a party house and the quiet peace that the place emanated was always one of the things Tyler liked most about it. This has always been a place of sanctuary, a bolthole that he could come to when things were at their worst.

He stares out of the car window, looking up at the imposing Victorian architecture of the townhouse. He first came here as a child and it seemed much bigger then.

He remembers looking up at the attic and thinking how far away it seemed. He always raced up the stairs to that window first, to stare out across the city at the rows of terraced houses, thinking how each one of them was full of people he didn't know, going about lives he could only guess at.

It was the attic window he sat in that first evening he came to stay here. He was sixteen. It was late that night too. And cold, though it hadn't been snowing. It was cold in a different way. He had come home after school that day to find his father hanging from the hallway banister. Somehow – he's a bit hazy on the details of this – he'd managed to call for help and he remembers Diane being the first one there. As an adult, now well versed in police procedure, he suspects that wasn't the case, but he doesn't remember any of the first responders or the paramedics or anyone else. Just Diane, putting her arms around him and pulling him away. She drove him straight home to this house. Her house. He'd gone to the attic window, curled up on the bench seat and watched the sun drop behind the hills.

Diane had fetched him drinks and food that he didn't touch. She draped a blanket around his shoulders and tried to talk to him. Eventually she'd left him alone but he was aware of her walking around the house below. He sat there all night waiting for the tears to come. Waiting for the sun to rise. Waiting for the world to make sense.

He was still waiting.

Tyler snaps back from the past at a sharp tap on the

window. He turns to see Doggett looking in at him, his hairy nose pressed up against the glass. Tyler hits a button and the window slides down, letting in a blast of cold air.

'I thought you were going home,' Doggett says, his eyebrows twitching.

After they'd caught up in the office and discovered that neither of them had anything more that they didn't already know, it had been Doggett's idea to call it a night. Tyler had agreed readily enough, knowing full well that he'd be coming back here.

'Let me in then,' Doggett moans. 'It's bloody freezing out here.'

Tyler unlocks the doors, closes his window and watches Doggett hustle around the front of the car to the passenger side. He jumps in, closes the door and sits there shivering, rubbing his hands together.

Tyler reaches forward and turns up the heat. 'How did you know I'd be here?'

Doggett blows on his fingers. 'I'm a bloody detective, son. You've been here every night since she disappeared.' His legs are jiggling up and down, although it isn't clear if it's an attempt to keep warm or just his usual fidgeting. 'Not sure what you're hoping to find.'

Neither is Tyler. Does he really think Diane's going to turn up and ask him to put the kettle on? Explain that she took an unexpected holiday to the Bahamas and just got back? Have a reasonable explanation for why she hasn't thought to ring him in all this time? No, even he's not that deluded.

'I feel closer to her here. I keep hoping I'll think of something.'

Doggett's quiet for a moment but his legs keep up their characteristic rhythm. Finally, he says, 'I think we need to tell Franklin what we know.'

So this is why he's here. Tyler knew there'd be a reason. 'We don't *know* anything.'

In the year since Doggett first came to Tyler and told him what he knew of his father's death, the two of them have gone over every aspect of Richard Tyler's final days, as well as all the notes Doggett made in the intervening years. Richard had been worried about something. He'd used the word conspiracy. He'd been looking into past cases. Cold cases, many of them, with no discernible link. And that one fresher one, the robbery at Demeter. What had Richard found that meant he had to be silenced? And now this body turns up frozen in ice. A tangible piece of physical evidence that might link to whatever his father had been investigating. After all this time were they finally getting closer to finding out?

'I still don't see anything that links the Demeter robbery to the others,' Tyler says. But they'd gone over all this earlier. For all that they've taken a step forward they're still going round in circles. 'What was Richard's interest in it?'

'I was thinking about that after you left,' Doggett says slowly. 'There is one person we could ask.' He seems reluctant to go on but after a few moments he says, 'Joey McKenna.'

Once a minor member of one of Sheffield's infamous east side gangs, Joey McKenna was an old school villain who had reinvented himself over the years into one of the city's most successful, if not entirely squeaky clean, entrepreneurs. A few months ago McKenna had offered Tyler information on the death of his father. All he had to do in exchange was walk out of police headquarters with hundreds of thousands of pounds of recovered cash that McKenna believed was his. Tyler refused. He should have done more than that, but he hadn't.

'No,' Tyler says. He has been thinking about this a lot over the past few months. What did McKenna really have in that file he'd been so intent on handing over? Was it really the answer to his father's murder? Whatever was in there, it was more likely to benefit McKenna than anyone else. 'All we know for sure is he wanted us to *believe* he knew something. For all we know the information he had was nothing new. And it isn't as though we can trust the man anyway.' He'd learned that the hard way. 'He might even have been involved in Richard's death.'

Doggett taps the tips of his fingers together. 'Maybe I should have a word with him. See if I can't shake loose what he's hiding. Or, like I said, we could make this official. Hand everything we know over to Franklin.'

Tyler glances at him. 'Are you really that sure we can trust her? We don't know much about her.'

'I know she put Slippery Stevens in his place the day she arrived. That puts a feather in her cap as far as I'm concerned.'

It was true the Superintendent hadn't been able to hide his displeasure when Franklin turned up in the wake of Diane's disappearance. The two of them had had at least three fairly public disagreements over the past weeks. But Tyler wasn't convinced. Was it coincidence she arrived so soon after Diane disappeared? 'We can't trust her. We can't trust anyone. And why would she take us seriously anyway? We don't know anything more than you knew all those years ago. They didn't take you seriously back then so there's no reason to assume they will now. We can't prove that this has anything to do with Diane's disappearance.'

'But you think it does?'

Tyler realises something. 'I do. I don't know why but I do.'

Doggett runs a hand over his face and breathes out heavily. 'We can't just sit on our arses doing nowt!' he says. 'Perhaps it's time we hand this over. We've done all we can.'

Tyler shakes his head. 'I'm not giving up.'

'All right, all right. But what do we have left?'

They sit in silence for a while, Doggett staring out of the passenger window while Tyler goes back to staring at the house he partially grew up in. In many ways this place was more of a home than his actual one.

'Jude,' Tyler says, finally.

'Eh?'

'*He's* the one thing we have left.' Tyler's been avoiding this for too long now. It's time to talk to his brother.

'From what you told me about the last time you met, it didn't go so well.'

Doggett's not wrong. Jude had turned up at Tyler's door a few months ago but the meeting had been ... fractious. They'd managed the best part of a pint with each other before Tyler had lost his temper and stormed out. He hasn't heard from Jude since.

'He could know something,' Tyler tells Doggett. He might not even know that he knows something. An overheard telephone conversation. Something Richard let slip in passing.

'From what I remember he didn't have the best relationship with your dad at that point.'

Tyler sighs. 'I know I'm clutching at straws but ...' He leaves the sentence unfinished.

'Do you have any way to contact him?'

Tyler looks again at the house. That's the real reason he came here tonight, he now understands. 'He was in touch with Diane a few months back. I'm hoping she has his contact details somewhere.' Tyler pulls the spare keys from his pocket. He's searched the house a number of times now but at the time he wasn't looking for Jude's number. He was looking for some explanation as to where she had gone.

'Okay. I suppose it's something. But if Jude can't help ... then we go to Franklin. Agreed?'

Tyler doesn't answer. Doggett's hand shoots out and grabs his elbow. 'Agreed?'

'Fine,' Tyler says, pulling his arm away.

'In the meantime, we still have a case to work on.'

Tyler nods. 'I haven't forgotten. But I'm not forgetting Diane either. She's out there somewhere and we need to find her. No matter what.'

It's Doggett's turn to nod. 'If she's still alive, she's more than capable of looking after herself, you know that.'

If she's alive. It's the one thing neither of them have allowed themselves to voice yet, the thought that she might not be. Tyler tries not to dwell on why Doggett's choosing to voice it now. He doesn't want to believe she's dead. He's *certain* she isn't. Even so, he can't deny the fact that if she isn't, her time is fast running out.

For the smallest of moments when she wakes, she forgets where she is. It really is the most infinitesimal amount of time, a sliver of a nanosecond where she isn't happy exactly, but she isn't afraid either.

And then she remembers.

It's always the cold that hits her first: the damp grit of the floor beneath her cheek; the chill of the urine that has now cooled between her legs and made the crotch of her under-wear scratch and blister her thighs; the freezing winter air that has crept up and under the blanket he left for her, and settled into the very marrow of her bones. These things combine to bring her crashing back to reality.

Then there's the smell. It's a dank, earthy scent caused by the white mould that coats the cellar walls like icing dusting a cake. This combines with her own sweet fetid odour as the bacteria that have gathered in her nooks and crannies run rampant. She despairs at the way her own body can betray her in this manner.

And then finally, the pain. She catalogues these ailments in a litany that reminds her to have hope. If she hurts this badly, she must still be alive. The plastic cable ties he used to bind her hands have cut into the skin of her wrists and are now stained pink with her blood. When she can stand the pain, she flexes her muscles in the vain hope that even one of them will snap but it isn't long before she's forced to give up. Besides, even if they did break, she would still have one arm handcuffed to the gas meter. She wishes she was stronger, more willing to cause herself permanent damage if it meant she could get free. But her will lets her down. Maybe she just hasn't reached that level of despair yet but the thought that there might be another, lower level of horror beneath the one she's trapped in, threatens to fully unravel her fraying mind.

The rope wrapped around her ankles would be easier to loosen were it not for her leg. She's certain now that it's broken. As long as she keeps still it pulses gently in the background of her mind, no worse than a toothache. But if she tries to move, it erupts in a volcano of agony that pushes away all other concerns. There's a bulge in the fabric of her trouser leg as well that's more than a little alarming. She can't see it all that clearly even now her eyes have adjusted to the dark, but she has a nasty feeling it's probably her tibia. When she'd finally given in and voided her bladder for the first time it had been the most amazing feeling in the world. But then the warm stream had reached her lower right leg and once again her body convulsed in waves of agony. The next time she managed to arch her body carefully to the left so that the stream flowed away from her bad leg. She suspects the growing pool of liquid beneath her is more than just urine, and she's sure she can smell that tell-tale metallic scent she's grown accustomed to over the years. The smell of life escaping.

But worse even than the leg – which is manageable as long as she stays still – are the incidental pains. The sudden cramps and violent spasms her body makes after so long confined without exercise. They hit without warning and have the knock-on effect of making her jump and setting the leg off all over again.

Then there are the minor ailments – her cracked lips, the dizziness and headaches – and she knows that these are the most serious of all. The hunger pangs are long passed and she no longer even thinks about food. But water is another matter. He left her three bottles on his last visit. Not even the big two-litre bottles but the poxy little ones you get with a meal deal. She'd tried to ration them but they hadn't lasted anywhere near as long as she'd hoped. Since she drained the last drops from them she's only had to pee once and that must have been hours ago now, maybe longer. With the blood loss and everything else ... No, it won't be hunger that kills her.

She wonders how long she has before her body gives out. *Three days without water.* But time has no meaning down here in the dark and there's no effective way to measure it since he stopped coming.

When she first woke here, however long ago that was, she'd been in almost the exact same position she's in now. Except the cable ties had been looser then and her leg was still intact. He would visit her regularly, bringing food and water twice a day, and emptying the bucket he'd left for her last thing at night. She thinks back to those heady salad days of her early incarceration almost fondly. Sometimes he'd stop and chat for a few minutes and that gave her a chance to talk him round. Not that she held out much hope that he might suddenly release her but at least it prevented him thinking about trying to kill her again.

She rubs her fingers across her bruised but healing throat, wincing as the movement causes her wrists to chafe. That was the first injury, caused when he tried to half suffocate, half strangle her. At least that one is fading. She still doesn't know for sure whether he bottled it or botched it, whether he failed to kill her accidentally or by design. Her money's on the former. He always was a cowardly little shit! Either way she'd woken up down here, trussed up like the Christmas turkey while he decided on his next move.

Stevens. Superintendent *Bloody* Stevens. *The Eel!* How could she have been so stupid? That might be the thing that hurts most of all. She'd walked straight into this and she really had no one to blame but herself. And then she'd compounded matters by being overconfident. It had taken her well over a week before she realised he wasn't going to let her go. He couldn't afford to. And once she figured that out, she knew it was only a matter of time before he would figure it out too, if he hadn't already. She had to make her move before then.

She'd waited until his second visit of the day, the evening one when he would be tired and hopefully paying less attention. He un-cuffed her from the gas meter so she could stretch her legs and that's when she went for him. She grabbed the toilet bucket as she stood up and slammed it into his head before he'd even got his hands up, taking only mild satisfaction that the contents of the bucket slopped into his face. But his instinctive backlash had caught her off-balance from the swing and she'd gone down backwards and pulled him with her. The rest was bad luck. Somehow her leg got caught between his and pinioned under the gas meter. She doesn't remember hearing the snap but maybe she was screaming too loudly.

He came back with the cable ties less than twenty minutes later and then he'd left for the second to last time.

It was in this period that she properly lost track of time, falling in and out of consciousness, no water, no food, her leg burning in agony. She doesn't know how long he was gone but she guesses it was days rather than hours. And then he'd come back for the final time, bringing the three bottles of water with him and an old duvet of all things. For a moment she thought he'd taken pity on her and was bringing her something for the cold but then he'd stuffed it into the coal chute, closing off the last of her light. She put away her pride at that point, begging him for help, pleading with him to let her go, to call for an ambulance. But he hadn't said a word, wouldn't even look at her. She'd screamed at his hunched back as he climbed the stairs, shouted until she was hoarse. Then she fell asleep again.

She woke to the sound of voices upstairs and her instinct had been to cry out but something stopped her. It was a gut feeling, that was all. Something instinctual that told her however much she thought things couldn't get any worse, there was a distinct possibility that they could. He hadn't replaced her gag. Why? So she would be able to drink the water presumably. Did that mean he wanted her to be found? Eventually. Maybe she should just wait a moment. She'd listened but couldn't make out the words. It was him – Stevens – and another male voice. Still she hesitated. Was it worth shouting again? Was it worth a try? And then they were gone and she's been cursing herself for her cowardice ever since. Because that was the last she heard of him.

How long ago that was she has no idea. Hours? Days? She's lost track. But she knows one thing now, he isn't coming back. Her water is gone and so is he. And time is beginning to unravel.

She sleeps too often and she knows that's not a good sign. When she's awake she plans and plots. She goes through every conceivable scenario in her head. She slips free of the cable ties by dislocating her thumb and sloughing the flesh from her hand. She wrenches the gas pipe from its mooring and sends herself to a sleepy peace. She hauls herself up the stone staircase, dragging her useless leg behind her only to find the door is padlocked from the other side.

She cries out, now that it's too late and there's no one to hear her. She screams until her lungs burn and her throat rasps and she convinces herself that this time there's a chance a neighbour might hear something and raise the alarm.

And then she sleeps again. A fitful sleep full of dreams of lakes and waterfalls and ice-cold glasses of crystal clear water. She dreams of Adam too, looking down on her with pitiful eyes.

But when she wakes he isn't there. There's only the cold and the smell and the ever-present pain. How much time has passed since Stevens brought her here? Since he left? She has no way to tell and it wouldn't help her if she did.

All she knows is that she can't have long left before the end. It's getting harder to think ... harder to move. Even the pain is fading away now. She wishes she could see Adam just one more time. If she did, she'd tell him the truth. She promises that, prays it even. If she gets out of this she'll tell him the truth about his past.

Detective Chief Inspector Diane Jordan's head slumps to one side and she falls into dreams once again.

day two

The ICER recordings #113

(Archivists' note: Voice analysis confirms this is the same caller as heard in recording #112 [03/05/18])

Call received: 06:34 Tuesday 6th Mar 2018
Duration: 1 minute 54 seconds

Partial Transcript:

ICER   Yes.

UC4   Erm ... Is it ... ? Is it done?

(Recording is silent for 4 seconds)

ICER   This number is to be used only in emergencies.

UC4   Yes, it's just ... Look, mate, I'm just doing what I'm told, all right? They need to know if the problem's been dealt with. Only, on the news they said only one body had been found. A male.

ICER   There were complications. I'm dealing with them.

UC4   Oh. So the DCI, Jord—

ICER No names!

UC4 Right, yeah. Sorry. The thing is, the information she received might just come back and bite us all on the arse. *(laughs)*

ICER Your inside man assured me he dealt with her. She wasn't at the house. He gave me the folder of information and seemed confident no copies were made.

UC4 Okay. Only . . . our other asset said the scene at the reservoir wasn't quite what we discussed. Apparently there was blood found by the body? *(pause 2 seconds)* We're assuming that's—

ICER Like I said, there were complications. The ultimate outcome will be the same.

UC4 Okay, so this won't affect the rest of the plan?

ICER It would be simpler just to plug this leak of yours. Permanently.

UC4 No, no, they don't want him . . . plugged. They just want to remind him what he stands to lose if he doesn't get back on board.

ICER Fine. It's your money.

UC4 So we're still on? The plan's still on track?

(recording is silent for 4 seconds)

He ... hello?

ICER   I said I'd handle it. Are you questioning my abilities?

UC4   No, no, of course not. It's just—

ICER   Then I think we're done here. Unless ... that other matter we discussed has become part of the agenda?

UC4   No. No, they don't want to act on that yet.

ICER   It might be sensible to deal with him now, while we're tying up loose ends. He isn't going to give up, you realise? The man was his father.

UC4   Jesus! Haven't we got enough dead cops to worry about? *(laughs)* Look, let's just stick to the plan, yeah? Anyway, I guess that's it, er ... for now. Thank you very much then. Goodbye.

Call ends 06:35

'Right then,' Doggett says, hopping up onto the desk and folding his arms. 'What do we have so far?'

Tyler nods his head to Rabbani, giving her permission to take the lead on the briefing. She stands up and walks across to the information on the wall. The picture of the frozen body stands out starkly in front of her. 'We have this bloke,' she says. 'And we need an ID on him.'

'How's Dr Ridgeway getting on with the autopsy?' Doggett asks.

'Not great. She said something about having to get the body back to room temperature without compromising evidence. It's gonna take a while, I think. Her preliminary findings, though, indicate he definitely wasn't shot.'

Doggett sniffs. 'So our blood spatter *does* belong to someone else.'

'We should have some results from the lab on that later today but other than blood type it's only going to help if our victim's on file somewhere.'

Doggett gets up and moves across to the board. 'Might be worth starting with the uniform then,' he suggests. 'Demeter Fabrications.'

'Yes,' Tyler says. 'I did think of that.'

Doggett grins. 'Of course you did.'

Rabbani clears her throat. 'The robbery at the factory was a bit amateurish. The guard was killed by a single blow to the head. DI Johnson thought it was probably accidental. They meant to disable the guard but someone got a bit heavy-handed. The weapon wasn't recovered but the pathologist thought it was some kind of pipe or bar. A crowbar maybe. They searched the nearby drains, got divers into the canal but no joy.'

'Did Johnson have any suspects?'

Tyler presumes Doggett's asking for Rabbani's benefit. He already knows the details of the original case backwards. They both do. Tyler shakes his head. 'He didn't make much of an effort to look at the company finances though so Mina's going to have a crack at it.' It was something they'd discussed before. The inside job was a fairly standard avenue of enquiry but Johnson hadn't followed it far. In fact, the whole investigation was a bit thin. Out of all the cases Richard was looking into, this one had the least to it despite being the most recent. Was that significant in some way? Regardless, without the authority to look into the case officially they hadn't had the time or the resources to investigate properly. Now all that has changed.

'Is this Whitehouse fella still around?' Doggett asks.

Tyler nods. 'We'll start with him. General background check, another interview.'

He crosses back to his desk and looks out at the snow that has begun to fall again. His thoughts stray once more to Jordan. Is she out there somewhere? Lying frozen in a heap of snow? Last night, at her house, he'd managed to find a mobile number for Jude scribbled down on the back of an envelope and stuffed in the back of a drawer. But when he'd tried it, the call had gone straight to a voicemail with no recorded greeting. He couldn't be sure it was the right number and he'd rung off without leaving a message. Could his brother really have the answers they're looking for? It's more than a stretch.

'If I were you,' Doggett says, 'I'd keep it vague for now. So far we've managed to keep the details of the uniform from the press. See how you go but it might be best not to mention the link between the two cases at the moment.'

Tyler agrees. 'Just a routine re-examining of a cold case. It's what we're here for, after all.' He turns back to Doggett. 'What about you?'

Doggett shuffles his way off the desk and takes his turn at the board. 'SOCOs found plenty of footprints but . . .' He shrugs. 'Might help with identity once we have a suspect but nothing to go on otherwise. There were also some minute traces of blood leading up to the road. Whoever moved the body was careful but not quite careful enough. My guess is he got the body up there and loaded it into a vehicle.'

'A bit risky,' Rabbani says. 'I mean, it's quiet round there but he could easily have been spotted.'

'Right. So why take the risk? Why not leave the body with the other one?'

'Because he didn't want it identified, presumably,' Tyler suggests.

Doggett looks at him. 'No shit.'

'So what *have* you got?' Tyler asks.

'Sweet F.A.' Doggett blows out his cheeks. 'I'll concentrate on CCTV footage on the roads and in the nearby village. There's a housing estate not far away. See if we can identify any vehicles in the area yesterday morning or the night before.'

'Rather you than me.'

Doggett grunts. 'I'll co-opt a couple of constables to help me since our new ACC seems intent on throwing the budget to the wall. Might as well take advantage of it. I've got DS Vaughan as well, for whatever use she turns out to be.'

'You'd better look into the boatshed as well, see who the owner is.'

'Yes,' says Doggett. 'I did think of that.'

'Of course you did.'

Rabbani tuts and rolls her eyes.

'And you,' Doggett tells her. 'I hope you've got a better coat on than yesterday.'

She shakes her head at them and Doggett gives Tyler a wink behind her back.

The company called Demeter Fabrications may not exist anymore but the building that housed it still does, now home to a very different sort of business. Unusually, Tyler lets Mina drive. She raises a questioning eyebrow at him and he offers a minimal explanation. 'I want to do some research on the way.'

This effectively cuts off any chance she might have had of quizzing him further. He sits fiddling with his mobile the whole way there, answering her tentative questions with grunts of acknowledgement at best.

Mina had found a mobile number for Whitehouse on file which turned out to still be current. He'd sounded pleasant enough on the phone, suggesting they meet at the old factory so that they could 'see the scene of the crime' for themselves. She had been surprised when Tyler had agreed to the unorthodox arrangement. And even more surprised when Whitehouse told her he would sort things with the current owners of the place.

Tyler directs her using the address she forwarded to him. It's a large industrial area on an estate in the Don Valley. The business is now called Delight! and a bright pink illuminated sign tells them they've found the right place. They're met at the very ornate front gates by a security guard. After Mina shows the woman her warrant card the guard goes into her little hut and makes a phone call.

'All a bit old school, isn't it?'

She was thinking aloud more than anything but Tyler answers her anyway. 'There must be a lot of money in ice cream these days.' He speaks without looking up. 'Unless they have some other reason for keeping people out.'

The guard puts down the phone and presses a button. The gates begin to swing open for them as the guard returns to Mina's window. 'Straight up and past the main building there, car park's on the left, love.'

Mina thanks her and drives through the gateway. The 'main building' is the original steel factory, Mina assumes, while off to the right-hand-side of the property there are a number of stacked containers, some of which have been converted into other businesses – she spots what looks like a dispatch office for a cab firm, and a design studio among others.

At reception they're met by a red-haired woman with a sharply angled bob and an even sharper suit. 'I'm Harriet Spencer. Welcome to Delight!' she tells them, her tone of voice somehow managing to convey the over-indulgent exclamation mark from the company logo. She shows them into a small, cosy room just off the reception area. It's plush with comfortable tub chairs and sparklingly clean glass tables, with menus laid out on them.

'What can I get you?' Spencer asks. 'Coffee? Cronut? Anything you fancy, on the house.'

Mina flicks through one of the menus. The choice is extensive, ranging from the sort of cakes and pastries that might be found in any coffee shop to far more elaborate desserts and ice-cream based products. She recognises a few of them from that place on London Road that she goes to with her family sometimes. Her dad's always had a particularly sweet tooth and although Mina's tried to dissuade him from these kinds of choices since he had his heart scare, she suspects he goes there a lot more often than he lets on.

She's about to decline when Tyler surprises her by smiling widely at the woman and saying, 'Just coffee, thanks. Black.' Both he and Spencer turn to look at her.

'I'm fine. Thank you.'

Spencer dips her head as though to tell her it's her loss and moves to a pink slimline telephone by the door. She lifts the receiver off the wall and speaks for a few moments, although her words are lost to Mina.

When Spencer returns she ushers them into a couple of tub chairs and takes one herself. 'Now,' she says. 'How can I help?'

Tyler acknowledges her cooperation with a long dip of his head. 'I'm not sure you can,' he tells her. 'It's Mr Whitehouse we were hoping to speak to.'

Spencer smiles widely. It's a curiously unsettling expression but Mina can't work out exactly what's wrong with it. 'I'm sure Gareth won't be long. He's always been ten minutes late to everything as long as I've known him.'

'How long has that been?' Tyler asks, smiling just as deeply and, to Mina's mind, unnervingly.

'We go way back.' Spencer waves her left hand through the air and Mina notes the lack of a wedding ring. 'I bought the factory off Gareth ... ooh, let's see ... almost ten years ago now ...' No jewellery of any kind, in fact. No earrings, no necklace ... She supposes that isn't so remarkable if the woman works with food but everything else about her is kind of glamorous. Her hair is so on point it could be a hairpiece. The suit is clearly designer, and professional but with a flattering cut. Priti would be envious of it, for sure, and would probably be able to tell her what brand it is. Mina wonders if she can engineer a way to take a photo of the woman so that she can ask her cousin later. *Why does it matter what the bloody woman's wearing?* She's not even relevant to their case, as far as they know. Except that . . . there's something wrong here. A wrinkle in the picture that stands out. No doubt Tyler would call that a mixed metaphor but . . . but what?

And then she realises. It isn't Spencer that has her senses alert at all. It's Tyler. She's picking up all of this from him. The way he's sitting there quietly listening to Spencer talk about how she founded the desserts company. Lapping it all up like he's really interested, accepting offers of refreshment . . . *smiling*!

He's up to something.

The coffee arrives, wheeled in on an ornate wooden trolley by a young woman in a tight pink T-shirt. The word *Delight!* is emblazoned across her chest in tall yellow letters. Mina makes eye contact with her for a moment but she quickly looks back at her trolley. There's something familiar about her and Mina wonders if she knows her from Mosque, or even from school – there can't be that many years between them. She's very beautiful, but effortlessly so, unlike the over-engineered Spencer. And she's far less sure of herself.

'Thank you, Binita,' Spencer tells the waitress. 'I'll manage.' The young woman flinches at her name and makes a hasty withdrawal towards the door. Spencer turns back to them. 'I took the liberty.' She lifts a filigreed silver cloche to reveal a plate loaded with pastries, which she then insists on serving to them on tea plates. They both accept the offerings but Mina follows Tyler's lead and pushes her plate onto the glass table in front of them.

'Are you sure you won't have anything to drink?' Spencer asks her again, but before she can answer the young waitress, Binita, yelps slightly and draws their attention.

The door is opening in her face, pushing her backwards, as a large balding man with a fat belly enters the room. He glances at the waitress briefly and for a moment Mina sees a look of utter contempt on his face. It's gone quickly though, and then he's moving towards them, smiling. Mina watches Binita slip through the doorway and once again their eyes meet across the room. Then the door closes quietly and the young woman is gone.

'I'm so sorry to have kept you,' Gareth Whitehouse tells them, reaching across the table to shake Tyler's hand. Tyler handles the introductions and Whitehouse looks Mina up and down before dismissing her importance almost as quickly as he had Binita's.

Mina can feel her face flushing at the familiar dismissal. She's met plenty of Whitehouses in her time but that doesn't make it any easier to deal with. Under normal circumstances she would take the opportunity to put him firmly in his place and she can already see Tyler hesitating, aware of what's just happened and giving her a chance to take control of the situation. For all his faults, his lack of empathy at times, he's very good at spotting things like this. But she has the feeling he will get far more out of Whitehouse than she ever could. Besides, she has something else to look into.

'Sorry,' she says, standing up and addressing herself to Harriet Spencer. 'I don't suppose I could use your loo, could I?'

'Oh, of course. If you'd like to follow—'

'That's all right,' Mina says, waving away the woman's hospitality. 'I saw it on the way in, other side of reception, right?' She doesn't give the woman a chance to answer but hurries towards the door.

'I—'

'Ms Spencer,' Tyler cuts in. 'It would be helpful if you could stay. I may have a few more questions for you.'

Yes! He gets it. She catches Tyler's eye as she slips out of the door. *Well done, Sarge!*

Tyler watches Rabbani close the door behind her. He hopes she knows what she's doing. He'd been surprised when she didn't take the opportunity to deal with Whitehouse. He has no idea yet if the man is sexist, racist or a little of both but Rabbani wouldn't normally suffer either. But then he'd noticed her eyeballing him and he realised she must have something up her sleeve. The least he could do is back her up.

Whitehouse is helping himself to tea and pastries and settling down in the tub chair across from Tyler's own, very much at home. He's a big man with a large paunch that he carries in front of himself like a statement of intent. He's in his early sixties, perhaps. Greying, not quite fully bald, and with an old-fashioned goatee beard that's still mostly dark. Tyler decides to take the man down a peg or two, but not just for Rabbani. There's something about the man he finds . . . unwholesome. Perhaps he's being unfair, but he's learned to trust his instincts and his instincts are telling him this man is already hiding something. He starts slowly though. No point in getting off on the wrong foot. There's plenty of time to get to that later.

'Thank you for seeing me, Mr Whitehouse.'

'Gareth, please,' Whitehouse tells him magnanimously through a mouthful of pastry crumbs. 'And it's really no inconvenience.'

'I'm truly glad about that.' Tyler's smile feels like a mask but Whitehouse doesn't appear to notice. Spencer does, though. Something about Rabbani's abrupt exit has put the woman on edge. She's perched herself on a chair arm and is watching him closely. Much of the professional cool of earlier has worn off now that Whitehouse has arrived. She seems nervous and has taken to turning her teacup on its saucer in her lap.

'I must admit,' Whitehouse says, shovelling a mini croissant into his mouth, 'I'm curious as to why you asked to meet me this morning. Your colleague wasn't all that forthcoming on the phone.' He chews between sentences and Tyler can see the mashed-up food moving across his tongue. 'Is there some new evidence about the robbery? I haven't heard anything from the police in years.'

Tyler smiles but chooses not to answer. 'I'm curious myself,' he says. 'Why did you suggest meeting here?'

'Well,' Whitehouse tells him, wiping flakes of pastry

from his goatee with a two-fingered pincer movement, 'scene of the crime and all that. I thought it would give you a feel for the place, even after all these years. Although of course it's very different now.' He liberates a Viennese slice from the cake stand. 'And in fairness, I don't need much of an excuse to come here.' He sinks his teeth into the pastry and the contents burst from either side. He performs a little juggling act, catching blobs of cream and licking the tips of his fingers.

'And you two obviously know each other,' Tyler says, taking advantage of Whitehouse's indisposition to turn back to Harriet Spencer. She flinches slightly at his returned gaze and he notes the way her eyes flick reflexively to the older man before she answers.

'As I said, I bought this place off Gareth in '09.' She smiles at the man who's still licking his lips and chewing. 'Since then we haven't been able to get rid of him.' She laughs to show she's joking but there's a tightness around her eyes that tells Tyler there's some truth to the statement as well. These two aren't the bosom-buddies they're trying to make out they are. He wonders how deep this friendship really runs or whether it's more one-sided. And if so, why? A marriage of convenience, perhaps. He lets it go for now. He needs to find out more about the robbery and, more importantly, why his father was so interested in it.

'It would help if you could take me through everything you can remember. I appreciate it was a long time ago.' Tyler sees Whitehouse eyeing up the cake stand again but he's damned if he's going to watch the man devour another morsel. 'That is, if you've finished your breakfast?'

Whitehouse opens his mouth to say something but obviously thinks better of it. 'Of course.' He sits back in his chair and brushes the last remains of the sticky sugar from his hands with a circular motion. 'It was the 23rd of August, 2002. A Friday—'

Tyler immediately jumps in. 'You're very sure of that. You must have a remarkably good memory, Gareth.' He keeps his tone polite and friendly.

Whitehouse pauses with his mouth open, aware something's changed, that he's lost his audience, perhaps, but unsure how he managed to lose them. 'Well, it was the second to last Friday of the month. Week before payday. And, to be honest, it was the beginning of the end for me. With the capital I lost in the robbery it was only a matter of time before I lost the business as well. When something that life-changing occurs, one tends to remember the details.' He's more serious now and Tyler believes him. This was a seminal moment in the man's life. But for the reasons he's stating or for some other reason?

'Please, go on.'

'I came in on the Saturday morning—'

'Was that usual? Working on a Saturday.' Tyler's starting to enjoy himself now. He notes the trace of frustration that crosses Whitehouse's face at being interrupted again so quickly.

'Not usual, but not unusual either. If we had a big order

on we'd often work through the weekend.' He stops, waiting for Tyler to jump in again. 'Do . . . Do you want me to continue?'

'Yes, yes, of course. Carry on.'

'Right . . . Well, I came into the office and I saw the safe straight away, door standing wide open, a few documents strewn across the floor and minus fifty grand, or thereabouts.' There's a false jollity about Whitehouse that's really beginning to get on Tyler's nerves.

'Was anything else stolen?'

'No, no, just the cash.'

'You seem very calm about that.'

'It was a long time ago, Detective. But no, at the time I was far from calm. I think a little bit of me knew even then that it was all over. The ramifications of that robbery meant that I was about to lose everything I had, not to mention the fact I would have to make more than two dozen employees redundant. I'm not saying all that went through my mind right in that moment but on some level I knew it.'

Tyler finds it hard to believe Whitehouse's employees ever featured in his thoughts, not even fleetingly. 'Yes, it must have been a terrible shock,' he says stonily. 'And finding a dead security guard can't have been easy either.'

Gareth Whitehouse narrows his eyes. 'Yes, I was the one who found the guard, but that wasn't until later. I'd already phoned the police and I realised I hadn't seen the man anywhere. I went looking for him and found him in the corridor at the back of the building. There was a smashed window. The police said the guard must have stumbled across the perpetrators as they made their escape and intervened.' Whitehouse does his best to fix a troubled expression onto his face but it's not all that convincing. 'I wish he hadn't. No amount of money is worth the loss of the guard's life.'

'Kevin,' Tyler says quietly.

'Sorry?'

'You seemed to be struggling to remember *the guard's* name. It was Kevin. Kevin Linville. He worked for you for five years.'

'I'm well aware of that.'

'You didn't know the man all that well then, I take it?'

'No, not really. We were on speaking terms, obviously, but I didn't have much to do with him on a daily basis. He worked the night shifts so other than a few words of greeting as we passed . . .' He leaves the sentence hanging.

'But no words on that particular day?'

'I'm not sure I understand what you're asking me.'

'I find it interesting, Gareth, that's all. You didn't see him that morning but you weren't overly concerned?'

'I assumed he was doing his rounds. There was nothing unusual about that. I didn't see him every day.'

Spencer squirms on her perch. 'I'm really not sure if I'm needed for all this, am I? Perhaps I should leave you two—'

'If you could hold on a few moments longer please, Ms Spencer.'

The woman settles back in place with a sigh and crosses her ankles.

Now,' Tyler says, turning back to Whitehouse. 'Something that's not very clear from the original investigation is why you were keeping such a large sum of money in a safe in the factory. Do you not trust banks, Gareth?'

Whitehouse is looking at him intently. The pleasant façade is crumbling away. 'As it happens, I don't, particularly. But at the time, as I said, the following week would have been payday and—'

'And you paid your employees in cash? Which you with-drew from the bank a whole week in advance?'

'This was a good few years ago, you realise. Different times and all that. There were always a few of the lads after a sub and most of them preferred to be paid in cash.'

'Even so, if you were paying them all in cash for a month's work, all two dozen or so, that still doesn't account for that large sum, does it? Unless you were extremely generous in your remuneration package.'

Whitehouse adjusts himself in his seat, the plastic squeaking under him. 'Look,' he says, 'I'm not sure what all this attitude is for. I'm the victim here. Of a crime that has never been solved, I might add. I feel like you're accusing me of something.'

'I'm just trying to work out the specifics of the situation.' Tyler waits. If he has to, he'll ask the question again but he suspects it won't be necessary. Whitehouse is only buying time to come up with a plausible reason.

Sure enough, he goes on, 'Many of our suppliers also operated in cash, and I liked to keep a healthy bit of capital to hand in case it was needed. It was the nature of the business.'

'I see,' Tyler says. 'Well, I suppose I'll have to take your word for that.'

He wonders how much luck Rabbani's going to have with those financial records after all these years. If only DI Johnson had dug a little deeper at the time. Was that Richard's interest as well? He hadn't made any reference to it but then he hadn't had long to look. A few weeks after the robbery, Richard was dead.

'So that leads me to wonder who knew the money was there.'

Again Whitehouse fidgets in his seat. 'It weren't a secret that I kept a slush fund handy.' Now he's dropped the pleas-antries Whitehouse sounds much broader, the Sheffield roots he was hiding beginning to break through.

'Amongst your employees, you mean?'

'Well . . . I suppose, but I can't imagine any of them—'

'Can't you? I would have thought that would be the first thing you might imagine. Someone breaks into your factory, goes straight to the office and steals fifty thousand pounds from a safe they clearly came prepared to break into. They don't steal anything else and then they murder a guard in cold blood for no apparent reason. Unless, of course, the reason was to hide their identity. If I were investigating this case – and I am now – the first thing I would consider would be an inside job. But you can't imagine that? You haven't once imagined that in the past sixteen years while you lamented the loss of your business?'

Whitehouse is leaning back in the chair now, his hands

folded neatly over his expansive belly. He smiles again but this time making no attempt to hide the insincerity of the gesture. 'It sounds very much as though you suspect me of something, Detective. Do I need to speak to a solicitor?'

Tyler lifts his hands in a small shrug. 'That's entirely your call, *Gareth*. But we're just having a chat and discussing possibilities at the moment. I'll let you know when we uncover any specific evidence.'

'Very well,' Whitehouse says, shuffling forward and putting his hands on the arms of the chair in preparation for levering his ample bulk upright. 'In that case, if there's nothing else . . .' He waits for Tyler to give him leave to stand.

Tyler hesitates. He isn't sure he wants to play this card so early in the investigation, and Doggett had warned against it. But on the other hand, given the way the interview's gone, he wants to gauge Whitehouse's reaction, and he won't be able to do that once the man's read about events in the papers. 'I wonder if you wouldn't mind looking at a photograph for me.' Tyler locates the relevant picture on his mobile. 'I should warn you that it's a photo of a dead body. We've yet to identify the man in question and I wondered if you might know him.'

Whitehouse is wary but he can hardly say no. He's curious as well, Tyler can see that much. He passes his phone across and Whitehouse takes it gingerly, fixing his eyes on the screen. He grimaces and turns his head away before looking back.

'Sorry, it's just . . .' He shakes his head.

Tyler's disappointed in the reaction. It certainly doesn't indicate anything substantive either way. It could just be the shock of the dead body. 'Do you recognise the man?'

Whitehouse shakes his head. 'No . . .' He's hesitant at first, then, surer of himself. 'No, should I? What is he, frozen?' He tries to pass the phone back.

'Perhaps you could take another look. It's not obvious from the photo, but the overalls the man is wearing have your company logo on the arm.' Tyler leans forward and flicks the screen to the left, revealing the picture he took of the logo. 'That *is* Demeter Fabrications?'

Whitehouse looks puzzled, nods. He flicks the photo back again. 'Yes, I can see that they're our overalls but . . . I mean we must have ordered hundreds of these over the years. I certainly didn't keep track of them. And I don't recognise this man. He didn't work for us. I mean, by the looks of him he wouldn't be old enough to have worked for us back then. He couldn't have been, what? Eight, when the robbery took place? Or . . . Hang on, you're not telling me this is a picture *from* back then, is it? I don't understand.'

Tyler has no intention of explaining. This isn't getting him anywhere though and he's beginning to regret showing his hand. He turns to Spencer. 'Perhaps you could have a look?'

'Me?' Spencer asks. 'I . . . I wasn't here then . . .'

'Of course,' Tyler says. 'But you were in Sheffield, weren't you? It's a long shot, granted, but there's a small chance you might recognise the man.'

'Well . . . if you really think it's necessary.'

Whitehouse passes her the phone and Spencer looks at it coolly. 'No,' she says, immediately passing the mobile back to Tyler. 'No, I don't recognise him.' But her lack of reaction is a reaction in itself. She's remarkably composed for someone who's just been shown a picture of a dead body. Spencer stands up. 'Now, I really should be getting on.'

Tyler hesitates for a moment. 'One last thing, was DI Johnson the only detective you spoke to at the time of the robbery?'

Whitehouse frowns. 'I'm not sure I follow.'

'There's a chance another officer went back over the case a few weeks later. Just to review progress. He didn't speak to you at all.'

Whatever patience Whitehouse has seems to have evaporated. 'Really, Detective, what's this all about? Don't you have records of that sort of thing? No, to my knowledge I've not spoken to anyone else about the case but . . . it was a long time ago.' Whitehouse spreads his hands in a gesture of helplessness.

Tyler's not buying this sudden loss of memory but he's not about to risk mentioning Richard by name either. He stands up. 'Okay, thank you both.'

Whitehouse hauls himself up out of the tub chair. 'I don't suppose . . . There isn't a chance you might recover the money after all this time?'

'I think that's rather unlikely, Mr Whitehouse, don't you? But there's still a good chance we might catch Kevin Linville's murderer. Sometimes second best is all you can hope for.'

This time Tyler's sarcasm isn't lost on the man and his top lip curls up in distaste.

'Now, since you've been kind enough to offer, perhaps we might have that little tour you promised me? How did you put it . . . *the scene of the crime, and all that?*'

Spencer struggles to hide her disappointment that the interview's still not over but she recovers quickly enough. 'Of course,' she says. 'If you'll follow me.'

Tyler gestures for Whitehouse to go ahead and the big man waddles after his so-called friend. Tyler follows him back into reception. There's no sign of Rabbani. He just hopes that whatever she's up to, he's given her enough time.

Mina emerges into the reception area in time to see the back of a pink T-shirt disappear through a set of double doors on the opposite side. She can't be sure it's the nervous-looking waitress, Binita, but it's worth a shot. She nods at the receptionist and mouths the word 'toilet' at the woman as she crosses the foyer. The receptionist acknowledges her with a nod of her own and looks back down at her computer. Mina sidesteps the corridor leading to the toilets and slips through the double doors in pursuit.

She finds herself in a long corridor lined down one side with huge floor-to-ceiling windows. The building they're in has been repurposed over the years but was probably some sort of mill at the turn of the previous century, the ceilings high, the windows vast, and the stone walls cold to the touch. The glass is frosted so there's no way to see outside but, assuming she hasn't got too turned around, they must look out over the car park at the front of the building. She moves down the wide corridor and is reminded for a moment of one of those old zombie games Ghulam was always playing. He'd made her have a go once, when she was far too young, and watched intently as she made her way down a corridor in a mansion just like this. Except for the fact that when she was halfway along, the windows burst open and a couple of zombified Rottweilers had jumped into the corridor and set upon her with their flesh-eaten muzzles. She'd screamed and ran out of the room crying and Ghulam had laughed at her for days. She never told him she'd actually wet herself, or that their mother had told her off for it.

Mina shivers and shakes off the image.

At the far end of the corridor there's another set of double doors and through the windows set into them she sees a large kitchen area with three employees in chefs' whites going about their baking business. She spots Binita on the far side of the room washing dishes.

Mina slips into the room and one of the chefs looks up. She flashes her warrant card to the woman. 'South Yorkshire CID,' she tells the woman. 'I just need to talk to Binita for a moment.'

The woman nods knowingly, perhaps already aware that the police are visiting the premises today. ''Nita!' she shouts across the room. 'This young lady wants a word with you. I hope you haven't been up to any mischief!' She grins at her own joke. 'Why don't you take your break now?' And with that the woman turns back to her business.

Binita still looks nervous, maybe even more so. She stands there with her arms covered in soap suds, dripping all over the floor while Mina crosses to her.

'Hi, Binita, I just wanted to ask you a couple of questions if that's okay. Do you want to dry off? Is there somewhere else we can go?'

Binita nods, grabs some paper towels from a dispenser attached to the wall and leads Mina through another door into some kind of staff changing facilities with lockers and benches. Mina notices a fire door at the far end of the room with a sign on it that says, 'Please make sure this door is <u>closed</u> when you leave!' Intuiting that Binita is more likely to talk to her openly if they are further from her work environment, Mina suggests they pop out for some fresh air. Binita agrees, fishing an anorak from a peg and pushing her way out through the fire door. Mina follows and immediately regrets her decision as they step back into the bitingly cold air. She really needs to speak to Priti about her jacket.

'I'm Mina, by the way. That's a pretty necklace you're wearing.'

Binita smiles and touches the thin gold chain with her hand. Her nails are painted dark red but most of them have been bitten down to the cuticles.

'We're here about something that happened here years ago, so I don't suppose you'll be able to tell us much.'

The young woman shakes her head.

'Have you worked here long?'

'Few months.'

'Right. Straight from school?'

Binita shakes her head. 'I did an access course at college. Catering level one.'

'Oh, right, brilliant! So that's what you want to get into, is it, catering?'

Binita shrugs, her hand still twisting the necklace. She still hasn't looked at Mina properly. This isn't going to be easy.

'Look, Binita.' She reaches out and gently touches the woman's arm. 'You can trust me, you know. If there's anything you want to tell me. I saw the way you reacted when that man came in. Mr Whitehouse? He's not done anything, has he?'

Binita's eyes widen. 'Nooooo! Nothing like that. He's just . . .' She lets out a deep breath and shakes her head. She's clearly been carrying this around for a while. Maybe all she needed was someone to ask. 'You won't say I said anything?'

'Promise.'

'He just . . . he's a bit . . . over-friendly sometimes.'

Mina swallows down a wave of revulsion. She'd seen it all in that one look he'd given her but she was hoping she was wrong.

Binita flushes. 'He hasn't done anything, really. Nothing . . . bad. It's just brushing up against you sometimes and saying things and . . . once . . .'

'Go on, you can tell me.'

'He patted me . . . here.' She touches her own behind with one rough-nailed hand.

Mina feels the blood rush to her head. If Whitehouse was there in front of her she's not sure she would be able to control herself. Thankfully, for her career anyway, he's not. 'That *is* bad, Binita. No one has the right to do that to you.'

'I know. But it's not like ... I mean it never went any further. I just got away from him. I told Ms Spencer though. I mean, I wasn't trying to make a big deal out of it or anything but ... well, she got upset and told me I must have got it wrong. That I misunderstood.'

'But you didn't misunderstand.'

'I don't know ... Maybe ... She ... she told me if I ever said anything like that again, I'd lose me job. I can't afford to get fired, me dad'll kill me!'

Mina takes a deep breath to steady herself. 'Listen,' she says. 'No one has a right to do stuff like that. And certainly not to fire you if you complain. You need to talk to the HR people.'

Binita shakes her head. 'It's not that sort of company. Anyway, what am I supposed to do if she fires me? I can't exactly afford to sue them.'

The worst thing is Mina knows she's right. What chance does she have in a fight like that?

'It's all right, honestly. I'm just gonna stay out of his way from now on.'

'You shouldn't have to stay out of his way!'

'No,' Binita says, finally dropping the necklace. 'But there's lots of things we shouldn't have to do, isn't there?' She suddenly seems much older. There's a pain in her eyes that horrifies

Mina. As though the girl's already given up, accepted her lot in life. 'I should probably get back. I only get twenty minutes.'

Mina nods but then, as Binita turns to go, she says, 'Hang on.' She digs out a business card and thrusts it at the young waitress. 'Here. Take this. If he tries anything again you tell him your friend's a police woman and she'll have his bollocks on a spike by the end of the day, you get me?'

Binita laughs. 'Yeah,' she says. 'I'll tell him.' But Mina doesn't think she will.

'I mean it. You can ring me. Any time. Even if you just want to talk about your options.'

Binita nods. 'Thanks,' she says, and slips back through the fire door, closing it behind her.

It's only then that Mina realises she has literally been left out in the cold. *Oh, bollocks!* She tries banging on the fire door but gives up when it becomes clear Binita isn't going to open it. She supposes she can just wander back round to the front door but the receptionist is going to be more than a little confused. *Well, bollocks to her and all!* She's going to find a way to help Binita, Mina thinks, as she starts her way round the building. And if she can find any reason at all to arrest Whitehouse – or Spencer, for that matter – she'll do it. She's learned something though. Whitehouse has something on Spencer, or else the two of them must be pretty close. Why else would the woman stick up for him?

The Delight! factory is a strange mixture of the old and new. The converted steelworks are still visible beneath the modern equipment. The building has high ceilings, red brick walls, and enormous leaded windows. There are huge stainless steel vats and shining ovens where the baked goods are turned out, and punctuating everything are the lighted neon signs that brand the place. Connecting one industrial-sized kitchen to another are long, wide corridors and walkways, and spiral metal staircases and gantries. The whole place seems like a cross between some futuristic sweet emporium and a nine-teenth century workhouse.

It's Harriet Spencer who leads the tour, with Gareth Whitehouse occasionally pointing out how things were different in his day – here were the offices, now transformed into racks of cooling croissants – there was the packaging area, now an overflow car park that's rarely used. Tyler begins to notice that actually very little of the original steelworks facility is currently being used.

'What's through here?' he asks, gesturing to a door marked with a yellow triangle. The sign underneath says: DANGER! RISK OF FALLING. NO ENTRY EXCEPT IN EMERGENCY. FOLLOW MARKED EXIT PATH ONLY.

'We just don't need that much space,' Spencer tells him. 'So there are large areas of the old steelworks that haven't been converted to anything yet.' She pushes on the emergency exit bar and the door opens.

Tyler pokes his head into an enormous warehouse lined with further metallic staircases and gantries. In the centre of the room is a gigantic smelting pot standing idle. The stomach-pleasing smells of the bakery are almost instantly replaced with a dank, metallic odour – the scent of industry.

They walk on, eventually descending an interior staircase and emerging on the far side of the building into the staff car park.

'I suppose I just don't understand why you didn't get somewhere smaller?' Tyler asks.

Spencer bristles slightly, perhaps taking his inquiry as an accusation. 'Land is cheap out here and the place suits our purpose.'

'And the containers over there?' He gestures across the car park.

Spencer crosses her arms. 'Some we use for longer-term storage. Some we rent to other businesses. It was more cost effective than renovating the rest of the factory.' She checks her watch. 'Look,' she says, 'I think we've been very reasonable about all this but I do have a business to run. I'm not sure what you're hoping to find after all this time but ... well, if there isn't anything else ... ?'

Tyler pauses for a moment, considering whether to remind her that they're investigating a murder, but he decides against it. 'You've been very helpful. Thank you.' He smiles at her but something about her expression tells him she's not convinced by his sincerity.

'I can show the detective out, Harriet.' Whitehouse gestures back along a path at the side of the building and Spencer takes her leave with a curt nod.

'I'm sorry about that, Detective,' Whitehouse says, as they

meander their way through the laurel bushes that flank the path. 'Harriet's got a lot on her plate at the moment. Perhaps I shouldn't have suggested we meet here after all. I was trying to help but maybe it would have been better if you'd come to my office.'

'Yes,' Tyler says. 'What business are you in now, exactly?'

'This and that. The service industry primarily but we're starting to branch out into deliveries. Takeaways, that sort of thing.'

'That's a far cry from the steel industry.'

Whitehouse smiles. 'Isn't it? Unfortunately there's just no money in steel anymore. I started with selling cars after the bankruptcy and it sort of snowballed from there. It was Harriet, funnily enough, who gave me the idea for starting a delivery business. It's all the rage these days, ordering online, home delivery.'

'So you deliver for Delight?'

'Not me personally but yes, my drivers do. She was the first to sign up.'

'That must have taken a fair bit of start-up capital.'

'Not really. The drivers are self-employed so it was just the IT infrastructure. We have a small office where we handle things but it's small potatoes compared to the old days. I'm fine with that though. Far less stress.' Whitehouse rummages around in his jacket pocket and pulls out a card. 'In case you have any more questions,' he says, handing it over.

Tyler takes it and slips it into his own pocket.

When they reach the car park they find Rabbani waiting by the car.

'Well, I'll leave you to it,' Whitehouse says. 'Like I said, anything more I can do, anything at all, just give me a bell.' He seems remarkably willing to be helpful now that the interview is over.

'We'll do that.' Tyler watches him cross to his own Land Rover parked up against the wall of the building.

'Well?' Rabbani asks.

'Mr Whitehouse and Ms Spencer were both extremely helpful and accommodating.'

'So they were in it up to their eyeballs then?'

'They're certainly hiding something.' Tyler glances over at the buildings on the far side of the car park. 'Have a look into these businesses, would you? It makes no sense to me. How the hell can they manage to afford all this space when they only need a part of it?'

'Maybe Whitehouse was desperate and sold it cheap.'

'Maybe. But then why the friends act? There's something about these two that doesn't add up. They seemed like they were close at some points but then ...' Tyler's thoughts trail off and he looks back at Rabbani. 'What about you? Find anything?'

'Whitehouse is a sleaze-bag. Gets a little too handsy with the staff and Spencer has his back for some reason. They must be close friends unless ...'

'Unless he's got something on her.'

'Maybe. But it could just be she doesn't want her under-lings causing trouble for the company. She wouldn't be the first shitty boss to not back her employees. Just because she's a woman, that doesn't mean she isn't a sleaze-bag too.'

Tyler laughs. 'Okay, let's get you back to the office and you can spend a bit of time looking into their finances.' He passes her Whitehouse's business card. 'Don't spend too long on it though, this might have nothing to do with what happened sixteen years ago.'

'What are you gonna do?'

'I'll go talk to the wife of the security guard who was killed. She still lives in Sheffield. Let's see if she recognises our mystery corpse.'

'Did you show those two the photo?' Rabbani asks as they watch Gareth Whitehouse drive his way out of the car park with a nod and a little wave. 'I thought we weren't gonna do that?'

Tyler nods. 'I changed my mind.'

'And?'

'Whitehouse overreacted and Spencer didn't react enough. I don't think either of them recognised him as such but there was something not quite right.'

Rabbani grunts. 'Doggett would say they were ringing his bullshit bell.'

'Indeed, he would,' says Tyler. 'And he'd be right.'

Edith didn't usually go out to the playground at lunch break, not if she could avoid it, but her options for hiding within the school were limited.

Her top choice was the computer room where she could happily while away forty-five minutes practising her coding and still manage to sneak a sandwich in when no one was looking. The computer science teacher – 'Call me Phil' – was the sort of teacher who wanted to be mates with everyone so he often left the room unlocked and turned a blind eye to students hanging out there.

This week, however, Call-Me-Phil was on administrative leave pending an investigation. The rumour mill had it that he had been found with a collection of animal porn on one of his terminals and Edith was 90 per cent sure that, if the rumour was true – and that was a big if – he wasn't the one who put it there.

Regardless, that meant they had a supply teacher in who, while perhaps not as up on cyber security as his predecessor, knew the benefit of a locked door when dealing with teenagers.

That left her wandering the corridors looking for spots under stairwells where she could hunker down and read for a bit. It wasn't easy to concentrate on the Brontës though, when you had to keep one eye and ear open for potential threats. The kids were easy to hear coming, they telegraphed their presence with jungle catcalls long before they were in sight, but many of the teachers moved at a far stealthier pace and Edith would often find herself staring at a pair of scuffed brogues and a wrinkled trouser hem while the owner cleared his throat from above meaningfully.

And that was precisely what happened today, leaving Edith standing dangerously exposed at one end of the netball court, once again regretting her close-cropped hair and her lack of hat and gloves. Thankfully, there was no sign of

Alice Clitherow and her gang, who were no doubt smoking in the bushes on the far side of the kitchen bins. People had a tendency not to notice her unless she wanted them to but she kept a wary eye on the corner of the building just in case. If they turned up, she would slip away easily in the crowd.

There were a few girls from one of the younger years throwing snowballs on the court but no one she knew. No one who was a significant threat. The boys kept exclusively to the football field, although it was rare that any of them bothered her anyway. And Mrs Khatri was huddled chatting with Dr Erikson by the door, as usual paying very little attention to what was going on but somehow always aware of it nonetheless. Edith suspected that was probably the way most teachers got by, by pretending to ignore the vast majority of rule infringements they witnessed and saving their wrath for the truly serious ones. Most of them would only intervene when things reached a serious level, their assumption being that name-calling and insults weren't all that serious. Edith knew full well that that wasn't always the case.

'Al, she's here!' shouts a voice from the corner of the science block and Edith realises she's taken her eye off the ball. She starts moving straight away but the other girls are faster and manage to intercept her long before she reaches the relative safety of the classroom.

There are three of them, Alice, Sophie and Carmel, but as always it's Alice who takes the lead. 'Where you going in such a hurry, *Darke?*'

The others snigger as though something funny has

been said. Edith supposes it's probably in connection with her name. It's a difficult name to find an insult for since it doesn't shorten very easily, leaving Alice no weapon but her tone of voice to insinuate how ridiculous it is. Edith had to agree with her on that. She'd much rather have her father's name . . . whatever that was.

'Oi, she asked you a question, bitch!' said Carmel. Always the least subtle and probably the cruellest, though she never takes physical action herself, preferring to egg on her co-conspirators.

Edith, aware there's no good answer to the question and that she's been silent too long for them to believe it anyway, says, 'I told Mrs Peters I'd help her with something.'

'Fucking teacher's pet!' Carmel snarls.

It would be easy to hate Carmel except for the fact that Edith saw her once, outside of school, getting slapped hard in the head by her father behind the fish and chip shop. It probably didn't help matters that Carmel knew Edith had witnessed this private shame and perhaps had misinterpreted the look of horror on Edith's face. That had been almost a year ago and there was no way either of the girls would ever broach the subject with the other. In her coldest, most reflective moments, Edith thought it was probably quite interesting how one such tiny moment could establish either a friendship or an enmity that would last a lifetime. It was just a shame it hadn't gone the other way.

'Oh my God, Al, look at her. She's not even fucking listening.'

'Crazy bitch.'

Edith realises her mind has wandered again. 'I really need to go now,' she says, without the slightest sense of hope.

She starts forward again but Alice stands in front of her and puts a hand on her shoulder. From a distance Edith imagines it probably looks comradely. She glances across at the two teachers by the door but they've moved on. She can still see Mrs Khatri but much further away now and with her back to them. She feels the hair rise on the back of her neck as the adrenaline starts to course through her body. Fight or flight. Always flight.

'No need to go all tense, *Darke*,' Alice says. 'I was only asking about your mum. That's not a crime, is it?'

'What? No—'

'What is it she's got again?'

'AIDS!' says Sophie, sniggering and putting a hand over her mouth as though she's said something taboo rather than just horrid.

'*Super* AIDS!' says Carmel.

'She has M.E.' Edith says quietly with her head down.

'Oh yeah,' Alice goes on. 'I remember now. That's that made up one, innit? Where they can't find anything wrong with you? I don't mean to be rude or anything but how do you know she's not just making it all up?'

Edith hates that expression, *I don't mean to be rude or anything but . . .* because of course you mean to be rude. Why else would you say it? It doesn't help that at times the thought has crossed her own mind. And it's the worst thought in the world. What if her mother *is* making it up? It's called Munchausen syndrome, a rare mental disorder where someone fakes illness for attention. Edith knows this because she's done her own research on the internet. She doesn't really believe it. Her mother loves her and she wouldn't put her through all this unnecessarily. And anyway, a mental disorder is still an illness. It wouldn't change anything.

'She sounds like a basket-case to me.' Carmel laughs.

Edith clenches her fist. Maybe it won't be flight this time, she can feel her blood pumping wildly through her heart.

'Ew,' Sophie exclaims suddenly, drawing Edith's attention. Edith assumes the comment is directed at her but she realises quickly that Sophie's actually looking out of the playground towards the street.

'Perv-alert!' Sophie points through the wire fence towards a car parked by the opposite kerb.

The girls all turn to follow her gaze. There's a man sitting in the driver's seat of the car making no effort to hide the fact he's watching them. He's wearing a baseball cap so it's difficult to make out his features but the window is down despite the cold weather and he's close enough they can see he's watching them. Edith feels the hair stand up on the back of her neck.

'Miiiiiiss!' Sophie shouts, running towards Mrs Khatri.

Alice looks mildly irritated at this unsanctioned, precipitate action but then she turns back to the man in the car. 'See anything you like, you dirty old skank!' She shouts it loudly and pushes her pubescent breasts together with both hands.

The car window rises silently and the man turns and starts his car engine. Sophie's returning now with Mrs Khatri but by the time the teacher arrives the car's already turning and is lost from sight.

Mrs Khatri splutters and fusses, taking things far more seriously than the occasion warrants given the track history of the informants. Most teachers take anything Alice Clitherow tells them with a pinch of salt but Mrs Khatri is painfully gullible. But Edith's not really being fair. After all, on this occasion, they're not making it up. Or maybe it's just the fact that Edith is with them that makes her take things more seriously. Whatever the reason, Mrs Khatri starts asking for details on the make of the car and whether or not the girls can describe the man.

Edith, however, is already slowly backing away, taking the opportunity of her tormentors' distraction to escape. It's sad in a way because it's shared experiences like these that can change everything. Just like the ill-fated trip to the fish shop when she saw Carmel, this predatory incident could have been just the thing that brought them all together. Something that built a bridge between them, a common enemy for Edith and Alice. But there isn't really time to consider that now because she's turning and running, her trainers slapping down hard on the icy tarmac, desperate to get her away. Because, despite the cap the man in the car was wearing, she could still somehow manage to see his eyes and she's absolutely positive that it was the man from the reservoir. As she runs, she wonders how he's managed to find her. What does he want? She really wants to believe that he could be her father, that he's come to say how sorry he is for scaring her yesterday. But the ice coursing through her veins tells her something very different.

After dropping off Rabbani back at the station Tyler tries Jude's number again. It's the same as before, straight to voicemail, no recorded outgoing message. He takes a chance. 'Jude, it's me. We really need to talk. Ring me back, yeah? Please.' The last word sticks in his throat but at least it's done.

Debbie Linville lives in a fairly utilitarian semi-detached house in Waterthorpe, a housing estate built in the 70s on the far southeast of the city. She answers the door to Tyler still dressed in her work suit and takes only a cursory glance at his warrant card when he offers it.

'What's this about?' she asks.

'We're looking into the robbery at Demeter Fabrications sixteen years ago,' he tells her, and then, when she appears to not fully take in what's he's saying, he adds, 'The death of your husband.'

She nods her head slowly and lets him in, escorting him into a front room that is largely clean and tidy but clearly not loved. The walls are well overdue another lick of magnolia and the carpet could do with an upgrade. A few scented candles and a couple of IKEA throws add a modicum of personality to the place but this clearly isn't a woman who takes a great deal of pride in her home. Tyler imagines that's probably what people would say about his place as well.

'Can I get you a cup of tea?' she asks. 'Or water?'

'I'm fine, thank you. Perhaps we could just sit? I only have a couple of questions. This shouldn't take long.'

She nods and perches herself on the edge of a tired-looking sofa leaving him the choice of joining her at the far end, or settling for a footstool covered in cat hair. He steps round the glass coffee table and sits down next to her.

Debbie clears her throat. 'Is . . . Is there some new evidence or something?'

'We're not sure yet. Something has come to light in another case we're investigating that might have a link with Demeter.'

She starts to look a little more animated than she has so far and Tyler wonders if that's hope he sees flaring up in her eyes. He hurries to qualify his words.

'Of course, it might not be linked at all but we have to examine every possibility.'

She nods and clears her throat again but this time she doesn't speak. It's a nervous habit, he realises.

'Can you tell me what you remember about that day? The day your husband was killed.'

She smiles for the first time but there's no humour visible. 'I haven't forgotten anything about that day,' she says. 'Kev had gone to work the night before as usual. That was the last time I saw him. About an hour before I went to bed. Then the next morning I went to work. I was a cleaner, offices mostly so it was an early start.' She must see his eyes flick down to her suit. 'I was studying to be an accountant as well

123

but I hadn't passed my exams back then.' He nods and she goes on. 'Normally I'd get back about the same time that Kevin got home but I was later than usual that day. It was gone nine and I was stuck in traffic. So I was surprised that he wasn't there when I got home.' Again she does a gentle clearing of her throat. 'I remember being concerned, obviously, but not massively. I just figured he'd got stuck in the same traffic I did, or got held up at work or something.' She pauses for a moment. 'Then the doorbell went and I knew. I already felt sick by the time I reached the door and opened it to find you lot standing there. They asked if they could come in and I didn't even ask them why. I knew he was dead. I don't know how. I just knew it.'

Tyler's read Phil Johnson's original report many times over the past year. It feels odd to finally be meeting the faces behind the names. He makes mention of Debbie Linville's stoic nature when they arrived to tell her that her husband was dead but Tyler's seen people react to bad news in all kinds of ways so he isn't about to blame the woman for that.

'I'm guessing you know the rest. After they left, I had to ring Kevin's mum.' Tyler tries to interrupt her to tell her he doesn't need the whole day's events but before he can speak, Debbie says, 'And after that I took a pregnancy test.' She has another little nervous cough. 'It was negative. We'd been trying for a while and my period had been due the week before so we were excited that maybe it was all happening finally. I'd been meaning to take the test for a few days but kept putting it off. But then it just seemed the most important thing in the world, to know, right then, like … if I was pregnant then he wasn't completely gone, you know?' She stares at Tyler for a moment and he says nothing. 'But it was negative, of course, and he was gone.'

'I'm sorry,' he tells her.

Debbie takes a deep breath. 'Ancient history,' she says, but he can see that it isn't. She has no wedding ring on and there's no evidence of children anywhere in the small part of the house he's seen so far. He suspects there wouldn't be anywhere else in the house either but he can't bring himself to ask her outright.

Tyler stands up and crosses to the windowsill. There's a picture of a much younger, more carefree Debbie with her arms draped round a young man. Not handsome exactly but full of life. 'This is Kevin?'

She stands up and follows him. 'It's the last picture I have of the two of us together. It was our two year anniversary the month before.'

'You look very happy.'

'We were.'

He can't help but compare the woman in the photo with the one in front of him. That story about her phantom pregnancy, he wonders how many times she's told it, how much it has become the defining moment of her life. He replaces the photo frame and they sit down again.

'Can you tell me a bit more about Kevin?'

She frowns at him. 'In what way?'

'Just … what was he like? Did he have any hobbies? Mates?'

She still looks puzzled and he can't blame her. It's not a particularly obvious line of questioning but he suddenly wants to know more about this man. He and Doggett have looked into this case a dozen times or more over the past year, looking for connections with the others. But up until now Kevin Linville was a means to an end; a name on a page in a file, a breadcrumb on the trail to Richard Tyler's killer. But Debbie's story has brought him to life. This man deserves justice too, he realises. And maybe then his wife will finally be able to move on with her life.

'I guess he wasn't anything all that special,' she says, smiling genuinely now. 'I mean, he was no Einstein and he couldn't bloody dance for toffee. He liked his sports, and drinking down the local with his mates.' She pauses for a moment. 'Mum always thought I could do better,' she says, reluctantly. 'She never understood why Kev didn't want to do more with his life. She kept trying to get him to join your lot. The police. Or to retrain or something. But he was happy as a security guard. He liked working nights 'cos he said it was quiet. He got lots of reading done. He read Westerns, used to get them from this specialist bookshop place in London that handled American imports.' She speaks with a reverence in her voice and Tyler realises something – Debbie Linville is still in love. She doesn't mention the fights and the worries about money, the doubt that sets in when you begin to wonder whether this person you've hitched yourself to for the rest of your life might not be quite the best one for you. She doesn't talk about the money trouble this couple must have had with him working as a security guard and her as a cleaner. The disapproving mother is a small slip but it's defensive as well. He wonders how much Debbie once shared that disapproval and how far the intervening years have transformed her memory of this man who 'wasn't anything special' into the revered figure she's now describing.

While she talks, Tyler's thoughts stray to Guy Daley's young bride. He hadn't met Sam until the funeral and even then he'd kept his distance. He caught her eyeing him when he first arrived and there was something in the expression that made him sure he wasn't welcome. No doubt Daley had told her something of their fractious working relationship, putting his own personal spin on things. But now he wonders how much of that was his own worries about being there. How egotistical of him to assume Sam Daley's thoughts touched on him at all when she had just lost her husband, her future happiness, her hopes for a family. Is she pining away in some suburban family home somewhere like this? Will she somehow manage to move on with her life now she has said her goodbyes? Or, in sixteen years' time, will she remain like Debbie, a fly trapped in amber, reminiscing about a mythical perfect past?

Tyler's suddenly aware that Debbie's stopped talking. 'That's helpful,' he says. 'Can you think of anyone who might have wanted to harm him?'

'No, of course not,' she says vehemently. Perhaps a little too vehemently.

'A friend he'd fallen out with? Anything unusual from

around that time. Anything at all. Maybe you didn't mention it at the time because it seemed insignificant but now, after the passage of time ...'

She's shaking her head but fails to meet his eye. 'Why are you asking this? It ... it was a robbery gone wrong, wasn't it? That's what you said back then.'

'The evidence certainly points that way but we have to ask these things. Just in case.'

She looks up now and he can see she's picked up on his meaning. 'You think Kevin was involved, don't you? That they killed him to keep him quiet.' Tyler says nothing, waiting for her to fill the space. 'The other guy ... the one who investigated before ... he tried to say the same thing.'

There's nothing in Johnson's notes to that effect. The inside job was an obvious line of inquiry and it surprised Tyler that Johnson hadn't considered it more seriously. 'DS Johnson said that to you?'

'Oh, he was very circumspect, but I knew what he meant. Asking questions about Kev's movements, who he hung out with, where he'd been over the past few weeks.'

None of this in Johnson's report. Why would he leave it out?

'He wouldn't do that. He was a good man!' Debbie's getting herself worked up and Tyler's worried he's going to lose her; best if he comes back to this later and gets to the real reason for his visit. Still, he hesitates. He doesn't want to cause this woman any more distress but there's a chance she could know the victim. 'The reason I'm here,' he tells her, 'is that we've found another body. It's a man, wearing a Demeter Fabrications uniform, but we haven't been able to identify him yet. There's no evidence to suggest he worked with your husband, but I'd like to show you a photograph of the body, to see if you recognise him. Is that okay?'

After a moment or two, she nods. He warns her about the state of the body. He doesn't want to shock her too much. But in fact, when he hands over his mobile she takes in the grisly photo without batting an eyelid. She stares at it without any visible reaction.

'Do you recognise him?' he asks.

'Yes,' she says, after another lengthy pause. 'Yes, I think I do, but I can't remember where from.' She passes the mobile back but he stops her.

'Take another look, please.'

She does so, but with a heavy sigh that conveys her fatigue at the whole subject. 'I ... Maybe, I don't know. He looks familiar, that's all but ...'

Could the body really have been frozen for sixteen years? 'One of your husband's work colleagues?' Although that can't be the case because as far as they know no one else is missing. 'Or a friend maybe?'

She shakes her head. 'I'm sorry. I'm really not sure.'

'Okay, thank you.' Tyler takes back his phone. He wants to push her but he gets the feeling she isn't being deliberately evasive. Maybe better to give her some time to think about it. 'You've been really helpful, Mrs Linville.' He stands up. 'I'm sorry for raking up bad memories.'

She escorts him back to the front door but then stops him by reaching out and touching his arm. 'Please,' she says. 'There's no way Kevin would have robbed that place, you have to believe me.' There's such a desperation to her request that he finds himself wanting to believe her. She certainly wants to believe it. But does she? Really?

'He wouldn't,' she says again, clutching at his sleeve. 'He wouldn't do that to Mr Whitehouse. He . . . He was like a father figure to Kev after he lost his own dad.'

'They knew each other?' Tyler asks. 'More so than just as employer and employee?'

She frowns, perhaps worried she's gone too far. 'Well, they weren't like close friends or anything but Mr Whitehouse looked out for Kev after his dad died. They'd known each other back in the day. He came to our wedding, for God's sake! Why would Kevin steal from someone he invited to his own wedding? He just wouldn't. I don't believe it!'

She's protesting too much now. Still, he lets it go and, after passing her his card and extracting a promise that she'll ring him if she thinks of anything, he allows her to close the door in his face.

As he's walking back to the car, connections begin to form in his head. Whitehouse lied about how well he knew Linville, distancing himself from the murdered security guard. And Linville's own wife clearly suspected he'd had something to do with the robbery. Interesting.

But more interesting, more disturbing if it came to it, was

the information she'd let slip about Johnson. Once again, Tyler finds himself working on a case where the original notes contradict what the witness is telling him. Johnson lied, or at least failed to detail in his report the full extent of his interest in Linville's role in the robbery. Is this the same place his father reached? And if so, what did he do about it? One thing is for sure, if he had any money to speak of, Tyler would bet the lot on who was overseeing the case. Everything always leads back there. To Stevens.

The slimy bastard has been at it again.

Doggett's still at the station, despite the late hour, so Tyler heads straight there and finds him knee deep in paperwork in their shiny new office. The room smells of curry and Tyler notes the half-dozen plastic containers that are open on his own desk, and a half-eaten naan lying abandoned on the printer. He picks it up and drops it into the bin.

'Help yourself,' Doggett says without looking up.

'What have I missed?' Tyler asks him.

'Not a lot. No ID on the corpse. Our American friend is still trying to thaw out the body. She said something about turkeys and Thanksgiving, and having to do things slowly. She did manage to tell us one thing though. She's certain the body was frozen before it was put into the water.'

Tyler voices his thought from earlier. 'If the body was frozen elsewhere, could it have been frozen for sixteen years?'

'Since the robbery, you mean?' Doggett shrugs. 'I suppose

it's possible. But no one else from Demeter Fabrications is missing.'

'That we know of,' Tyler muses. 'What about the blood trail?'

'No handy footprints, unfortunately. Or rather, far too many of the bloody things. The world and his wife must have tramped round that reservoir. The speccy-techies are still analysing the DNA from the blood and bone matter found on the wall.'

'CCTV?'

Doggett just looks at him and blinks.

'I'll take that as a no then.'

'How about you? Any progress?'

Tyler outlines his and Rabbani's trip to the desserts factory and his later chat with Debbie Linville, including the revelation regarding Johnson's suspicions of an inside job that didn't make it into the case file. 'Do you think that's what Richard was looking into?'

'Johnson's report wasn't exactly detailed but if anything, that set it apart from the other cases your dad was looking into.' Doggett scratches his stubbled chin. 'You said the wife recognised our new victim?'

'She said he looked familiar but she couldn't place him. I pretty much believe her. She could have easily denied knowing him altogether. But she's hiding something, or at least not telling me everything. I got the sense that she also felt Linville was involved in the robbery somehow. Johnson questioned her about it and she's had sixteen years to consider the possibility. Maybe she's come to her own conclusions.'

'You think this is something to do with Stevens again?' Doggett asks.

'I checked the records and Stevens oversaw the investigation into the robbery and murder.'

'Bloody hell!' Doggett stands up and moves over to the curry cartons. He grabs another chunk of naan and slops it around in some dark red sauce. 'You think we've got another situation like Cooper's?'

A few months ago, their investigation into the death of a student unearthed a number of mistakes that were made during the original investigation into her disappearance. DCI Cooper had been the lead investigator and had pretty much told Rabbani that Superintendent Stevens had pressured her to drop the investigation quietly. They'd assumed that it was because the student was a foreign national and the Superintendent hadn't wanted any fuss. Dodgy as hell but not necessarily indicative of a deeper conspiracy.

'Well,' Doggett says, stuffing his mouth full of bread and talking as he chews, 'there's no way we're talking to Johnson.'

'Why not? Maybe he has info on Stevens we can finally use.'

'Maybe so, but if he does he took it to the grave with him.' Doggett smacks his lips. 'Heart attack. Three years back.'

'Damn it! Someone must know something. What about Cooper?'

'Worth a try, I suppose. But she wasn't particularly cooperative the last time Rabbani spoke to her.'

Doggett uses his tongue to wipe the last of the cold curry
from around his teeth.

Tyler can almost see him thinking. 'What?' he asks.

'I've just had a nasty thought,' Doggett says. 'Maybe someone did know something.'

Tyler doesn't follow at first but there's a gravity to
Doggett's expression that takes his mind to the right place.
'Diane,' he says.

'I don't like it but . . . it makes a certain sort of sense.'

'But we didn't tell her anything about the conspiracy
my father mentioned to you. Or about Rabbani's chat with
Cooper last year.'

'Diane's clever enough to have come up with this on
her own. She was around at the time of your father's death,
remember. When I tried to convince her years ago that he
wouldn't have killed himself she didn't want to know. But
she was in mourning then. Maybe she's been investigating
your dad's death just as we have, but somehow managed
to get further than us. If she found something out about
Stevens . . .'

'And if she told the wrong person . . .' Tyler doesn't want
to think about it but it would explain a lot. Diane's just not
the sort of person who would disappear without trace. 'We
need to ask Rabbani if she said anything.'

'Said anything about what?' Rabbani asks as she strolls
into the office.

Tyler and Doggett look at each other.

'You're here late,' Doggett says.

'I've been going over Whitehouse's finances and it makes for some interesting reading.'

'Where?' Doggett barks the question. 'I've been here for a couple of hours and I haven't seen you.'

'I was talking to Amber down in Fraud. She was helping me with the National Crimes Agency and . . .' Rabbani stops and crosses her arms. 'What does it matter *where*? What's going on?'

Again Tyler and Doggett look at each other. They've talked about this so many times. They've kept her out of all of this to protect her, and if their suspicions about Diane are accurate, then they were right to do so.

'Said anything about what?' Rabbani asks again, firmer this time and louder. That infamous temper of hers bubbling away.

Doggett cocks his head on one side as though to say, *it's your call.*

Tyler turns back to her. 'Did you tell DCI Jordan about your conversation with Cooper last year? About your suspicions about Stevens and how he was closing down cases?'

Rabbani frowns again. 'No, of course not. You told me to forget it.' But there's something in the colour that floods her cheeks that tells him differently. She's a terrible liar, Rabbani. But the thought, far from annoying him, actually gives him comfort. At least there's no way *she* could be involved in any conspiracy, she'd give herself away in seconds. 'Mina . . .'

'I didn't!' she says. He waits for her to go on. 'But I did keep digging. I know you told me not to but . . .'

Tyler feels the relief flood through him but it's short-lived. Diane's a resourceful woman.

'It doesn't mean she didn't find out some other way,' Doggett says, echoing Tyler's thoughts.

'Found out what?' Rabbani's frustration is building, perhaps stoked by her embarrassment at her confession.

'You didn't say anything to Stevens, did you?'

'No! Of course not. I'm not a complete numpty!'

'We really do need to talk to Franklin,' Doggett says again. 'If Stevens is behind all of this we can't deal with him on our own.'

'We still don't know if we can trust her?'

'Behind *what*?' Rabbani asks again.

Doggett blows out his lips. 'Can we afford not to? At this point?'

'Oh, for fuck's sake!' Rabbani brings her right hand down on the desk with a loud bang, then rubs the base of it with her left. She recovers quickly enough though. 'For once, will you two *please* just tell me what's going on?!'

Doggett and Tyler exchange another look. Finally Doggett nods.

'We think Superintendent Stevens might have something to do with Jordan's disappearance.' Saying it out loud makes it sound even more ridiculous but it also makes it real and the silence stretches around the three of them, wrapping them up in the possibility that they might be right.

'In that case,' Rabbani says after a few moments, 'there's something you really need to know.'

Tyler and Doggett both turn to look at her.

'I just heard in the Murder Room. Stevens didn't come into work yesterday.' Rabbani bites her lip and looks Tyler directly in the eye. 'They think he's gone missing, too.'

Mina hears them talking as she's coming along the corridor. She finds herself slowing down and even as she begins to listen she wonders if she's really doing this. Spying on her colleagues. Spying on her friends. But are they friends? If they don't include her in anything?

She hears Doggett ask Tyler about his interview with the guard's wife and Tyler tells him that he thinks she recognised the photo of the victim. She's moving so slowly now she's virtually stopped. If anyone sees her it will be more than obvious what she's doing, so she forces herself to actually stop, inches from the doorway but not yet in view. A few seconds later she's glad she did.

She doesn't understand it all. Something about a conspiracy involving Stevens. DCI Cooper's name gets mentioned. So she was right! Despite the fact Tyler warned her off, he did at least take her seriously. And then they're talking about DCI Jordan and Tyler's father, Richard. And then her name comes up.

Mina jumps and pulls backwards, flattening herself against the wall as though she's trying to make herself into a smaller target. Ridiculous. They've got it all wrong. She did talk to someone about her suspicions concerning Stevens but it wasn't Jordan. A wave of heat moves through her body and floods her cheeks. A ripple of shame. She can't do this any-more. She hears Tyler say, 'We need to ask Rabbani if she said anything,' and before she even thinks about it she finds herself stepping forward and through the doorway.

'Said anything about what?

The two of them look exactly like Ghulam and her cousin that time she caught them climbing up onto the work surface in the kitchen trying to reach the sweet treats cupboard.

They say nothing at first, retreating to their comfortable silences, but she's going to wait them out this time. She's going to force their hand. It feels right. She hadn't planned on confronting them this way but she knows she can't spy on them anymore, not really. No matter what leg-up Franklin offers her, she just isn't that sort of person.

And then, all of a sudden, she's the one on the back foot again as Doggett begins quizzing her about her own actions. She has nothing to hide but she's always struggled with talk-ing to Doggett. There's just something about the man that makes people nervous. She suspects that's why he's such a good cop. He has this inbuilt ability to unsettle people. She feels herself reddening even as she stumbles over her words and tries to explain, the memory of her standing outside lis-tening to them a few moments ago burning in her thoughts.

Then they do that look again, the one she's seen so many times over the past year or more, like two schoolboys sharing a dark secret. Like they suspect her of something. She's so sick of this.

'Said anything about what?' she says again and she can hear it in her own voice, how close she is to snapping. But unusually, this time they take her seriously. Tyler actually answers her. 'Did you tell DCI Jordan about your conversation with Cooper last year?'

She can answer honestly that she didn't. She'd thought about it, several times, but she knew she didn't have enough to prove Cooper did anything wrong. The woman had an online gambling problem and, according to her, Superintendent Stevens shut her case down before she'd even begun investigating, but they only had her word for that. And in any case, the investigation moved on and then Daley was killed and . . . well, then there really wasn't time to think about anything else.

But honest answer or not, she did talk to someone about it and the thought of that makes her cheeks flush again. She has to tell them about Franklin. Tyler's reaction is one of relief more than anything, especially when she tells him she didn't involve Stevens. It's then she realises he hasn't forgotten about what she told him. So this is what the two of them have been up to? Investigating Stevens in some way. It's obvious they were only trying to protect her from him but it's still annoying. And what was all that about Tyler's father's death? As they continue to argue about whether to tell her more she snaps again.

She swears and brings her palm down hard on the table top. The skin stings and she winces. 'For once, will you two *please* just tell me what's going on?'

139

And for once they do. 'We think Superintendent Stevens might have something to do with Jordan's disappearance.'

A number of things slot into place and suddenly she's sure they're right. It was this piece of gossip she'd been on her way here with when she'd caught them. The breakroom was buzzing with the news. Not only was there still no sign of Jordan but now Stevens was missing as well.

'What do you mean, missing?' Doggett asks her.

'That's all I know. He didn't come into work yesterday so they sent someone round to his place but there was no sign of him.' She hesitates for a second but there's no point hiding anything now. 'Stevens is the reason Franklin is here.'

Tyler snaps his eyes up. 'What?'

'When ACC Franklin first turned up she spoke to each of us, yeah? She asked if there was anything going on that I wanted to talk about. Off the record. Anything at all. I told her what I knew – or suspected, anyway – about Stevens closing down cases early, changing details in the reports and all that. I mean, I only had what Cooper told me but Franklin seemed to take it seriously.'

'Why didn't you say anything?' Tyler asks.

Mina folds her arms in front of her. 'Why didn't you say anything to me?'

He nods at that, without any attempt at self-defence.

'Stevens,' Doggett says quietly. The piece of naan in his hand drops into a tub of curry with a faint plop. 'Mina, when they sent someone to his place, did they get in?'

'What? No, I think they just sent Uniform to check but

there was no one home. The word is Franklin's arranging a warrant to search the place. She's put an All-Ports out on him so she must reckon he's guilty of something.'

'His place,' Doggett says, speaking so quietly now dogs would have trouble hearing him. 'We all got invited there a couple of years back for some team-building barbe-cue shite.'

'So?'

Doggett turns to Tyler. 'It's at the top end of Eccy Road. Maybe half a mile further on from that last camera sighting of her. The petrol station.'

Jordan. He's talking about DCI Jordan. Mina feels like she's playing catch-up but then, that's often the way with these two. 'You're not serious? I mean, Stevens is a bit of a twat, maybe even dodgy but you can't think he's . . . what?' She doesn't want to say it. Kidnapped her. Killed her.

But Tyler's already moving for the door.

'No, son!' Doggett shouts. 'Wait!'

But he's already gone.

Tyler's just about to get in the car when the realisation comes crashing home. He has no idea where he's going.

'Shit!' he says, slamming the car door. He's going to have to go back and speak to Doggett. He'll look like an idiot for just tearing off like that and Doggett will try to stop him. Tell him he's putting his career on the line. Again. But he doesn't care about any of that. The alternative is worse. They're wasting time.

But in the end he doesn't have to do any of that because he sees Doggett and Rabbani jogging towards him across the car park.

'Don't try and talk me out of this,' he tells the DI. 'Just give me the address.'

'I don't know the bloody address,' Doggett tells him, moving round the car to the passenger side. 'But I can find it. Come on.'

Rabbani reaches for the back door but Tyler shoots out a hand and stops her. 'No,' he says.

She pulls her arm away from him. 'For fuck's sake, will you stop cutting me out of this? Maybe if you'd talked to me sooner . . .' She doesn't finish the sentence but he knows what she was about to say. Jordan might still be alive.

'I know,' he says, taking some of the wind out of her sails. 'But this is different. You could lose your job.'

'So could you. I don't care.'

'Yes, you do.' His words stop her short. 'And that's a good thing. Stay here and be our link with Franklin. If we find anything, if we need backup, I'll call you first.'

'You're trying to protect me,' she says, but her temper seems to have dampened again and there's no heat in her words.

'Of course I am.' He can't lose another one.

Doggett raps on the side window and speaks, his voice muffled by the glass. 'Are we going, or what?'

*

They both glance at the petrol station that was the last known whereabouts of DCI Diane Jordan but neither of them say anything.

Stevens. Tyler has his foot to the pedal and is driving like a maniac but for once Doggett isn't complaining. Why didn't they consider Stevens sooner? But neither of them would ever have believed he could be capable of something like this. He was the first to take them seriously when they went to him with their concerns about Diane's disappearance. But then, if he was responsible for it that's exactly how he would act. They've let her down and they both know it. Tyler glances at Doggett. He knew the man lived out here. Why didn't he say anything?

That's not fair. There are thousands of houses out this way, no reason to assume Diane was visiting one of them rather than on her way out across the Peaks. And even if there was, no reason to think it was Stevens. They still don't know for sure that it was. Maybe this is some bizarre coincidence, or it's possible that whatever happened to Diane happened to Stevens as well. Did she confide in him about something? Why else would she be out this way? She must have been on her way to see Stevens. And if she was, then why didn't he say anything?

'Here,' Doggett says suddenly. 'Stop here.'

Tyler slams on the brakes and heaves the car over into a layby. The car behind sounds its horn, a long blast of irritation. But if the guy had time to hit the horn he had time to brake. The car flies past them, the horn sounding long into the distance.

Tyler parks up and gets out. Doggett joins him from the far side of the car and they stand there for a moment staring up at the Victorian townhouses that tower above them on the opposite side of the road.

'It's one of these,' Doggett says, but he doesn't sound sure.

They cross the road, dodging the traffic, and Doggett walks up the row of houses clearly looking for some hint of a memory from the time he came here.

'That one,' he says finally, pointing to the third house from the right with a stubby little finger.

'You sure?'

'Not in the least.'

They trot gingerly up the frozen steps and Tyler presses the doorbell. From somewhere deep in the house the tinkle of some classical tune comes to him. Sounds like Stevens' taste. 'No lights on,' he says.

'Wherever he's gone I guess he took the family with him.' Doggett peers at the house next door. 'Hang on, I'll have a word with the neighbours,' he says, and hops over a low stone wall.

There's a narrow path of gravel skirting the front of the house and Tyler crunches along it, stepping over an old coal grate as he tries to look in through the bay window. Looks like some sort of living room but it's hard to tell in the dark with the street lights reflecting from the road. There's a gate at the side of the house that leads round the back. He tries it but it's locked. He hears Doggett chatting amiably with the neighbour.

Tyler sizes up the front window. It's a relatively modern uPVC frame and thick double-glazed glass so they would need some kind of tool to get in that way. Same with the door – uPVC, multiple locking mechanism. Even with an Enforcer that would take a while, and they don't have an Enforcer.

Doggett finishes up with the neighbour and joins Tyler at the front door. 'Deaf old bat,' he mumbles through tight lips. He turns and waves a thank you at the woman who eventually takes the hint and goes back inside out of the cold. 'She could barely hear me over the noise of the traffic but this is definitely the right place. Says she hasn't seen him for a few days though. Thought he'd gone away somewhere.'

Tyler looks up. The windows on all three floors are modern and closed, even if they had a way to get up there. 'Let's try round the back.' He jogs back to the gate, his sense of urgency undiminished despite the neighbour's report of a lack of activity.

They have no bolt-cutters for the padlock and the wood looks sturdy. They might be able to break it down between them but Tyler has a better, more energy-efficient idea. He reaches up, takes hold of the top of the wooden slats and hauls his body weight up using the stone wall next to him as a boost for his foot.

'Hang on a minute . . .' Doggett says, but Tyler's already up and has one leg swung over. He drops down onto the path the other side and hears Doggett swearing through the gate. 'I'm getting too bloody old for this.' The gate shakes as Doggett launches himself skyward. Despite his words and his diminutive stature, he's over the top almost as quickly as Tyler. There's a sharp ripping sound as his wiry frame drops down the other side and more swearing as he examines the torn shirt under his jacket.

The back garden stretches away from them and is as unkempt as the front. It's clear that Stevens has been garden-proud at some point in the past. There are flower beds at either side of a large expanse of lawn, a koi fish pond off to the right-hand side, a rockery, fruit trees, and a garden shed that's probably large enough to consider another room of the house. But all of it has the air of neglect. Even under a layer of snow, that much is obvious. As they get closer to the pond Tyler looks down to see several fish floating on the half-frozen surface of the water. Something must have happened recently to make the Superintendent less house-proud than he used to be.

'Not a good sign,' Doggett says mournfully.

The three-storey house towers above them and has an equally large number of closed uPVC windows. There's a conservatory attached to the rear that juts out in a hexagonal shape onto the patio. Tyler tries the door but it holds firm.

'Any ideas?' he asks.

'We really breaking in?' Doggett has a concerned expression that Tyler hasn't seen before. 'There's no way back from this. If we're wrong . . .'

'We're not wrong,' Tyler tells him. 'She was here. I know she was.'

'We should wait for Franklin and her warrant.'

'She could still be here.'

Doggett hesitates and then nods. He examines the lock on the door and runs his hand down the frame. 'We're not getting through that. Or the windows. Not without something a bit more heavy-duty than a flowerpot.' He glances up at the guttering running along the low roof of the conservatory, then back over his shoulder down the garden. He points to the shed. 'See what you can find down there. Something sharp, and something that might give us some leverage.'

Tyler jogs down the garden, his feet crunching through the virgin snow. The door to the shed is padlocked but the wooden frame doesn't look as though it will hold up to much. He takes a few steps back and runs, his shoulder connecting with the wood and sending a shudder through his body. The door holds but something cracked. He just hopes it was the door and not him. He backs up and goes again. This time the door flies open and rebounds into his elbow as he stumbles into the dark interior.

Tyler rubs his arm as he roots around looking for tools that might fit Doggett's description. He manages to find a couple of trowels, a garden hoe and a pair of shears, and by the time he's got back up the garden, Doggett has dragged a large stone flowerpot across the patio and has used it to climb up onto the roof. He reaches down with a beckoning hand and Tyler passes him a trowel. Doggett wobbles as he takes it and Tyler can see the plastic roof panel bowing slightly under his weight. A sheet of frozen ice slides loose and falls to the stones below.

'You sure you're safe up there?'

Doggett jams the trowel down into a gap behind the guttering. 'Well, on the bright side,' he says, 'if this doesn't work, I reckon all I need to do is jump up and down a bit and we'll be in.' He grunts as he levers up the panel next to the one he's balanced on. 'Course, you might have to phone me an ambulance before you properly search the place. Hoe!'

Tyler passes him up the requested equipment and Doggett jams it into the gap he's made with the trowel.

After that, it's remarkably simple. Doggett levers the panel up in one easy movement; whatever glue holds it in place gives without causing Doggett to strain very hard. The panel flips over and clatters to rest on the gently sloping roof. He looks down and wiggles his eyebrows. Then he chucks the tools onto the lawn behind Tyler and clambers down into the conservatory. He blows warm air onto his wet fingers and grins at Tyler through the window. Then he reaches out and turns the key in the lock, swinging open the door. 'Piece of cake,' he says, but Tyler can see the DI's hands shaking a little as the adrenaline wears off.

Tyler steps into the room and bangs the slush off his shoes on the linoleum. 'What sort of idiot leaves the key in the door?'

Doggett's reply comes as he reaches the back door to the house and opens it. 'The same sort of idiot who leaves his back door unlocked. Either he was in a hurry to leave or . . .'

'Or he's still here.' Tyler still has the other trowel gripped tightly in his fist. Doggett looks down at it but refrains from passing judgement.

The conservatory leads into an expensively equipped kitchen-diner, all chrome fittings and sleek grey tiles. It's remarkably clean and tidy given the state of the garden. There's a small weathered dresser next to the fridge that's not exactly in keeping with the rest of the fixtures. A relatively new addition from some antiques trip, no doubt, waiting to be upcycled; there's a can of white paint resting on one of the shelves, and a pile of newspapers stacked up next to it. But other than that there's not a thing out of place. Unless you count the wet footprints they leave trailing behind them across the gleaming floor.

Tyler takes the lead as they move through the kitchen doorway and into the corridor. The house is deathly quiet, only the sound of a clock ticking coming to them from somewhere and the much quieter hum of traffic on the road outside. Tyler can smell bleach. The place is spotless but from what he knows of Stevens' nature that's nothing out of character. There are two doors off the corridor and a staircase leading up to the next floor. The first room is another, more formal dining room, and the next one is the sitting room with the bay window that looks out over the front garden. Both are clean and tidy, meticulously so, as though the place is a show home rather than that of a family of four. The only thing that stands out as personal is the array of framed photographs on the mantelpiece but a scant glance along them confirms the thing that Stevens holds most dear – his career. They are all pictures of him in uniform with various members of the great and good.

Then one photo jumps out at Tyler. He leans in to examine it closer. The picture shows Stevens out of uniform, on some kind of adventure away day. In the background there are rope bridges strung between trees, and all the photographed participants are wearing casual sports gear. One or two are even in camouflage. But it's one figure in particular that draws his eye. Right in the background, not part of the group who are posing for the photograph, is his father, Richard Tyler.

He feels a shudder run down his spine and along his arms. Finding this here seems . . . incongruous . . . bizarre. And yet, it shouldn't. He knows that Stevens was around in his father's day, he and Doggett have even discussed – and rejected – the idea that he might have had something to do with Richard's death, but seeing them framed together in this way brings the whole thing much closer.

Doggett touches his shoulder making him jump. The DI points upstairs and Tyler nods, following him out of the room.

They move slowly through the house, examining each room in turn. There are three bedrooms on the first floor, a master and two kids' rooms as scrupulously tidied as the adults'. Tyler finds it vaguely depressing. The beds are all made, the clothes folded neatly and put away in drawers and wardrobes. In the bathroom and the smaller en suite, there's not so much as a toothpaste stain in the basin. The shower cubicle and bath are both dry and clearly haven't been used in the past twenty-four hours at least.

Tyler's hopes begin to fade as he leaves Doggett searching cupboards and bounds up to the second floor attic conversion. There are only two rooms left up here and Diane is in neither of them.

One is a junk room of sorts and it's the one place in the entire house that shows some level of disorganisation. But even here, though there are cardboard boxes and plastic storage containers full of personal items, everything is neatly stored and stacked. It's as though the Stevens moved in and left everything personal to them here. Some of the boxes are still labelled. *Maureen. Toys. Photographs.*

The second room is clearly Stevens' home office, as tidy as everything else, nothing on the desk but a small reading lamp, a keyboard and a mouse. There's no PC though, or laptop, but the charging wire plugged in under the desk tells Tyler that there was one.

Doggett appears in the doorway. 'I think the Mrs did a flit,' he says. 'There's a whole load of empty hangers in her side of the wardrobe and it looks like a lot of the kids' clothes are missing as well.'

'I didn't even know he had kids.' Tyler says. 'Isn't he a bit . . . ?'

'Past it?' Doggett folds his arms and leans against the door jamb. 'It's his second marriage. Or third maybe . . . I forget. He's got older kids too. A daughter and a son. Both of them moved away.' He stares around at the sparse, blank walls. 'I don't suppose you can blame them for that.' Doggett moves across to examine the bookcase that runs along one wall.

There's a noticeably empty shelf towards the bottom. He squats down and peers at the dark wood. 'First sign of dust I've seen in the place,' he says. 'Looks like there were some box files here until recently.'

He's gone. And taken the evidence with him. Any last chance they had of finding out where she is.

Doggett reads his mind. 'If she ever came to this place, she isn't here now. We've searched everywhere.'

Tyler feels that shudder again, a pulse of sudden fear that travels through his body from top to bottom pushing out the last of the hope. She isn't here. He'd been so sure that she was.

They retrace their steps back downstairs but leave via the front door rather than the back.

'So what do we tell Franklin?' Doggett asks as they step outside. 'That someone else broke in?'

Tyler leaves the door on the latch. 'We can't lie about this, it could disrupt the investigation.' He looks up at the house. 'This could still be a crime scene and it's no longer secure. I'll wait here until they arrive. I'll tell her I came here alone.'

'Don't be daft, lad!' Doggett pats him on the arm and pushes past him down the path. 'We're in this together.' He pulls out his mobile to make the call.

Tyler follows Doggett back down the treacherous steps. Why had he been so sure she was here? Sheer desperation? It was a ridiculous leap of intuition and he'd got it wrong. He smiles to himself when he thinks what Diane would say about that. No use crying over spilt milk. The damage is done and they'd have to face the consequences. *She'd* have to face the consequences. The smile dissolves.

Doggett picks his way across the busy road and gets back into the car. Tyler decides he might as well join him, no point freezing to death while they wait. He looks back once more at the modernised Victorian house, begging it to reveal its secrets. Was she ever here? It's similar to her place, although much more modern with its double-glazed dormer. No draughty gable window to stare out of here.

Something about this thought nags at him. Why? Was it something about the attic? There hadn't been anything all that unusual about it. A great number of the houses in Sheffield date from this era and are very similar. Three storeys. Often with the attic converted, that wasn't at all unusual. A lot of modern families needed a third or fourth bedroom. And even bigger houses like this one would make use of the extra space if they could. Some people even decided to convert their cellars into . . .

Tyler feels a chill ripple through him. He turns back to see Jim getting back out of the car. They stare at each other for a moment as Doggett absorbs the look on his face and then Tyler turns and runs.

His right foot skids out from under him as it comes down on the first step and he falls forwards, his hands slamming hard into the concrete steps, but he's up again in moments, skidding and sliding his way up to the top. He stops for a moment at the gravel path and crouches down at the old coal grate he'd seen when they'd arrived. How could he have been so stupid?

'Diane!' he shouts. He can't see down into the cellar. It looks as though it's been partially blocked with something but it's too dark to see with what. A lot of homeowners blocked up their coal chutes though, to prevent anything falling or crawling in. Was that the reason here? Or was it to stop noise escaping?

He's up and running again, pushing open the front door and barrelling along the corridor. He stumbles into a console table, knocking over a vase and a bowl of keys that both shatter loudly on the parquet flooring. He can hear Doggett shouting at him from behind.

There's no door to the cellar in the hallway, which means it must be in the kitchen. He turns as he enters the room and sees the incongruous dresser. Surely not?

Tyler grabs one side and pulls hard, pivoting the antique away from the wall. And sure enough, behind it is the cellar door. He turns and pulls on the metallic doorknob but it doesn't budge. Locked. It opens outwards as well, which is going to make it virtually impossible to break down. If he can find a screwdriver maybe he could . . . Then he remembers the keys. He doubles back to the broken remnants at the base of the stairs and searches through them. There's a couple of Yale keys and a combination padlock that might be used for a gym locker of some kind, and a longer, metallic old-fashioned key that has a crumbled paper label attached to it with string. The words written on it, if there ever were any, have long since rubbed off but it's the only thing that fits.

Doggett's puffing his way through the front door as Tyler snatches up the key and runs back to the kitchen. The key fits, and turns with a grinding crunch and a loud squeak. The door swings open silently.

Only now does Tyler hesitate, as the stench hits him. Decay. There's the usual damp, the familiar earthy scent of a Sheffield cellar, but overlaid with something far more noxious. He gags at a smell he's all too familiar with, the sour stench of evacuated bowels, the putrid odour of decay. This is the scent of death.

He pauses, one hand splayed out against the flaking plaster of the wall as he tries to steady legs that threaten to give out under him.

He feels Doggett's hand on his shoulder. 'Leave it, son,' he says. 'Come away.' But he shakes the hand off and pushes himself forward down the stone steps into the dark stench. One foot after another, the smell growing stronger in his nostrils, the bile gathering in his throat.

He stumbles at the bottom, his foot coming down hard on the flagstones. His hand is raw where he's dragged it down the rough wall. His eyes are beginning to adjust to the darkness and despite Stevens' best efforts to block up the coal chute — an attempt at soundproofing? — there are thin cracks of light coming in from the road. Below it Tyler can see a sinister black shape huddled low against the back wall. Then he realises it isn't just his eyes adjusting, there's actually a faint light coming in from some other grating, despite the fact it's already dark outside. He's glad about that. That she wasn't in complete darkness at the end. Bad enough she was alone.

He covers his mouth with the crook of his left elbow and knows that if he ever sees Stevens again, he will kill him. Instantly. His hands wrapped around the bastard's throat until he's choked the air from his lungs. He can see her in more detail now. Her leg is bent out at an odd angle, jutting out from under her, but the rest of her is curled small, her body hunched in on itself, as though, at the end of her life, she tried to curl back into the same position in which she came into it. He can't fully make out her face but he can see enough to know that it's her. That scraggly grey hair that was always wafting around her head as though it had a life of its own.

He crouches down beside her, ignoring the stench now, focused only on her face, bloodied and smudged, the skin darkened from multiple bruises. 'I'm sorry,' he tells her, reaching out to brush the hair from her face. And as he touches her skin Diane opens her eyes and coughs.

'Adam,' she says, before closing her eyes again.

day three

The ICER recordings #114

(Archivists' note: This is a different voice to the caller in the last transcript but voiceprint analysis suggests a high probability that it is the same man heard on some of the earliest recordings, labelled as Unknown Caller 2. Interestingly, this voice is heard more often than any other. The identity of the caller has yet to be determined and he remains a high priority for identification [03/05/18])

Call received: 06:16 Wednesday 7th Mar 2018
Duration: 2 minutes 29 seconds

Partial Transcript:

ICER   Yes.

UC2   This is C1. Can you confirm I am speaking with the same individual we have dealt with in the past?

(Recording is silent for 2 seconds)

ICER   I don't exactly have staff, you realise?

UC2   This is not a laughing matter. I assumed that there must have been a change in ownership of the business or something. I can't think of another reason you would have disappointed us in this manner.

ICER   I don't appreciate the—

UC2   And I don't appreciate shoddy service. I was told the matter regarding the last target would be dealt with expediently and with your usual attention to detail.

ICER   Stevens told me he'd dealt with her and—

UC2   And yet, today, I'm reliably informed, the person in question is recuperating at the Northern General Hospital under police protection.

ICER   I see. (*pause 2 seconds*) Well, the contract still stands, with or without police protection, whatever the location.

(Recording is silent for 3 seconds)

UC2   Unfortunately, the damage is done. She's had ample time to reveal whatever she's learned so removing her from the field of play now would seem to be—

ICER   Overkill? That's your prerogative, of course. You understand the situation regarding my refund policy?

UC2   Yes, yes, we're painfully aware of how attached you are to money.

ICER Watch your tone! I told the last bloke, I'm retired. Perhaps it's time we dissolved this partnership for good.

UC2 Okay, okay, let's not be too hasty. (*pause 1 second*) Perhaps I was being a little unfair.

ICER Perhaps you were.

UC2 May I suggest we call it an exchange rather than a refund? The file of information you retrieved for us, given its nature, can only have come from one source. Joey McKenna.

ICER No names!

UC2 Oh, yes, right. Anyway, obviously our original hope was that the situation you created at the reservoir would be traced back to him, but it's clear now we can't rely on him to keep his mouth shut even if he does go down. If you could deal with him instead, perhaps we can—

ICER Are you sure that's what you want? I was led to believe a long time ago that you had other plans for the man.

UC2 Plans change.

ICER He's not exactly an easy target. Wouldn't it be better to deal with the bloke who's at the heart of all this? McKenna's contact. Wouldn't that be enough to make him think twice? After all, that's where all this started.

UC2 Hmm. I was told you were pretty keen to clean up that particular loose end. What exactly is he to you?

ICER   Fine. Forget it. But McKenna's going to take some time to sort out.

UC2   Very well. But not too long, I hope. I could remind you that you have as much to lose as we do, if not more.

ICER   You could do, but I wouldn't recommend that you do.

UC2   Yes, well … As long as—

Call ends 06:18

Tyler can see her through a half-frosted window, lying in a hospital bed, her grey hair fanned out around her blue face. She's never looked older.

He's been aware for a while now that she must be getting close to retirement. Or half-aware, perhaps, since the idea of this woman stepping down to prune roses in the back garden is so foreign to him he can barely picture it. He can't imagine what she would do with herself. Take up art? Travel? Nothing seems quite right. She has no family to take up her time, no partner, no hobbies or pastimes or anything other than her work. He has a sudden image of her in five years' time, shuffling around the city streets she used to patrol on foot, looking for some kind of purpose. And he realises that it could be an image of him as well, his future.

But all of that assumes she will make it through the next few hours. She nearly didn't make retirement at all. Better for now to stay focused on that. The consultant seems to think she'll be okay, though he refuses to be drawn on anything much beyond that.

Tyler glances along the hospital corridor towards the nurses' station but they seem content to ignore him for now. He's here under sufferance and thanks, no doubt, to his warrant card. This is not an area of the hospital that they normally allow people to hang out in, regardless of the circumstances surrounding how Diane was found or his relationship with her. He isn't family. That was made abundantly clear. And even if he were, there are strict visiting hours.

'DS Tyler.' The voice bounces along the corridor, unashamedly loud in a place that doesn't welcome noise. ACC Franklin strolls towards him. Out of uniform she looks a completely different woman. Still composed, still small of stature, still so precise in all her movements. But wrapped in an outdoor fleece, her legs in tight jeans and walking boots, she looks as though she'd be more at home out hiking through the Peaks. It's a glimpse behind the curtain, at the woman she is beyond the police. He wonders for the first time if she has anyone to go home to. Anyone waiting for her to retire so that they can get on with a quiet life together. He hopes she has.

'How is she?' she asks simply as she reaches him, glancing through the window with a frown etched on her face.

'Dehydrated,' he says. 'Dangerously so. And suffering from chronic hypothermia. The doctors seem to think we found her in time.'

Franklin puts a hand on his forearm. '*You* found her in time.'

'She's still critical but . . . well, the nurses check on her less often so I'm taking that as a sign they think the real danger has passed.'

'And her leg?' Franklin points to the gruesome metal contraption wrapped around Diane's right calf.

'Compound fracture. They still need to reset the bone but they can't operate until she's stronger.'

Franklin nods, still effortlessly efficient in the face of a crisis. But then, she doesn't really know Diane. Although . . . he realises she probably does. A younger Diane, from years ago, not the accomplished DCI she is now.

'All things considered then, it could be worse.'

'Yes,' he tells her, 'she could be dead.'

She steps away a few paces, thinking, her hands thrust into the baggy pockets of the fleece. She turns. 'And how are you?'

'Fine.'

'No,' she says. 'Of course you aren't.'

'Really, it's—'

'Because if you were fine you would be okay to talk to the Professional Standards officers who are waiting for you downstairs. And I'm not sure you're ready for that. At least . . . not quite yet.'

He looks at her. Something is being offered but he's not sure what.

'You look well enough to talk to me though,' she goes on. 'Then, depending on your answers, I'll decide if you're ready to talk to them. Or whether it's better for you to head home and get some sleep.' She glances at her watch. 'After all, you're still actively involved in a murder investigation and I have to think of my officers first.' There's something in her voice that tells him this isn't all about his welfare. He has the distinct impression that the outcome of this conversation will decide whether he *is* still involved in the investigation. Or any other.

There's a row of four chairs on the opposite side of the corridor and she sits down in the one furthest from him, gesturing for him to take a seat next to her. He does so, suddenly aware that the only sleep he's had for twenty-four hours is about twenty minutes or so dozing off in this very chair.

'How did you find her?' she asks.

'Mina told us Stevens was missing. It seemed too big a coincidence so we decided to search his place.' It was as much of a story as Doggett and he had been able to concoct in the panicked minutes they'd spent waiting for an ambulance. But no doubt Franklin knows this much already. He doubts Doggett's managed to avoid her questioning.

'So without a warrant you took it upon yourselves to break into Stevens' home?'

'We—'

'I expect you were heading there first to check on him, isn't that right? What with him being your superior officer and everything. It would make sense that you were worried about his welfare, especially in light of the fact DCI Jordan was missing as well.'

'No one who knows my relationship with Stevens is going to believe that.'

Franklin waves a hand in the air. 'Ancient history. Regardless of your ... documented differences, you were looking out for a fellow officer.'

'If you say so.'

'I do. Then, when you arrived, I imagine you heard DCI

Jordan calling for help from the cellar and that's when you decided to break in.'

'It's almost as though you were there.'

A nurse wanders by and shoots them a questioning glance but she doesn't say anything.

'Tell me,' Franklin goes on, once the nurse is out of earshot. 'Has DCI Jordan regained consciousness yet?'

Tyler turns to look at her. 'Why do you ask?'

'It's important we know what happened to her.'

'It seems fairly clear to me. That maniac Stevens locked her in his cellar and did a bunk. Maybe you should be looking for him and asking him what happened.'

'You can rest assured I have every available resource looking for him.' She leans back in her chair and lets out a sigh. 'Although I have a nasty feeling he's already long gone.'

'What do you mean?'

She examines him for a few moments, as though trying to work out whether she can trust him. Whatever she sees must reassure her. 'I shouldn't be telling you this but I think it's time the two of us were a bit more candid with each other, don't you? Last week, Stevens bought a one-way ticket to Buenos Aires from Heathrow. The flight departed yesterday afternoon. We know he has a son who lives in South America so we can only assume that's where he's headed. As you know, the UK does have an extradition treaty with Argentina but it may still be difficult to get him back.'

'Bastard!' Tyler jumps up out of his seat and steps back to the window to check on Diane. There's no discernible change.

'We've been looking into Stevens for some time now,' Franklin says from behind him. 'It was one of the reasons I was sent here in the first place. A few too many questions have popped up surrounding his career.'

'How long?' he asks.

'What?'

'How long have Professional Standards suspected him? Months? Years?'

'A few months.'

Tyler turns to face her. 'Long enough then that this could have been avoided,' he says, gesturing over his shoulder at the unconscious form in the bed behind him.

'You know these things aren't easy. Stevens has had plenty of people looking out for him over the years. People who would prefer to cover their tracks than say what they know. We can only go where the evidence takes us.'

That hits a little too close to home for Tyler. Is he responsible for this? If he and Doggett had voiced their suspicions earlier, turned over the information they'd amassed, could this whole horror have been avoided?

No, he won't accept responsibility for this. No one listened to Doggett all those years ago and they wouldn't have listened now.

'Adam,' Franklin says, again reaching out to take his arm. 'What did she know? There's a reason he did this to her and we need to know what it was.'

'I don't know,' he tells her, and he doesn't even have to lie. But even if he did know, he still wouldn't have told her.

Because he's had time to think about this through this longest of nights. His father called it a conspiracy. And you can't have a conspiracy of one. Stevens wasn't in this alone. Nothing has changed. He still doesn't know who he can trust. Except Doggett, of course. And Mina. He trusts Mina. But does he want to draw her into this?

His head's spinning, his thoughts going round in circles. It's all he's been able to think about all night, in between worrying about Diane. Did Stevens kill his father? What did Diane find out that made him take action?

'Tyler!'

'What?'

Franklin shakes her head. 'Go home. Get some sleep.'

'I'm fine.'

'No, you're not.'

He flicks his eyes towards Diane, willing the fluids that are flowing into her arm to go faster.

'She'll be fine. I'll make sure someone from Professional Standards stays with her until you get back.'

'No . . . I can't leave her alone again.'

'You have two options, DS Tyler. You can go home now and get a few hours' sleep to clear your head, or I can call Professional Standards and they'll take you back to the station for questioning. Either way you're going to have to entrust her to me.'

Franklin is eyeing him closely, her face blank of expression. How much does she know? How far can he trust her?

'If anything happens to her . . .' He trails off.

'It's a good job you didn't finish that sentence. Now go home.'

He takes one last look at Diane, trying to reassure himself that they can't touch her here, in a hospital surrounded by nurses and doctors. Especially now it's getting light and there will be more people coming and going. So why doesn't he feel more sure of that?

As he's walking away, Franklin calls after him. 'And don't forget you still have an appointment with OH. I've bumped it back to twelve for you but miss it and I *will* be forced to take action.'

Tyler waves his hand behind him in acknowledgement but refuses to turn round.

He makes his way down a back staircase and steps out near the entrance doors to the hospital. He's not sure if Franklin was entirely serious about Professional Standards waiting downstairs for him but best not to risk it; the last thing he needs right now is them questioning him. He's too tired to think and he might just let the wrong thing slip.

When he steps out into the cold dark of the morning and a hand touches his shoulder, he's so tightly wound he spins on the ball of his foot and brings his fist up ready to defend himself.

'Whoa, bro!' Jude says, lifting his hands up in front of him in mock surrender. 'I know we've got our differences but . . . ?'

Tyler relaxes a little, letting the tension go out of his arm. He's glad he didn't just clock his brother; things are bad enough as it is. Mind you, even that would have been preferable to punching someone from Professional Standards. He isn't thinking straight. He glances back at the hospital doors and then looks around, seeing if he can spot anyone who looks official.

'You need to get out of here?' Jude asks, correctly interpreting the worry that must be etched on Tyler's face. 'Come on, where's your car?'

Tyler leads him away from the building and across the car park.

'How is she?' Jude asks.

It's a measure of how tired he is that Tyler hasn't even asked what Jude's doing here.

Again his brother somehow manages to read his thoughts. 'I heard it on the local radio. They didn't name her but I put two and two together. I figured you'd be here but they wouldn't let me in.'

Tyler frowns. 'Bit early to be listening to the news, isn't it?'

Jude shrugs. 'I sometimes have those talk shows on. I don't sleep all that good these days. So, Diane, is she . . .'

'She's not great.'

'Sorry, mate.'

'Do you really give a shit?'

They'd been young when their mother walked out on them but not so young they weren't aware of the rumours. Jude had always chosen to blame Diane for their parents' problems. Tyler chose to blame Richard.

'Hey!' Jude grabs his arm and spins him round. 'Diane and

I might have had our differences but do you really think I'd want to see her get hurt?'

Tyler rubs his eyes with his thumb and forefingers. 'Sorry. That was unfair.'

'Come on, let's get you home. I'll drive.'

'You don't need to do that.'

'Yeah, I do actually,' Jude says, a smile playing at the corner of his mouth. 'Look at the fucking state of you.'

'Hey, it's Binita, isn't it?'

The girl looks up from the crate she's sitting on and Mina smiles at her. Her biggest, warmest, most disarming smile . . . she hopes.

'I thought it was you. Mina,' she says. 'We spoke at Delight! yesterday.'

'Yes, of course. I remember.'

'I knew you looked familiar. I must have seen you in here.' Mina picks up a basket in the hope it adds credibility to her flimsy explanation. It hadn't taken a great deal of detective work to find her. Just a call to Delight! with a cover story about needing a list of employee names and then a bit of asking around in the community. 'Just doing a bit of shopping,' she adds, and immediately regrets it. *Who says that?* She grabs a butternut squash from the display and makes a show of squeezing it to see if it's ripe. She has no idea if that's what you're meant to do with them.

But if Binita picks up on anything she doesn't say so. 'My dad's the owner,' she says.

'Oh, really? That must be it then. I'm guessing you help out here sometimes.' Mina feels her cheeks colouring again. She should probably never go undercover.

'Yeah, not so much anymore. I'm just watching the place for a bit while he's at the cash and carry.'

Mina hesitates but this is what she's come here for, and there isn't anyone else in the shop who could overhear them. 'Any more trouble at work?' she asks.

Binita's eyes dart left and right as though her dad might appear at any moment. 'No,' she says. 'I really shouldn't have said anything.'

Mina's instinct is to tell her she should definitely say something but they've been over all that already and anyway, she reminds herself, she's here for work. She just wishes she could help Binita in some way.

'Does he come to the factory very often,' she asks. 'Mr Whitehouse, I mean?'

Binita shrugs, looking up at her again with wide, pretty eyes.

Mina's not surprised she gets unwanted attention; there's an innocence to her that's exactly the sort of thing some men would find irresistible. *You need to toughen up, girl! Fast!*

'He's there a bit, I guess.'

'But he doesn't have any financial interest in the company, does he? I thought he just sold the factory to Ms Spencer?' She regrets this as soon as it's out of her mouth. *Too formal. You'll only scare her off.*

Again, Binita shrugs.

Besides, by this point, Mina probably knows more about the financial situation at Delight! than she does. She'd spent most of yesterday digging into the company. It had taken a bit of doing which is why she'd needed help from Amber in the Fraud department. There didn't seem to be anything specific on Spencer or on Whitehouse, but she had discovered one thing: Whitehouse had sold the factory to Spencer's company for £1. That had struck her as very weird but Amber had seemed less excited. She'd spent a lot of time lecturing Mina on fulfilment of legal contracts and nominal fees and so on. She really hadn't understood most of it but the gist seemed to be that Spencer got a good deal and in return Whitehouse avoided the costs involved in getting rid of other liabilities – machinery, staffing, all the rest of it. He also got a free space to operate the so-called 'car' business he mentioned to Tyler, which turned out to be the cab firm they'd seen at the factory. Another fact he'd failed to mention to them. It was all a bit shady. And despite all of the upsides for Whitehouse it seemed as though Spencer was getting the best part of the deal. Would that be enough that she felt she owed him something? Surely, there was more to it than that.

'He's always been there,' Binita says, 'as long as I have anyway. I figured ... well, I mean, I'm not sure but I thought he and Ms Spencer were related or something?'

'Related?'

'I don't know ... I just ... It must have been something they said once. I mean, they definitely see each other outside of work. Mrs Spencer has parties sometimes and we do the catering. Mr Whitehouse is always there.'

'You mean there's something romantic between them?'

Binita grimaces. 'No! You wouldn't think that if you'd seen the way she looks at him sometimes. Anyway, she's married.'

Married. Mina hadn't thought of that. She mentally berates herself. She'd assumed from the lack of a ring that Spencer was single, but maybe she just didn't want to announce her marital status to the world. If Spencer was a nicer human being Mina would wish her luck with that. But the question remains, is Spencer a woman who stands on her own two feet and doesn't feel the need to identify herself as someone's wife? Or is she hiding the fact she's married for some other reason?

And, of course, the fact that she's married doesn't stop her from being romantically connected to Whitehouse as well. *When did I get this cynical?*

'One thing did confuse me,' Mina says, as though she's just thought of it. 'What are all those other buildings for? All those containers.'

Binita frowns as though she's never considered that before. Maybe she hasn't. 'A couple of them are for food storage. I think the rest are rented. I've seen a few people coming and going but I'm sure Mrs Spencer would be able to—'

'Oh, I don't want to bother her, I was just curious. Anyway, I'd better be off.'

'What about your shopping?' Binita points to Mina's basket and its sole vegetable occupant.

'Oh, yeah. Duh.' Mina pays for the unwanted squash,

picking up a tube of toothpaste from near the till and a packet of pecans. She can feel her face growing steadily redder. 'Right, I should be getting back to work then.'

She hurries out of the shop with a mortifyingly pathetic wave.

Tyler sleeps fitfully, plagued with dreams that make little sense, random images: Diane hobbling towards him holding a baby in her arms, yet when he looks at it he sees it's her own severed leg, the bone sticking out of the flesh with a jagged edge. Someone who might be Doggett but is somehow also his father, Richard, knitting with rope in place of wool. Tyler himself, running alongside a steam train, desperate to outdistance it because he knows, deep in his gut, that if he doesn't the people closest to him will be gone forever.

He wakes to the smell of fresh coffee and bacon and forces himself up and out of bed. Something's wrong. There shouldn't be anyone else here.

In the kitchen, Jude is standing at the hob cooking bacon in a pan, clouds of blue smoke billowing up from the hot oil. 'Shit!' he says, grinning. He pulls the pan from the heat and wafts the smoke away with his hand. 'I never was much of a cook.'

Tyler pours himself a coffee from the cafetiere. He'd forgotten he even had one of those. 'What are you doing here?'

'I wanted to make sure you were all right. I nipped out to that garage up the road and got some shit. You don't keep much in, do you? Anyway, I thought you might want breakfast before work.' He looks down at the pan. 'I think it's still salvageable.'

'What time is it?'

'Just gone eleven.'

Tyler rubs his face with one hand, trying to wake himself up. 'I have to get back to the hospital.'

Jude fiddles around in the pan with a pair of tongs, snapping the burnt rashers of bacon even as he tries to fish them out. 'Your colleague rang,' he says. 'Doggett?'

'What?' Tyler finds himself automatically patting down his boxer shorts, as though his phone is tucked in there somewhere.

'Here.' Jude retrieves the mobile from the kitchen work surface, disconnecting the charger. 'You tried to take it to bed with you but I managed to pry it off you.'

Tyler always sleeps with his phone next to him, just in case. It's a sign of how far gone he was that he allowed Jude to take it off him. Especially under the circumstances.

'He's been to the hospital and she's fine. They're still not letting anyone in though. He said not to go to the office but that he'd meet you in the usual place at lunchtime. Make sense?'

Tyler nods. The usual place means the bacon butty van that parks just outside the station. For Doggett, a creature of well-defined habit, lunchtime is one o'clock. It seems his day is going to be filled with fried food again.

He moves across to the wide living-room window and looks down at the semi-frozen car park. It seems there's been another snowstorm in the night and the ground that was beginning to turn brown and slushy in the thaw has firmed up again with a fresh white blanket of virgin snow. The concierge is out spreading grit on the paths with a giant yellow spade. If he'd been one day later . . . if Diane had had to sleep in that cellar for just one more night . . .

Jude gives up on the breakfast and joins him at the window with his own mug of coffee. 'Looks bleak out there.'

Tyler looks at him properly for the first time. His brother does look older, much more so than he did in the pub the night of their first reunion. He was never a particularly big man but he's skinny now, almost slight, the skin of his face loose and drooping. Tyler wants to ask if he's okay but where do you start after all this time? And if they do start . . . if he begins once again to poke at the scab of their relationship, he runs the risk of breaking the wound wide open. On the one hand, he's not proud of the way he stormed out of the pub that night but on the other, he knows he's only a few wrong words away from doing the same all over again.

The silence stretches on between them and Tyler can see his brother wrestling with the same dilemma. Where to start.

'I guess . . . er . . .' Jude manages eventually. 'I should probably leave you to get ready.'

They both stand staring out of the window for a few more moments and then Jude turns and heads towards the door. Tyler can feel his brother pulling further away from him and the pain is almost physical. He's right back there in Jude's old bedroom, desperate for him not to leave, with no idea that this would be the last time he would see his brother for more than a decade. But he won't beg Jude not to go. Not again.

'Why?' he blurts out, turning round to face his brother. 'Why didn't you come back?'

Jude has stopped by the door, his back to the room. He speaks without turning around. He doesn't answer straight away, maybe because he's aware everything hangs on his answer, or maybe just because he doesn't have one. Then, without turning, he speaks, his voice so low it's almost a whisper. 'Because you were better off without me.'

It's not good enough. Tyler knows it, and Jude knows it too. That's why he hasn't turned round. That's why he's speaking so quietly, ashamed that he doesn't have anything better to say. But it seems honest. Whatever else, Jude believes it to be the truth.

'You were wrong,' Tyler tells him. 'I wasn't.'

Jude starts moving towards the door and again Tyler feels his brother slipping away. 'So that's it? You're leaving?' There's still so much he needs to ask. About Richard, about exactly what happened between them all those years ago and whether he remembers anything that could help the investigation into their father's death.

Jude turns now and Tyler can see his eyes are brimming with unshed tears. 'I can stay if you want? I thought you had to get to work.'

He does. He checks the time again. He's already pushing it if he's going to make his meeting with Occupational Health at twelve. He needs to talk to Doggett too, and Rabbani. He has to check on Diane, find out exactly what happened to her. And of course, he still has a murder to solve . . .

'Meet me tonight,' he says. 'Same pub. Nine o'clock. If you're there, I know you're serious about putting things right. If you're not . . . then don't bother coming back.' *This is your last chance, Jude. Last chance to make it right.* He doesn't say it but he can see from the glint of hope in his brother's eyes that he gets it.

'I'll be there,' Jude tells him, and God help him, Tyler thinks he believes it.

The offices for Occupational Health are tucked away in a dark corner of the building. The entrance is an understated door accessible from the street, presumably so that serving officers can pop in and out without it being too obvious to their colleagues. At least he won't have to dodge Professional Standards at every turn. There's a small plastic sign to tell him he's in the right place but not much else. At the top of a narrow flight of stairs he finds a receptionist and a waiting room. There are several posters on the walls with calming landscape scenes and inspirational quotes about the benefits of talking.

He doesn't want to talk about anything to anyone, and he's mentally preparing himself as he sits in the waiting room, compartmentalising his thoughts, trying to paint a smile on his face that says, 'I'm okay! Don't worry about me. Nothing to see here.' He has a nasty suspicion that this isn't a skill he has in spades. He's never seen anyone from Occupational

Health before but he has a nagging sense it's going to be a bit like seeing a psychologist and the guy is probably going to get fixated on his mother. Which is fine as far as Tyler's concerned – he can barely remember his mother. And no doubt the bloke will have a field day with that.

'DS Tyler? I'm Scott Austin.'

Tyler looks up to see a man standing over him, smiling. He's wearing a tightly fitted white shirt with the sleeves rolled up and a buttoned-up waistcoat over the top. Somehow he's both the very stereotype of a therapist and a long way from it. He's much younger than Tyler would have expected, late twenties, early thirties perhaps, and although he has a beard, it's cropped short and well-maintained, emphasising his jawline rather than hiding it. As Tyler follows him into a small office, trying to not be too aware of his stretched check trousers, he half expects to see the real therapist sitting behind the desk and find that this guy is actually an intern or something.

But he gestures for Tyler to take one of two seats positioned by the window either side of a small coffee table, and then sits down himself, crossing one leg over the other and putting further strain on the already burdened trousers.

Austin smiles and the word enigmatic has never taken on greater meaning for Tyler. The man actually has dimples appear either side of his mouth. The top two buttons of his shirt are undone and Tyler can't help noticing the dark veins that stand out on Austin's neck against the crisp white fabric.

The next hour is excruciating. Austin . . . *Scott* starts with a few general questions regarding his work situation. How stressful is his job? Does he find himself struggling to sleep at night? Tyler bats them away with generalisations of his own but becomes increasingly aware of the man's penetrating gaze. Then, after a couple of attempts to draw him out in more specific detail Austin lapses into silence. Tyler's been expecting this too; after all, it's a trick he's used himself on enough occasions when interviewing suspects. But being ready for it doesn't make it any less uncomfortable. He feels as though those bluey-green pupils are boring right into his soul. He refuses to be drawn out though, and even as he thinks that Austin smiles again, as though he can read the very thought in Tyler's head.

'Okay, let's be honest, shall we? You don't want to be here. I get that. But you have to be here. And at the end of this session I have to tell your –' He looks down at his notes for a moment, '– ACC Franklin, whether or not you should be allowed to continue in your current capacity or –' And here he pauses, more for dramatic effect, Tyler imagines, than anything, '– whether you need to take a leave of absence.'

'What?'

The smile remains fixed in place, the dimples creating two lopsided mini smiles of their own. 'I'm not here to make your life difficult, Detective Tyler. But you do need to talk to me. Like I said at the top of the meeting, anything you say is confidential. I only report back my recommendation, nothing else.'

Can Franklin really do this? He's not sure. Maybe it's time

to talk to the union. On the other hand, she could have just handed him over to Professional Standards and she didn't.

Austin checks his watch – a black-strapped Fitbit fastened so tightly Tyler can see the golden hair on his wrist sprouting underneath. 'Okay, we're running out of time so I'm going to ask you one more question and my hope is that you'll answer it honestly. If you do, you can go straight back to work. But if I think you're giving me the runaround . . .' He spreads his hands wide.

Tyler watches Austin watching him. He should just walk out. Forget this nonsense and get back to work, after a quick chat to his union representative. But if Franklin suspends him he won't be able to go anywhere near the case. And this case could finally give him the answers he's been looking for. He feels like he's closer than ever to finding out the truth and he's not about to let some jumped-up little tosser get the better of him, no matter how fit the bastard is.

'Ask your question,' he says, trying to keep the growl from his voice and failing.

Austin pauses, the smile still in place, the eyes watching him so closely. 'This is my question,' he says, resting his elbows on the arms of his chair and steepling his fingers together in front of him. 'Did you kill DS Guy Daley?'

It's so far from anything Tyler's expecting that for a moment he thinks he must have misheard. 'I don't . . . Is that supposed to be funny?'

Austin doesn't answer directly. 'Out of everyone involved in the case, you're the only one who hasn't been to see me.'

'I don't need to talk about it.'

'ACC Franklin believes differently. But you haven't answered my question. Did you kill Guy Daley?'

'No! Of course not.'

Austin nods. 'But you feel responsible.'

It isn't exactly a question so Tyler says nothing.

'From what I understand, you weren't even near him at the time. And you tried your best to save him. Carried out all the appropriate first-aid treatments you were able to. You did everything anyone could have expected of you.'

Tyler stares at Austin's shoe bobbing in the air in front of him.

'I gather you and DS Daley weren't very close. That there'd been some animosity between you. Did that affect your actions in some way? Did it make you hesitate? Maybe you thought you'd be better off if he wasn't around anymore?'

'Wha—? No, of course I didn't. I did everything I could but . . .'

'But what?' Austin remains calm, his hands clasped on top of his note pad. 'But he died anyway?'

Tyler watches the shoe gently bobbing and suddenly he's back there in the Gardens, watching Daley's face grow paler and paler as the blood cools and thickens on the ground around him. 'He shouldn't have even been there,' he says. 'I made him come.'

Austin breathes out heavily, as though he's been holding his breath. He opens his notebook and flips back a page or

184

two. 'The official report says you left him in the car, and that he followed you of his own volition.'

'Yeah, but . . .' He'd cajoled Daley to go with him, using Mina as bait. He could see the man was suffering. He knew he wasn't fit for work but he used him anyway. 'I guilted him into it.' The last words he'd said to Daley were '*Look after yourself for a change*'. He'd spat sarcasm at the man when he knew he was on the edge.

'And you think if you'd done things differently he'd still be here.'

'I don't know.'

'And I imagine you don't like not knowing things.' Austin uncrosses his legs. 'Maybe you're right.'

Tyler looks up. 'What?'

'I'm not here to absolve you. Only you can do that. But consider something else. Maybe if you'd acted differently Guy Daley would still be alive. But it's possible DC Rabbani wouldn't be, or you might not be, or an innocent bystander might not be. There's really no way to know for sure.'

'Is that supposed to make me feel better?'

Austin beams again and Tyler feels the smile reach him somewhere deep in his stomach. 'It's not my job to make you feel better,' he says. Again, he looks at his watch. 'Time's up, I'm afraid, but you'd better get on anyway. Don't you have a murder to solve?'

For the first time since he entered the room Tyler feels himself relax. 'You giving me a clean bill of health then, *Doc*?'

'Hardly. I think you're a complete fucking mess.'

Tyler laughs. 'Don't sugar-coat it, or anything.' He holds the man's gaze for a moment. Long enough to know he isn't imagining anything. 'You're not exactly what I expected an OH officer to be.'

Austin inclines his head in acknowledgement of that. Perhaps he's used to the reaction. But then the wry smile disappears and he gets more serious. 'You need to talk to someone about this hero complex of yours.'

'Hero complex?'

'In my opinion I think you would benefit from speaking to a counsellor. There's someone I could recommend if you want?'

'I don't need a counsellor.'

'Well, I can't force you but think about it, please?'

Tyler nods.

'Okay, I don't see any reason why you can't go on with your job. For now, you're free to go.'

He gets up and Austin escorts him to the door. 'Think about the counsellor. It could help.'

Tyler leaves Austin at the door and walks along the corridor but when he gets to the top of the stairs he can't resist turning back. Austin is watching him, that smile still fixed firmly in place. Then, for the first time, he shows a moment of doubt and the smile dissolves. He retreats into his office and closes the door behind him, leaving Tyler to wonder if that intense gaze represented something more than just professional curiosity.

*

By the time he gets out of his session with the curious Scott Austin, Tyler's late to meet Doggett but as it turns out he has a missed call and a voice message telling him to meet the DI at the hospital. His stomach flips over when he hears that but then Doggett must have realised the assumption Tyler would make so added that Jordan was awake and asking for him.

He rushes over to the Northern General, no easy achievement given the state of the roads and the always present gridlock of traffic. At the ward entrance there's no sign of Doggett but he expects to be waylaid by Professional Standards as soon as he steps foot anywhere near Diane. In fact there's only one plain-clothed officer playing with his mobile, lounging on the same chair Tyler himself occupied just a few hours before. He looks up and appears to recognise Tyler but makes no attempt to waylay him. Tyler has no doubt who the man is, though; he doesn't recognise him from the station.

'She's been asking for you,' he says. 'ACC Franklin said to let you in.'

Again Laura Franklin surprises him. But he has to wonder whether she's actually on his side or whether she's lulling him into a false sense of security.

Diane still has her eyes closed but she looks more peaceful than she did earlier. She has a bit of colour back in her face that is more reassuring than any words. For the first time he allows himself to believe that she's going to be okay.

There's a chair propped against the radiator under the window, which he pulls up to her bedside. As he sits, he glances back out into the corridor but the guy from Professional Standards has turned his attention back to his phone, on the face of it entirely unconcerned with any conversation they might have.

When he turns back, Diane is looking at him.

'Hey!' he says, and when she lifts her arm he takes her hand and lets her squeeze his. It's a feeble action but it conveys everything it needs to. 'I know,' he says. 'I know.'

She tries to speak, though nothing comes out but a croak. She stops, closes her eyes and swallows. She points to her neck and looks at the bedside unit. 'Throat . . .' she manages.

He tops up the empty glass of water from a jug and passes it to her. It becomes clear she won't be able to support the weight on her own so he holds the glass to her lips while she drinks.

After a few more minutes and a few more sips she seems a little more like her old self. She must notice his eyes drifting over to her trussed-up leg because she croaks, 'Looks like my dancing days are over.' Then she smiles. 'Thank you,' she says, squeezing his hand again. 'Thank you for finding me.'

She tells him the story slowly, stopping occasionally for more sips of water. How she went to Stevens' house to confront him. How she realised how stupid she'd been but just a moment too late.

'He . . . He was really going to kill me.' She puts her hand to her throat, raw with red and purple bruises where he'd tried to strangle her.

'But he didn't,' he reminds her.

She closes her eyes and he knows she's reliving that moment. When she opens them, she says, 'He was always an incompetent bastard but on this occasion, I'm glad he bottled it.'

'Is that what you think happened?'

She nods. 'I think so. That's why he dumped me in the cellar. Didn't have the guts to finish me off himself so he left me there to ...' She trails off and Tyler imagines what that must have been like for her, lying there all those days, broken, dying, knowing no one was coming for her.

'Why?' he asks. 'Why did you go there?'

She shakes her head and then regrets the movement, has to drink some more water before she can go on. 'It was an anonymous file,' she says, and Tyler feels the hair go up on the back of his neck. 'A folder, outlining all the crap Stevens has been involved in over the years. I didn't believe it at first.' She coughs. 'I mean, I knew he was a crooked bastard but I just thought he was massaging the figures a bit. Ignoring cases that wouldn't bring in a favourable result.' She takes another sip of water. 'But this dossier ... It had dates, specifics, information about how he was altering records, putting pressure on people.' She breaks into another coughing fit.

'Let's do this later,' he says, passing her the water again.

She waves him off. 'I started piecing things together. Some of the cases were familiar and I'd had doubts about them at the time. Reading this ... dossier made me realise he wasn't just incompetent, he was actually falsifying records. I was so furious with him but ... well, I got cocky too. You know he'd been looking at restructuring things, your department was going to be the first to go and I suddenly saw a way out.' She sighs heavily. 'You've always been my bloody Achilles' heel, haven't you?'

She means it as a joke but now he knows. This is his fault too.

'Oh, Adam, no!' she says, realising her mistake. 'I didn't mean that. This is my own stupid fault. I should have gone straight to Professional Standards when that folder first landed on my desk. I just thank God I'd at least had the presence of mind to call Laura. God knows what he might have got up to if she hadn't been here!'

'You called Franklin?'

Diane nods. 'I wanted to ask her advice on how to play things. But she wasn't there and I ended up leaving a message on her voicemail.' She closes her eyes. 'If I'd just said more . . . mentioned Stevens by name . . .' She shakes her head again. 'I've been a complete fucking idiot.' Diane rarely swears but he can see the anger bubbling away beneath the surface. Anger at herself.

'Where's the folder now?'

'It was in my car. He must have got rid of it. Along with the car as well, apparently, since I gather there's been no sign of it. They've gone over his place already but they haven't found anything. It looks as though he did a pretty thorough job of cleaning up after himself.'

That explained the missing laptop and box-files, and how clean the place was. Tyler can't understand why he'd go to all that trouble though, knowing full well they'd find a body in his cellar. He shivers at the thought.

'It's not your fault,' he tells her, and he knows that it isn't. It's his. The folder on her desk has to be the one Joey McKenna tried to give him. First, he'd tried to black-mail Tyler into taking it and then he'd given it directly to Jordan. Why? Unless there was something in it that benefitted him. If Tyler and Doggett had come clean a few months ago when McKenna first contacted them, or at any time in the months between, Diane wouldn't be in the hospital right now. Another one for the guilt column. He wonders what platitudes Scott Austin would have for him about that.

'Adam,' Diane says, and her face is creased in so much pain he wonders if he should call for someone. 'Adam, there's something else. Something I didn't realise ... No, something I didn't want to accept until I was in that ... that place.'

'Shh,' he tells her, reaching out to take her hand again. 'There's plenty of time for all that. You just concentrate on getting better.'

But she shakes his hand away. 'No, you don't understand. I tried telling Laura earlier but I don't think she took me seriously. It's your father, Adam ... Richard.'

Tyler freezes.

'It's ...' She's crying now, tears she can't afford to lose in her dehydrated state rolling down her cheeks. 'I think he killed him, Adam. I think Roger killed your father.'

He doesn't know how to respond.

'Adam? Did you hear me?'

'Yes.' He looks away from her, his eyes travelling of their own accord towards the corridor and the bloke from Professional Standards still looking at his phone. 'Was there something in the folder that indicated . . . ?'

'No, it wasn't that but . . . Richard came to me shortly before he died to tell me he was worried about something but he wouldn't tell me what. After he . . . After he died I assumed that whatever it was that was worrying him was the reason he . . . did it. Killed himself. And then that stuff came out about money in his account. I didn't want to believe it, but . . . Oh, God forgive me, I didn't even want to think about it!'

She breaks off and he has to wait a moment while she gets her tears under control. He passes her a box of tissues and she wipes her eyes. Eventually she goes on.

'This stuff with Stevens, it goes back years. There have been rumours circulating about him for as long as I can remember. He didn't get that nickname of his for nothing. But it was more like a running joke. Everyone knew he massaged the figures but, well, that sort of thing goes on all the time and it's above my pay grade to worry about. Then I got the folder and I finally had actionable evidence I could use against him. I went to see him, out of courtesy, I suppose, more fool me. But it was only when I was there in his house that it clicked. It was Stevens that Richard had been worried about. I think your father already had something on him way back then.'

She stops and waits for him to respond. When he doesn't, she frowns.

'Adam, do you understand me? Richard wasn't suicidal. He never would have killed himself ... It was Stevens. I think he killed him.' She's fully crying now. 'I'm so sorry, Adam. I should have listened to Jim all those years ago. I got it wrong.'

He leans in and holds her while she cries, telling her not to worry, not to blame herself. He tells her it's okay, that he doesn't blame her, but he wonders if some part of him does. Doggett had never believed Richard killed himself. What might they have achieved if she'd believed as well? How different could his own life have been?

Eventually she cries herself back to sleep, her eyes closing even as she babbles her continued apologies at him. She must be exhausted and he realises the conversation with him has taken a great deal out of her, more than she has to give at the moment. He shouldn't have let her talk for so long. He needs to reach Doggett and tell him about this latest development, assuming he doesn't already know. But he doesn't want to leave her. He doesn't want her to wake up alone and think she's back in that place. He's wondering what to do when the decision's taken out of his hands. The guy in the corridor raises a hand and beckons him outside.

'The Gaffer wants a word with you,' he says, as Tyler joins him. He speaks with a London accent that convinces Tyler he was right about the man not being local.

'Your gaffer or mine?'

'Both, from what I can gather. They want you back at the station ASAP.'

Tyler nods. He can't avoid Franklin forever and he could really do with talking to Doggett as well but . . . He glances back through the glass at Diane's sleeping form.

'Don't worry, I'm not going anywhere. I'll keep a good eye on her.'

'Cheers.'

'DS Todd,' says the man, holding out a hand for Tyler to shake. 'Most people call me Toddy.'

'Thanks, Toddy.'

'I heard you two are close?' Toddy asks.

Again Tyler nods. 'She's my godmother.' And then he feels like that isn't quite enough so he adds, 'She's my friend.'

'Tell you what, mate, why don't you give us your number and I'll let you know if there's any change.'

Tyler hesitates, wondering if this is some way of getting info from him. But then it's not as though his mobile number is a secret. He must still be tired, seeing conspiracies around every corner. The guy's just trying to be friendly. Probably. They swap numbers and Tyler shakes Toddy's hand again.

'Any idea how much trouble I'm actually in?' Tyler asks before he leaves.

Toddy moves his mouth to one side and raises his eyes heavenward. Tyler knows he won't tell him anything but it was worth a try.

But then Toddy takes pity on him. 'I'd prepare myself for a roasting if I were you, mate, but I don't think it's all that major. If the Gaffer was looking at you for anything serious you'd already be toast.'

'Good to know,' Tyler tells him.

Edith slips out of school at lunchtime to check on her mother. It's fairly easy to do. She's become so adept at hiding in plain sight that even the teachers don't see her if she doesn't want them to.

She doesn't always do this but today she has a nasty feeling something bad is coming. She can't work out if this is because of the Reservoir Man or whether it's some other, more subtle sign she's noticed about her mother. She's picked up on things like that in the past, little signature tells that Melanie lets slip when she's on a downward spiral. She's been good for a while now as well, which probably means she's overdue a bad spell; her mother's health is as predictably unpredictable as a volcanic event and similarly Edith has begun to realise that the signs are there if you know what you're looking for. Sometimes.

Whatever the reason, it seems as good a day as any to duck out and head home to check on her. Besides, it's PE this afternoon and there's no way they'll let them run in this weather. She'll be stuck in the school hall with Alice Clitherow and whatever sports equipment she decides to throw at her. Sure, it's technically truancy but she reckons she'll get more exercise on the run home than she will in the hall and it will ultimately be safer for her.

Or at least it would be, were it not for the Reservoir Man.

She keeps an eye out for him all the way home, positive he's about to pop up at any moment and grab her. She takes a longer route, circling around the village and coming onto the estate from the other side. She watches the traffic as it passes but she's never been that interested in cars and, try as she might, she can't remember what the car was that she saw him in outside of the school.

Last night, she'd tried telling her mother about what happened at the reservoir but Melanie was far from in a talkative mood, far more interested in the episode of *Quincy* she was watching. 'It's the waitress,' she kept saying, and Edith knew she was right having seen the episode at least a dozen times herself.

When she reaches the parade of shops just outside her estate Edith remembers that they need toilet roll. She's already left it too long and despite reminding Melanie last night and this morning she knows full well her mother won't have bought any. She nips into Mrs Abassi's place. She might as well pick up a few bits for tea while she's here, and those biscuits Melanie likes so much.

Mrs Abassi beams at her as she comes through the door and Edith smiles back.

'It is good to see you, Edith! Where have you been?' she asks. And then, as though answering her own question, continues, 'Why are you not in school, eh?'

'Lunchtime, Mrs A.'

'Ah.'

Edith grabs a few bits and pieces and only at the last minute remembers the toilet roll she came in for. It's that horrible *scratch-your-bum* stuff that Melanie hates but it's cheap so they'll just have to make do. Mrs Abassi taps the prices into her old-fashioned till, squinting through the glasses that hang round her neck on a fabric cord. Edith bought that for her for Christmas last year because Mrs A had packed her own glasses into Edith's shopping three times in the past six months. At least Edith always brought them back, which was more than many of the customers did.

'Eight pounds and fifty-six,' Mrs A says in her rich, deep accent. She has a very comforting voice.

Edith opens her wallet and pulls out her last tenner. She'll need to get Melanie's bank card off her tonight or they won't have anything to eat tomorrow.

'So,' Mrs Abassi says as she pushes everything into a white plastic bag. Edith's lost count of the number of times she's asked her not to bother. Mrs Abassi's sense of environmental science is as weak as her ability to hold on to her glasses. But for once Edith doesn't have a bag with her so she doesn't complain today. 'Did that man find you?'

Edith feels something icy shoot down her spine. 'What? Who?'

'The man!' Mrs Abassi says, as though this explains everything. 'He came in this morning and ... oh!' Mrs Abassi's face crumples as she sees the look on Edith's face. 'Was this not a good thing? He isn't your friend?'

Edith says nothing.

'He asked for a girl. No hair. Metal in ear. I knew he meant you but ... Oh, I'm sorry, I've been a silly woman, yes?'

'No, no, it's all right, Mrs A. I'm sure it's nothing.'

'I didn't tell him where you live, just . . . on the estate.' Mrs Abassi seems sure this is a distinction worthy of high praise although Edith finds it hard to agree with her on that point. 'Is he . . . government man? Taxes!'

Edith knows from previous conversations that this is the worst fate Mrs A can imagine. 'No, nothing like that but . . . If he comes in again, could you, maybe, not tell him anything else?'

'Lips sealed,' Mrs Abassi says, drawing a be-ringed finger across her mouth.

Edith steps back out onto the street hesitatingly. She finds herself scouring every direction. Is he out there somewhere, watching her? Why is he following her like this, it makes no sense! Unless she hadn't imagined the gunshot after all. Edith slips between the buildings, feeling his eyes on the back of her neck all the way home.

Tyler watches as Doggett puts away the best part of an all-day breakfast. He's pushing it now, not heading straight back to Franklin, but he wants to speak to Doggett first.

This very much seems to be his life now, watching Doggett eat. As interests go it isn't the most scintillating. Nor is it all that easy to stomach. The man eats as though someone might take the food away again if he doesn't get it inside him as quickly as possible. Maybe he grew up in a large family. Tyler realises he actually knows very little about this unlikely ally. He's probably been closer to this strange, prickly little man over the past couple of years than anyone else in his life, and yet he knows almost nothing about his past. Or his present for that matter.

'Penny for 'em!' Doggett splutters through his final mouthful, as he wipes a crumbling white slice around a plate of cold bean juice.

'We need to come clean,' Tyler tells him. 'About McKenna and the file he tried to give us. If it's the same folder that ended up on Diane's desk then they need to know where it came from.'

Doggett picks at a tooth with the nail on his little finger. 'I'm not so sure that's a good idea.'

'Why not?'

Doggett leans back in his chair and washes down his meal with a slosh of weak tea. 'Because nothing's changed. We still don't know who we can trust. Your father called it a conspiracy. That means more than one person. Stevens wasn't in this alone.'

The thought is an echo of Tyler's own from earlier.

'We don't even know if Stevens was the one in charge,' Doggett goes on. 'Personally, I never thought the bloke was clever enough to fight his way out of a wet paper bag, so you'll have to forgive me if I don't jump to any conclusions about this. We have no way of knowing if he was the biggest fish in this murky little pond, or if there isn't someone bigger behind him.'

Tyler can't argue with that but there's more at stake now. 'They need to know the providence of the information they're working from. We can't trust McKenna. Why did he just hand over the folder to Diane after making such a song and dance about giving it to me? He must have his own reasons. He wants whatever was in that file to come out.'

'Of course he does. But Professional Standards aren't stupid, they'll treat an anonymous file with a certain level of scepticism. And anyway, they don't actually have the information, Stevens took care of that. They only have Diane's memory of it.'

That's another concern Tyler has. What if Diane knows something but has forgotten it? There might be a reason for them to come back and finish what Stevens started. He appreciated Toddy agreeing to keep an eye on her but Tyler has no idea how far he can trust the guy to keep his word. And he isn't going to be on shift forever. What if the next guard assigned isn't quite as concerned with doing his or her job? Or worse, what if they have an agenda of their own?

'But that's my point,' he tells Doggett, unwilling to let it drop. 'McKenna might know more. If Franklin and Professional Standards bring him in they can get him to tell them what he knows.'

'No, they'll *try* to bring McKenna in and he'll get his very expensive solicitors to cry foul and then whoever's really behind this will quietly pack up shop and disappear.'

Again, it isn't as though Tyler hasn't considered this. Was he really expecting Doggett to just roll over and agree with him, or is this what he really wants? For Doggett to talk him out of doing the right thing. He can't think straight anymore.

'We let her down,' he says. 'If we'd told her about McKenna earlier, about all of this ... conspiracy stuff, she wouldn't have gone near Stevens. She wouldn't be lying in that bloody hospital bed at death's door!'

'You don't know that,' Doggett says, but he no longer sounds quite as sure of himself. He frowns and uses the edge of his knife to pick at some dried egg yolk left on his plate.

'I can't avoid Professional Standards forever. As soon as I step foot back in the station they're going to be all over me.' He pauses but he's sure of his decision now. 'I'm going to tell Franklin the truth, about the conspiracy Richard suspected and about McKenna's involvement. Diane trusts her and we should too.'

Doggett looks at him and nods. 'Your choice,' he says. 'But before you rush into anything, you might want to consider something else.' He puts down the knife and laces his fingers together on the table top. 'Franklin went to see Stevens at home a few days ago. While your godmother was languishing in his cellar, bleeding out.'

'What?'

Doggett nods. 'Aye. Not so sure you can trust her now, are you?'

'Where've you got this from?'

'Professional Standards might think they run a tight ship but word still gets round. She was questioned this morning about it. Reckons she went to ask him something about some procedure or other. Didn't notice anything out of the ordinary.'

'It's possible.'

'Anything's possible.'

Doggett gets up and heads to the counter to pay his bill. Tyler waits outside, the cool breeze a welcome relief after the stuffy fried air of the café. He watches Doggett through the condensation on the window. He'd like to think the man's just being paranoid but he can imagine the DI's response to that. *It isn't paranoia if the bastards are out to get you.* The problem is, once you start thinking like that, you start to doubt everyone. Doggett's right about one thing though – they really can't trust anyone.

When Tyler finally answers his phone with a curt, 'What?' Mina has to resist the urge to swear.

'Where are you?' she demands instead. Sometimes it feels like she's the only one working this case.

'I've been at the hospital,' he tells her, which takes the wind out of her sails a bit.

'Oh, yeah. Right. How is she?'

Tyler takes her through the prognosis. He seems optimistic about DCI Jordan's chances of a full recovery but he's distracted by something as well. Maybe it's Jordan. But maybe it's something else.

'At least she's awake and talking,' she says when he finishes his update.

'Did you want something, Mina?'

She bites her tongue. 'I've been looking into Whitehouse and Spencer. She's his sister-in-law. She married Whitehouse's brother but obviously kept her own name.'

'O-kay?'

'Don't you think that's significant?'

'It might explain why their relationship seemed so mixed. She doesn't like him very much but at the end of the day, he's family?'

'But they didn't tell us.' Granted, neither of them had asked but Mina knows there's something dodgy going on at that desserts place. 'They didn't tell us he sold her the factory for a pound either. Or that his cab firm operates out of the same site. From what you told me, he kind of implied he worked somewhere else. I think they were trying to hide the fact they were connected.'

The line goes quiet while Tyler thinks about this. 'Why?'

'Well, I . . . I dunno.'

'Okay, maybe keep digging then. See what else you can find. Good work.' And with that he hangs up on her.

Mina throws her mobile down on the desk. *Why does he have to be so bloody infuriating?* Okay, so it wasn't much, but he's always using his intuition and talking about what his gut is telling him. Would it kill him to back her when she does the same?

When her phone starts vibrating again her first thought is that he's rung back to apologise. But when she sees who's calling, she feels a wave of dread creep up her spine. She gets up and puts her head out into the hallway but there's no sign of anyone on their sparsely occupied floor. She pushes the door to and returns to her desk, the phone still buzzing in her hand like an irritated insect. She has a nasty feeling she's about to get stung. She takes a deep breath and answers it.

'Ma'am.'

'What have you got for me, Mina?'

'Er.' How to answer that? Nothing would be the correct response but certainly not a wise one. As always, Franklin's voice sounds professional and to the point. Not at all as though she's pissed off or anything but … But. There's always just a hint with her, as though the bomb might go off at any second.

'I see,' Franklin says, and Mina hears the ticking grow just that little bit louder.

'I've been talking to them,' Mina says, her eyes flicking towards the door. A door that could open at any moment. 'It's just … well, now DCI Jordan's been found I thought—'

'Mina, the situation with Superintendent Stevens was clearly much bigger than either of us suspected.'

'You can't think they were involved with—'

'Now more than ever, I can't have my officers going off half-cocked to their own agenda.' She pauses for a moment but Mina keeps quiet. 'I'm not saying that whatever they're up to is related to Stevens' misconduct but I need to know what it is. Better that I find out before Professional Standards do.'

The threat is palpable but Mina has no idea what to say next. She's aware the silence is stretching to breaking point but then Franklin takes the problem away from her.

'All right, Mina. I can't say I'm not disappointed but I can see I've put too much pressure on you. Perhaps I was wrong. Maybe this isn't your time after all.'

Mina's not stupid – she knows the woman's playing her, trying to get her to do what she wants. But the truth is this is still an opportunity. And Tyler, much as the two of them might have developed a grudging respect for each other, just isn't going to help her. He made that clear enough last night when he stopped her getting in the car and again just now. He doesn't take her seriously. She's always going to be the one left behind. If she wants to get on in her career she can't rely on him.

But can you throw him to the wolves?

'I heard one thing,' she finds herself saying.

'Go on.'

'It wasn't really anything serious . . .'

'Detective Constable Rabbani,' Franklin's voice is harder now. 'I'll be the judge of what is or isn't serious. Your DCI – your *mentor* – is currently lying critical in a hospital bed. I'm not suggesting DS Tyler was responsible for that, but if he has information that could pertain to this case it's his duty, no, more than that, it's his moral obligation to come forward with it. As it is yours.'

Mina swallows and clears her throat. 'I heard him talking to DI Doggett last night. I think . . . they've been looking into the death of Tyler's father.'

'His father?'

'Richard Tyler?'

'Yes, I know who his father was.' Franklin's tone betrays her impatience. 'He killed himself.'

'Tyler doesn't think so. *Richard* Tyler was looking into some sort of conspiracy and they think that DCI Jordan might have found out and . . . well, that's pretty much as far as I've got.'

The silence on the other end of the line lasts for so long Mina begins to wonder if the ACC has hung up on her. 'Ma'am?'

'Yes,' Franklin says. 'Okay. Well, I'll take that under advisement. Thank you. I'll be in touch.' And then she hangs up on Mina too.

'That sounded intense,' says Emma Ridgeway from the doorway.

'Shit!' Mina jumps, dropping her mobile.

'Oh, my God,' says the pathologist. 'I'm sorry. I didn't mean to make you jump.'

'It's fine,' Mina says, but then she realises her hands are shaking and shoves them into her lap. 'Sorry. It's . . . nothing.' She smiles. 'Hi. How are you?'

'Better than you by the look of things.' Emma frowns but doesn't ask anything else. She perches one buttock on the edge of the table and opens a plastic bag. 'I come bearing gifts.' She pulls out a tiny cactus and presents it on the palm of her hand. 'For your new office.' She looks around the room. 'If I'd known how gigantic the place is I'd've gone for something bigger.'

Mina smiles. 'That's kind. Thank you.'

'You sure you're okay?'

Mina leans back in her chair and throws her head back. 'No, not really. I think I've just dropped Tyler in the shit.'

'Oh.' Emma puts the cactus down under Mina's screen. 'Well, he's a big boy who's been in the shit before. I'm sure he can drag himself out of it.'

Mina lets out a hollow laugh. 'I'm not so sure about that.'

'In that case you better come with me.'

'Huh?'

'There's some stuff I need to tell you about the case.'

'Oh, right.' Mina's confused. 'What . . . really?'

'No, not really. I've already sent you an email. But you look like you could use a drink and I get to decide where I take you for the debrief. I'm thinking something fruity with umbrellas in. I'll tell you what I've discovered and you can tell me all about how deep this shit is that you pushed Tyler into.'

Mina looks at her watch. 'It's barely two.'

'So we'll call it lunch. Come on, up you get.' Emma drags her up out of the chair.

'Okay, okay.' Mina grabs her jacket and bag and takes a last look at Tyler's empty chair. *Ah, to hell with him.* If he was so bothered about getting into trouble he shouldn't keep so many secrets.

Toddy's 'gaffer' turns out to be a short, portly DCI called Giles Ledbetter. A ruddy-faced copper from the Home Counties who seems like he'd be more at home on the back of a horse or a ride-on mower negotiating the wide lawns of his country estate than dealing with the great unwashed heathens of the North. There's something off about the man's appearance that Tyler can't quite put his finger on.

He assumes Ledbetter will be the one to lead the inter-rogation, if that's what this is – he's still not a hundred per cent sure – but in fact, it's Franklin who takes centre stage at the court martial.

He's invited to sit at one end of the long conference table in the incident room that Franklin has commandeered since her arrival. She takes the seat at the opposite end of the table, with Ledbetter at her right-hand side.

She leads him through his actions of the previous night and he explains how he and Doggett came to arrive at Stevens' house, how they heard a noise in the cellar, and broke in to discover DCI Jordan incapacitated. It feels like a horribly understated word to be using, given the state she was in, but he gets the sense it will be more effective for that. After all, they know full well what Diane's condition is. They let him go through it without contradicting or questioning anything in any detail. At one point the Home Counties DCI blows out his moustache in a manner that conveys he doesn't believe a word of Tyler's explanation but he doesn't go as far as to contradict him and after a sidelong glance from Franklin he goes back to examining his fingernails. Tyler wonders exactly who's in charge here. The ACC clearly has the higher rank but that doesn't always matter when Professional Standards are involved.

They seem to be coming to the end of the interview and Tyler has the sense it's gone pretty well. Ledbetter doesn't look happy but maybe he can trust Franklin after all. She's done everything she can to show him she's on his side. He's pretty much decided to tell them the truth about McKenna and the folder, despite Doggett's protestations. But then Franklin blindsides him. 'When did you start investigating the death of your father?' she asks out of nowhere.

'What?'

'DCI Jordan has told us that she believes Stevens might have been involved in his death. Is that what you believe?'

Tyler looks at each of them carefully but neither are giving anything away. He notes that Ledbetter has finished with his fingernails though, and suddenly appears to be paying closer attention. How does she know? She's always one step ahead. He supposes she could just be guessing from what Diane told her but it seems more than that.

'DCI Richard Tyler took his own life in 2002,' Franklin says, evidently addressing Ledbetter since Tyler himself knows full well the details of what happened that day.

'I don't believe that,' Tyler tells her, and it feels good to say it out loud for the first time. 'I believe my father was murdered.' He won't let the shame he's been living with for all these years win. 'I think Stevens, or possibly someone working with him, killed Richard and staged it to look like a suicide.'

'Adam,' Franklin says, not ungently. 'He took a whole bottle of pills and hanged himself. There was no evidence of foul play.'

Tyler feels the old rage bubbling up inside him but he pushes it down. 'There was no evidence otherwise either. No suicide note, for example. He cancelled the cleaner that day but neglected the fact his sixteen-year-old son would come home to find his body.'

'I'm sorry, Adam. That must have been hard for you.'

He's trying to keep his voice steady but he can feel his heart racing in his chest. 'My point is that that isn't consistent behaviour. There was a receipt left out for the paracetamol that he'd bought that day even though the house was full of the stuff.'

Franklin and Ledbetter share a look. On Ledbetter's side he seems puzzled, confused as to the turn things have taken. But Franklin seems more . . . what? Embarrassed, maybe. Ashamed that her officer is behaving in this way. Not that he is one of *her* officers. *She's* only been here five minutes.

'Is this what you've been doing all this time, Detective? Investigating Superintendent Stevens when you should have been working on—'

He cuts her off. 'I just told you that I think one of your senior officers killed my father – the same officer who very recently held another of your officers hostage for weeks in torturous circumstances and then ran off to leave her to die. You can't see that there might be a connection?'

She studies him for a moment and he wonders if she's taking him more seriously than he first thought. She did bring this up, after all. He needs to keep his temper in check.

'Do you have any evidence to produce?' she asks.

'What sort of evidence?'

'I understand you've been looking into your father's death for a while. And there's the matter of the folder of information that was left on DCI Jordan's desk. Understandably, her memory of the details is a little fuzzy at the moment. It would be useful if we could see this folder for ourselves. Or at least find out where this information came from. You wouldn't be able to help clarify that for us, would you?'

How does she know he's been looking into Richard's death? Other than him there was only one other person who knew about it. What is she playing at? 'No,' he says. 'I have no idea what was inside.' And at least he doesn't have to lie. He never got to see what was in it.

'Then I'm sorry but I can't help you. Your father's death was investigated at the time. His bank account had a number of unaccountable deposits from overseas. It seems quite likely that he had reasons for the actions he took.'

'All the more reason to look into it, surely? If you believe Richard was on the take, and you know full well Roger Stevens was, then these men were contemporaries, connected to each other. You don't think that's worth investigating? That seems a bit odd, to me. Especially since you were also one of their contemporaries.'

Franklin's face drops and the kindly boss demeanour evaporates. 'Be careful what you're insinuating, DS Tyler.'

'I'm not insinuating anything. I'm asking you outright. Do you have a reason not to investigate the link between my father's death and Roger Stevens' actions?'

The silence hangs heavy in the air for a moment and, surprisingly, it's Ledbetter who breaks first. 'We've already looked into your father's death.'

'Giles, I'm not sure—'

Tyler's question as to who is in charge is finally answered as Ledbetter cuts Franklin off with a raised hand. 'We've been looking into Roger Stevens' actions for some months now. He wasn't quite as clever as he thought and a number of inconsistencies have raised flags over the years. Your father's death was one of the first things we examined. You can thank your good friend DI Doggett for that. The fuss he made all those years ago was quite something and it's all still on record.'

Tyler can feel the blood pumping in his ears.

'Given the sheer number of other case files Stevens doctored, including the case you're currently investigating, if anything, the fact that DI Doggett's complaints are still a matter of record only convinces me Stevens wasn't involved. But that's by the by. I've personally looked into your father's death and despite the inconsistencies you have documented, the physical evidence and the pathologist's report are quite clear. Your father hanged himself. There's no doubt.'

Tyler can barely hear the man's words through the thick pounding rush in his head. 'The case I'm currently investigating ... You knew about it already.'

'ACC Franklin recognised the uniform on your body in the ice. It's one of a number of cases we suspected Stevens and Johnson were responsible for shutting down.'

'But if you were already suspicious of Stevens why didn't you go to his house? You might have found her sooner.'

'Tyler,' Franklin warns him.

'It's all right, ma'am,' Ledbetter tells her. 'We have a number of ongoing investigations into serving officers,' he says meaningfully. 'Until Stevens went missing himself, we had no reason to assume he was responsible for your DCI's disappearance. It could easily have been someone else.'

Ledbetter stands up. 'Well, I'm satisfied we're done here. For now. DS Tyler, thank you for your time. I'm sorry I couldn't provide you with the answers you were hoping for.'

The cocktail bar is on the rooftop of an office building in the city centre and Mina's not at all sure about the wisdom of sitting outside in this weather. But as Emma pushes her into the lift, she reassures Mina that the terrace is covered. 'It'll be fine.'

They end up sitting in quite a cosy little swing chair contraption with a heater right next to them so despite the clumps of snow gathered in the corners of the patio, and the biting wind that intermittently engulfs them, it's actually not too bad. There are twinkly lights strewn under the canopy, and three plastic palm trees do their best to add to the tropical feel. All in all, it's a bit kitsch but kind of fun.

'I'm ordering,' Emma says. 'Let's see . . . something non-alcoholic for Mina, and something *very* alcoholic for Emma.'

The drinks arrive surprisingly quickly for cocktails, draped in pieces of exotic fruit and tangled plastic straws. Mina's has a paper umbrella stuck in a cherry and Emma's a red plastic monkey with a curly tail.

'Cheers!' Emma says. She'd once told Mina that she got a kick out of that very British expression and Mina suspects she revels in using it whenever she can. They clink their glasses together.

'So,' Emma says. 'The frozen body finally thawed.'

'Oh, we're actually doing this here?'

'Why not? Don't worry, I won't actually put down the bar tab as expenses.' She liberates a piece of pineapple from her glass and chews off the flesh. 'So. Male, mid-twenties, but I guess you knew that already. Anyways, nothing really that remarkable about the body. He was in good health. He had a tattoo on his upper left arm of a skull with a snake passing through the eye socket so I guess that might help with ID. Nothing back on DNA just yet.'

'Okay, well I guess that's something.'

'You're so welcome. But I'm not done. I'm pretty sure that cause of death was from extensive internal injury. He'd taken a massive beating and had several broken bones consistent with being hit by some long cylindrical object. Like a tyre iron maybe, or a wrecking bar. None of the bones showed any signs of healing so all the injuries were sustained perimortem. There was massive head trauma as well but probably not enough to kill. I think his heart probably gave out first, but his liver and lungs were punctured too so it's possible he bled out internally. I haven't gotten back the toxicology reports yet but I'm pretty sure this was just a good old-fashioned beat down.'

'That's some beating.'

'Yeah. There were pre-mortem marks on his skin where he tried to break free of his restraints.'

'Meaning his wrists and ankles were bound before he was beaten to death?'

'Uh huh. The poor guy didn't even have a chance to defend himself. This was brutal, Mina. Savage. I know I'm not supposed to make comments like this but somebody hated this guy. Or was some kind of sadist.'

Mina realises how cold her hands are, wrapped around the glass, and puts down her sugary drink. She sits on her hands to warm them.

'One more thing,' Emma tells her. 'He was frozen shortly after he died. Given that that can't have been in the lake I think he must have been kept somewhere cold. Real cold. Like a freezer.'

'Any idea how long he was kept there?'

Emma shakes her head. 'It's impossible to say. It could have been a long time.'

'Like sixteen years long?'

Emma shrugs. 'Like I said, there's no way to tell.' She takes a sip of her drink before she goes on. 'There were lividity marks on the skin of his buttocks and parts of his arms and legs. From the positioning of them my best guess is some kind of reach-in freezer. Something big enough to fit him in but not without contorting the body into a foetal shape. This must have been done before rigor mortis set in for the blood to pool like that so he was frozen within an hour or two of death, max. One other thing, there were serious abrasions on his arms and legs as well. These occurred post-mortem. Some were consistent with freezer burns but others better resemble tool marks. Someone had a helluva job carving him out of the ice.'

They sit quietly for a moment while Mina absorbs all this. 'Why would someone tie him up, beat him to death, then freeze him only to dump him in a frozen lake some time later?'

'The only thing I can think is maybe they hid the body rather than risk disposing of it, but that the hiding place was compromised in some way. Maybe they put the body in the reservoir hoping they'd confuse us about time of death.'

Mina sighs. 'Okay. I'd better ring Tyler and tell him about this.' But she's not thrilled at the prospect of talking to him given what she told Franklin.

Tyler spends the rest of the afternoon in the office with Rabbani, trying to put together what they've got so far. He keeps getting distracted by his conversation with Franklin and Ledbetter, and its abrupt ending. In light of what they said he seriously considers going back to tell them about McKenna and the folder but he's still not sure if he can trust Franklin. Did she really recognise the Demeter uniform? She wasn't even at the crime scene, although he supposes someone else could have sent her a photo. She's only been with them five minutes though, could she have a network of informants already? And if so, what did that say about her?

He's self-aware enough to realise that the real reason he

doesn't go back is that he's annoyed at how easily they dismissed his claims about Richard's death. He won't believe it. He *can't* believe it. Neither will he believe that Doggett betrayed him. But if Doggett didn't say anything, the only other person who knew he was looking into Richard's death was McKenna. Has *he* been talking to Professional Standards? Surely not. But if he has, Tyler really should go back and tell them what he knows about the folder that ended up on Jordan's desk.

His thoughts go round and round in circles like this and he doesn't have Doggett to use as a sounding board. Even if he wanted to, the DI's been dragged back to the Murder Room to help with a triple shooting in Stannington. He hadn't realised until now how much he'd got used to leaning on Doggett. Just the thought of the man betraying him is crippling.

Rabbani's obviously pissed off with him again for some reason. She fills him in on her chat with Ridgeway – at least they have the tattoo as something to work with – but after that she's unusually quiet, almost morose. He can't work out if he's done something or if she has. In the end he decides she'll tell him if and when she's ready to.

By the end of the day he's more than ready to head home but he still has a couple of visits left to make. He stops by the hospital to check on Diane and she seems much improved. The nurse tells him she's sleeping a lot but that that's probably a good sign so that improves his mood somewhat even though it means he doesn't get to talk to her. Then he just about has time to grab a burrito and he's off to his final port of call for the day.

Jude's already waiting at the bar when he arrives. The Jude he remembers was never early for anything. It's another mark of how little he knows about his brother anymore, or perhaps a mark of how much his brother has changed. Maybe he really does want to make amends. So why does Tyler find that so hard to believe?

They take a table not far from the one they sat at a few months ago and the spectre of that evening hangs heavily over the both of them. This is comparable with some of the worst dates Tyler's been on, Jude in the role of suitor, trying to make small talk about how Sheffield has changed in the time he's been gone, and Tyler the unimpressed date responding with monosyllabic answers. He knows he isn't being entirely fair but neither can he pretend he's okay with all this . . . reconnecting, or whatever it is.

Jude changes the subject and asks after Diane. Given how much Jude always hated her, Tyler sees it as yet another olive branch so he does his best to fill him in on the details and Jude, for his part, does his best to look as though he really cares. Maybe he does.

But after that they fall back into an impenetrable silence. It doesn't help that Tyler's still a bit distracted. Jude becomes increasingly downcast and Tyler begins to wonder if his own mood is infectious. First Rabbani and now his brother. He goes to get more drinks from the bar and tries to think of a way of getting things back on track. He needs to find a way to ask Jude about Richard, whether he remembers what happened all those years ago. But when he gets back, it's Jude that opens, making the effort to build bridges once again.

'I'm sorry, bro,' he says. 'I really mean that. I'm sorry.' He avoids eye contact with Tyler and something about the hang-dog expression makes Tyler believe him. He remembers his brother well enough to know when he's feeling guilty about something.

'What you have to remember, mate, is, whatever you thought at the time, I weren't much more than a kid me'sen. I was a fucking idiot. I got in trouble and I ran away. I should have come back when Dad died but . . . I dunno, something stopped me.' He stops for a moment but Tyler stays quiet, letting him work out what he wants to say. 'If you wanna know the truth, I was ashamed. I guess I thought it was my fault that Dad did it, you know? After all the shit I put him through and . . . No, that's not strictly true. I mean it is, but it isn't the real reason.' He stops again and looks up for the first time. 'I was scared, mate. Of you.'

'Me?'

Jude grins. 'Yeah, sounds stupid, eh? I mean, you might have filled out into a handy bastard these days but back then I could have taken you with my little finger.'

Tyler's face must betray his thoughts because Jude holds up his hands in mock surrender.

'All right, mate. I know, no jokes. What I mean is, I knew you'd want me to look after you.'

'What are you on about?'

'It was too much pressure. I could barely look after *me*, and the thought of having to be there for someone else and all ... well, it was too much. I couldn't do it. I know that makes me a selfish twat but that's the truth of it. I knew you'd be all right with Diane but if I came back you'd insist on us being together and there was no way I was living with that ...' Jude bites off whatever choice expletive he'd been about to use. 'Sorry. Force of habit. I don't hate Diane anymore, even if she did split up our family. She's been good to you over the years and, well, I owe her for the help she's given me these past few months as well.'

This is more like the Jude that Tyler remembers, spitting venom at the whole world for things he can't control. But as much as Tyler wants to, this isn't the time to dig into that particular hornets' nest. Whatever reason Jude has for hating Diane can wait for now.

'So I stayed away from the funeral. And then I figured I'd come back for Christmas, once you were settled a bit. But then that felt too soon as well. I kept putting it off and putting it off and soon enough it became easier to put it off than to do it. That's one thing the army's good for, I guess. It kinda takes your mind off all the other shit.'

Tyler can't help feeling hurt by that. Is that how Jude always saw him, as part of all 'the other shit'?

'I left it too long, and the longer I left it the harder it became. I know that's not good enough but it's the truth. The whole fucking kit and caboodle. I let you down. Big time. I know it and I'm sorry.'

'Fine.' He doesn't mean it and Jude picks up on his tone.

'Is it, though? 'Cos it don't sound like it.' Jude grins to take the sting out of his words. But Tyler's still not in the mood for joking or ready to let bygones be bygones.

'You're my brother, the only real family I've got left, whether you're here or off somewhere doing fuck knows what, that doesn't change.' Tyler takes a drink to calm himself down. 'But I don't trust you, Jude. I'm always going to be waiting for you to disappear again, you know that, right? If there was one person in my life I thought I could count on it was you. And when it counted, when I needed you most, you weren't there. You weren't fucking there!' He shouts it without meaning to and a number of drinkers stop in mid-conversation to turn and look at them.

'Yeah,' Jude says as the hubbub around them picks up again. 'I know.'

They sit in silence again. But it's a different kind of silence, without the tension of earlier. They've both said what they came to say and maybe it's the start of something different.

'I'm not going away again,' Jude says. 'I mean, if you don't want me in your life that's one thing but ... I'm gonna be here if you want me to be. Here.' Jude picks Tyler's mobile up from the table. 'Open this for me.'

'What?'

'Just open your bloody phone, will you?'

Tyler reaches across and slides his fingerprint over the sensor. Jude presses the screen a few times, poses for a selfie and snaps a photo. 'There you go,' he says, typing on the screen. He passes the phone back to show the contacts page. He's entered his own number and labelled it 'Jude – Bollock-head'. It was a nickname Tyler used to call him when they were kids, because of the huge head of curls he had then. At the top of the screen Jude's winking face looms out at Tyler. 'That's me. So you know I'm sticking around this time.'

For the first time Tyler smiles.

'There he is,' Jude tells him. 'There's my annoying little brother.' He ruffles Tyler's hair.

Tyler has a thought. 'Where are you staying?'

'Eh? Oh, just kipping on a mate's couch.'

'Why don't you come and stay at my place for a while?'

Jude's mouth falls open with shock; he clearly hadn't been expecting this. Neither had Tyler at the start of their conversation, but it suddenly seems right. What better way to quiz Jude on the past than if he's there, to ask questions of when he thinks of them. Not that he's about to sell it to his brother that way.

'Look, it could be good for us. A chance to properly catch up. You'd have your own room and I'm not after rent or anything. You can just get some food now and again. Take-out though. I've had enough of your cooking.'

Jude's frowning as though he can't find the right words to tell Tyler what a stupid idea this is.

'It was just a suggestion,' Tyler says. 'I'm not trying to control you or anything. Forget it.'

'No,' Jude says, smiling. 'No, I reckon it's a great idea. Just for a few weeks though, eh? Till I've saved up a bit of cash for my own place.'

Given that Jude has been couch-surfing for the past few months it's clearly going to be a bit longer than that but Tyler lets it go. The important thing is that he has Jude where he wants him, available to answer questions.

And with that in mind something Jude said earlier is still playing on his mind. 'What did you mean when you said you thought it was your fault Dad died?'

'Eh?'

'You said something about all the shit you put him through. And that you were in trouble.'

'It's ancient history. Let's not get into it, eh?'

'Jude, it's important. I need to know. I always thought you ran away because you were sick of all the arguments with Rich . . . with Dad.'

'Well, yeah, but it was a bit more than that. I did a few things I weren't proud of and that Dad didn't like. I mean, it was easy for me to blame him then but looking back I was a right little bastard. I know he could be a pain in the arse what with his job and all – no offence – but it wasn't all his fault.'

Tyler's never thought of it that way before. All he remembers is Jude moaning about what a hard time Richard gave him about stuff but of course it was never that simple. They were both teenagers, and Richard was a single father with a job that kept him out of the house all manner of hours. Neither of them were saints and Jude . . . well, at the time Tyler had kept his eyes closed to all the shit Jude got up to but as an adult looking back he can see how worried Richard must have been. Why has it taken him so long to see that?

'What was this trouble you were in?' Tyler asks.

Jude fails to make eye contact with him. 'We don't need to go into all that now. Like I said, ancient history. And besides, you're a copper now, aren't you? I'm not about to turn myself in.' He grins.

'That serious?'

'Nah. I mean, it could have been. But Dad got me out before anything bad happened. I didn't exactly appreciate him interfering though and to be honest it just felt like the last straw. I wanted to live my own life, make my own decisions. Dad made that impossible so the army was the next best choice. Turns out the army aren't so hot on you making your own decisions either. I ended up exchanging one totalitarian regime for another. But hey, what else was I gonna do? I mean, it isn't like I had any academic stuff to fall back on like my clever-clogs little bro.'

'How did Dad interfere?'

'Honestly, just leave it, eh?'

But he can't let it go. This is what he's here for. 'Jude ... There's stuff you don't know about Dad's death.'

'Eh?'

'I can't give you all the details, I'm still looking into it but ... I don't think Richard killed himself.'

'What? You mean ...'

'I think he was murdered. I think he found out about something and someone killed him to keep him quiet.'

224

'No,' Jude says. 'No! He . . .' He covers his face with both hands. 'Fuck! That bastard!'

Tyler feels a wave of cold dread sweep through him. 'What bastard?'

But Jude's lost in the past. 'Fuck! Fucker! When I said I thought I was responsible . . . I mean, I didn't *really* think I was . . . Shit!'

'Jude. Calm down. You need to tell me what happened.'

Sweat has broken out on Jude's forehead and his eyes dart about the room as though he's looking for someone. His left knee is pumping up and down with nervous energy and his hand keeps covering his mouth as if he's going to be sick.

'Jude!' Tyler shouts, grabbing his brother's attention. 'Just focus on me. Tell me!'

Jude nods and lets out a deep breath.

'You know what I was like back then. I'd started getting into some pretty dodgy shit. Drugs, a bit of shoplifting and that. The first time I met them was at Elly's place.'

Elly was Jude's ex-girlfriend. Well, Tyler doesn't know for sure exactly what their arrangement was but the woman was older and heavily into drugs. He'd once gone there to hang out after school and watched Jude stick a needle in his arm. After that he'd never gone back and the way he remembered it, it wasn't long after that that Jude stopped visiting as well. He'd always figured his brother got a taste of what his life might have been and ran away from it.

'You remember what that place was like,' Jude goes on, 'all kinds of people coming and going. It was a party and I got chatting to these lads. They wanted to know if I wanted to make a bit of extra cash and ... well, I was eighteen, of course I fucking did! But it was kids' stuff really, shoplifting, flogging gear down the pub, that sort of thing. I didn't know it was linked to anything bigger. Anyway, someone must have seen us together down the pub, me and these blokes. Next thing I know, Dad's going bat-shit crazy at me, talking about organised crime and how I'm heading down a dangerous path and all that shit he liked to lecture us on.' Jude looks directly at Tyler for the first time. 'Mate, honestly, I'd never seen him so mad. I thought for a minute he was gonna arrest me! Haul me down the cop shop and get me charged with something.

'Then suddenly, my mates are telling me what a cunt I am and how they want nothing more to do with me. Turns out Dad spoke to the boss of this organisation they worked for and word had come down that no one was to give me the time of fucking day ever again.'

Tyler's stomach feels as though it's full of ice. Somehow he knows what's coming.

'I was so mad with him. That's why we argued and I left. I couldn't believe he'd interfered. But then, later, after he ... after he died, I began to think about it a bit more and I thought ... Oh God, mate, I'm sorry but I thought he'd done something for them. You know ... fiddled something or got someone off a charge or summat and that's why they agreed to keep away from me.'

Jude looks at Tyler with dark guilty eyes. 'That's the real reason I never came back. When they said he was bent and found that money in his bank account I figured he must have done something dodgy to protect me.' There are tears in his eyes now. 'Mate. Was it me? Did I get him killed?'

Tyler can't speak but he shakes his head. For years he blamed himself for his father's death, assuming Richard had killed himself because of his wayward teenage son. It never once occurred to him that Jude might have been living with the same guilt. Even if it was true, he wouldn't want Jude to live with that.

'No,' Tyler says, quietly. He doesn't want to get into the conspiracy stuff now but he can't leave Jude thinking that. 'It wasn't your fault. But I need to know. Who was this guy? This boss guy Dad spoke to.'

Jude shakes his head. 'I can't believe he killed him.'

'Jude!'

'What? Oh. His name . . .' Jude pauses as though the word he's about to speak is forbidden in some way. 'McKenna,' he finally manages, spitting the word from his lips. 'Joey McKenna.'

The ice shifts as Tyler's fears are realised. 'Okay,' he says, 'you're gonna come home with me now and we're gonna talk this through properly. I need to know everything you know. You leave nothing out.'

Jude nods. 'Then what?'

Tyler glances down to see his knuckles are turning white where he's clutching his pint glass too hard. He lets go. 'Then I'm going to find out the truth.'

227

day four

The ICER recordings #Supplementary1

(Archivists' note: This call was recorded on a different phone line, presumably by mistake. We have filed it here, chronologically, in the event it may contain information pertinent to the case [04/05/18])

Call placed: 18:34 Thursday 8th Mar 2018
Duration: 2 minutes 27 seconds

Partial Transcript:

Robert Hello?

ICER Robbie? It's Dad.

Robert Oh. Right. Hi.

ICER How's everything?

Robert Everything's great. Couldn't be better.

(Recording is silent for 4 seconds)

ICER So you've got a new number then?

Robert Yeah. Six months ago. (*pause 1 second*) How did you get it?

ICERI   . . . I spoke to your mother.

Robert Fucking hell! That's a turn up.

ICER Robert!

Robert Come on, Dad. Bit late to be lecturing me on my language, isn't it? So, was there a reason for this call or . . . ?

ICER I just . . . I wanted to . . .

(recording is silent for 3 seconds)

Look, I might have to go away for a while.

Robert Is that supposed to be news?

ICER I'm not sure when I'm likely to be back.

Robert Okay, well, it's been real. Thanks for the update—

ICER Robbie, please. It's work.

Robert Yeah. It always is, isn't it? What is it you do again? 'Cos you've never really told us, have you? Something to do with finance, that was the line, wasn't it? I used to think it was MI5 but even the security services would let you say something to your family. Or they'd at least come up with a better cover story.

ICER Rob—

Robert Lucy had a theory. She reckoned you had another family somewhere, maybe more than one. I think she still thinks that, to be honest.

ICER It's just work.

Robert Maybe she's right. Anyway, we're all pretty much past caring at this point. Truth is, you don't give a shit, so why should we?

ICER If you're not even going to be civil I guess there's not much more to be said. I just wanted to let you know that I won't be able to make the wedding and I wanted to wish—

Robert Jesus Christ, are you serious! Dad, you're not invited to the wedding.

ICER Robert, you might hate me but we're still family. Look, I wanted to give you something. How much do you need for—?

Robert *(laughs)* You really believe that, don't you? That stuff about family? Dad, we don't want your money. Me and Suzie's dad have got it covered and when the baby gets here . . . well, we'll cope. I don't want your money. I never have.

ICER Please, son. Let me help. All of this . . . the work . . . everything . . . it's all been for you. For your new family. My grandkid.

Robert You've already got family you make no effort to see. Why should it be any different with my kids?

ICER   Robbie, don't . . . Look, I'm retiring. I want things to be different . . .

Robert You said you were going away.

(recording is silent for 4 seconds)

Goodbye, Dad. Thanks for everything but I'll take it from here.

ICER   Robbie! Robert—

Call ends 18:36

Tyler should be on his way to pick up Rabbani as arranged, but he can't let go what he learned last night. He barely slept going over it all in his mind and he needs to talk to the man himself.

He really shouldn't be seen here but luckily, there are very few people who continue playing golf in winter and even fewer who go down to the course when the entire place is covered in two feet of snow. Tyler knows Joey McKenna will be there though. The self-styled reformed gangster heads down to the club at least three times a week to play a round and even on a day like today he'll be on the covered driving range, practising his swing. Tyler knows this because, in the months since they met, he has gone out of his way to look into every part of McKenna's life, both business and personal. And the golf course is the place where those two worlds overlap.

Interestingly, it's also a place that Roger Stevens used to enjoy frequenting. That fact didn't seem so relevant before, given that half the senior officers in South Yorkshire Police have memberships here as well, but now it gives Tyler pause. Is this where the conspiracy was born, perhaps? Like-minded men hatching plots on the fifth hole and cementing them at the nineteenth? Who knows how many more of those officers are involved? Is Franklin a member here? It seems unlikely since the ACC has been living down south for the past decade but not impossible.

The woman at the front desk is reluctant to let him in and he ends up having to flash his warrant card. He'd much rather have not left a trail but she waves him into the club as though she's not in the least surprised nor interested in a visit from the police. He imagines she's well used to turning a blind eye to things. The membership fees this place charges guarantee a certain level of anonymity.

He finds the driving range and sees McKenna straight away. He's the only person there. He's chosen the lane at the far end of the range and so has already clocked Tyler before he reaches him. Perhaps that's why he chose this one. The two men in tracksuits leaning up against the wall behind him certainly begin to pay closer attention as it becomes obvious Tyler is heading their way. One drops the cigarette he's smoking and the other squares his shoulders and steps between Tyler and McKenna.

'Detective Sergeant!' McKenna shouts, most likely for the benefit of the heavies, and their demeanour visibly relaxes. 'What a delightful surprise!' He does not interrupt his practice however, and continues to send white balls spinning down into the net at the far end of the lane. 'Boys, why don't you take five, eh? Get yourselves a wee drink from the lassie out front.' They hesitate for a moment until McKenna raises a thick white eyebrow that brooks no disobedience. Still, their movements are sluggish and reluctant, and the one who'd stepped in front of McKenna continues to glance back at them even as they move away. Tyler gets a whiff of orange-scented cologne as he passes and is painfully reminded of the last time they'd met. McKenna had had the man beat him up for no other reason than because he knew it would pique his interest. It's a sober reminder too of the fact McKenna always has his own angle. And of how ruthless he is.

'Ah, they're good lads,' McKenna says, turning back to concentrate on his swing. 'But they do worry so. Especially our Danny. I swear, the man's as fretful as a mother hen, that one.'

Tyler wasn't sure exactly what he'd do when he saw McKenna. He's been back and forth over it time and time again during the night. Is this the man who killed his father? Or had him killed? He knows the man's capable of it but he can't see how any of that fits with what they know about Stevens and the conspiracy. If Richard really was onto him, Stevens had a strong motive. But just because they don't yet know of one doesn't mean McKenna didn't have one as well.

What exactly did he hope to achieve by coming here? Doggett would be furious with him, and rightly so. If McKenna is his father's killer then just by being here Tyler could be scuppering any chance they have of bringing him to justice. Is justice what he really wants though? Or is it something darker? He can feel his fists clenching by his sides but now the moment is here he's frozen with indecision.

McKenna pauses mid-swing and turns to look at him with a frown on his face. Tyler's very aware of the fact he hasn't spoken in some time. McKenna smiles and nods, coming to some internal realisation. 'I see,' he says. He steps away from the putting lane and opens his arms wide. 'Well, here I am, Detective. Whatever it is you've learned that's sent you back my way I assume by the look on your face that it's not so pleasant. Are you here to have a pop at me, son, is that it? If so, come on then, give it your best shot.' McKenna plants his feet and raises his fists in a mock boxing stance. He gestures with his fingers, inviting Tyler to take the first punch. Tyler's sorely tempted but apart from the fact that, however the fight ended, any attack would be a disaster of epic proportions for his career, he's also not entirely sure he can even take the man. Joey McKenna has been bare-fist fighting for decades and even in his seventies is a big, fit man. He's also still holding the golf club and Tyler has no doubt he'd be willing to use it.

McKenna laughs at his hesitation. 'No? All right then, maybe we should just talk like civilised individuals then, eh?' McKenna pushes past Tyler, back towards the entrance way. 'Come along, Detective, let's grab a drink and you can tell me what's bothering you.'

He hates giving the man the upper hand but then he did that the moment he walked in here without any semblance of a plan. Talking to him more will only make things worse but he needs some answers.

He'd stayed up until the early hours wringing every tiny detail he could from Jude's memory. It hadn't been easy. Jude, by nature, was not a man who took well to being questioned and for his part was more interested in reminiscing about their childhood. Tyler had to keep dragging him back on topic but in the end he hadn't learned anything more than Jude had already revealed in the pub. He'd never even met McKenna and knew of the man only by reputation. Neither could he remember ever overhearing any phone calls or conversations Richard had had about the gangster, or anyone else for that matter. Tyler decided that if he was going to learn more he'd need to go straight to McKenna. Which is what has brought him here.

There's a small drinks lounge back in the reception area and McKenna helps himself to a complimentary bottle of Evian, throwing one to Tyler in the same motion. Tyler catches the bottle but doesn't open it. McKenna sits in a large tub chair and gestures for Tyler to sit as well. When he doesn't the gangster barks at him, 'Sit down, man! For the love of God, don't push any more buttons, I think I'm being pretty restrained under the circumstances.'

Tyler sits. He has seen McKenna's infamous temper before but he's still chilled by how quickly the man can turn from charming to dangerous. It's a reminder, if the two heavies who have taken up a defensive stance over by the window isn't enough of one, that he made the right decision not to fight him earlier.

'Now then,' McKenna says, once again all sweetness and charm. 'What's this about?'

'Did you kill my father?' Tyler doesn't know he's going to ask the question until it's out of his mouth.

'No. I did not. And I've told you that already. Ach, why on Earth would I want to kill the man? I had nothing to gain by it.'

'You had some kind of working relationship with him, didn't you? Enough that he could come to you and warn you off my brother, and you listened.'

'Ah, the prodigal has returned, has he? Is that what this is all about?' McKenna runs a hand across his jaw, considering something. 'I've never lied to you, Adam. In fact, I gave you an opportunity once before to learn what I know and you rejected it.'

'And then you arranged to have the information delivered to my boss anyway, didn't you? That folder that mysteriously appeared on Jordan's desk almost cost her her life. That's another thing I'm landing squarely at your door.'

McKenna has the good grace to look chastened, pursing his lips in a grimace. 'Aye. Well, I am sorry about that. But I had no idea the Superintendent would do anything so bloody foolish as to kidnap someone, least of all his own DCI.'

'What's going on, McKenna? If you want to tell me something then just bloody tell me! Stop all this nonsense.'

McKenna glances across to his men and picks up his water bottle. He takes a long swig and works his mouth as though he's washing away a bad taste. When he speaks his voice is softer. 'There's a code, Tyler. You know that. There's a limit to how much I can just come straight out and tell you.'

'Then I'm going to arrest you.'

McKenna shakes his head. 'We've been down this road

before. Assuming you even have anything, which you don't, I'll be out in a matter of hours and I can promise you that's the last you'll ever hear from me.'

'Off to South America with your pal, Stevens.'

'Aye, if I'm lucky.' Again McKenna's eyes flick towards his two bodyguards. 'These people, Tyler. You don't mess with them. Just by sitting here talking to you I'm taking a helluva risk. It isn't like the old days anymore. You can't bloody trust anybody.'

'Who are *these* people?'

'All right. I'm going to tell you a story, strictly off the record, mind. You can decide what you do with it, but I can tell you one thing, I won't be speaking to you again so listen carefully.

'A long time ago I fell in with the wrong crowd. Got myself into a bit of mischief, I'm sure you know this bit already. Anyway, there came a time when I decided it was best if I cut my losses and got out of the game. It seems some of your colleagues had put together quite the case against my old . . . business partners. So I saw which side my bread was buttered and I jumped ship. I spoke to a young DI who was making a name for himself at the time, aye, Richard Tyler. He scratched my back and I scratched his.'

Tyler opens his mouth to call the man a liar but McKenna holds his hand up and ploughs on.

'It was all above board on your dad's side and if you want to check out my story I'm sure there are files somewhere documenting everything. Old Dickie was always a meticulous record keeper. That's assuming Stevens hasn't destroyed them of course, but he'd have nae reason to.

'So I helped him . . . put a case against some of my old gang and in return I got to keep my nose clean and stay out of the big house. Afterward, your dad and me, we decided to keep the lines of communication open, just in case. I cannae speak for the man but I also got the strong impression he thought he could keep his eye on me and make sure I was still on the straight and narrow.' McKenna chuckles and then trails off when he sees Tyler's stony face. 'So like I told you once before, me and your dad, we go back a ways.

'Now. Cut to a decade or so later and along comes Richard with a request for me. Well, it was a wee bit more than a request but like I said, we had a history, your father and me, so I cut the fella some slack. He meets me and starts ranting and raving about how I'm leading his eldest son into a life of crime. Well, this is the first I've heard of the matter and after a not wholly pleasant exchange between the two of us I assure him that I've never had any business dealings with his precious boy.'

'I thought you said you'd got out of the game.'

'There are always more games, son. Don't be naïve.' McKenna's smile has no humour in it. 'But no, I'm being honest with you here. It was my eldest boy, Joseph Junior, who'd got your brother mixed up in something. Boys stuff, nothing heavy, but it was enough to rile your father up. So I offered to do your father the not inconsiderable favour of letting it be known amongst my lads, that they were to have nothing to do with your brother ever again. On pain of . . . well, extreme pain.'

'And you did this out of the kindness of your heart.'

'No, you wee heid-the-baw! I did it because I didnae need your father taking any closer an interest in my affairs. We might have had a truce but it was a fragile one. So I read the lads the riot act and that was the end of it.'

It's a good story and much of it makes sense but Tyler knows that isn't the end of it. 'Then why did you seek me out last year? What was in that folder that you so desperately wanted us to know? Surely not just that Stevens was a bent copper. There were already plenty of suspicions about that. What possible reason could you have for turning him in? And don't go feeding me any bullshit about civic duty.'

McKenna hides a smile behind the shaft of his golf club. 'I know I've said it before but you really are a chip off the old block, aren't you?' McKenna checks his phone and frowns. 'Fine. Just hang on a minute.' He calls over the thickset heavy – Danny. 'Who's with Tina?' he asks.

Danny looks as though the question might be hurting his brain. 'Nate's with her. Pilates or something.'

McKenna nods but he looks thoughtful. 'Give him a bell, will you? She hasn't checked in yet.'

Danny nods and heads back to the window with his mobile pressed to his ear.

'What was that about?'

'Just checking up on the next Mrs McKenna. She's a daft wee lass and if I'm not careful she'll have bought something expensive.' But it isn't just money worries that are etched on McKenna's face. Not unless he's in some very serious financial difficulties.

'Aye, Stevens,' he goes on. 'Well, we've all known that bugger was a crook for decades. Your dad came to me a few weeks before he died and asked me about him. I told him what I knew, which amounted to suspicions and hearsay more than anything, and then off he went and that was the last I ever saw of him, and that's the God's honest truth.

'I'll admit, I never took your old man as the sort who would top himself but then who really knows anyone, eh? Not these days. But when I heard you and the Yorkshire Terrier were looking into your dad's death I got to thinking. It occurred to me you could do worse than look at Stevens so I asked around and gathered together the info I eventually gave to your DCI Jordan.'

'Where did you get this evidence? And how did you know we were looking into it?'

'Come on, Tyler. A man's got to keep some mystery, eh?'

'And you did all this – what? – because you owed my father?'

'I liked Dickie. He could be a pain in the backside but he was a good man. I didn't like the thought someone might have offed him.'

'I don't buy it.'

McKenna shrugs. 'That's your prerogative, of course.'

'How did my father find out about this so-called conspiracy of his?'

Another shrug. 'I cannae tell you any more than I have.'

Danny has returned and is hovering nearby with his mobile in his hands. McKenna looks up and the heavy shakes his head slightly.

'Right,' McKenna says, 'I'm afraid that's really all I can help you with.'

'Just a minute, we're not finished.'

'Yes, we are, son.' McKenna stands up.

'I should take you in. We need to know exactly what was in that folder and where you found the information.'

McKenna smiles. 'And what folder would that be? Oh, this . . . info you tell me your DCI Jordan was careless enough to lose. I'm afraid I don't know anything about that.'

'McKenna—'

The charm evaporates again and suddenly McKenna's standing right in front of him. He's a tall man, and despite his age he has no trouble making himself look threatening. 'No, DS Tyler. That's more than enough. Whatever else you need I suggest you get from the horse's mouth. Perhaps a word with your misplaced Superintendent. Or maybe your DCI Jordan has remembered something?'

Tyler's aware of the heavies standing tense and ready to involve themselves. He watches McKenna walk away from him and out of the building. Outside, he tries calling someone on his mobile but there's clearly no response. He gestures violently and the other heavy – not Danny – rushes off to fetch the car. Less than thirty seconds later a Land Rover is sweeping away from the golf club in a cloud of gravel.

*

The Grapes of Rotherham is about as classy as its name implies. It's on the outskirts of the town, not far from the M1 junction with the Meadowhall Shopping Centre. It's a surprisingly big place with an expansive car park and at some point in its dim and distant past must have operated as one of those child-friendly Sunday lunch places offering an all-you-can-eat carvery for less than a tenner. Tyler can still see the faded remains of a slide in the garden although to reach it you'd have to cross a lawn peppered with steaming dog turds that have melted holes in the snow. Tyler's glad the cold weather has tempered the smell.

Rabbani's quiet as they cross the car park. She's barely said two words to Tyler since he picked her up this morning and he wonders what he's done to upset her now.

She looks bleakly at the flaking paint peeling from the door. 'You sure this is the right place?' she asks him.

He shrugs. 'According to Debbie.' She'd rung him last night, while he was walking home with Jude trying to get more information about their father's relationship to Joey McKenna. She said she'd been racking her brains, trying to remember where she knew the person in the picture he'd shown her from, the picture of the body from the reservoir. She couldn't remember precisely but she seemed to think it might have been at their local pub at the time. She couldn't be sure though.

'It's the right pub,' he tells Rabbani. 'We just have to hope it's the right man.'

'If it is,' Rabbani says as she raps hard on the front door, 'then it's a big coincidence that our victim drank in the same pub as the murdered security guard.'

'Isn't it?'

The sound of dogs barking comes from somewhere deep inside the pub but not very much else. While they wait, Tyler tries his best to build some bridges. 'That was great work,' he tells her. 'Finding out about the tattoo. Should help with an ID.'

She looks at him with that deep frown that's always plastered over her face. 'It was Emma came up with that, not me.'

'Yeah,' he says, 'but . . . well, it's good that you're working well with Emma, you know . . . building a rapport and that.'

She looks at him as though he's sprouted a second head. 'Right,' she says, then turns back and hammers on the door again. This time the furious barking is accompanied by the voice of a man shouting at them. A minute or so later they hear a chain being undone and a key turning, then the pub door opens and a man's face scowls out at them.

'What?'

'Mr Ashworth?'

'Yeah?'

Rabbani shows the man her warrant card and handles the introductions. 'We just wanted to ask you a few questions about someone who might have been a customer here. Can we come in?'

Ashworth looks back and forth between them. 'You got a warrant?'

'We're only asking questions, not searching the place.'

Rabbani slips her warrant card away and Tyler hears her voice change. 'Look, I doubt any of this has anything to do with you, we're just after a bit of info.' She speaks like she's an old friend, looking out for his best interests. 'Of course, if you prefer we could come back during opening hours, question some of your customers, check for ID, that sort of thing—'

'All right, all right, just hang on a minute, I've got no keks on.' The door closes in their faces.

'Nicely done,' Tyler tells her.

She nods an acknowledgement of his compliment this time. He supposes that's a slight improvement. 'What do you suppose he's really doing in there?' she asks. 'Hiding evidence of a lock-in?'

Tyler grins. 'Maybe. Although judging by the state of his eyes I'd say he's probably flushing his stash.'

Rabbani smiles back. 'Shame. Looks like we've ruined his day already then.'

Ashworth returns a few minutes later and lets them into the saloon bar. It's not quite as run down as the outside of the pub but it's getting there. Considering the premises will be opening in a couple of hours, there's a distinct lack of cleaning going on. Pint pots tower on the bar, their insides still pooling with amber liquid. Tyler reckons there are probably more crisps left lying crushed into the carpet than there are behind the bar and the whole place stinks of stale beer and sweat. Ashworth offers them a seat but one look at Rabbani's horror-filled face convinces Tyler to stay standing. Not that he needed convincing.

'This really won't take long,' he tells the landlord. This time he doesn't bother with any niceties or explanations but goes straight for the jugular. 'I wonder if you recognise this man.' He holds his mobile screen out and the publican squints at it through red-rimmed eyes.

'Jesus! Fuck!' Ashworth turns away from the picture. 'Is that ... Is he ... ?'

'Dead. His body was fished out of a reservoir a few days ago. Do you recognise him?'

Ashworth shakes his head. 'Can't say I do.'

'Are you sure? Take another look. We were led to believe the man might be a regular of yours, or used to be. You've had this place for a while now, haven't you?'

Ashworth peers again at the screen. 'Yeah. Twenty year next June.'

'You should hold an anniversary celebration,' Tyler says. 'Nothing, then?'

'We've had thousands in here over the years. I can't say he definitely hasn't been in but ...' He raises his hands. You don't have to be a trained psychologist to see that he's lying.

'Looks like we'll have to come back after all then,' Rabbani says from behind them. She's sniffing round the bar area, and poking her head into nooks and crannies. 'See if any of your regulars recognise him. Hope it doesn't put anyone off their pint.'

'He had a distinctive tattoo,' Tyler says. 'A skull with a snake coiled through the eye sockets. Maybe that helps.'

Ashworth is sweating heavily but that could just be

whatever he was on last night. Still, he starts to nod, his eyes flicking over at Rabbani who has disappeared down the corridor towards the toilets. 'Give me another look,' he says. Tyler holds out the phone while Ashworth makes a show of examining it more closely. 'Could be Jake Baker,' he says. 'Tattoo sounds about right. He hasn't been in here for fifteen year though, I reckon. At least.'

'What did he do, this Jake Baker?'

'I dunno. We don't ask for a potted biography of every customer.'

'But you remember his name,' Tyler says. 'Just like that, after all this time.'

Ashworth sighs and rolls his eyes. 'He was a builder, I reckon. Labourer or summat. Look, I don't want no trouble. Whatever he's done, it's nowt to do with me. I'm telling you I haven't seen him in years. Where's the lass gone? Oi.' He heads off to follow Rabbani who reappears from down a corridor. 'You can't just come in and search the place without a warrant.'

Rabbani smiles sweetly. 'I was just having a look around. Lovely old building, isn't it?'

'I've answered your questions. I've got work to do.'

'All right then, Mr Ashworth. Thank you for your time. Do give us a ring if that razor-sharp mind of yours remembers anything else, won't you?' Tyler hands Ashworth a card.

Back outside, Ashworth has the door shut almost before they're fully through it.

'Jake Baker,' Tyler says. 'Well, that's a start.'

Rabbani's grinning at him from ear to ear, evidently desperate for him to ask.

'Go on then, what did you find?'

'Oh, nothing much. Just one of those hall of fame noticeboards. I think it was for darts or summat.'

'And?'

She pulls out her mobile and presents him with a picture. 'And guess who was halfway up the leader board.'

Tyler looks down at the phone and the picture of a sweating Gareth Whitehouse with his arm around a young woman. 'Well, well, well,' he says. 'Those coincidences just keep stacking up, don't they?'

'It was me,' Rabbani says out of nowhere.

Tyler's driving and has to flick his eyes from the road. She's sitting with her arms crossed, usually a pretty good sign that she's pissed off with him about something, but he recognises the frown on her face as that particular expression she reserves for herself when she thinks she's fucked up. It's an unusual mix of emotions he's not sure he's seen on her before. He wonders if this is whatever had her so worked up yesterday afternoon.

'I've been spying on you.'

Tyler's foot slips from the accelerator and the car behind honks at their sudden deceleration. 'O-kay.' He has to admit, whatever he had been expecting it wasn't this.

'I told Franklin you and Doggett had been looking into your dad's death. I overheard you talking about it the other night.'

The first thing Tyler feels is relief. It wasn't Doggett. At least half the reason he hadn't slept was the thought that he might truly be on his own now.

'And you decided to go straight to Franklin with that?'

'No! I've been spying for her, I told you.' She huffs but Tyler knows this expression well enough. It's frustration aimed at herself not him. 'She asked me to keep an eye on you. She knew you were up to something with Doggett.'

'Did she, now?'

'Look, I was pissed off, all right! You and Doggett leave me out of everything and I'm sick of it!' The arms tighten slightly across her chest.

'Right,' he says, trying to keep the smile on his face in check. He supposes he should be more upset; it's still a betrayal. But for some reason he's not. 'Well, thanks for the apology.'

She whips her head round to look at him. 'You're not pissed off with me then?'

'I guess you had your reasons.'

She sighs heavily. 'I *am* sorry. It was a dick move and I shouldn't have done it. I was just so mad at you both and then when I realised what you'd been up to all this time – without bothering to include me – and . . .' She trails off and then, after a pause, 'I'm sorry. Really.'

'It's okay,' he says. 'I got the feeling Franklin already knew most of it anyway. And it was only a ticking off. Not my first and undoubtedly not my last either.' He glances to the side to see Rabbani examining him again. 'What?'

'I'm never gonna understand you, am I?'

'I hope not. Wouldn't want our relationship to get boring.'

'You're annoyingly reasonable this morning. What's wrong with you?'

'Nothing,' he says, and realises that he means it. His run-in with McKenna has left him strangely satisfied, as though it was a catharsis of sorts. He doesn't believe McKenna told him everything but what he did say had the ring of truth to it. McKenna has deceived him before though. He needs to remember that.

So why this sense of closure? The reconciliation with Jude, his realisation that there was stuff going on in Richard's life that wasn't just about him ... it's almost as though this lets him off the hook. At worst he was no more responsible for Richard's death than Jude was. Somehow sharing the blame has lifted the weight slightly. It's ridiculous. He doesn't blame himself for his father's death anymore, he hasn't done for years. If anything all his anger and blame was centred on his father. But then Doggett had come along with his theory, and Tyler realised that a part of him never really believed Richard killed himself. And if he couldn't blame Richard anymore then who else could he blame but himself? At least now he has a place to target his anger. Stevens. He'll find the man. Somehow.

'She played me,' Rabbani says, drawing his attention back to the present.

'Huh?'

'Franklin.'

'What about her?'

The heavy sigh makes another appearance. 'I told you I went to see her when she first came here, to tell her what I discovered last year about DCI Cooper and the way Stevens shut down her investigation. She took it seriously and then she was telling me what a bright future I had as long as I knew whose side I was on and . . .'

'She asked you to spy on us.' It makes sense and he's glad now that he didn't tell Franklin anything about McKenna. She may or may not be bent but he's more convinced than ever that he can't trust her.

Rabbani squirms a bit in her seat. 'I mean . . . she didn't say spy exactly but . . .'

'Really, Mina, it's okay.' And it is. He wants her to know he forgives her. In fact, he doesn't want to be alone in this anymore. Maybe it's just this new-found euphoria making him reckless but . . . it feels right.

Tyler pulls over into a layby. There's a burger van up ahead providing an array of fried foods to a queue of white vans.

'Do you want to know what's going on?' he asks.

Rabbani hesitates.

'Because if you do, I'll tell you now. All of it. Not just what I told Franklin. And then you'll have to decide whether you want to tell her the rest or not. But you need to know something before you decide. The reason Doggett and I kept this secret, other than the fact we're shit communicators, is because it's dangerous.'

'I don't need protecting.'

He nods. 'I know. I'm sorry. You're a serving officer, a good detective and you don't deserve to be left in the dark. But I want you to know that not letting you in had nothing to do with us not trusting you or anything, okay? So, you need to decide now. You want in, or not?'

She thinks about it and he's glad about that even though he's pretty sure he knows what her answer's going to be.

'Tell me,' she says.

So he does.

Jake Baker's mother lives in a terraced house on the outskirts of Rotherham. She's a small woman who has that lost look on her face that Mina's begun to recognise in the relatives of the cases they work. She wonders, not for the first time, whether this is the worst thing that can happen to someone whose loved one has gone missing. A visit from the police. Tyler's always telling her that they're helping, giving closure to the family, rescuing them from the never-ending nightmare of wondering what happened and why. But sometimes Mina isn't so sure. Is it really closure? Or does their grief just morph from one monster into another?

And for the first time she gets it, right there in Mrs Baker's tired front room as she fusses over them and offers to fetch them tea, and tries to put off the moment that she must by now know is coming. Mina finally understands him. She understands Tyler.

She watches him talk Karen Baker through the news, doing his best to minimise the gruesome details, asking if he can see a photo of her missing son. Karen begins rifling through an old photo album, clearly eager to be able to help, even if it's only in identifying her dead son. Mina sees the hope in the woman's eyes as Tyler tells her they'll still need to do a formal identification, and the pain when he describes the tattoo.

She sees that pain reflected in Tyler's eyes and considers what he told her about the manner of his father's death. She knew some of it already but second-hand, never directly from his own mouth. She didn't know, for example, that he'd been the one to find his father's body, swinging by a makeshift noose from the banisters. She hadn't really ever considered the personal human tragedy of it all, what it must feel like to be cut off from all the family you've ever known at the age of sixteen. She can't imagine where she would be right now if the same thing had happened to her at that age.

And then to find out years later that the formative moment from your past, the moment you were forced to become an adult, was actually all a lie . . . No wonder he's been acting so strangely over the past year. If she felt bad about betraying him to Franklin before, it's nothing compared to the guilt she feels now.

Mrs Baker cries and Tyler passes the photograph to Mina. She looks down at the cheeky, smiling face of 21-year-old Jake. Just a boy really. Nothing like the frozen corpse they dug out of the reservoir a few days ago and yet close enough that she has no doubt it's him.

Tyler lets Baker cry herself out and then starts the

questioning. He goes in gently – What was Jake like? What did he do for a living? Can she think of anyone who might want to harm him? All the usual stuff with the usual answers – *such a lovely lad . . . finding his feet . . . no, of course not, I can't imagine . . .*

The questioning continues. Did he have any close friends? Other family members that might know more of his life? It becomes clear that Mrs Baker knows very little of what her son got up to outside of the family home. She knows he had friends but doesn't remember their names. She mentions a girlfriend, although she can't remember the girl's name either, if she ever knew it. And there's no one else.

'It was always just me and Jake,' she says. 'Just me and Jake.'

Mina can almost hear the woman's heart breaking with her voice.

Tyler's so gentle with her but somehow still manages to get answers to his questions. He gets her to talk them through the days leading up to Jake's disappearance, and the day itself, the last time she saw him. He's good at this, Mina realises, in a way she's never fully appreciated until now. It's as though she's seeing him for the first time today. This man, who struggles so much with the social stuff and manages to offend his colleagues so easily with his blunt single-mindedness, somehow manages to navigate the world of the victim in a manner she can only marvel at. Because he's one of them. And so he understands them. She wonders what he might have got from Binita if he'd been the one to question her. Perhaps the girl would have opened up to him about Whitehouse in a way she couldn't with Mina.

In the end they spend the best part of an hour talking to Mrs Baker, most of which consists of the woman taking them through childhood photograph albums. They learn next to nothing of importance and Mina can feel Tyler's frustration building, but still he treats her with kid gloves, making no attempt to rush her. Occasionally he brings her back to the topic at hand when she meanders too far but otherwise he seems content to let her have this moment, this chance to talk in a way she hasn't for sixteen years.

Only once does his voice harden a little and it comes near the end of their conversation.

'Mrs Baker,' he says, drawing her attention back from a frame on the wall that holds a plaster of Paris imprint of Jake's hands and feet as a toddler. 'There's something I don't quite understand.' She comes back to join them and perches on the arm of a chair, ready once again to be of service in whatever small way she can. 'When Jake went missing, why didn't you report it?'

It's the first thing they checked for once they had his ID, or at least, the first thing Mina had checked for after Tyler had questioned her as to why Baker's name hadn't come up in her routine check of the missing persons database. There was no file on Jake Baker. He had never been reported missing.

'But I did,' she says, and Mina feels a sliver of ice form deep in her belly.

'You reported him missing to the police?' Tyler asks.

Mrs Baker nods. 'The day after the night he didn't come home. They told me it was too early and I had to wait because he was an adult and he hadn't been gone long enough.'

'But you didn't go back again?'

'Well . . .' Mrs Baker's face crumples as though she's worried she did something wrong. 'I didn't need to. A policeman came round later that day and spoke to me. He was very helpful although . . . to be honest, I wasn't all that nice to him.'

'How so?'

'Well, he just kept telling me that Jake had probably gone off somewhere with his girlfriend. I tried to make him understand that he wouldn't do that. Not Jake. He wouldn't just leave without telling me.'

'But the policeman thought otherwise?'

Mrs Baker nods. 'He said he saw it all the time, youngsters like Jake, just picking up and disappearing. He said it was pretty common and he'd do all he could but often there really wasn't much to be done in these cases. I got very upset but he was lovely and helped calm me down. He came back . . . oh, maybe a dozen times all told until . . . well, he stopped eventually. I would call him now and again but there was never any more news after that.'

Tyler meets Mina's eye and she can see the silent fury in him. He turns back to Mrs Baker.

'Do you remember his name?' he asks.

'Of course. It was Detective Stevens.'

The ice in Mina's stomach twists into a knot.

*

Edith's stopped going out on her morning constitutionals. She came across that word in a play they studied for English last year. She googled it and thought it was just the right phrase to describe what she does every day. Something that is good for the constitution. And now, since her self-imposed abstinence from walking, she has begun to realise just how apt the word is.

At school she's jittery and forever on guard, even more so than she would be under normal circumstances. She has taken to hiding in the toilets at break times, rather than risk the playground and anyone who might be watching it. She eats her pack-up from its Tupperware container with her legs pulled up under her on the toilet seat. It's not the most pleasant way to eat food, given the smells that waft around her, and she can't help thinking about something Dr Erikson told them a few weeks ago. About how, if you think about it, whenever you smell something, that means that particles of whatever that thing is are inside your nose. Tiny, minuscule molecules of matter. She rarely makes it through a whole sandwich.

At home, she stays in more, but this is not good for her or Melanie. With Edith around, Melanie gets worse. As though, if Edith's there to do it, Melanie doesn't have to. She doesn't think her mother's doing it on purpose but it's getting to the point where Edith has to do everything: cooking, cleaning, laying out Melanie's clothes in the morning. Yesterday she came home to find her mother hadn't even bothered to get dressed. She's taken up residence on the settee, watching her worn out TV shows and speaking only when she needs something, with a voice as thin and cracked as her VHS tapes.

She can't deny it, the more she's around, the worse Melanie is. But worse than that, Edith can feel herself growing more bitter about it. She doesn't want to hate her mother. She loves her – *needs* her, badly. But not this mother. This shell of the woman she once was. But if she asks for help ... if she does the unthinkable and tells someone, one of her teachers perhaps ... ? No, she couldn't bear it if they took her away.

This morning she decides she just has to get out. The snow seems to have finally passed and the temperature is up a few degrees. Under normal circumstances she would be out there already. So what's stopping her? The man with the hate-filled eyes, obviously. But maybe he's given up. And she's still not a hundred per cent sure she hasn't got this all wrong. She can't help thinking about her father. She knows it's absurd but ... even if the man isn't him he might know him. If he's connected to the boatshed in some way too.

Once again she thinks about telling her mum. With this extra information would she finally get something out of her? She's not stupid. She's often wondered why Melanie is so reluctant to talk about her dad. Given the only other thing she knows about him, that her grandad didn't like him, she suspects she wouldn't like the answer. On her more fanciful days Edith likes to pretend her dad works for MI5 or something and that's why he's not around anymore. Or maybe they're in witness protection and he'll join them once he's finished giving evidence against the bad guys.

But in truth she knows it's far more likely that he's the crook. Or a wife-beater or in prison or . . . Melanie is only trying to protect her but she'd rather know. However bad he was, at least she'd know who he was.

'Mum, I'm going out for a bit.' She shouts it and receives a pitiful whine in response, but whether Melanie is tired or hungry or sad, she doesn't wait to find out. Her mother will be fine for an hour or two.

Outside, the day isn't quite as warm as Edith thought, the weak sun that has broken through the cloud cover, deceiving in its brightness. Still, she's not about to go back for a thicker coat now. She'll walk faster, maybe even jog for a bit if she finds a stretch of ground that isn't too icy, and that will keep her warm enough.

She doesn't realise she's going back to the reservoir until she's almost there. She stops, not far from the place where she first saw him. Her heart's racing now but she realises this is more than just a careless choice, more than muscle memory that has brought her to this place. Subconsciously she meant to come here. She needs to confront this strange occurrence that has set her life so off balance.

She moves down the trail slowly, her heart thudding in her chest and her feet ready to about-turn and sprint in the opposite direction. When the boatshed comes into view she stops for a moment. There's no one around and she can't decide if that's a good thing. It means *he's* not here, but then neither is anyone else who might help her if he were to appear suddenly out of the bushes.

Edith treads onward, her feet taking her closer to the run-down building. A part of her screams that this isn't sensible, that she should be nowhere near this place. But another part urges her on. It's the part that has so often brought her to this place, the place her mother told her was so important. The place she was conceived. She tries to imagine it as Melanie had described it that one time, on that uncharacteristically candid afternoon.

It was a summer night, she'd said. The sun was setting and there were water boatmen whipping around in circles across the surface of the lake. She'd stripped naked and plunged into the water, cold enough, even at that time of the year, to take the breath from her lungs. Her lover came up behind her, wrapped his strong arms around her and whispered into her ear, telling her this was their special place. Melanie had been nervous that someone would see them. This was a well-worn path with dog-walkers and joggers, especially in mid-summer, but her lover had told her to relax, that they would be out of sight soon enough.

They swam round to the front of the boatshed and dipped their heads under the water and under the doors. It was thrilling for Melanie, taking that risk that there would be air to come up to on the other side, but she trusted him. She trusted him more than she had ever trusted anyone. And then they were breaking the surface in the dark interior of the shed, the evening sun shining through the slatted walls and lighting the place up like some fairy grotto.

Melanie had been a little less forthcoming on the details

from that point, which Edith was grateful for, but she could still read between the lines. They lay down and made love between the canoes. He told her he loved her, that she was all he wanted. He pulled a tarpaulin cover over her when she began to shiver. He admitted he had a friend in the rowing club who assured him the place would be empty this evening. Melanie realised this spontaneous event had been a little more planned than she'd thought but it didn't matter. She was his now. She'd had other lovers, of course. Some of them more suitable than others, but no one who made her feel like this. She lay there with him until morning and as the first light began to chase away the dark she saw the tattoo on his upper arm and traced it with her finger. He laughed and asked her if she liked it. She didn't. She thought it was a hideous thing, a gruesome smiling skull with a snake crawling out of its eye socket. But she told him she loved it. She loved every part of him, even the bits she didn't like.

Edith shivers. She can't imagine the man with the hateful eyes can possibly be the same man her mother described that time. But then she realises something. The tattoo. If she ever does meet her father, or someone she thinks is her father, there will be a cast iron way of discovering if it's really him. All she has to do is get a look at his shoulder.

She smiles to herself; finally, a concrete lead. Taggart would consider that tangible evidence she could use to determine his identity. She feels closer to finding him than ever.

It's then that Edith notices the tape, strung across the doorway of the boatshed. It's yellow and has the words

CRIME SCENE — DO NOT ENTER written in large black letters all across it. She moves closer and reaches out a hand, her curiosity fighting her instinct for self-preservation.

So it *was* a gunshot she heard, and the man with the hateful eyes is not who she thought. Or rather, he's exactly who she thought because she realises now she's been kidding herself. Why would this random man be her father? Even if she did come across him in her mother's special, sacred spot. All these years later, of course he had nothing to do with her mother or her. He was just a bad man up to no good, who she stumbled across at the worst possible time.

She has to go to the police. It's her responsibility to tell them what she knows. But if she does that they'll talk to Melanie. They'll see what's happening and they'll take her away and then Melanie will have no one and ... she can't take that risk.

Edith hears voices coming towards her along the path. She hesitates a moment longer and then turns and runs.

Mina can't believe it.

But of course, she *can* believe it. It makes perfect sense Stevens would be involved in this. He's involved in everything. Jordan's kidnapping, Tyler's dad's death, most likely, pretty much every case they've examined over the past two years! But what does it all mean? What the hell was he up to?

'Why don't you take the lead on this?' Tyler suggests as she pulls up at the entrance to the desserts place. The gates themselves are open this time but there's a barrier across the road. It's the same guard on the door who recognises them, smiles, and waves them through as the barrier rises.

'Any particular reason?' Mina asks him, pulling forward into the car park. This time they don't pull up by the main building that is the hub of the desserts business but at a smaller Portakabin on the far side of the car park.

'You were the one who realised something was up with these two,' Tyler tells her, and then, after a brief pause, 'And it'll throw Whitehouse off his game.'

Mina smiles to herself. 'Yeah, I thought that's what you had in mind.' She's not displeased though. She wouldn't mind throwing Whitehouse off his game. If what Binita told her is true – and if anything she suspects the girl was underplaying it – then she wouldn't mind throwing Whitehouse off a building. She'll settle for unsettling him though. She realises she wants the man to be guilty. *Please let him be our killer!* She wants to see him put away somewhere he can't intimidate young women anymore. Where he's the one being intimidated, and he can have a taste of his own medicine.

As they get out of the car she looks up at the very temporary looking sign over the door. *City Kabs.* From what Tyler told her of his interview with the man, Whitehouse hadn't actually lied, but he certainly didn't volunteer the fact he still worked on the same site as his old factory. Why? Unless he has something to hide.

The parking spaces on this side of the car park are full of the firm's cabs and there are one or two men idling about smoking and chatting to each other. Mina can feel their eyes trudging all over her as they approach the door to the office and she makes a point of staring straight at each of them in turn. She's not sure it makes all that much difference but she won't allow them to intimidate her.

She pushes open the door without knocking. The interior of the cabin has two desks, behind each of which sits a middle-aged woman with an elaborate hairstyle. They're both talking into their headphones. Presumably these are the radio operators.

At the far end of the cabin a thin plasterboard wall and window separates this area from another inner office and behind the window she sees Whitehouse notice them and jump up out of his chair. She's glad he's on the defensive straight away.

He gets to the door in time to greet them.

'Detective,' he says, talking directly to Tyler.

'Detectives,' she corrects him. 'Can we come in, Mr Whitehouse?' She doesn't wait for him to respond but pushes past him into the inner office. The room is hot, a portable heater blowing stale air out from behind the desk, and it smells of body odour and days' old sweat. There are wet patches staining the pits under both of Whitehouse's arms. Mina can't help twitching her nose in revulsion.

'You lied to us, Mr Whitehouse,' she says, as the businessman retakes his seat behind his desk, leaving them both standing on the other side.

'How so, Detective?' If the man's equilibrium is disturbed

by their sudden appearance, he's over it quickly enough and now presents a calm, stoic expression to them.

'When we came to see you the other day, you implied that you had nothing to do with this place anymore and now it turns out you work here.' Behind her, Mina can sense more than see Tyler turning about in the small office, making a show of examining the shelves. She knows he'll be glancing out of the window, picking up books, and generally look-ing as though he's barely paying attention. In truth, he'll be watching Whitehouse closely.

'I rent this small area from Harriet, as do any number of other people. All the units on this side of the property belong to different businesses. I really don't see what any of that has to do with what happened at my old factory all those years ago.'

Mina stares down at him, trying not to break contact despite the fact that staring into the odious creep's eyes is curdling her soul. She can feel them moving over her like they're an extension of his fat, sweaty fingers. 'You also failed to mention that Harriet Spencer is your sister-in-law. You sold this whole place to her for a pound not long before you declared bankruptcy.'

For the first time since he sat down, Whitehouse hesitates. 'Yes, Harriet's married to my brother but I don't see what relevance that has on anything. As to the rest, that was all a long time ago and I really can't remember the details. I'd have to go over the financial records and I'm afraid I won't have anything from that far back.' He's almost smirking, positive that from any legal standpoint he's untouchable and, in fairness to the man, he hasn't actually done anything illegal. Nothing they can prove anyway.

Mina forces a smile and picks up a small paperweight in the shape of the Eiffel Tower from the desk. 'That's all right, Mr Whitehouse,' she says, turning the statue in her hands. 'We're not all that interested in your financial dealings anyway. Tell me, do you ever drink at the Grapes of Rotherham? It's a public house on the—'

'Yes, I know where it is. I've been in there a few times over the years. Not so much lately.'

'We've managed to identify the man we found frozen in the reservoir as Jake Baker. Does that name ring a bell?'

'Jake . . .' It's an artful performance of a man searching his memory.

'He also used to drink in the Grapes. And coincidentally – or not – so did your old employee, Kevin Linville. You remember him? The man who had his brains bashed in while he was protecting your property.'

Whitehouse stands up. 'Really, Detective Sergeant,' he says, making it clear he's addressing Tyler over her head but Tyler steadfastly ignores him. 'I've tried to be cooperative but this is—'

'Sit down!' she tells him sharply, and almost to Mina's surprise, he does. 'You also implied you only knew Kevin slightly, and yet his widow tells us you went to his wedding?'

'I'd . . . I'd forgotten that . . .' Whitehouse seems a lot less sure of himself now. 'No, it was nothing like that. We weren't close or anything. I was just the boss. I'd often go along to events to pay my respects. That doesn't mean ...'

'Doesn't mean what?'

Whitehouse looks up at her.

'Doesn't mean you conspired to steal from your own failing business?'

Whitehouse shakes his head violently and Mina sees him sit up straighter, ready for a new attack. 'Lots of people used to drink at the Grapes. There was a time when it was the place to go. Now, if you're telling me that Linville was in on this robbery, well, I suppose I'd have to accept it, much as it would pain me to believe a man in my own employ could be capable of—'

'Jake Baker!' Mina shouts, slamming the paperweight back down on the desk and making Whitehouse jump. 'You used to play darts with him!'

'I ... I played darts with lots of people ...'

'Oh, for—!'

Tyler clears his throat loudly and Mina bites off the expletive. She takes a deep breath.

She starts again with a milder tone. 'A man is dead, Mr Whitehouse. Two men, in fact. One of them your employee, the other dressed in your company's overalls. So it seems highly plausible that the two of them conspired to steal a large amount of money from you. Now either you were involved as well, or you were a victim of their betrayal. Either way ...' She pauses for dramatic effect. ' ...that gives you a significant motive for murder.'

'What? Now hang on—'

The door to the office opens and Harriet Spencer walks in, her eyes brimming over with fury, followed by a man in a suit carrying a briefcase who might as well have lawyer written all over him.

'Stop talking!' she says in much the same tone of voice Mina used earlier.

Whitehouse falls silent instantly.

'What's going on here?' she demands.

Tyler steps forward. 'This is a private conversation, Ms Spencer. I'll have to ask you to wait out—'

'This conversation is over,' says the solicitor, stepping forward. 'Unless you intend to arrest my client?'

Tyler looks at each of the players in turn. 'I see,' he says, but when he speaks his eyes are resting squarely on the face of Harriet Spencer. He turns to Mina, deferring to her, giving her the chance to save some face.

'All right, Mr Whitehouse. We're requesting that you come into the station and give us an official statement. Otherwise, we'll be back with an arrest warrant.'

'We'll come in,' the solicitor tells her. 'I will telephone you to arrange a *mutually* convenient time.'

Whitehouse is openly smirking at them now and she wishes she had a way to wipe the expression off his face. But then he catches Spencer's eye and the confidence is gone. He cowers there, pale and sweaty in his chair as Mina and Tyler file out of the room. She can hear Spencer talking behind them and she glances back over her shoulder. She can't make out the words exactly, but the intent is clear enough. Spencer is telling him off, like he's a child who's been caught getting up to mischief again.

And, just before the door closes, the last glimpse she catches of Whitehouse tells her something else. He's truly scared of his sister-in-law.

Diane is looking much more like her old self when Tyler goes to see her that evening, despite the fact her leg is still raised in the air at a very odd angle. She does her best to question him about the case he's working but he makes vague noises about it being a missing person's case and she lets him off the hook. He has no doubt she knows he isn't being entirely honest with her but it's a mark of how shaken she is that she doesn't pursue the matter further. He's glad of that, he doesn't want to tell her what they've learned about Stevens' involvement in yet another cover-up, but it worries him to see her like this. She has always been the capable one, the lynchpin in his otherwise chaotic universe. To say he's relieved to have her back in . . . well, almost in one piece, would be a colossal understatement but for the first time he wonders if he has got her back, really. Will she ever get over the trauma of an event like this? He shivers and shakes off the morbid thought.

He chats to her for an hour or so until it becomes clear to him that she's fighting her tiredness. Then he stops talking and it takes only a matter of minutes for her to fall asleep. He gets up and leaves quietly, nodding to Toddy who's back on watch outside her door.

'I heard you got a bollocking,' Toddy says, smiling.

'It happens,' Tyler tells him.

Toddy does a good impression of an amateur spy checking up and down the corridor with his eyes to see who's in earshot. 'Listen,' he says. 'I thought you might want to know, my gaffer wants me back. They're lifting the twenty-four watch on her.'

'Damn!' Tyler kicks out at a chair, risking the wrath of a passing nurse. The guy eyes him up and down but Tyler can't decide if the look is meant to be an admonishment or flirtation – either way he ignores it.

'If your Stevens has fled the country then there's no reason to worry he'll be back for her.'

'He's not *my* Stevens.'

'Yeah, sorry, mate. Bad choice of words. But anyway, I can't see that she's in all that much danger now. Surely?'

Tyler shakes his head but what can he say? There's a chance Stevens wasn't working alone? There's a chance ACC Franklin has Jordan right where she wants her? 'Thanks for telling me,' he says.

Outside the hospital the night air is crisp. Tomorrow is going to be another frozen morning, assuming it doesn't snow again in the night. The only parking space he could find when he arrived was on the far side of the building and he's halfway round his circumnavigation when he senses someone following him. He glances back over his shoulder but there are a number of people milling about – staff, visitors, no one he recognises – so it's hard to say which of them if any have set off his early-warning system. He turns back and moves on.

Maybe Rabbani's right, maybe he *is* getting paranoid. *It isn't paranoia if the bastards are out to get you!*

They'd talked over what Mrs Baker had said in the car on the way back to town and she'd been adamant that they needed to take what they'd learned to Franklin.

'You can't think she's involved in all this, surely?' she'd asked when he'd tried to convince her against the idea.

'She was here, back in my father's time. She knew Stevens. She went to see him while Diane was in his cellar. It might be coincidence she got called in when Diane disappeared. Then again it might not.'

Rabbani had given him a look he can only describe as pity and that disturbed him more than any of the other many looks she has in her repertoire. The last thing he wants from her is pity.

'You've got to learn to trust people,' she'd told him, to which he'd carelessly responded, 'Because they're not all spying on me?'

He meant it as a joke but regretted it when she turned away from him with her cheeks reddening. But then they'd arrived at the station and he'd shouted after her that they'd talk later and she'd waved a dismissive hand at him without turning around.

Tyler turns the final corner and is setting out towards his car when he smells the distinctive scent of overpowering cologne. He turns without even thinking about it and lashes out, his fist connecting with Danny's nose.

McKenna's henchman says, 'Fuck!' but before Tyler

can follow up the man responds, punching him hard in the stomach and bending him over. Tyler collapses to his knees, winded.

'He only wants to fucking talk!' Danny tells him. 'Jesus Christ! If you've broken my nose I'll fucking kill you me'sen!'

And then a car pulls up and Tyler's lifted onto his feet and shoved into the back of the vehicle.

McKenna's house is a palatial Georgian-style detached property likely built in the early 90s. It's surrounded by a wide gravel drive that in another era would probably have been a moat. McKenna's waiting for them by the colonnaded front door picking leaves off a bay tree.

'What the *fuck* happened?' he asks, taking in Tyler's dishevelled appearance and Danny's swollen, bleeding nose.

'The bastard clocked me one!' says Danny, pushing Tyler forward.

'I told you to ask him nicely! Not belt the man.'

'I never got a chance.'

McKenna steps forward, tensed for violence, but in the end he just clenches his fists and says, 'Get out of here,' so quietly Tyler's not sure exactly who he's talking to. Nevertheless, Danny makes a swift exit in the direction of the garage. McKenna loosens his fists and takes Tyler by the arm. 'I'm sorry, Detective.'

'You know assaulting an officer is a serious offence.'

McKenna nods. 'Aye, and if you want to press charges against the wee dobber I'll not stand in yer way.'

Nothing would give Tyler greater pleasure but it would be something of a hollow victory. 'What do you want, McKenna?'

McKenna's eyes pass over the driveway and the surrounding gardens. 'Inside,' he says, gesturing Tyler in.

The hallway is a wide open vestibule with several doors leading off it and a sweeping staircase that curves up around the wall. It's perhaps not as grand as a country estate but the place must have five or six bedrooms at least. There are oversized photographic portraits of McKenna's children and grandchildren leading up the stairs. There's an ornate oak table in the centre of the hallway with an arrangement of semi-wilting blooms and an incongruent rubber ball of some kind. Tyler can't decide if it's a dog toy or one of those executive stress balls people have on their desks.

There's something different about the man tonight. McKenna moves around the table as though heading towards one door before apparently changing his mind and doubling back. He seems unsure about the best location for their chat and ends up turning back and standing where he is, in the middle of the hallway, his right hand stroking his chin, the elbow supported by his left. It's the first time in their, albeit relatively short, relationship that Tyler has seen him agitated. Not angry or calculating but truly out of sorts.

'It's our Tina,' he says finally, presumably deciding there's no better place for their interview than the entranceway. 'She's missing.'

It isn't in the least what Tyler was expecting. 'Your

girlfriend?' He's never met the woman and all he knows about her is that she's significantly younger than McKenna.

'Fiancée.'

'Congratulations.'

'Look,' McKenna says, picking up the rubber ball and squeezing it tightly. 'I'm not gonna mess you around. I need your help, Tyler.'

'You're kidding, right?'

'She's missing . . . I'm worried about her.' The admission seems to stick in his craw.

'So file a missing persons' report.'

McKenna breaths out his irritation. 'Aye, and invite your lot to come in here and go over the place with a fine-tooth comb. You know I cannae do that.'

'That's your choice.'

'Just . . .' McKenna gets his temper back under control. The rubber ball distends even further. 'Please! You know I wouldn't ask this if it wasn't important. Just find her for me. I need to know she's safe.'

Tyler considers the man in front of him. He really does seem worried. 'How long has she been missing?'

'Since this morning.'

'In that case—'

'I know what you're gonna say but this is our Tina. She never goes anywhere without me or one of the lads. And the fella who was with her, Nathaniel, he's not answering his phone either.'

'There could be any number of reasons for that.' Tyler

stops short of naming them; he doesn't want to rile McKenna any further.

'Look, lad,' McKenna says. 'I've managed to amass a fair number of competitors in my time and Tina's a good way for them to get leverage over me. She might be a daft wee lass some of the time but she's not stupid enough to go off on her own, especially . . .' McKenna trails off.

'Especially what?'

'She just wouldn't, that's all.'

'McKenna . . .' Tyler says, while the man refuses to meet his eye. 'Joey!'

McKenna looks up sharply, as though he's unused to hearing his Christian name. Tyler imagines he is. Even the prodigal Tina probably only calls him by some sweet endearment. *Babe* or *puddin'* or something.

'If there's something else going on here I need to know about it or I can't help you.' He has no idea how he can help anyway. If McKenna doesn't want the police involved officially there's very little he can do. But he keeps that to himself.

McKenna makes a noise of frustration in the back of his throat which turns into a growl. Then he turns and fires the rubber ball across the room where it bounces hard against the wall and ricochets back into the vase of flowers. The glass smashes and water cascades across the table.

Tyler stands very still, once again aware of this big man's temper and his infamous reputation. It's easy to think only of the charming ex-con in his dotage, the loving family man with his extended brood lining the stairwell behind him. But there are still flashes of the younger, more dangerous man with a short fuse.

Danny's head appears around the front door, presumably alerted by the noise.

'I told you to fuck off!' McKenna shouts and Danny disappears again.

Tyler stands perfectly still at the heart of the maelstrom, patiently waiting for the wind to settle. Finally McKenna manages to pace out his fury and nods to himself. He crosses to Tyler and closes the front door.

'There's always someone in charge,' McKenna says. Moving back to the table he begins collecting up the broken pieces of glass from the vase and putting them in a pile. 'Sometimes it's those Tory scum, eh? That Eton lot who think they run the country. Then there's the unions. Oh, they have good enough intentions, I suppose, but sooner or later they get used to being in power and they make the same mistakes as the other lot but for different reasons. And in some places, it's organised crime, my old lot, for example. But like it or not, someone has to be in charge. That's the way of the world.

'This particular lot call themselves "The Circle". A group of wealthy industrialists who began snatching up land and power after your father and his colleagues finally put a nail in the coffin of my old gang. No one, not even I, know how many of them there are but they run things all right, behind the scenes, buying people off here and there, greasing the pole so it slides in their direction. Your old friend Gerald

Cartwright was one of them, a long time ago. Membership changes over the years, they come and go, but their stranglehold over the city continues. And they succeed because no one knows they exist, not as a group. Most of these people have very little to do with each other on a daily basis. You'd struggle to find two of them in the same room at the same time. And that's the secret to their success.'

'But somehow you know about them?'

'Aye,' McKenna says, sweeping water onto the floor with a flat palm. 'I know a lot of things. I've never been part of the club, so to speak, they're too good for an old lag like me, but our interests have aligned over the years and we've done occasional business together.'

'So what's changed?'

McKenna drops the pieces of glass in his hand onto the table again. 'They've gone too far. We had an agreement. The east side was mine but they're clearly not happy with that. They've started coming after my assets, closing in on my land. Building their hideous concrete monstrosities and filling them with foreign students. Ah, before much longer they'll have ripped the heart out of the place and it will be a soulless money-making machine like everywhere else. I may not have been born here but it's the city I've made my home for the past forty-five years and I want something to pass on to my lads when I've gone.'

'I'm confused. Is this a civic pride thing or good old-fashioned financial hardship?'

McKenna grins savagely. 'Let's call it a bit of both.' The

grin fades. 'It might not sound so bad to you, what's a bit of gentrification among friends, eh? But I'm telling you, what they get up to puts my old lot to shame. They're ruthless fuckers and life has no value to them. At least we used to look after people. All right, we charged them for the privilege, but it meant something. You remember that fire over Attercliffe way a year or so back?'

Tyler nods. 'The old guy who set fire to his tailoring business?' He can't remember all the details but he knows an extended family were killed in the blaze, Grandparents, parents and kids. It was a terrible tragedy, big enough to make the national news. 'Insurance job, wasn't it?'

'Aye, that's what they want you to believe. Only, I happen to know old Ranveer had had plenty of offers for his place. The sort of offers that would have kept him and his family in chapatis for years. Fact was, he didn't want to sell. He might not have been making much money but he loved that business, almost as much as he loved those poor wee grandkids who died in the fire.'

'You're saying this Circle killed him and his family?'

'I'm saying Ranveer's place was the last open business on that block. Now the whole site's being redeveloped. There'll be a Tesco Superstore there by the end of the year, you mark my words.'

'There's no way they could get away with that.'

'They can if your Superintendent decides that it's case closed.'

Tyler shakes his head. Despite all the evidence they've

amassed on Stevens' activities, he can't believe it. 'But the fire brigade would be involved too, surely they would know—'

'You think Stevens is the only one? They have people everywhere. Ranveer and me went way back. He'd been paying me for protection since the 90s and I'm telling you he'd slit his own throat before he'd put those grandkiddies of his in any danger.' McKenna's mouth curls in disgust. 'When they threatened him he trusted me to protect him. I thought I could trust them to keep to our agreement but in the end they did whatever the hell benefited them the most.'

Tyler shakes his head again. 'Assuming I believe this tall tale, what's all this got to do with Tina?'

'It hasn't,' McKenna says. 'Not directly. It's to do with you.'

'Me?'

'What happened with Ranveer was the last straw. That's what made me come to you. I needed them to go away. Or at least, to be so preoccupied with their own affairs they backed off from interfering in mine. So I threw you a bone last year, hoping you'd pounce. Unfortunately for me, you were a bad puppy.'

'The folder.'

'The conspiracy your father was looking into was the Circle. He only had one part of the picture though. Stevens. He's been their man since the beginning, shutting down cases they didn't want investigating, arranging for evidence to disappear when necessary. Your father picked up on it and came to me. I did my best to warn him off but it was too late.'

'They had him killed.'

'And now they know I've been talking to you. I've had a few warnings, a few shots across the bow as it were, but I never thought they'd go as far as to go after Tina. Not really. I knew there was a chance they'd come for me but . . . well, they wouldn't be the first.'

'Did Stevens kill my father?'

McKenna leans back against the wall and sighs. 'That wee pisspot? No, he couldn't even bring himself to wring the neck of your godmother, could he?' Tyler steps forward. 'No offence. No, the man's a long streak of piss and no mistake. They have a gopher for that sort of thing. A fixer. A hired assassin. They call him the ICER. In Case of Emergency, Ring. The fuckers have a warped, if underdeveloped sense of humour. He's called in when they need . . . extreme measures to be taken.'

'A hired killer? Seriously?'

'Do I look like I'm joking, man? If he's got Tina . . .'

'McKenna, do you have any proof of this?'

'All the proof I had went in the folder I gave your DCI Jordan. Nothing about the ICER, but as much as I could dig up on Stevens and his exploits. I hoped it would be enough to put you on their trail. And now, if they find out I've told you this . . . Ach, we'll worry about that later. For now, all I care about is Tina.'

Tyler really has no idea how much of this to believe. It all seems a bit far-fetched but on the other hand, it fits with what he knows already. When he and Doggett began look- ing into Richard's conspiracy they went over every case file he had been re-examining and could find no link between them. But if what McKenna says is true there wouldn't be. Yes, Stevens was the one running interference on the cases but not for himself, not even for one other person but on behalf of a range of masters with a variety of interests. It fits.

Of course, on the other hand, it could all be designed to fit. If nothing else though he can tell one thing – McKenna really is worried, and he doubts it takes much less than the most extraordinary trouble to worry this man.

'What do you know about this ICER?'

McKenna shakes his head. 'Nothing, and that's the God's honest truth.'

Tyler's not convinced. 'You're going to have to come in and make a statement.'

McKenna laughs. 'Don't be fucking daft, lad.'

'It's the only way I can protect you. And Tina. And if what you say is true—'

'Of course it's true! Do I look like a fantasist?'

'*If* what you say is true, then the best way to make sure you're not a target anymore is for other people to know the truth. If this Circle are as fixated on secrecy as you say then once the secret's out they'll have no reason to come after you.'

McKenna leans forward and picks up the rubber ball, brushes it clean of glass fragments. 'If I tell you any of this officially I'll be dead or disappeared within hours, trust me. They have eyes everywhere. Among your lot, in the prisons, even among my crew.' He glances out the window, moving aside a lace net curtain with one meaty hand. 'And when they decide to act they don't piss about. After I spoke with your father, three of my best lads disappeared within a week. And I never even told him anything.'

'I really don't know how I can help then. I can't use official resources to look for Tina without a reason.'

McKenna squeezes the ball hard. 'Damn it, man! I came to you because I don't know who I can trust anymore, can't you see that? Nathaniel, Mick . . . even that pillock, Danny.' He waves a hand in the general direction of the front door. 'He's less than feckin' useless but he's been with me for years. I always thought he was loyal to a fault but . . . I just don't know anymore. I . . . I don't know what I'd do if anything happened to her . . . She's all I've got left now. She's the only one I can trust.'

Tyler refrains from pointing out that McKenna has any number of children and grandchildren as well. Surely, he could surround himself with people he could trust if he wanted to . . . A sudden thought occurs to Tyler. 'When did you find out Tina was missing?'

'I told you, man, this morning. She's supposed to check in every four hours but she was gone when—'

'And you sent everyone out to look for her?'

'Everyone except Danny and Mick.'

Tyler moves to the window next to the front door and inches back the fussy net curtain. 'Where are they now?'

'Mick'll be parking the car and then he'll head upstairs until I need him. He has a place over the garage.'

'And Danny?'

'What are you getting at?'

'I'm saying, if someone wanted to get to you, what would be the ideal way to make sure you had minimal security around you?'

McKenna's tossing the rubber ball up and down in his hand and frowning. 'Aye. I'm with you, but—' McKenna fumbles the ball and they both jerk their arms in an effort to catch it. Tyler isn't sure which he hears first, the *phut phut* of the bullets firing, or the screech of exploding glass that shreds the net curtain. He feels something rip into his arm and turns instinctively, diving to the floor. The bullets slam into the plaster behind McKenna but the man's already falling, blood arcing from his shoulder.

Tyler sees the black shape of the muzzle beginning to poke through the nets, aiming directly for McKenna. He jumps up, ignoring the pain in his arm, and throws himself at the gun. Even as his hands close on the killer's arm, there's another double tap – *phut phut* – and the door to their left showers fragments of wood over McKenna's head.

'Stay down,' Tyler shouts, as he wrestles with the gun. He slams the killer's wrist against the jagged glass and hears the guy grunt. There's a *click, click, click* as the chamber empties and then something slams hard into the left side of Tyler's face. He loses his grip and the arm and the gun withdraw. Tyler's head is pounding and his vision blurred but he turns in time to see the man running away from the house, dressed entirely in black, the silenced pistol still in his hand. He turns, still dazed, to check on McKenna. The gangster's lying on his side, clutching his bloodied left shoulder.

'Get after him, man! I'm fine!'

Tyler grabs the door handle and runs out into the night, his shoes tearing into the gravel. But as the blood starts pumping through his veins he becomes aware of the aching pain in his left arm even over the ringing in his head. He glances down to see the blood pooling on his shirt. It's just a graze though; if it wasn't it would hurt a lot more. Ahead of him the figure reaches the end of the driveway and launches itself at the metal gate. Tyler begins to gain ground as the figure scales the gate, but as he drops down the other side, the black-clad assassin notices his pursuer for the first time. The gun comes up in one level movement and Tyler dives to his right. He hears the sound of the silenced gun crack in the cold night air — somehow the guy must have reloaded as he ran — and then he's hitting the icy ground and rolling, the pain in his arm sending shockwaves through his body. There's some scrubby bushes running the length of the driveway and he rolls behind them in the hope they'll give him some cover.

He comes to a stop, lying on his back in the snow and panting for a moment before he flips himself over onto his stomach and peers up towards the gate. The figure is gone. Tyler gets slowly to his feet and jogs carefully down the rest of the drive, clutching his injured arm and using the trees for cover where he can, ready to dive at the first sound of anything even vaguely like a gun firing. Using the big walled gate post for cover he looks out through the bars. Despite the darkness he can see pretty well onto the well-lit street and there's no sign of their attacker. He could have taken off in any direction now and the ground is too frozen to reveal any tracks.

Tyler runs back to the house still nursing his arm. He thinks about McKenna's story. It's still possible the whole thing is a load of nonsense that the man's made up for unknown reasons of his own, but if he has, then staging an attempt on his own life seems like overkill. Not beyond the realms of possibility though.

But as he reaches the house to find McKenna on the porch he can see the raw fear in the man's eyes. Unless McKenna is a brilliant actor, this wasn't staged.

Danny comes stumbling across the driveway clutching at his head.

McKenna screams at him. 'Where the *fuck* were you?'

'Sorry, boss, I . . .' He pulls a bloodied hand away and looks at it. 'You said to . . . The fucker must have clocked me . . .' He falls to his knees on the gravel.

'Shit!' McKenna says, and then, as Tyler pulls out his mobile, 'What the fuck are you doing? No polis!'

'McKenna, there were shots fired. Besides, we need an ambulance. The only way you're keeping this quiet is to kill me.'

Even in his dazed state Danny manages to raise himself to one knee and shoots a questioning look at his boss, and for a moment McKenna hesitates. Tyler wonders briefly if he's pushed things too far but then McKenna's body language relaxes.

'Feck!' he shouts, and winces as the movement jolts his shoulder. 'Get Mick out here, I need the two of you to . . . clean up a bit.' His eyes flick towards Tyler and then he disappears into the house.

But Tyler's not interested in whatever else the man's hiding. As he presses the call button and raises the mobile to his ear he's only thinking of one thing. Did he really just meet his father's killer? And, more importantly, did he let him get away?

day five

The ICER recordings #115

(Archivists' note: This is the first female voice catalogued and appears to be a new recruit of some kind. As such we have catalogued her as Unknown Caller 5. Given her close connection to Stevens she remains a person of strong interest [04/05/18])

Call received: 06:59 Friday 9th Mar 2018

Duration: 1 minute 58 seconds

Partial Transcript:

ICER   Yes.

UC5   This is ... er ... well, I was told not to use any names but ...

(recording is silent for 2 seconds)

ICER   How did you get this number?

UC5   They said I should ring you direct if there was any more information about the incident at the lake the other day.

ICER   You're Stevens' colleague?

UC5   I thought we weren't supposed to—

ICER   Yes, all right. From now on you're P2.

UC5   Eh?

ICER   Stevens was P1. That makes you P2.

UC5   Oh, right, yeah. Cool.

ICER   What's the information?

UC5   Right, yeah. A woman rang the helpline. We put a sign up near the reservoir for anyone with information pertaining to—

ICER   Yes, thank you. I'm aware of how these things work.

UC5   Right. So ... anyway, this woman rings in, says she saw someone running from the reservoir. Early hours of the morning. Reckons she was moving like a bat out of hell.

ICER   Description?

UC5   What?

ICER   Is there a description of the girl?

UC5   How d'you know it was a girl?

ICER   (*pause 2 seconds*) Listen to me, P2. I know all sorts of things and though I don't know it yet, it really wouldn't be hard for me to find out your identity. Understood?

UC5I   ... Yeah, yeah, man. No worries. It's all good. So yeah, description. Young, teenager, the woman reckoned.

Skinny, shaved head. Thought maybe she had her ears pierced but wasn't sure. Dressed in jeans and some sort of boots, and a fleece.

ICER   Yes, that's her.

UC5   You knew? Shit! You never said anything about a witness. If we'd known I could have—

ICER   Is that everything?

UC5   No, one more thing. The woman thought she knew who the girl was. Couldn't remember her first name but she knew the mother from way back. Name of Darke, with an e on the end. Is that helpful?

(recording is silent for 5 seconds)

Hello?

ICER   Tell them I'll deal with it.

UC5   They're gonna be pissed, you know that, right?

ICER   Just tell them.

UC5   So ... anything else you need, you just let me know, yeah? I mean, I know Stev– P1 let you down a bit on that last business but I'm here now so, you know, we're good, yeah? Any more info you need, you just give me a ring and—

Call ends 07:01

It's a little after midnight and Tyler shivers in the early morning air. They've sent two ambulances, one for him and one for McKenna. The paramedics have patched up his arm. The wound isn't all that serious but they make noises about the risk of tetanus when he refuses to go to the hospital. He promises he'll follow things up with his GP.

McKenna's wound is a little more serious. The bullet passed right through his left shoulder but he too refuses to go to the hospital. He claims to be waiting for news about his beloved Tina, and makes several loud exclamations about her welfare. In truth, Tyler thinks his main concern is allowing the police unfettered access to his home. There has been no sign of Danny and Mick since he sent them off on some unknown errand and Tyler suspects they are busy removing anything from the property that might cause McKenna embarrassment.

Uniform were the first to arrive but McKenna's lawyers weren't all that far behind and so far no police officer or forensics technician has made it any further into the house than the hallway where the shooting happened.

'Well, well, well. You don't half manage to land yourself in it, don't you?' Toddy says when he arrives, a big grin plastered across his face.

'I didn't expect Professional Standards to be here quite so quickly. Good news travels fast.'

'Mate, when you're involved, the Gaffer likes to know about it *before* it happens. So in this case, I'm late.'

'Noted.'

'Do you want to tell me why *you're* here?'

'I invited him, Detective . . . ?' McKenna shouts from his perch. He's sitting on the step at the back of the ambulance. After a valiant effort to convince McKenna he should go to the hospital, the bearded paramedic has been forced to settle for applying a field dressing but doesn't look happy about it. Tyler follows Todd over to them and the paramedic withdraws to talk to his colleagues.

'DS Todd.'

'Aye, pleasure, I'm sure. I contacted DS Tyler because I was worried about my girlfriend.' McKenna gives Todd an expurgated account of their relationship, including the connection between him and Tyler's father. It's close enough to the truth but leaves a wide area of wriggle room.

Toddy nods along as though he doesn't believe a word of it and then looks to Tyler for confirmation. Tyler says nothing and thankfully Toddy doesn't push it but heads off to negotiate with the lawyers.

A taxi drives through the open gates and pulls up by the house. A blonde twenty-something gets out with her arms full of packages and begins shouting at the uniformed officer who tries to stop her. 'What the fuck? This is my fucking house!' followed by 'Oh, my God!' when she sees McKenna.

Tyler waves at the officer to allow her through and she rushes to McKenna, shedding her shopping bags as she goes. He seems genuinely relieved to see her. Whatever else the man is or isn't, he's loyal to his women.

'Jesus! Thank God!' McKenna says, wincing as she throws her arms around him.

After some fraught negotiation with the unpaid taxi driver and hurried explanations all round it turns out that Tina has been visiting her mother in Scarborough all day.

'But why didn't you tell me, you daft wee lass?'

'What?' Tina looks confused. 'But ... it were your idea. Nate said you needed me out of the house for the day. He dropped me off and told me not to come back until the morning. I'm only back now because me and mam had a row.'

'Nathaniel? That fucking ... !'

'I'm sorry, baby.' Tina looks on the edge of tears. She checks her watch. 'It is technically morning ...'

'Don't worry, hun, eh? It's just ... Why didn't you answer your phone?'

'I ... I lost it. I mean ... I thought I had it with me but then I couldn't find it. I must have left it in the car. Oh baby, I'm so sorry. I didn't mean to do anything wrong.' Then the tears break and the young woman begins to cry, her inflated lips quivering in time with her partially exposed chest. She begs forgiveness for whatever transgressions she has committed while McKenna does his best to soothe and reassure her.

It's a convincing display, the level of hysteria pitched just right for someone who's suffered the shock of coming home to find their loved one seriously injured. But it's not lost on Tyler that she's one of those individuals who manages not to look ugly when she cries, and the whole performance would be a great deal more believable if it wasn't all over so quickly. At McKenna's insistence Tina gathers up her shopping and prepares to head into the house.

'This is still a crime scene, McKenna. She'll have to stop somewhere else.'

McKenna shoots him daggers but Tyler holds his ground. 'Fine,' he says, eventually. 'Tina, love. We'll get a hotel room for the night. Just hang fire a minute, eh, lass?'

'But what about my shopping?' Tina demands.

'Well, we'll take that with us.'

This seems to do the trick and McKenna ends up showered in another volley of kisses.

'Who's this Nathaniel?' Tyler asks after the barrage of affection dries up and Tina agrees to go and wait in the unpaid taxi. 'He's got some questions to answer.'

McKenna shakes his head and spits on the ground. 'Aye, the wee *bastard*! He must have taken her phone this morning. That fucker'll be long gone by now. Whatever they paid him better be worth it 'cos he's not gonna have long to enjoy it.'

McKenna suddenly sways to the left and Tyler grabs his right arm to steady him. 'I'm fine.' McKenna brushes the hand away.

Tyler calls back the paramedic who tries again to get McKenna to go to hospital. 'Mate, you could have internal bleeding.' He turns to Tyler as ally. 'I can get some TXA in him here if he lets me cannulate but he really needs to be looked at properly.'

McKenna glances at the house.

'Don't worry,' Tyler tells him. 'I'm sure your lawyers will keep us out.'

Finally McKenna nods. 'Where's Danny? I'm not leaving Tina alone and there's no way she'll wanna go to a hospital.'

Danny is found chatting up a young female paramedic who has helped patch up the back of his head and, despite his earlier worries as to the man's loyalty, McKenna now seems content enough to leave Tina in his hands. Tyler watches as the taxi heads away down the driveway followed by the first of the two ambulances. At the gate it narrowly avoids a front-end collision with Doggett's battered Saab.

'You all right?' Doggett asks, noting the padded dressing on Tyler's arm as he gets out of the car.

'He got away.'

'He?' Doggett turns back to look at the ambulance disappearing at the end of the road.

'That's McKenna. It's not too serious as far as I can tell but it might mess up his golf swing for a while. I meant the shooter.'

'Who was he?'

Tyler looks round. 'There's a lot we need to discuss,' he says quietly. 'But not here.'

'Yeah,' Doggett says, still watching the ambulance's rear lights fading into the darkness. 'More than you realise.'

Tyler looks at him but the DI shakes his head. 'Like you

said, not here.' Doggett frowns down at Tyler's injured arm again. 'So who was the target?'

'McKenna. Probably.'

'What about Diane?'

'I thought of that. They've taken the twenty-four hour watch off her so I called Rabbani.' It had been the second call he'd made after phoning in the shooting. 'She texted me twenty minutes ago to tell me she was there and everything was fine. She'll stay until I can get there.'

Doggett lets out a breath of relieved air. 'Okay, well it looks to me like you're taking a turn for the worse. It's my informed opinion you better head to Casualty too, get yourself properly looked at.' He arches an eyebrow at the second ambulance.

'I can't just leave.'

'You can if I say so. We need to talk before you get hauled in to see Franklin again.' He nods towards Toddy, watching them silently from the front door of the house. 'If he's here then his boss isn't going to be far behind. Get yourself checked out and then get home and get some sleep.'

'What about Diane?'

'I'll get some Uniforms on her. Franklin said we could have some extra hands, didn't she? Let's make the most of it. I'll be round early doors so we can put our heads together before the shit properly hits the fan.'

'That good, eh?' Tyler nods. 'Listen, one more thing. I asked the forensics lot to go over that broken window, there's a chance the guy cut himself while we were struggling.

We could have his DNA. Make sure it happens and that it's logged properly.'

Doggett frowns again. 'All right, I'm on it.'

'And bring Rabbani with you.'

'Really?'

'She knows what we've been up to. I've told her everything.'

'Fair enough. You sure you want her involved in this though? Could get messy.'

Tyler hesitates. 'Yes,' he says. 'I trust her, and I think we need her.'

'Right then,' says Doggett. 'See you in the morning.'

'It is morning.'

Tyler suspects that he gets his tetanus booster far quicker than the average civvy would but he's not about to complain about dodging a long night trapped in A&E. While he's at the hospital, he takes the opportunity to check on Diane, slipping up the back stairwell he used before. Rabbani's already gone but there are two young uniformed officers in her place. He vaguely recognises them and they take great pains to let him know what a good job they're doing. They're pretty wet behind the ears, which Tyler reckons is probably good thinking on Doggett's part. Less chance they're corrupt if they haven't had time to become disenchanted with the job. And with two officers, the chances of them both being bent are lesser still.

At home he manages to get a few hours' sleep until just

after five when he wakes to the sound of screaming. He leaps out of bed and rushes into the spare room to find Jude thrashing beneath the duvet.

'Hey, hey!' Tyler tries to wake him gently but Jude's lost in a world of past pain. His forehead is soaked in sweat and he's muttering to himself, the words unintelligible. Then he screams again and sits bolt upright with his eyes wide. He flinches slightly as he sees Tyler standing over him.

Slowly Jude comes back to himself. 'Sorry, mate,' he says after a minute or so. 'Did I wake you? What time is it?'

'Early. Don't worry about it, just get yourself back to sleep.'

Jude nods and Tyler leaves him be, but it's less than ten minutes before his brother follows him out into the living room. Tyler gets out another mug and makes them both some coffee.

'Does that happen a lot?' he asks as they sit together watching the city skyline lit by the setting moon.

'Pretty much every night,' Jude says, and smiles weakly. 'I don't sleep a lot these days.'

'Maybe you should get some help.'

'Been there, done that, bro'. Bought the T-shirt and woke up with it wringing in sweat.'

Tyler lets it go for now. Jude gets up.

'Where you headed?'

'Just gonna have a quick shower if that's all right? I've got an interview this morning, figured I'd get some prep in, you know, research the company and all that?'

'That's brilliant, Jude! Congratulations.'

'Yeah, well, it's just a part-time security thing.' He shrugs. 'I haven't got it yet.'

'Anything I can do to help?'

'Not unless you know the manager.'

'I meant . . . do you need any cash or—'

'I'm fine,' Jude says a little too quickly.

'Sure. Okay.'

Jude slips out of the apartment an hour or so later without saying goodbye, leaving Tyler to wonder if he's said the wrong thing again.

Doggett and Rabbani arrive together just before seven, Rabbani clutching a tray of steaming coffees and a paper bag of pastries.

'How's the arm?' Doggett asks as they gather around Tyler's couch.

'Fine.'

He takes them through the events of the previous evening, detailing what McKenna told him about Richard and the hired assassin.

Doggett whistles loudly through his front teeth when Tyler's finished. 'That's one tall story.'

'Meaning you don't believe him?'

'About his relationship with your dad? Yeah, that much I can believe. Your dad had a few informants he never let on about. And their paths would certainly have crossed back in the day when Richard was helping to bring down McKenna's gang. So that much tallies. But a shady conglomerate operating behind the scenes? Arranging the city to their own

305

requirements. Well, it's possible I suppose but I don't see how it puts us any further ahead, given that he's offering no proof.'

'Rabbani?'

She looks shocked that he's asked. 'Er . . . I guess. I dunno.'

'Come on, Mina. We said we'd be honest with each other.'

Rabbani crosses her arms in that familiar defensive position she manages so well. 'Fine. It sounds like a load of bullshit to me.'

Doggett grins. 'No, come on, lass, tell us what you really think.'

'Don't *lass* me! I'm just saying, it sounds pretty convenient that he tells you this story about a killer and then they come for him while you're there.'

'That thought did occur to me,' Doggett says.

Tyler shakes his head. 'He was scared. He wasn't faking it.'

Rabbani tuts. 'That doesn't mean this killer had anything to do with your dad's death. Maybe McKenna told you that to get you involved.'

Doggett inclines his head in agreement. 'It wouldn't be the first time McKenna told you what you wanted to hear to get something from you though, would it?'

Rabbani frowns. 'What does that mean?'

'That's not important right now,' Tyler says, and when Rabbani opens her mouth to object he adds, 'I'm not saying I won't tell you, just that we don't have time right now.' If he has to explain the full details of McKenna's involvement in the Botanical Gardens case last year, they'll still be at it when Franklin arrives to arrest him. Not to mention the fact that if Rabbani finds out just how much he kept from her back then she might decide to re-evaluate this new détente they've reached.

'Still,' Doggett says, 'Mina's right. McKenna could well have his own motivations for dragging you into all this again and muddying the waters. There's something you don't know yet which might make you re-examine what he's told you.'

Tyler lifts his hands. 'Go on.'

'We finally got the DNA results back from the blood spatter we found at the boatshed.'

'And?'

Doggett hesitates. 'It's Stevens'.'

There's a palpable silence in the room and then Rabbani says, 'So . . . you mean . . . he's dead?'

Doggett nods. 'Unless he walked out of that boatshed leaving half his brain matter behind then yes. No cosy South American retirement for the Superintendent after all.'

Tyler tries to work this into what they know. 'Stevens panics when Diane turns up at his door with McKenna's folder. He tries to kill her but he bottles it. Who does he call for help?'

'The Circle,' Rabbani says.

'Right. Maybe they tell him they'll get him out, first class ticket to South America to visit his family. But instead they call in this ICER to clean house for them. Stevens knows too much and Professional Standards are already investigating what he's been up to.'

'How could the Circle know that, though?' Rabbani

asks as she tucks into a croissant. 'I mean, we didn't even know that.'

'They've got people everywhere, according to McKenna.' He doesn't name her but a glance at Doggett tells him they're both thinking of Franklin.

'Hang on, though.' Rabbani brushes the crumbs from her fingers. 'Wouldn't the ICER . . .' She stumbles over the thought. 'Wouldn't he have . . . dealt with DCI Jordan as well?'

'She was in the cellar,' Tyler tells her, 'the door hidden by a dresser. I think that ultimately Stevens couldn't go through with it. He left her with bottles of water. Why do that if he didn't expect her to be found? Diane told me she heard him talking to someone.'

Unless the voice she'd heard was Franklin paying Stevens a visit. Diane had seemed adamant it was a man's voice but she had also been pretty out of it. Professional Standards seemed to have taken Franklin's explanation of her visit at face value and so had Diane. Tyler just wishes he could.

'I'd like to think Stevens had a change of heart,' Rabbani says. 'Maybe he told the ICER he'd already got rid of her body, and then later he was going to ring in a tip about her once he got safely to the airport?'

'Only he didn't make it that far.'

Doggett shakes his head violently. 'Listen to yourselves. Maybe this, suppose that. The man's got you thinking on his terms already. The Circle? Hired assassins? More likely McKenna was the one involved with Stevens. Maybe that's what your dad found out and it's McKenna who's cleaning house. What about this Danny fella? Maybe he shoots at you and McKenna, legs it, doubles back and then bashes himself on the head to make it look like he's a victim as well.'

'That's ridiculous!'

'Hey, I'm just saying we can all play make-believe.'

Tyler thinks about it. He supposes there might just have been enough time but ... 'It would have been too tight.' McKenna had been a bit inconsistent, worrying about the loyalty of his lieutenants one minute and then sending his beloved Tina off with Danny the next. Was that just because he'd already found out Nathaniel was the informant and so he assumed the rest of his men were loyal, or because he'd set the whole thing up in the first place to throw them off the scent? Nathaniel could have been in on the whole thing, even Tina could have been. But the figure that ran away from him was slighter in build than Danny. Wasn't he? He knows what Doggett would say to that. It was dark, the bloke was shooting at you, you were injured and distracted ... He winces at a sudden stabbing sensation from his arm. He doesn't know what to think anymore.

'You think I'm crazy for believing McKenna, is that it?'

'No one thinks you're crazy,' Rabbani says, and Doggett wiggles his head back and forth as if to say, *the jury's still out on that one.*

'All right,' Tyler says, trying a more conciliatory tone. 'Let's go back over it. What was Stevens up to? If you look at all the cases Richard was looking into there's nothing they have in common. We should know,' he says directly to Doggett, 'we've been looking at them for more than a year now. You've been looking into them for a decade or more. The whole point of the problem we had was that they don't correlate – kidnappings, robberies, murders, missing people. They can't all be for the benefit of one person, certainly not Stevens, and not McKenna either. Not to mention the fact we have nothing linking McKenna to any of them.'

'That doesn't mean there isn't a link,' Doggett reminds him.

'I'm just saying that if we start from the hypothesis that these cases remaining unsolved might benefit a *group* of people, rather than just one, then perhaps there is a way to draw links between them. Richard told you he was looking into a conspiracy. We assumed that meant a conspiracy on the force but what if it didn't? What if it was this Circle? A conspiracy of business people.'

Doggett nods as though conceding the point but then turns it around. 'And Stevens could equally have been working for a number of different people. We know he was bent. There's no reason to assume he was only taking backhanders from one person. Maybe he made a habit of it. It finally caught up with him and one of them got rid of him.'

'And left a frozen corpse behind at his murder site?' Rabbani asks. 'That's the bit none of us have an answer for. If the ICER – or McKenna – killed Stevens why do it in the boatshed and then cart his body away leaving Jake Baker in his place? All we've got are *hypotheses*.' She puts extra emphasis on the last word as though trying to point out that she can use big words too. 'Okay, you don't like maybes,' she tells Doggett. 'Let's forget the theories then, and focus on what we do next.'

'She has a point,' Doggett says. 'When did you get so wise?'

'When I was running around after you two muppets.'

'What about the story McKenna told me about the tailor whose business was torched?' Tyler says. 'That's something we could look into. Who benefitted?'

Doggett nods. 'I can take a look at that. You're going to have enough on your plate today.'

Tyler turns and walks over to the window. 'How much shit am I in?'

Doggett huffs. 'A fair bit, I should imagine. They can't prove you've done anything wrong but you *were* at the home of a known criminal when someone tried to shoot him. Professional Standards are gonna want to rake you over the coals about that.'

Tyler turns back. 'Suspension?'

'Maybe. But doubtful as long as you give a semi-reasonable account of yourself.'

'No pressure then.'

'Mind you, given that the case is now officially linked to Stevens, there's a chance they'll take over completely. Try to keep things impartial.'

Tyler places his hand over the dressing on his arm, putting pressure on it and taking perverse pleasure in the pain. 'Or try to cover it all up.'

'So what *do* we do now?' Rabbani asks.

'Same thing we always do,' Doggett tells her. 'We work the case anyway.'

Rabbani fixes him with that long-suffering expression she manages so well, a sort of half sigh, half eye-roll with a liberal dose of contempt. 'We should tell ACC Franklin what we've found out. We can't keep this from her.'

'No,' Doggett says, 'we don't know how far we can trust her.'

'I still can't work out how she recognised the Demeter uniform so quickly,' Tyler says. 'Unless someone sent her a photo from the reservoir?' He glances at Rabbani.

She hurries to shake her head. 'DS Vaughan,' she says. 'She was at the crime scene, and I saw her that evening when I went to meet Franklin. I guess I'm not the only one she promised to help.' Her cheeks flush crimson.

Doggett tuts loudly. 'I'll have to keep an eye on that one. Still, that doesn't let Franklin off the hook. And even if we do trust her, we don't know how many others Stevens had in his pocket.'

Tyler sometimes wonders if Doggett says the opposite of whatever anyone suggests just out of some kind of principle. 'Now you sound like you believe in McKenna's Circle.'

'I never said it wasn't possible, just unlikely. It makes sense to assume the worst.'

'But we have to trust someone, sooner or later!' Rabbani crosses her arms again.

'Maybe,' Doggett goes on. 'But at the moment we have

one advantage. Professional Standards don't know that you know what we know.'

Rabbani frowns. 'What?'

'All the cases Richard was looking into were cold cases. That means even if Tyler's suspended, or we get shunted, there's nothing stopping you looking at them.'

'Now, hang on—'

'Maybe you can see something we couldn't.'

'He's right, Mina,' Tyler tells her. 'We need to prove that McKenna's Circle exists before we go to anyone with this. Otherwise it's just a story made up by some old crook with an axe to grind. If you can work out who benefitted from Stevens' attempts to muddy the waters, then maybe we'll know who to look at more closely.'

Tyler watches Rabbani thinking it through. That's what makes her such a good copper, he realises. This habit she's developing for examining every angle before rushing in. It's the opposite way to the way he usually works but maybe that's not such a bad thing.

'All right,' she says. 'I'll look at the cases, but if I don't find anything we take the lot to Franklin. Promise me.'

Tyler sees Doggett gently shaking his head.

'Fine,' he tells her. 'I promise.'

Mina has the new office to herself for the first time and is enjoying the peace and quiet after the frenzied hubbub of the Murder Room. Doggett's taken himself off to look into the arson attack and as far as she knows Tyler's still making statements to Professional Standards. She hopes that isn't a bad sign.

She hasn't officially been taken off the robbery so she's nervous at first, looking into cases that essentially have nothing to do with the case they're supposed to be investigating. But she's seen no sign of Franklin all day and suspects that even if she did, Mina is way down her list of priorities by this point. Franklin got what she wanted from her and now she's moved on.

There's not much to the case files themselves given that Stevens shut them down before they could really get going. There are seven in total, eight if you count the robbery at Demeter Fabrications. She can see where Doggett and Tyler might have tried drawing parallels between the lives of the victims – this robbery happened in a similar part of the city to the school that child attended, a young boy left for dead on the railway tracks might have gone to the same school as the sister of a sex worker who was strangled under the Wicker arches. But it isn't hard to draw connections in a city like Sheffield; it might have a huge population but the city centre itself is small and its people's lives crisscross each other like the footprints in the snow she saw on her way in this morning. The connections are spurious at best and Mina reckons she could probably come up with a dozen more if she let herself get drawn into their crusade, all of which would probably turn out to be equally useless. No wonder the two of them never took this further up the chain, their reluctance perhaps born out of lack of evidence rather than concern over Richard Tyler's so-called 'conspiracy'. There's just nothing that seems to link these cases together, any more so than she might link them to any other case they've looked into over the years. Not the slightest sign of conspiracy other than the fact that each of the cases was ultimately overseen by Superintendent Roger Stevens and, since he oversaw pretty much everything, that doesn't mean anything either.

Mina sighs. It's still early days. Tyler and Doggett have been working on this for a year; did she really expect to find the answer after a couple of hours? She leans back in her chair and throws her head back, working the muscles in her neck. She can't believe the Eel is really dead. It's a relief as much as anything and that thought shames her to her core. Her mother wouldn't approve of such an immoral thought. But after Doggett's announcement, she realised just how much she'd been living in fear over the past few months. Ever since last year when the case they'd been working on brought her into contact with the disgraced Suzanne Cooper. Cooper had told her that Stevens effectively ordered an end into her investigation of the disappearance of a young international student. She intimated that it wasn't the only time he'd messed with her too, and then, when she was involved in another disappearance and the missing boy had turned up dead, Stevens had hung her out to dry, a convenient scapegoat for the media.

It was this information Mina had taken to Franklin when she arrived, after Tyler and Doggett had steadfastly attempted to throw her off the scent (at least she knew the reason for that now, though if they went on acting like she was some kind of delicate flower who needed protecting they'd be hearing about it). She'd taken the info to Franklin, not because she felt some moral obligation to report wrong-doing – even *she* wasn't that naïve – nor because she thought it would give her a leg up the ladder as Franklin's protégé. Not really. She'd done it because she was scared of him. DCI Jordan was missing, she couldn't talk to Tyler or Doggett, and she'd never felt so alone. Had she had some inkling, even then, of what he was capable of? Surely not. And yet something about Stevens terrified her and for that reason she couldn't be sorry he was dead.

Of course, if she carried that thought through to its ultimate conclusion then there was someone else out there who was even scarier, and that person was whoever splattered Stevens' brains across the wall of the boatshed. McKenna's ICER? A hired gun who worked for the great and not so good of Sheffield. The idea was ridiculous but not impossible. There were plenty of hitmen out there, some of whom could be hired for as little as a few hundred quid. Maybe less, if they were desperate enough for the cash. But they were amateurs and invariably got caught when they made stupid mistakes. Whereas, if McKenna was to be believed – and who the hell would believe a semi-reformed gangster? – then this man, or woman, had been operating under the radar for at least the past sixteen years.

That was another thing that bothered her. Joey McKenna. She'd heard the stories, of course. The old guard around the station loved telling tales of the good old days in the 80s and 90s when men were men, and there was honour among thieves, and there was no political correctness or snowflake politics. Thankfully these people were few and far between nowadays. She used to think Doggett was one of them but he turned out to be a far more complex version of the classic misogynistic bastard.

But Joey McKenna was a living fossil from an epoch that, up until now, Mina had only ever experienced on TV detective shows. And then she finds out that Tyler has a working relationship with the man. What else has he not been telling her? On their way into work this morning, and after a great deal of cajoling from her, Tyler had filled her in on McKenna's involvement in the missing student case last year. She'd sat there in stony silence trying to take it all in but she just couldn't believe that all the time she was busy investigating, he was off chatting to gangsters. She'd had no idea.

Cooper. There's something about that case that's niggling away at the back of her mind. Cooper told her that Stevens had intervened and told her to stop investigating the girl's disappearance. Did that make *that* case one of Richard Tyler's 'conspiracy' cases as well? Of course, the events took place long after he was dead but that doesn't mean it isn't connected. They'd assumed at the time that Stevens had shut down the case at the behest of the girl's father, a high-level diplomat in China who was unwilling to lose face with the Party. But McKenna also had a reason for the police investigation to go away quietly. After all, it was his money the girl had stolen.

Tyler wouldn't like that. It only added to Doggett's preferred theory that McKenna was behind all of this. Maybe they didn't have to look all that far for Stevens' killer after all.

Mina taps the desk with her pen and stares at the board in front of her without really seeing it. Then she picks up her mobile, finds the relevant number and presses the call button.

She doesn't think Cooper will answer and even if she does, the last time they'd spoken hadn't ended well and she'd received a ticking off from Jordan about her attitude. Still. That was months ago now, surely—

'Hello.'

'DCI Cooper? It's DC Mina Rabbani here, we spoke last year.'

There's a short pause and then Cooper says, 'I remember you.'

Mina's not sure exactly how the woman means it but she presses on. 'Look, I'm sorry to bother you, I know you've got a lot going on . . .'

Cooper breathes out a laugh, a bitter, hollow sound that Mina imagines has nothing to do with the quality of the line.

'I thought . . .' Mina begins, and then worries that perhaps she shouldn't be making this call. *Too late now.* 'I thought you'd want to know that Superintendent Stevens is dead.'

The silence goes on for so long that Mina wonders if Cooper has hung up but then, just at the point she determines to speak, the DI responds. 'You're sure?'

And Mina knows that she guessed right. Cooper's feelings are not so far removed from her own. 'We haven't found his body yet but they scraped up enough of his blood and brains to make it pretty concrete.'

This time the laugh sounds lighter. 'Good. Good riddance.'

Cooper's bitterness is so palpable that, again, it makes Mina question her own morality. 'Anyway,' she says, 'I don't know how this affects your case.' She's not even sure what's happening with Cooper. The last she'd heard the woman was suspended pending an investigation. 'But I thought you'd want to know.'

'Yes. Thank you.' Cooper's voice is noticeably brighter. Mina can almost hear the woman's brain ticking over, thoughts processing one after the other as to how this affects her and her chances of reinstatement. Assuming she wants to be reinstated. Mina really doesn't know her well enough to say.

'I thought ... well, Professional Standards are looking into Stevens in a pretty big way and ... maybe if you came forward now, with what you know. I mean, it could only help your own case, right?'

Again there's a silence while Cooper processes this. 'I'll think about it,' she says.

'Okay, well. That was all, I guess.' She thinks about telling Cooper not to mention where she got her information from but that seems cowardly. If she gets into trouble for this, so be it.

'Mina,' Cooper says. 'Thank you for letting me know.'

'No problem.' And then, at the point she's about to hang up, the thought that's been niggling away at her jumps forward. 'Missing persons,' she says.

'What?'

'Oh, sorry, it just occurred to me. You ran the Missing Persons unit and there's a case we're looking into at the moment that wasn't on file even though the man's mother reported him missing. We think Stevens was involved again. You wouldn't know anything about it, would you? The man's name was Jake Baker.' There's another long silence and then Mina adds, 'I'm really not trying to get you in trouble here. I just thought maybe you'd remember . . .'

'No,' Cooper says sharply and Mina thinks she's fucked it up again. But then Cooper goes on. 'When was it?'

'Er . . . it would have been . . .' Mina checks the board in front of her where the gruesome picture of Jake Baker's corpse is still hanging. '2002.'

'No,' Cooper says but this time she sounds calmer. 'No, that was before my time. It's not one of mine.'

'Okay. Well, it was a long shot.

There's a brief pause and then Cooper says, 'There was another case though.'

Mina finds herself holding her breath. *Just give the woman room to speak.*

'A young woman, an Asian girl from Rotherham. Asma Ali. She disappeared in 2014.'

'And Stevens made you shelve the case?'

'Yes.' The DI's voice is small and weak. 'He said there was little-to-no evidence and it would be best if I "turned my sights to something more lucrative". Those were his exact words. But that's what he was always like, wasn't he? More bothered about results than the fact a young girl was missing and potentially in danger.'

'Can you tell me any more about the case? I'd like to take another look at it. If you don't mind?'

'You won't find it. Stevens removed the file.'

'How do you know?'

'Because I tried going back to it the following year.'

If she knew that . . . Mina tries to moderate her tone; accusing the woman of something isn't going to help matters. Even so, she can hear the judgement in her own voice. 'Why didn't you come forward? You could have proved—'

'What could I *prove*?' Cooper breathes heavily down the phone and Mina wonders for a moment if she's hung up. Then she finally speaks, her voice quiet again. 'You're right. I should have come forward but I didn't.'

The regret in her voice is palpable. Is this what started the woman down the self-destructive road she'd been on when they met last year?

'I can tell you one thing though,' Cooper says. 'The name of the man who I believe raped and murdered her. His name was Gareth Whitehouse.'

Mina's heart leaps in her chest. The first thing she thinks of is Binita. 'Cooper, you need to come in, immediately. I'm sure if you agree to tell them what you know it can only help your own position and they need to know what you've just told me.'

'I'll think about it,' Cooper says, and then she hangs up.

Tyler's back in the same boardroom facing Franklin and the unusually quiet representative from Professional Standards, Ledbetter. He realises what it is about Ledbetter that seems off. He's missing a handlebar moustache but, other than that, he's the perfect picture of the old English statesman, the retired Boer war colonel, as robust and mottled as a thick slice of gammon.

Tyler sits quietly, the wound on his arm pulsing under its dressing, and awaits the verdict as they exchange notes and whisper with each other. He can't hear them but he doubts the conversation is actually about him. It's standard procedure for unsettling him. They've already heard his story about McKenna, a variation of the truth he'd concocted with Doggett and Rabbani. That McKenna approached Tyler because of his relationship with Richard and because he was concerned that a hired killer was after his girlfriend. The three of them had decided not to mention the Circle for now but the ICER was too great a threat to keep hidden.

'Do you believe what McKenna told you?' Franklin asks eventually. 'This story about a hired assassin working with Stevens? And that this is the man who killed your father?'

Tyler thinks before answering, Doggett's voice is sharp in his head, telling him to be careful. 'I'm not sure,' he says. 'He hasn't offered any evidence to support his theory.'

'But you *do* still believe your father was murdered. And McKenna's story fits that narrative rather neatly.'

This is clearly a test of some sort. But it's one he hasn't studied for and he has no idea what the right answers are. 'Yes,' he answers honestly. 'But there are other possibilities.'

'Such as?'

He can see Doggett smiling smugly at him. 'McKenna could have killed my father. Or had him killed. Stevens might have been his man all along. Assuming this hitman who tried to kill him is real, and there's always the possibility McKenna staged the whole thing, but if he is real, they could have fallen out in some way. At any rate, I've absolutely no doubt McKenna knows more than he's saying. Perhaps he knows too much and this hitman has decided to silence him.'

Franklin turns and exchanges a look with Ledbetter, who rolls his eyes and shrugs.

'What else?' she asks.

'I'm sorry?'

'What other possibilities are there?'

Tyler knows what she's waiting for. He presses his fingernails deep into his palms. 'It's possible my father was working with McKenna and Stevens all along. That the money you found in his account when he died was a payoff for something. That he killed himself because he couldn't bear the shame.'

Again, his two inquisitors exchange a look.

'But you don't believe that,' Ledbetter says. It isn't a question.

Franklin meets Tyler's eye. 'No,' he says. 'I don't believe that. But that doesn't mean I'm right. If the evidence supports that, I'll have to learn to accept it.'

'You don't believe the evidence supports it?' Ledbetter asks.

Before Tyler can answer, Franklin ends the discussion. 'Enough, Giles. I'm satisfied. Can we move on?'

Ledbetter puffs out his cheeks in indignation but sits back in his chair and nods.

Franklin also sits back in her chair, and some of the tension seems to go out of the room. Has he passed? She looks straight down the table at him. 'We have some new information,' she says. 'DNA results from some of the wounds on Jake Baker's body are a match for Joey McKenna.'

Tyler feels the blood pulsing in his arm again. What does that mean? That McKenna killed Baker? He feels like an idiot. Was this what Franklin was testing? To see if he was so blinkered by his father's death that he couldn't keep an open mind. He says nothing though, just waits for Franklin to go on.

Judging by the approving tilt to her mouth it's the right call. 'We want you to talk to him,' she says. 'He seems to have an interest in you and we could use that to our advantage. Maybe he'll try to show off and slip up. Regardless, I have a feeling that if anyone's going to get anything out of him, it's you.'

'I'm not suspended then?'

'Have you done something that warrants suspension?'

'No . . .'

'We have every confidence in you, Detective Tyler.'

Ledbetter grunts a little at this but Franklin goes on.

'And frankly, McKenna's not going to give anything to anyone else. His solicitors are already circling like buzzards. To quote an old hero of mine, you're our only hope.' She smiles at him but the expression is as unnerving as Ledbetter's frown of obvious displeasure. 'Your team will continue to investigate the Jake Baker case but given this new connection to Stevens you'll work alongside Professional Standards. Don't worry, I've already informed DI Doggett.'

Tyler can imagine Doggett's reaction to that.

'DS Todd will be your liaison. I want you to get him up to speed on everything you've discovered so far.'

Tyler suspects DS Todd is already more than up to date on what they've done so far. He wonders briefly whether to object, for the show of it as much as for anything else, but decides against pushing things any further. He has a nasty suspicion that he's dodged more than one bullet this morning.

'What do you mean, "you couldn't find me"?'

Mina hears Doggett shouting before she sees him. She slows down her approach, unwilling to insert herself into something she doesn't know the details of.

'I just thought . . .' The voice belongs to DS Vaughan. Mina would feel sorry for her if the woman hadn't been so standoffish when she bumped into her outside the restaurant. *Welcome to the Murder Team, DS Vaughan!* She catches herself smiling.

Whatever Vaughan thought, Doggett leaves her in no doubt she hasn't been hired to think, only to do the legwork and report back promptly to her superiors. Mina rounds the corner in time to see Doggett storming away from her and the look of utter contempt on Vaughan's face.

'DS Vaughan,' Mina says politely as she passes. Vaughan scowls at her too and turns on her heel.

Mina grins and hurries after Doggett. He's already a good way ahead, his wrath somehow fuelling those short legs of his and propelling him along the corridor. But it's clear he's heading back to CCRU and she isn't about to risk shouting his name out in case his anger at the hapless DS comes down on her. So she follows him at a safe distance, hoping some of his anger has dissipated by the time she reaches him.

'Have you seen Tyler?' she risks when she gets back to their room of operations. Doggett's standing at the window, looking out at the view.

He turns and for a moment Mina braces herself for another tirade but in fact he looks worried, if anything. 'I was hoping he'd be here.'

'You think they suspended him?' she asks.

Doggett shakes his head. 'It's not quite that bad. But we're working with Professional Standards now. I've just been unceremoniously informed that Tyler and that cockney fella are gonna interview McKenna. It seems his DNA has turned up on your dead body.'

'McKenna's?'

'This Franklin woman . . . I tell you, Mina, I haven't got a clue about her, and that worries me more than I can tell you. Anyway, we can't wait for him, we need to—'

'I've found a connection,' she interrupts.

'What?'

Mina can't help but enjoy the surprise on his face. 'Not between the cases you were looking at, but between our case and another cold case. A young girl who disappeared.'

Doggett's eyebrows go up in that familiar way that she's begun to realise she looks forward to. It's his pleased look. 'Good,' he says, grabbing his coat from the back of a chair. 'You can tell me on the way.'

'What? Wait!' Mina picks up her own jacket and hurries after him. 'Where are we going?' she asks, trotting after him down the corridor.

'Damn girl!' he says, but for once he's not talking about her. 'Bloody stupid woman!'

Mina follows after him and lets him get it out in his own time. There's no point asking any more questions.

'There's a witness,' he tells her finally. 'A young girl that some dog-walker saw running away from the reservoir in the early hours of the morning. Only, it turns out the statement was taken yesterday and I'm only just hearing about it.'

No wonder DS Vaughan had been read the riot act, as Doggett would put it. Mina reckons she was lucky not to get worse.

'I've no idea why Stevens insisted on bringing her over,' Doggett goes on with his crusade. 'Bloody woman's as useless as a cock-flavoured lollipop at a lesbian convention.'

A passing desk-sergeant overhears this last comment and shouts over her shoulder as she passes, 'Not cool, Jim, not cool.'

Doggett waves an apology at her but carries on with his tirade against the hapless DS Vaughan. As Mina follows him down the corridor listening to a variety of the usual expletives, and one or two she hasn't heard before, she wonders when she's going to get a chance to get her own news across. When Doggett's like this, he has a tendency to go on for a long time. She'll just have to be patient for now.

'So I gave the lad a hiding,' McKenna tells them, and his solicitor winces at the admission. McKenna silences the young man with a look of steel. The hapless solicitor has already had one telling-off from his client and Tyler thinks the man's sulking now.

'You're admitting that you beat Jake Baker?' Toddy asks.

'I'll admit I gave the lad a couple of taps. He was outta line and it was a good lesson to the others. But the wee fella was hale and hearty when I left him.'

'And you never saw him again?'

'Up and disappeared. What can I tell yer? Some guys just can't take their punishment. But hey, I'm not their keeper. If an employee wants to move on, it's nae my business.'

The solicitor pipes up. 'That would explain why my client's DNA was on the victim, although we reserve the right to refute that evidence. It certainly doesn't prove that he killed anyone.'

McKenna rolls his eyes for Tyler's benefit, as if he's saying, *Kids, eh?*

'So you admit Mr Baker worked for you?' Toddy asks.

When he answers, McKenna's eyes stay fixed on Tyler. 'An odd job man of sorts. Cash in hand. Am I in trouble with the tax man as well now, eh?'

Toddy goes on. 'So your lad, Jake, puts a foot wrong here and there and you decide to give him a beating to teach him a lesson, is that it?'

McKenna says nothing.

'Only this time you lose that temper of yours and the beating goes a bit too far. You end up putting poor Jakey down for good.'

McKenna snorts. 'Aye, well, if I had done, you'd no' have found him, I can tell you that much.'

The solicitor splutters. 'I'd like to make it clear that my client was being sarcastic just then and not admitting to any crime.'

'Ach, they know that, yer wee pratt!'

Once again the solicitor falls into a sulk.

'And how do you explain this?' Toddy asks, presenting a document for McKenna and his solicitor to look at. 'The boatshed we found your old employee in, Mr McKenna, is owned by you.'

'What?'

'Purchased as part of a collection of properties sold at auction back in 2002. Purchased by your company.'

McKenna seems genuinely concerned for the first time. 'You see?' he asks Tyler. 'You see what you're up against now?'

Toddy's phone trills and he checks the message without

showing it to Tyler. Then he suspends the interview and he and Tyler step outside.

'They're setting me up, man,' McKenna shouts after them. 'Can yer not see what's right in front of your face?'

'Well?' Tyler asks after he's closed the door behind them.

'We're getting nowhere and without a confession none of this is gonna stick.'

'I meant the message.'

'Oh,' says Toddy, grinning. 'Well, that's the good news. Your very delicious Amber down in Fraud just got back to me. What's the story with her, by the way? Any chance she's single?'

'The message?'

'At the request of your DC Rabbani, they've done a full forensic check into that desserts place you visited. Turns out this woman Spencer does own the freehold on the land but the leasehold on most of the storage units was sold off a while back. Guess who owns one of them?'

'Joey McKenna.'

'Bingo. Things keep coming back to your old gangster friend, don't they?'

'Yes. Convenient that, isn't it?'

'Not for him. So, how do you want to play this?'

'We get a warrant,' Tyler says. 'But let's take old Joey along with us.'

Toddy frowns.

'I want to be able to see his reactions.'

'You still think he might be innocent?'

'No,' Tyler says, 'he's far from innocent. I just don't know if he's guilty of this one.'

Toddy shrugs. 'Well, as my old gran used to say, maybe this makes up for one he got away with. What about Rabbani then? Is she seeing anyone?'

Edith has had a particularly bad day at school. She must have been careless and given away her normal routine because at second break Alice was waiting for her in the toilets. Before she could about-turn, the rest of the gang had followed her in and Edith found herself trapped in a pincer movement. All in all, it could have been worse. It was mostly name-calling and the odd bit of pushing and shoving that resulted in one of the sleeves on her school shirt tearing at the seam. That would be easy enough to sew up tonight so at least she didn't have to try to get Melanie to fork out for a new shirt. It was probably the tearing sound that brought the three of them up short, Edith thought, and made them realise they'd gone too far. And at that point one of the Year 12s had come in and Alice had managed to escape. She'd gone straight to Mrs Peters' classroom then and sure enough the door was unlocked. She'd hidden out there for a bit and when Mrs Peters returned from her own lunch break she hadn't even questioned Edith very hard. Edith suspected she knew, at least roughly, what had happened and taken pity on her. They'd talked about her GCSEs for the rest of break.

After school, Edith stays behind to help Mrs Peters with a classroom display. She can't face going straight home but neither does she want to risk running into the Reservoir Man on one of her walks. But eventually even Mrs Peters sends her packing, reminding her she has homework to finish.

It's nearly teatime when she finally makes it home. Her stomach growling reminds her that she'd left her sandwiches in the toilets earlier when she'd fled.

It's the lack of lights on that first makes Edith think something's wrong. She lets herself into the hallway and calls out for Melanie.

'Mum?'

There's no answer but that's not unusual in itself. It's possible Melanie took herself off for a nap this afternoon. She doesn't often sleep this late, but it's not unheard of either.

She checks the living room first, in case Melanie has fallen asleep on the settee, but there are no lights on and no television blaring away to itself. Edith feels the first fluttering of panic in her stomach. It doesn't mean anything but ... she shouldn't have stayed out so long. What if Melanie needed her for something? Maybe she was forced to go to the shops and has collapsed somewhere en route, though Edith can't think of anything they could be short of that would propel Melanie out of the house so quickly.

Edith forces herself to calm down. She's letting her imagination run away with her. Melanie will be upstairs, there's no reason to assume—

There's a loud thud from overhead and then a muffled cry. 'Mum!' She moves towards the door, even as the sound of footsteps travels across the creaking floorboards overhead.

'Edith!' Melanie's voice sounds faint and strangled.

'Mum!' She's in the hallway again now and there are more noises from up above. A scuffle, as though her mother is dragging furniture or—

'Edith! Run! Run, bab—' Her mother's sentence ends in a cry and then there's another loud bang. Edith sees Melanie tumble down the stairs in front of her, end over end, the awful sound of her bones crunching and cracking. Horror brings bile into Edith's throat and the sensation cuts off her scream before she manages to get it out. Before she can do anything Melanie's crumpled form hits the wall at the bend in the stairs with another loud crack and lies still.

Edith wants to help but her feet are moving so slowly. It feels as though she's running in treacle, fighting to reach her mother even though she knows she's too late. Melanie's neck is turned at a terrible angle. Edith knows she is gone. There's nothing she can do. She's at the bottom of the stairs now, her foot rising to the first step, her eyes fixed wholly on Melanie's pale, twisted face. And then she's turning, looking up the stairs, and there he is. A figure straight from her nightmares. The Reservoir Man. He's standing there, looking down at her, and for a moment they are both frozen, staring at each other. Edith thinks of a nature documentary she saw once, of a lion stalking a gazelle. There was a moment, before the awful bloody action started, where hunter and prey found each other's eyes. It was a fraction of a millisecond before the gazelle bolted, and maybe it's only that short a time now, but it feels so much longer. Time elongates, stretches out the distance between them. And Edith knows that as soon as she moves the lion will take her.

Then the front doorbell rings and Edith screams.

Doggett swears as he gets out of the car.

'How the bloody hell are we going to find her in this place?'

Mina looks around. The estate stretches away ahead of them, one 60s-built concrete block after another, connected by walkways and bridges and paths. There's a children's playground next to the car park that is at least in a better state than the one at the Grapes pub. There are some kids playing on the swings but she doubts they're old enough to help, even if they were inclined, and the way they're eyeing up the two of them suggests they wouldn't be.

'There,' Mina says, pointing behind the playground to a small row of shops on the ground floor of the concrete block closest to them. 'Shopkeeper always knows everyone.'

Doggett shoots her a dubious look but doesn't argue. He abandons the car, reluctantly, using sign language to convey to the kids in the playground that he's watching them. The kids giggle in a manner that's far from reassuring.

Mrs Abassi is a charming woman who likes to talk, and once Mina manages to establish that she has nothing to do with the tax office, the woman gives her the information she needs. She seems genuinely concerned for the wellbeing of one of her favourite customers and it takes Mina a further five minutes to get back out of the shop. Outside, Doggett is still staring hard at the kids in the playground.

'Edith Darke,' she tells him. 'Fifteen. Lives with her mum, Melanie. I've got the address. There was a guy here asking questions about her a couple of days back.'

'Description?'

'Nothing great. Average build, average height. Brown or black hair. She didn't have her glasses on apparently.'

Doggett gives her a short sharp nod. From anyone else it would be nothing but from him it's high praise. Mina can't help the pride that bubbles up in her. She finally feels as though she's pulling her own weight, as though she's a part of things, actually making a difference.

Past the concrete blocks of social housing they reach a smaller estate of brick houses. It's a nicely put-together little housing estate that reminds Mina a little of the place she grew up. Each property has a small turfed front garden with a little wooden fence. It's past its best though, and many of the houses are run down, the gardens overgrown and uncared for. She'd thought it was a shame when her dad and his brothers paved over the area at the back of their houses, creating one big communal space for family get-togethers and ball games. He'd promised her mum he'd build a separate vegetable garden for her to grow things but it never materialised and Mina suspected the whole thing was something of a ruse. After all, the vegetables and herbs her mother wanted to grow would never survive the northern British climate and they both knew it. Still, it gave Mum something to browbeat him about and they were both secretly content with that.

One or two of the properties have been looked after a little better, and one has the largest collection of ornamental gnomes Mina has ever seen in her life. But for the most part the unkempt front lawns just add to the rundown feel of the whole place. It takes them a ridiculously long time to work out the numbering system of the houses, which provokes another round of curses from Doggett as they double back on themselves, weaving their way along the footpaths, but eventually they reach what they think is the right door.

Mina presses the doorbell, her head still full of memories of her childhood. Which is probably why the scream shocks her so badly.

The doorbell rings, and Edith screams and bolts, as though the shrill sound of the electronic chime is the starting pistol Mrs Bellamy uses for Sports Day. She's halfway to the back door before she considers whoever's at the front door might be a potential ally. But it's too late by then. The lion could be right behind her and she's not about to turn around to check. Besides, there's no guarantee that the doorbell pusher isn't another lion. As though this thought has conjured it, she hears a loud knocking on the front door and the doorbell ringing again. Once, twice, urgently.

She careers through the kitchen, her hands out in front of her. If he is behind her, he'll catch her easily when she has to fumble with the lock on the door, but there's no other way. She pushes the kitchen door closed behind her, grabs the edge of the kitchen table and drags it backwards against the door. It will buy her a couple of seconds at most but it's better than nothing.

As she turns she hears a loud bang from somewhere deeper in the house behind her. The key's in the back door, as it always is. It grinds as she turns it, slowly, oh so slowly, and Edith imagines a thick hand on her shoulder, twisting her round, pulling her backwards. But then she's slamming down on the door handle and pushing open the door and tripping down the back step and running and running . . . Now she risks a backward glance and there's no sign of him. The flood of adrenaline threatens to push her down to her knees and she stumbles but finds her feet, and then she's off again, along the ginnel at the back of the house, darting from one path to another, crossing the cold, hard frozen lawns. She slows just once, when she thinks about her mum lying back there at the bottom of the stairs, but then she hears Melanie's voice screaming for her to run. She can't stop, she won't stop.

Edith runs.

The scream has Mina frozen momentarily. Then Doggett's next to her, banging on the door and pressing the door-bell again.

'Stand back!' he shouts and she moves without thinking. She watches him throw his meagre weight against the door but it holds.

'Together,' she tells him, finally catching up to reality.

They both charge the door and the wood around the latch plate splinters and breaks, sending Mina tumbling forward and down across the threshold. The metal frame slams into her knees and the pain is excruciating. Doggett fares better and manages to stay upright.

'Shit!' he says, and rushes up to the crumpled form Mina can now see hunched in a ball at the bend in the stairs. 'She's alive,' he says, feeling at her neck for her pulse. He pulls out his mobile and calls for help even as Mina's struggling back to her feet. 'Check the house,' he tells her, and then, as she turns away from the stairs, 'Be careful!'

Mina checks the front room first but it's empty. She doubles back into the hallway and follows it along to the only other door. It resists when she tries to open it but it moves a little, as though stuck. She puts her shoulder to the door and heaves, slowly; she doesn't think her kneecaps could take another fall. There's a loud groaning sound and a gap opens wide enough for her to slip into the kitchen. The room's empty but someone has pushed the kitchen table up against the door. She pulls it away to give herself a bit more space to manoeuvre. The back door's open but there's no sign of anyone in the yard, nor on the path that runs along the back of the houses. She's just turning back to the house when the fist hits her hard in the side of the face. She cries out and once again she's falling, her vision blurring, the world streaking past her eyes as she falls.

'Mina!'

Doggett arrives, puts his stubby little hands on her face, talks at her, pushes her back down even as she tries to stand up. 'Just stay still!' he's saying.

She wonders whether she lost consciousness. She doesn't feel as though she's lost any time but maybe she wouldn't. The only reference she has is that time Ghulam hit her in the head with a cricket ball and she woke up on the floor with her father screaming at her. She'd been out for almost ten minutes. But it doesn't feel like that. She vaguely remembers falling, hitting the ground, bouncing back up, seeing the black-clad figure running away from her ... but it's all jumbled and mixed up and—

'I'm fine,' she says, and now she's back in the present, a dozen aches and pains hitting her body at the same time. 'Ow.' Her head is spinning.

'Stay where you are,' Doggett says, but she bats his hands away.

'I'm fine,' she says again, and manages to get back to her feet. She still feels a bit woozy though. 'He's getting away!'

'He's gone,' Doggett tells her. 'Just hold steady. The ambulance is on its way.'

'We need to go after him.' Mina tries to pull away from Doggett but he has a firm grip on her arm.

'Mina! Stop! We need to get back to Mrs Darke. Backup's on the way.'

It isn't so much his words as the way the world spins when she tries to put one foot in front of the other that stops her arguing further and she allows herself to be escorted back inside.

'Upstairs window is open,' Doggett points out. 'He must have come down the drainpipe.'

'I didn't even see him,' she says, feeling oddly pathetic. 'I can't describe his face.'

'Never mind that.' He pulls out a kitchen chair. 'Just sit yourself down here and rest for a minute.'

There are dark spots appearing in front of her eyes now. Bloody hell, how hard did he hit her? If she hadn't been turning . . . if the blow had hit her from behind . . . 'He could have snapped my neck.' The thought turns her stomach over.

By the time the paramedics arrive, she's feeling a lot better. She joins Doggett back in the hallway. Melanie Darke hasn't regained consciousness and Mina and Doggett have to help the paramedics lift her gently to the floor, before they can get her onto a long yellow scoop stretcher.

One of the paramedics looks Mina over quickly before they leave and mentions something about concussion but they're far more concerned with getting Melanie to the hospital.

'Did you check upstairs?' she asks Doggett as they watch the ambulance pull out of the estate, its blue lights flicking on.

'No sign of the girl.'

'What do you think happened?'

Doggett looks back at the house. 'Whoever your friend was, I'm guessing he was after something. The question is, did he find it?'

'If Edith was a witness to what happened at the reservoir, maybe he was after her.'

'And the mother got in the way.'

'The kitchen door was barricaded and the back door open. I think she got away.' But Edith is still out there somewhere, with a killer looking for her. 'We need to help her.'

Doggett nods. 'If she's any sense she'll head straight to the police, but as soon as Uniform get here we'll send them out to search.'

'I can go . . .'

'You're going nowhere. I want you where I can keep an eye on you, Evel Knievel.'

Who? 'The paramedic only said *may* have concussion. I'm fine, honestly.' But Mina's voice doesn't even convince herself.

'We'll see about that,' says Doggett. 'Let's have a quick look round while we're here. If you're still standing at the end of that, we'll see what's what.'

Doggett heads back into the house, leaving Mina to follow him. One or two of the neighbours have turned out to see what's happening, including a thin, black-clad man in the house opposite. For a moment Mina's heart races as she wonders if it's the same man who attacked her. No, it couldn't be, surely. No one would be that brazen. The man smiles weakly at her and heads back inside. The man who attacked her was bigger, she's sure, but she wonders if every man she meets now is going to make her think of him. He's out there somewhere. If Tyler's right . . . if McKenna's ICER is real, then this man is a stone-cold killer who has gone undetected for more than a decade. And now he's after a 15-year-old girl. Edith doesn't stand a chance.

*

341

Tyler drives with Toddy in the passenger seat. A uniformed car follows behind them with its reluctant passenger.

They pull up in the car park not far from the cab company operated by Whitehouse. There's no sign of him but Harriet Spencer steps out to meet them.

'This is harassment,' she begins, pulling out her mobile. 'I'm calling my solicitors right now and unless you have a warrant—'

'We do in fact have a warrant,' Tyler tells her. 'But don't worry, it's not for your place. Not just yet anyway,' he adds, taking no small delight in her expression. 'We're here to look at Unit 4a,' he tells her, handing her the relevant paperwork.

She peruses the information. 'This ... This isn't one of ours. It's a company that bought the space from us ...' She trails off, perhaps unsure of herself or, at least, unsure of what it might be a good idea to reveal at this point.

'Yes,' Tyler says, glancing at McKenna's form hunched in the back of the patrol car. 'Can you just direct us to the relevant unit, please?'

Spencer escorts them along the row of containers and around a corner to a second row, and then a third. 'A lot of these companies are owned by others,' she tells him on the way, clicking along in her corporate heels. They use the units for temporary storage and ... we're not legally obliged to ask them what their operations entail.'

Tyler catches her eye. 'I'm not sure Customs and Excise would agree, but why don't we let the solicitors argue about that. For now, I'll be happy with a look in this unit.'

Spencer points to the next container and stops.

'Who deals with renting these places out?' he asks her.

'It's all handled by the women in the cab office. Gareth . . .' She trails off again. 'Perhaps I should go and call my solicitor.'

'You do that.'

He watches Spencer totter away in her heels. She passes Toddy, who's escorting Joey McKenna with one of the uniformed officers. He isn't cuffed, his left arm is strapped across his chest in a sling, but there's something reduced about the man. Tyler notes that Spencer watches him all the way but it's hard to know whether it's just curiosity or whether they actually know each other.

'Last chance, Joe,' Tyler says.

McKenna meets his eye directly. 'I'm telling you, I've no idea what this place is. It has nothing to do with me.'

'Even though your company name's all over the documents?'

'Tyler, man. I'm being set up here, can you really not see that?'

'No key then?'

McKenna just shakes his head but Tyler thinks it's probably frustration as much as an answer to his question.

'Okay, let's get that lock off.'

The uniformed officer steps forward with a pair of bolt cutters and the padlock to the unit is off in seconds. Tyler helps him with the roller shutter and it grinds its way upwards revealing the contents of the unit.

The container is about thirty feet long and eight or so

wide. There's nothing inside but four chest freezers running down one wall of the unit. Each of them is humming gently.

He turns to McKenna, who shakes his head again.

Tyler pulls on a pair of Tyvek gloves and steps carefully into the container. There are no locks on the chest freezers and he opens the first with a light tug upwards that breaks the cold seal. A puff of cool air reaches up to engulf his face but the freezer is empty. He moves to the next one and repeats the process. Again, empty. The third as well.

He has a sudden moment of hesitation when he gets to the fourth, the furthest from the door. Lying on the floor, tucked behind the freezer, are a couple of power tools. Then he tugs on the fourth lid too. The same puff of air hits him in the face but this time the freezer isn't empty. He turns away for a moment, pushing down the bile that's risen in his throat. He takes another look and then closes the freezer lid again. He retraces his steps back out of the container and meets Toddy's questioning glance. He nods at the DI. 'We need a forensics team, now. And more officers,' he adds quietly. 'We're going to need to search the whole place.' He pulls the shutter down behind him and then turns to McKenna. 'Joey McKenna,' he says, loudly and clearly, 'I'm arresting you for the murder of Superintendent Roger Stevens ...'

Edith runs and runs.

For a while she wonders if she'll ever stop. She has nowhere to go, no idea what to do or who to turn to, but this is something she can do. She can run. Maybe she'll just keep running forever. Last year, a woman had come in to speak to them at assembly. She'd run right around the world, crossed deserts and oceans, twenty-four borders, and burned through seventeen pairs of trainers. She'd had her tent stolen twice, suffered any number of illnesses including dysentery, heatstroke and – bizarrely – bird flu. 'I've been bitten by every creature known to man,' she'd laughed. Or woman, Edith had thought.

Afterwards, Mrs Bellamy introduced Edith as their 'best runner' and Edith had smiled and tried to ask the sort of questions she thought everyone wanted her to, like, 'Did you have any trouble with the locals?' and 'What's the worst weather to run in, hot or cold?' By the end of the meeting, Mrs Bellamy had single-handedly decided Edith was not just likely to follow in the woman's footsteps but had asked for her email address in case Edith might need any future tips. The woman had given it, grudgingly, as though she wasn't all that keen for some upstart 15-year-old to steal her crown just yet.

In truth, Edith couldn't think of anything she'd like to do less. Running wasn't about going anywhere, nowhere specific anyway, and certainly not in the quickest possible time. To Edith, running was just running. She enjoyed it for what it was. All that other stuff sounded gross. But maybe she was wrong. Maybe that woman knew something she didn't. Maybe she had a dead mother and a killer chasing her. Although if she did, stopping for the occasional school assembly didn't seem a particularly sensible thing to do.

She slows down when she reaches the lights of Middlewood

and Hillsborough. She's been keeping off the main road, for obvious reasons, but something's drawing her to the city. She consciously thinks about the reasons for this for the first time and guesses it makes sense. It's better to be around people. She could have lost herself in the woods or a field, bedded down under a bush for the night, although she worries that if she does that, given how cold it is, she might not wake up again in the morning. But something tells her that, weather aside, being in a populated area, while risky, is not as bad as finding herself alone on a road somewhere facing that man all over again.

She can't stop thinking about him now she's seen him again close up. She's rejected any thoughts that the man might be her father. She can't believe she's related to him in any way. And those eyes ... It was the one thing she'd remembered about him and yet, faced with them again, it was like she was seeing them for the first time. The cold, hungry way he looked at her. It had frozen her as effectively as Medusa's head.

She considers Hillsborough Park as a possible location for the night but it's too open; she really ought to try and find shelter. She runs on.

What is she going to do?

Melanie. The thought has been floating around somewhere but she hasn't let herself focus on it. Her mother can't be dead. She can't. Edith hasn't even cried yet. Does that make her a bad person? She wants to but she can't seem to summon the tears, not as long as she keeps running. Maybe she's in shock.

Without Melanie she has no one. She should go to the police, of course she should. She should just stop, find a phone – her own mobile is on the floor of the front room, assuming the man with the terrible eyes hasn't stolen it and used it to find out everything about her. She consoles herself that at least he'll struggle to learn much, given how few contacts she has saved in her address book. No social media accounts for him to rummage through. So, stop, find a phone, call the police. They'll pick her up and she'll tell them what she knows and then . . . Then they'll put her in a home somewhere and the man with the terrible eyes will find her. If she knows one thing for sure it's that. He found her at school, at Mrs Abassi's, at her home. He'll find her wherever they put her and then she'll have a dead foster mother as well as a dead real mother.

The same applies to her teachers. She thinks she can trust them . . . well, Mrs Peters, anyway. Given the circumstances she could probably even trust Alice Clitherow to take her in but he'd still find her. He'd come for her in the night and she'd wake up and look into those eyes and know that it was the end.

So Edith runs.

day six

The ICER recordings #116

(Archivists' note: Voice matches that recorded in #114 and earlier transcripts, and as such has been labelled Unknown Caller 2 [04/05/18])

Call received: 05:34 Saturday 10th Mar 2018

Duration: 1 minute 44 seconds

Partial Transcript:

ICER   Yes.

UC2   I need an update on the situation.

(recording is silent for 2 seconds)

ICER   The situation is being handled.

UC2   It doesn't feel very handled.

ICER   The police have arrested McKenna. That's what you wanted, isn't it?

UC2   Yes, originally. But that was before he started shooting his mouth off. I thought we agreed to . . . expedite matters?

ICER   Does it matter? He's out of your way.

UC2   For now, maybe. But he knows too much.

ICER   The contract stands. With his money and his fancy solicitors I'll doubt they'll be able to hold him long. I'll deal with him when he gets out.

UC2   What about the witness? This . . . girl?

(recording is silent for 2 seconds)

ICER   It's . . . complicated. She got away.

UC2   Yes, we're well aware of that. And you were seen as well, not just by the girl's mother but by a police detective.

ICER   The policewoman didn't see anything and the mother is dead.

UC2   You seem very sure about the former and you're entirely wrong about the latter, so forgive me if I don't feel reassured.

ICER   What?

UC2   The mother's in the hospital.

ICER   (*pause 2 seconds*) I'll handle it. The daughter as well.

UC2   Yes, you keep saying that but I fear we may have reached the end of the road. Perhaps it would be better if we just dissolved this partnership now.

ICER   If you really thought that you wouldn't have rung me.

UC2   To be honest, at this point we couldn't care less what happens to the girl or her mother, that's entirely up to you since it's your face. As for McKenna, perhaps that was a mistake as well. I doubt he'll tell the police anything now he's in the system. And if he does, we have other ways of reaching him. But there is one loose end remaining that we're going to have to deal with and this one shouldn't cause you too much trouble. He certainly can't run as fast as a 15-year old.

ICER   You mean—?

UC2   Try to contain your excitement. No, not him. I'll send you the details.

ICER   Fine. The usual terms then?

UC2   The usual terms.

Call ends 05:35

Tyler wakes early that morning to more screaming. He jumps out of bed and hurries into the spare room where Jude is writhing and thrashing under the duvet. Gently, he wakes his brother.

'Sorry,' Jude says. 'Maybe I should get my own place.' But they both know he can't afford that any time soon.

'Hey, it's fine. You can stay as long as you like.' Tyler hesitates. 'Do you want to talk about it?'

Jude doesn't answer. A bead of sweat streaks from his hairline down his neck.

'I'll get the coffee on.'

They don't talk about it, though. Instead Tyler tries to get Jude to talk about his interview, but that doesn't go well either.

'Fucking hell, mate! What's with the third degree?'

'I was only asking. If it didn't go well maybe I can help with . . . interview techniques or something?'

'Jesus Christ! You know who you sound like?'

Tyler doesn't respond and Jude doesn't elaborate. He doesn't have to.

On his way into the office Tyler makes a detour to the back of the building. He knocks on the office door and lets himself in.

Scott Austin is sitting at his desk in what may or may not be the same tight white shirt. Perhaps he has a wardrobe full of them, alongside those tight check trousers. His very own uniform.

'Hey. Any chance I can get a quick word?'

Austin's face creases into a big smile, bigger than is warranted given their very brief encounter. He stands up. 'Please, come in.' He checks his watch. 'I can give you a few minutes.'

'I was just wondering if you had the details of that counsellor you recommended.'

Austin nods and smiles widely. 'You're taking my advice. I'm glad, Tyler.' He picks up his mobile from the desk. 'Let me get you the details.'

'Yeah, sorry to disappoint you but actually it's not for me.'

The smile morphs into a frown.

'It's my brother. I think he may have some kind of PTSD.'

Austin puts down his phone and sits. He gestures to the chair in front of him but Tyler stays standing. He doesn't want to get pulled into another session like before.

'And you think by helping him you can make up for not helping DS Daley, is that it?'

Tyler opens his mouth to speak but Austin's appraisal cuts a little too close to home. 'I think Jude is really troubled. He keeps having these nightmares. Some kind of trauma in his past. He was in the army.' Saying this makes Tyler realise Austin's right. He can't get this wrong again. If he'd paid proper attention to Daley . . . 'Look, I just want to help him.'

Austin puts his hand to his chiselled jaw, the very image

of a TV psychologist. 'It doesn't work like that. Your brother has to accept that he needs to talk to someone. Just as you do. You can't just fix him, Tyler. You can't fix everything.'

'You're very personal for an Occupational Health officer, aren't you?'

The smile comes back, causing two dimples to appear in Austin's cheeks. 'I have my own special charm.' The smile dies. 'But maybe that's why I'm not very good at it.'

Tyler questions this with a slight incline of his head.

'It's my last month on the job actually. I'm retraining. To be a counsellor, believe it or not.'

Tyler smiles. 'You'll be good at that.'

'Thank you.' Austin stands up again. 'Here, give me your number and I'll forward you the details of my friend. When you – or your brother – are ready, you can contact him.'

Tyler gets out his phone. 'If you wanted my number you could have just asked the first time we met.'

Austin raises an eyebrow. 'If I thought you had the slightest room in your life for a relationship, I might have done.'

They exchange numbers and Austin forwards Tyler the contact details for his counsellor friend.

'Seriously,' Austin tells him. 'The best thing you can do for your brother is encourage him to talk.'

'Okay, thanks.'

On his way out the door Tyler stops and turns back. Austin is watching him, his appreciation writ large on his face. 'So if I did find some time in my life,' Tyler asks, 'would it be worth giving you that call?'

Austin holds his eye for a moment. 'It might,' he says, finally. 'But you should use the other number I gave you first.'

'Understood,' Tyler says, and walks out of the office.

Edith watches the house for a good half an hour or so before making her move. She thinks it's a student house as it has a sign on the wall that says 'You could live here! Avail Sep' and a telephone number. She creeps up the driveway, ready to run at the first sign of challenge but there isn't any. The back gate's unlocked and, although there is a lock on the garden shed, the rotten wood breaks easily enough even under her slight weight.

Inside, it's warmer, although a bit damp, but at least the slatted walls keep the wind at bay. She finds an old IKEA bag full of tools and after she's emptied them out, she uses it to cover herself as best she can. It's far from ideal and there are any number of unknown objects digging into her as she curls herself up and tries to sleep. She lies there for a while, thinking about her mother and wondering if the itches she feels are insects crawling over her or just her imagination. But then, despite all of that, she falls into a deep sleep.

She wakes once in the night, disorientated, and sits up, her body crying out with a dozen pinpricks of pain. She guesses it's the early hours of the morning and listens to the sound of the students arriving home and putting on music. Her stomach's aching badly. She thinks about walking up to the door and asking if she can join the party. Maybe they have pizza. Students eat pizza, right? But why would they let her in? Why wouldn't they just call the police? So she makes do with what's left of the packet of biscuits she bought at a newsagent's earlier. That had been the last of her money, apart from a handful of small change, and she has no idea what she's going to do for breakfast.

But even through her gut-wrenching hunger, and the thought that one of the students might come out into the garden and notice the shed, and the wretched knowledge she'll never see Melanie again, and the fear of the Reservoir Man and his evil eyes. Even through all of that, somehow, Edith manages to fall back to sleep.

She wakes early to the sound of birdsong in the garden, a window high on the right-hand side of the shed lets in the early morning light. At once she is sure of what she needs to do, as though the answer has come to her in the night. She has to go away, far away. It's the only chance she has of escaping him. But she can't just go like this. She won't survive a week without something more than the – she checks her pocket – 37p she has on her. It's a massive risk but what choice does she have, really? She's going to need a few things. Her phone, if he hasn't taken it. Money. Perhaps a change of clothes or two in a bag. Then . . . well, then she'll see. London maybe. Or is that too obvious? Everyone always runs away to London; it's the first place he'd look. Manchester then, or somewhere further north. Edith's always wanted to go to Scotland. She'll have to grow her hair out, which is not ideal but they'll be looking for a girl with a shaved head. *He'll* be looking for a girl with a shaved head.

Home. She has to go back. There's a chance he's still there but a chance he's not as well. Maybe going back is stupid but maybe it's so stupid no one would think of it. Or is that the sort of double bluff that a bad man like him *would* think of?

She lets herself out of the shed and feels bad about the damage to the door. She suspects the landlord can easily afford to fix it, assuming he ever notices it's damaged, but she hopes the students won't get the blame for it. One of them has left a khaki jacket lying abandoned on the single plastic chair that represents the sum total of their patio furniture. Edith takes it. Again she feels bad but not as bad as she should do. This is how it begins, she thinks. A life of crime starts with necessity.

She creeps carefully back down the driveway, slipping the jacket over her shoulders. Even though it has been out all night and is cold to the touch, it's beautifully warm when she shrugs it on. And it has the added benefit of changing her shape a bit, making her look bigger. She begins to retrace her steps. Her feet ache so she decides she can't possibly run, or even walk, all the way back, which means taking public transport. She'll have to risk getting closer to people again, but maybe that's not such a bad thing. Safety in numbers. And besides, the Reservoir Man can't have eyes everywhere. He isn't superhuman. Is he?

She has no money though, not even enough for a child's fare, and she doesn't have her pass so that means the bus is out. So it's the tram. Much more likely she can dodge the conductor, and even if she gets caught and thrown off she can always get on the next one. Then she'll still have to walk from Middlewood but that's a lot shorter distance than the whole way.

So home it is, she thinks, as she sets off back down the hill. But only briefly, and then it's on to a new life somewhere. It's not much of a plan but at least it *is* a plan. She's taking action. That's the important thing. Isn't it?

It's quite the team gathered in CCRU's new dedicated office with its view across the city. Tyler and Rabbani. Doggett and Toddy. Even a couple of Uniforms that Doggett managed to wrestle away from the Murder Team to help with the CCTV search for Edith Darke. If he wasn't so worried that Franklin was still out to get him in some way, Tyler might even take pride in the operation. Doggett's pacing back and forth in the window, channelling the frustration they all feel. Because, for as far along as they are with this case, it feels very much like they're standing still, as though the shadowy faces behind all this are still out there somewhere. 'Any news from the hospital?' he asks.

It's Rabbani who answers. She's sitting opposite Tyler at what they've all come to think of as 'her' desk. 'Melanie Darke still hasn't regained consciousness but they seem to think it's just a matter of time. She's out of danger for the most part.'

DS Todd is standing by the whiteboard, on the face of it trying to make sense of the connections. He's not as daft as he tries to make out though and Tyler had been right about him

being well informed. They'd caught him up on everything –
except for the Circle – including the info Rabbani had got
from DI Cooper regarding Gareth Whitehouse. Toddy had
let Rabbani outline the whole thing before calmly informing
them that DI Cooper had taken her advice and had already
been in and made a statement about it yesterday evening.
'We're looking into it,' he'd said, shutting down the conversation, and Tyler wondered just how far they could trust this
spy in their camp.

'Did you find anything at her place?' Toddy asks now.

Doggett makes a guttural grunting noise, which probably
means 'no' but is hard to determine. Thankfully he follows
it up with, 'Nothing of interest. This bloke – whoever he
was – was either there for her or the girl, or else he found
what he was looking for and took it with him.' Doggett's still
not on board with the whole ICER concept but Tyler thinks
the others have come round, Rabbani especially after her
run-in with the man. She has a dark bruise forming on her
left cheek as a visual reminder to all of them that whoever
this guy is, he means business.

'I left her mobile at the house,' Rabbani says, 'with a
message on it telling her about her mum and to contact me.
Uniform are keeping an eye on the place too, in case she
goes back.'

'And what if our new friend goes back? Will Uniform be
able to stop him?' Todd asks.

'We can't put armed response on hold all round the city,
just in case,' Tyler tells him.

Doggett chips in. 'You're not in London now, son,'

Toddy grins at the jibe. Tyler can't help liking the man. He has a positive energy about him that's not something you'd expect from someone who works for Professional Standards. It would be easy to underestimate him. Tyler has to remember that he's Ledbetter's man at the end of the day.

'Okay,' Tyler says, bringing them back on track. 'What have we got from the storage facility?'

Toddy clears his throat. 'Superintendent Stevens was shot once in the head at close range. Your doc reckons he's been there a few days although it's hard for her to tell given the body was frozen. There was enough flesh frozen to the sides of the freezer to prove Jake Baker was in residence there before him. Those tools you found had been used to chip him out. It looks as though we've found the place he was kept on ice for the past sixteen years.'

'But why?' Doggett's voice is strained with frustration.

Tyler has a theory but he's not sure Doggett's ready to hear it and he's not about to share it with Toddy, either.

'The way I see it,' Toddy goes on, 'McKenna sends in this ICER to help Stevens out with whatever they've got planned for Baker's body. They have a falling out of some kind at the scene and the ICER shoots him in the head.' Toddy looks at Tyler. 'You told me you thought Stevens had backed out of killing DCI Jordan. Maybe he was backing out of the rest of the plan too.'

Doggett scoffs. 'What sort of name is the ICER, anyway?'

'Call him what you like then,' Toddy says, defending

himself. 'But you've got to admit it's catchier than the Reservoir Killer.' That was the rather prosaic epithet the papers had come up with.

'ICER's a good enough name for now,' Tyler says. He heads off Doggett's objections by raising a hand. 'Regardless of whether McKenna's telling the whole truth about this guy, we do know he exists. I've seen him, Rabbani's seen him. Melanie Darke nearly died at his hands. McKenna's man or someone else's, he's real enough.'

Doggett looks as though he's trying to think of some way to disagree but can't find one.

'What about the blood on McKenna's window?'

Doggett shakes his head. 'Nothing yet.'

'Maybe we'll get lucky and he's on file,' Tyler says, poking masochistically at his injured arm.

Toddy picks up his theory. 'The real unanswered question is just what the two of them did have planned for Baker's corpse. Why move it to the boatshed?'

'And why move Stevens' body back to the storage unit?' Doggett asks. 'It doesn't make bloody sense, man! Why not shoot Stevens when he was already at the storage place and save himself the hassle?'

Tyler jumps in. 'He didn't intend to kill Stevens, not there anyway. Something changed.'

'Like what?'

'Something Stevens said?' Rabbani suggests. 'Or didn't say. He didn't give up DCI Jordan.'

'Or,' Tyler says, 'Stevens figured out he was for the chop.

Whatever else he was, he wasn't a stupid man.' He can see Stevens making a run for it, the ICER forced to take precipitate action. 'We were only supposed to find Baker there but his clean-up gets interrupted by Edith Darke. He gets the body away but doesn't have time to come back and deal with the blood spatter.'

'Why is he moving bodies about after sixteen years anyway?' Doggett's voice sounds more strangled with every sentence.

'There's one explanation,' Tyler says quietly, still undecided about how much he wants to say in front of Todd. Doggett looks at him. 'McKenna didn't do it.'

'Oh, bollocks!'

Tyler ignores him. 'Why would McKenna keep a body for all that time? Especially one that incriminates him. He'd have got rid of it. You don't think he's got rid of other bodies over the years? Why keep this one?'

'You were the one that bloody arrested him!'

'Yes, to make sure he was safe, and somewhere we could find him. But don't you think it's a bit convenient? McKenna starts dropping hints about ... Stevens, and the past.' He hopes the slight pause is enough for Doggett to read between the lines. 'Then suddenly this body turns up from a decade and a half ago, on McKenna's property, covered in his DNA. Maybe somebody else wanted us to find it.'

'Who?' Toddy asks.

Doggett falls silent. Tyler's not used to winning arguments with the man; it's slightly unnerving.

'What did McKenna say about it?' Rabbani asks Toddy directly, helping with the misdirection.

'He's saying he was set up,' Toddy says.

'Well, he would do, wouldn't he?' Doggett says, but Tyler can tell from the fixed expression on his face that he's got Doggett thinking about it.

Toddy leans against the whiteboard, eyeing each of them in turn. He's not stupid either. He knows he's missing something, aware of some new undercurrent to the conversation.

Silence falls on the room for a few moments and then Doggett scratches his head. 'None of this means McKenna didn't do it. He could still have killed the bloke and someone else kept the body on ice all these years as an insurance policy, just in case he did something they didn't like.'

Like dropping a folder of evidence onto DCI Jordan's desk, Tyler thinks, willing his thoughts to align with Doggett's. It's so frustrating not being able to talk openly about things.

'You think Stevens was the one with the insurance policy?' Toddy asks.

None of them disagree with him but they know they aren't talking about Stevens anymore. Rabbani's face is flaring again and giving them away.

'Stevens ... or whoever, decides to tidy up after himself,' Doggett goes on, 'leaving the body for us to find, implicating McKenna—'

'So the ICER works for Stevens then, not McKenna?' Toddy interrupts again. Tyler can see Doggett's frustration building within him. Another time it might be funny. 'But if that was the case there'd be no reason to move Stevens' body from the reservoir. With his boss dead he'd just cut his losses and get out, wouldn't he?'

Doggett nods. 'Right, that doesn't fit.' But his gaze never leaves Tyler's.

It does if someone else is pulling the strings. Someone who wanted rid of Stevens and McKenna both, in such a way that implied they were working together. The Circle.

'You're right,' Tyler says. 'I'm just trying to look at every angle. I'm clutching at straws though, McKenna's finger-prints are all over this. We should probably make another attempt at breaking him.' He's not sure Toddy's buying the sudden about-turn but he doesn't know them well enough to call them on it either.

It's Doggett's turn to change the direction of the conver-sation. 'Did you look into that airline ticket?' he asks.

'Yeah,' Toddy tells him. 'Online transaction with Stevens' credit card, purchased a few days before he died. But I checked with Heathrow. He wasn't on the plane.'

Doggett starts pacing again. 'No leads there then. He obviously intended to do a runner but didn't make it.'

'The others,' Tyler says.

'What?'

'McKenna said that Jake Baker's beating was a lesson for the others. If McKenna's not talking, and Baker's dead, maybe we can find one of these others.'

'And how do we go about that?' Doggett asks, narrow-ing his eyes.

Tyler has an idea but he needs DS Todd out of the way first. 'Danny,' he says, playing the game. 'McKenna's lieutenant. He would have been around back then. Maybe DS Todd can put those impressive interrogation techniques to good use.'

Tyler has no doubt it's a fool's mission. From what he's seen, Danny is McKenna's man through and through. He won't say anything, and certainly not to someone he doesn't know.

'Maybe,' Toddy says slowly. 'You don't want to be involved?'

'We had an altercation when McKenna invited me to his place the other night. He's not my biggest fan. I reckon you'll do better without me. Rabbani and I should focus on finding the girl.'

If Toddy picks up on the fact Tyler's getting him out of the way he doesn't say so. 'All right, I'll give it a go. I need to catch up with the Gaffer anyway. Let me know how you get on.' He seems all sweetness and light as he leaves the room but Tyler's not about to underestimate him. He sees far more than he lets on.

'I hope you know what you're doing,' Doggett tells him after they're sure Toddy's gone. 'What are you really up to?'

'I'd rather not say,' Tyler says. 'Find the girl. She's the key to this.'

Doggett nods. 'I'll chase up those DNA results as well. If we can find out who this so-called ICER is, it's job done.'

'Come on then, Mina,' Tyler calls.

She looks at him with that furrowed brow of hers.

'Don't worry,' he tells her. 'I'm just taking you for a pint.'

Edith lets herself in through the back door. There's a police car, or what she thinks is a police car, outside the front of the house. Two men sitting in a car for no apparent reason seems pretty suspicious to her anyway. Either it's the police or it's someone working for the Reservoir Man. Besides, she doesn't have her front door key so there would be no point going in that way. But she does always leave a spare key for the back door under a stone next to the drain, ever since she forgot her keys once and Melanie had been too far gone to let her in. She'd ended up spending the night curled up on the back doorstep. It was as uncomfortable as the night she's just spent in the shed but at least that night it had been summer.

Someone has moved the table and chairs away from the door and roughly back into their usual position. She finds her phone plugged in on the kitchen worktop. It's switched off. She wonders who could have plugged it in but slips it into her pocket anyway. Then she rolls up the wire around the charger and pockets that as well.

She moves into the hallway slowly, worried that her mum might still be lying dead at the foot of the stairs, but she's gone. If they've taken her mum away that means the police were definitely here. Unless the Reservoir Man moved her, and even if he didn't, that doesn't mean he didn't come back later. But after a quick search of every room, certain he might jump out at her at any moment, she begins to calm down. He's gone. The police are gone. Melanie is gone. She can afford a few minutes to make sure she gets everything she needs.

She gathers together a couple of changes of clothes and a washbag of stuff from the bathroom. She takes an extra couple of minutes to clean her teeth and immediately feels better. She considers taking a shower as well but decides against it in the end because getting naked feels like a place of vulnerability she's not willing to put herself into. Back in the bedroom she needs something for the clothes to go in. She considers using her school bag; it's bigger than anything else she has but on the other hand she thinks it probably looks exactly like what it is – a school bag. She needs to look different to the Edith Darke everyone knows. And it's then she realises she doesn't have only her own things to choose from.

She moves into her mother's bedroom and opens the closet, pulling out a rucksack that her mum sometimes used to wear when she went shopping. She thinks about wearing one of her mother's jackets as well but decides she's probably not old enough to pull it off. The student jacket suits her better. But she does pick up a bucket hat that Melanie used to wear in the summer. She said it reminded her of her festival days. It will have to do until her hair grows.

It's when she takes down the hat from the shelf that she sees the pretty box that was hidden behind it. Edith has to climb up on the chest of drawers to reach it. She pulls down the whole box and puts it on the bed, sits down next to it and lifts the lid. Inside are the collected treasures of her mother's life. She turns them over in her hands one at a time. A ticket stub for an old movie called *My Big Fat Greek Wedding*, a necklace of wooden beads, a polished stone. Lots of things that make very little sense to Edith. Why would her mother keep these things? Unless they had something to do with her father?

It hits her like a brick. Something detaches itself inside and drops through her belly. She's never going to know. She won't ever be able to come back here. She's saying goodbye to everything she's ever known. She's saying goodbye to Melanie.

And now, finally, she cries. She falls backwards onto the bed and weeps into the duvet. It smells of the washing powder Melanie loves her to use. Ylang Ylang. A tropical tree native to India. Edith had googled it when her mother told her how much she loved the scent. She cries for a good ten minutes or more and only stops when she thinks she hears a noise downstairs. She sits up abruptly and listens. Nothing. But it reminds her she can't be here. She needs to get out.

She grabs the box but she can't take it all. She drapes the wooden necklace round her neck and pockets the stone, she has no idea why. Then something else in the box catches her eye and she pulls out a glossy rectangle of photographic paper. On the back, written in blue ink in her mother's hand, are the words *Me and the 3 Jays*. She turns the photo over.

There are three men in the photograph, and her mother of course. She looks happy. Truly happy, in a way Edith isn't sure she's ever seen. They are standing on the front somewhere, the sea clearly visible behind them. Her mother is in the middle with two men on one side and one on the other. They have their arms around each other and the man pressed close against her mother is resting his cheek on her head. Is this him? she wonders. And then has the question answered for her as she notices he's wearing a vest top. The tattoo is clearly visible on his upper left shoulder, a skull with a snake twisting around and through it. Her father. Edith scrapes her finger over his face and down his torso. The second man is the other side of Melanie. He's leaning in closely and saying something to her that makes her laugh. That joke, whatever it was, is frozen here in this moment, for all eternity, but no one will ever know what it was. Edith feels the tears welling up again.

And then she looks at the third man, the one with his arm loosely around the shoulders of the man telling the joke. He's smiling just like the rest of them but the smile can do nothing to hide the coldness in his eyes. It's the Reservoir Man. The man who killed her mother. How can it be? It makes no sense. Her mother knew him somehow? And her father too! She examines the photo again and she's sure it's him. He's much younger but it's definitely him, she could never mistake those eyes.

Somewhere outside, a car door slams and Edith lets go of the photo. He's here, she thinks. He's come for her.

This time when they visit the Grapes of Rotherham, the place is open for business, which Tyler thinks makes it a slightly less depressing place than it was the last time they were here. Marginally. Possibly.

There's no sign of the landlord, Ashworth, but that isn't why they're here. They walk into the saloon bar and everyone looks up at them. It could be a scene from an old Western movie. 'Everyone' consists of three elderly gentlemen, a woman in her forties sitting at the bar and a small mongrel dog. The dog yaps once, which sets off the larger dog somewhere upstairs on the premises. The barmaid watches them but says nothing and neither Tyler nor Rabbani make any effort to speak to her either. She slips away out the back somewhere. Everyone else just watches them. Perhaps these people know police when they see them. Or perhaps it's just that they don't get strangers round these parts often.

'Down here,' Rabbani tells him and he follows her along the corridor towards the toilets. At the far end is another entrance that presumably leads out into the car park. And off to the right-hand side a doorway leading into a snug.

There are a handful of bench seats around the walls of the room and a couple of small tables with stools but the bulk of the room is empty. In the middle of the wall opposite the door there's an ancient dartboard, its cork pitted with thousands of tiny pinpricks. A rubber mat stretches out towards the centre of the room and the oche. The right-hand wall is taken up with a sea of faces and stats, leaders and runners-up reaching back over a decade or more judging by the faded nature of some of the photographs.

Tyler crosses to the wall and begins his search. Rabbani points out the photograph of Whitehouse with his arm around the young woman. An Asian woman.

'Do you think that's her?' Tyler asks. 'Cooper's missing girl?'

'Asma Ali,' Rabbani tells him, her face stern and brooding. 'I dunno.'

'Mina,' Tyler says, putting a hand on her arm to bring her back to the moment. 'I know you want to find her but that's not the case we're focused on right now.'

'It could be connected. If that is her,' she points to the photo, 'I'd say it *is* connected. And Whitehouse is certainly connected!'

'Cooper's spoken to Professional Standards, they're looking into it. Toddy'll keep us informed if there's any progress.' Tyler wants to believe that.

'I'm just worried about Binita,' Rabbani says. 'I rang and spoke to her but I'm not sure she took me seriously and there was only so much I could say.'

'Look, we'll find Asma. You'll find her, and you can enjoy breaking Gareth Whitehouse on the way. But for now we need to focus on Jake Baker.'

'Not your dad then?'

'What?'

'I just think it's a bit rich you telling me to focus on the case at hand when the only thing you've been focused on for the past year is your dad.' She's furious and for the first time Tyler sees what he's put her through. But the fury dies as quickly as it always does with her. 'I'm sorry,' she says. 'I shouldn't've said that.'

'No, it's a fair comment. You're right, I'm the one who should be saying sorry.' But he has so much to be sorry about he's not sure where to begin. 'I know I should have told you what was going on but when I first found out I barely knew you. And then, for the longest time there was nothing to tell, and then Daley died and . . .'

Rabbani nods. 'It's not your fault,' she tells him.

'What?'

'Daley.'

Tyler sees the body again, just as he always does, the blood pooling around him in the dark, soaking into the fertile grounds of the Gardens. By the time Tyler had reached him he was already gone but that's not exactly how he remembers it. He sees Daley looking at him, as he did in the car shortly before that, pleading with little-boy eyes that said, *please don't make me do this, I don't want to.* And he remembers, again, the sarcasm he'd spat at the man: *Look after yourself for a change.*

'I know you think it is,' Rabbani goes on. 'But it's not. Not entirely anyway. Did you fuck up? Yes. We both did. So did Jordan. So did Daley. There's plenty of blame for everyone so you don't have to take it all on yourself.'

He nods but he doesn't believe that. Maybe he will one day. Maybe he'll speak to Scott Austin's counsellor after all. He turns back to examining the photos on the wall.

But Rabbani's not finished. 'You never bloody talk about

it. About him! We tiptoe around it like it's not there but the more we ignore it the bigger it gets. He's gone, Tyler! He was an arsehole and a misogynist and a pretty shitty detective actually. But none of us wanted him dead. He's gone, but we're still allowed to talk about him. We *should* talk about him.'

'Shit!' Tyler says.

'Yeah, I know. But that's life for you.'

'No, I didn't mean that.' Tyler's staring at the photo that's just caught his eye. He tries to tell himself it doesn't mean anything, that hundreds of thousands of people must have drunk in this pub over the years, that there are a sea of at least a hundred faces or more on this wall alone. It doesn't mean they're all connected to the case. To the frozen corpse of Jake Baker and the murdered security guard Kevin Linville. They can't all be connected to Joey McKenna and his Circle and its hired assassin.

But he already knows this one *is* connected. He should have seen this sooner. He did see it, he just hoped he was wrong. It's the reason they're here right now.

Rabbani leans in to get a better look at the picture that's caught his eye, a yellowing photograph of two men raising their pints to the camera. One is ruffling the other's hair in a very familiar manner. 'Is that Jake Baker?' she asks, but the question's half rhetorical. 'Sorry, boss. I missed that last time.'

'It's not your fault. Besides, we already knew he drank here.' They should have spent more time on this but they were so excited to get a positive ID on the corpse they didn't bother to look any further. 'You'd better go find Ashworth though. We'll need to take all of these with us.'

As Mina heads off to fetch the landlord Tyler reaches out and unsticks the photo from the wall. Jake Baker's grinning face peers out at him, very much alive, full of himself for some grand darts-based achievement. But it's the man alongside him that really caught Tyler's eye. The man ruffling his hair in much the same way he ruffled Tyler's just a few days ago. It's his brother, Jude.

Edith dives over to the window. She can hear voices down below but not what they're saying, and whoever's there is tucked in too close to the house for her to be able to see them properly. She turns back to the bed, picks up the photograph and shoves it into her coat pocket. Then she grabs the rucksack and the summer hat and slips across the landing back into her own bedroom. She pushes the last of the things she's gathered into her mum's bag, the washbag, the change of clothes, but now she can hear someone pushing a key into the front door. She runs back out to the top of the stairs and looks down at the place where her mother fell. The man at the door is cursing as he struggles with the lock. The key always sticks if you don't get it right and you have to jiggle it a bit, and pull it slightly towards you as you turn it. If she can just get down the stairs before he manages it.

She creeps down each stair slowly and is halfway down when she realises her mistake. She should have run. The lock engages and the door begins to swing open. For a split second Edith freezes, unsure whether to run on or go back, and then she moves. Forward. It's her only chance, if she goes back she has no way out.

The door opens in her face as she passes it but the man is turned away from her, talking to someone behind him. '... think to keep an eye on the back, did you? That would be too much to bloody hope for!' And then she's past the door but now it's swinging wide and if she makes a break for the kitchen he'll see her so she keeps heading forward into the living room. Her mum's chair is the only conceivable place she can hide and she's behind it in seconds.

Edith crouches there, trying to breath without making a sound. The man is still muttering, but to himself this time, she thinks he's the only one who has actually come into the house. She feels his presence as he enters the room, hears his breathing over the sound of her own.

Edith's small for her age but she's not sure she's small enough. What if he can see her? She can't see him, she can't move, all she can do is hope. If he can see her she's finished anyway. The first she'll know about it is when he reaches down and hauls her out, his hands closing around her throat like they must have done on her mother's. The last thing she'll see is those eyes staring their hatred into her as her vision fades ...

The man clears his throat. 'All right, love, you can come out now,' says a voice. 'I can see your shoes. My name's Detective Inspector Jim Doggett. You can call me Jim.'

Edith lifts her head over the arm of the chair. A short, hairy-looking man is smiling at her.

'You must be Edith,' he says. 'Your mum's right worried about you, you know?'

Ashworth makes a fuss about them taking the photographs, bandying around words about warrants and solicitors and the like, but Rabbani deals with it all very well, calmly pointing out to him that if he really wants them to make this official they can, but implying heavily that that's a headache he doesn't want to inflict on himself.

Tyler's impressed. She's come a long way in the eighteen months or so he's known her. Has it really only been that long? It feels so much longer. She's grown into herself, put away her doubts and fears and sometimes even that enormous chip that she carries around on her shoulder, and now she's observant, competent, efficient. An all-round, more than decent detective who he's proud to have on his team.

Not so observant that she notices when he pockets the photograph of Jude, though. He does it without thinking, some protective brotherly thing, he supposes. But can he really hide this? He stays with her until she's dealt with the boisterous Ashworth and cajoled the barmaid into finding her a crisp box she can use to collect the photos. Then he tells her that he's off.

'You're leaving?'

'I just need to pop to the hospital,' he tells her, the lie burning his lips. 'It's Jordan's operation today and I wanted to see her before she goes down.' At least that bit's not a lie. 'You're all right here on your own, aren't you?'

'Oh. Right. Yeah, sure.' He can feel the disappointment radiating from her. If she can just learn to disguise the heart dangling on her sleeve she's going to make the most formidable detective.

'Don't worry, I'll organise a car for you.' And he's as good as his word on this, calling it in on his way to the car. Then he makes a second phone call.

'All right, mate?'

'Jude.' Tyler stops, realises he doesn't want to have this conversation over the phone. 'Where are you?'

'What? You checking up on me again?'

'Jude, I'm serious. I need to talk to you about something. Where are you?'

'All right, chill. I'm in the flat.'

'Okay. Don't go anywhere. I'm on my way.'

'Christ, mate, you make it sound—'

But Tyler doesn't wait to hear the rest of the sentence.

He makes it home in a little over twenty minutes, breaking several speed limits to do it. Jude's lounging on the sofa in a T-shirt and boxer shorts, the TV that Tyler never watches playing some music channel in the background.

'Jake Baker,' Tyler says without preamble. He pulls out the photograph and slaps it down on the coffee table.

Jude leans forward and picks it up. 'Jesus. Yeah, that takes me back.'

'You know him then?'

'Yeah, obviously. What's going on, bro'?'

'Jake Baker is the man whose murder I'm investigating.'

Jude swallows and the hand holding the photo begins to shake. 'Jakey's dead?'

'You didn't know?'

'No, of course I didn't bloody know! What the fuck?'

Tyler realises he believes him and he's glad of that. Had he really thought his brother was involved in all this somehow? Working for, or with McKenna? And the ICER? No, of course not but . . . there's a connection here, there has to be. Something beyond a bizarre coincidence. 'How do you know him?'

'What?'

'How did you meet Jake Baker?'

'Look, mate . . .'

'Just tell me, Jude. This is important.'

'I don't want to talk about it.'

'Tough. You don't get to choose. You talk to me now or my boss will be here in about half an hour's time.'

Jude's face creases up in fury. 'Are you threatening me? Jesus Christ, Adam?'

'This is serious. A man has been murdered. A man you knew.'

'I haven't seen Jake in years! Not since I left Sheffield.'

'He's been dead for years. I'm a cold case specialist, remember?' Although now he thinks about it, he's not sure he's ever told Jude that. 'That doesn't let you off the hook.'

'You're not seriously accusing me of killing the bloke? He was me mate!'

Tyler knows he isn't being entirely fair. He's handling this all wrong. 'I just ... I need to know how you know him. You could be a material witness.'

Jude visibly relaxes, the tension going out of his shoulders as the anger drains away. 'It was a long time ago ...'

'Jude, please! It's McKenna, isn't it? Jake was one of the guys who got you involved with him.'

Jude looks at the photo again. 'Yeah. I met him at Elly's place. Him and a couple of other lads. We hung out for a while. Did some shit I'd really rather not get into.'

'You might have to get into it.'

'He still lived with his mum,' Jude says, smiling down fondly at the picture. 'Always said she was a daft cow who thought the sun shone out of his arse but he loved her.' Jude looks up. 'How did he ... ?'

Tyler doesn't answer. 'You're gonna have to come in and tell us everything you can remember about him. About everyone else you knew back then.'

'No,' Jude says simply. 'Fuck that for a game of soldiers!'

'McKenna's not saying anything and you're the only link we have to what happened back then.'

'No. I don't want to get involved.'

'You're refusing to cooperate?'

'Yeah, I'm pleading the fifth or whatever you call it.'

'You've been watching too many US cop dramas. That's not a thing here.' Tyler runs a hand over his face. 'Jude. If you don't talk it makes you look guilty.'

'I *am* guilty, Adam. Not of killing Jake but ... I did stuff back then. Stuff I can't tell you about.'

Tyler sits down. 'All right, we'll get you a solicitor. All I care about is what you know about McKenna.'

Jude laughs. 'Seriously? And what do you think happens when I start pointing the finger at him? Do I look like I've got a death wish?'

'You said you wanted to help. This . . . this might be about catching the man who killed our father.'

Jude hesitates then. 'You're saying . . . it could be someone I know? From back then?'

'I don't know. It's possible. McKenna told me the man who did it is called the ICER. He's here in Sheffield now, and he's killing again. He tried to kill McKenna and he took a shot at me. There's a fifteen-year-old girl somewhere out there on the run from him. If we don't stop him he's going to keep on killing people.'

Jude says nothing but Tyler can see him thinking.

Tyler's mobile vibrates in his pocket. He pulls it out. Toddy's the last person he wants to speak to right now but if he doesn't answer it might look dodgy and he can't afford that either, not until he can work out what to do to protect Jude.

He takes the call.

'Where are you?' Toddy asks. He's talking quietly and sounds serious.

'Rabbani and I were looking into a lead,' Tyler says carefully.

'The Gaffer didn't want me to call you but . . . I'm texting you an address. Get here. ASAP!' Then he hangs up.

'I've got to go.' Jude's still looking down at the photo.

Tyler reaches forward and takes it back. 'I'll be back, soon as I can. Jude, look at me.'

Jude looks up.

'Everything you know from that time. Every*one* you know. It's important.'

Jude half shrugs, half nods, but it's the best Tyler's going to get for now. Tyler leaves him there on the sofa in his boxers but as he gets to the door, Jude calls out to him and Tyler turns back.

'I didn't kill Jake. I swear on Dad's grave. I'm telling the truth.'

'I know,' Tyler tells him, but he's not so sure Jude's telling him the truth about everything.

The address Toddy texts him leads Tyler to a detached house in Totley. It's a grand home in a similar style to McKenna's although not quite on the same scale. The sort of place whose owner no doubt would aspire to McKenna's place.

There are a number of emergency services vehicles outside the property, leading Tyler to believe this is something bigger than the usual callout for a property like this, burglary. Toddy is liaising with Jill, the crime scene manager, when Tyler walks up.

Jill looks him up and down suspiciously but that's her standard greeting for anyone she thinks is about to traipse over her crime scene. She hands him a pair of shoe coveralls without speaking.

'Who is it?' Tyler asks.

'Gareth Whitehouse,' Toddy says quietly.

The Circle are cleaning shop. He should have prioritised Whitehouse when Rabbani told him about the girl. He trusted Professional Standards to deal with it and somehow, as always, word got out. Cooper arrived with her story last night and Whitehouse is dead today.

Toddy looks round before he speaks, checking who's within earshot. 'I can't give you long, Ledbetter didn't want you here at all but—'

'Whitehouse is part of my investigation.'

'Yeah, and that's why I rang. That . . . and the manner of his death. You might want to prepare yourself, mate—'

'I've seen plenty of crime scenes,' Tyler tells him and heads into the house.

'Tyler, wait—!'

But he doesn't get any further because Tyler's already in the middle of the crime scene. The grand entrance hall is actually bigger than the one at McKenna's place with a broad staircase curling up the right-hand side of the oval-shaped room. There are four white-clad SOCOs already hard at work.

For a moment Tyler's taken back to another stairwell, sixteen years ago. He was sixteen and had just walked home from school with his best mate. He was later than he said he'd be and let himself in half expecting a bollocking from his dad. Only half though because odds were good his dad was still at work anyway. More than likely the place would be empty with Jude gone. But the place wasn't empty. His father

385

was there, hanging by his neck from a length of red rope, twisting silently in an air current disturbed by his opening of the front door.

Tyler stumbles to a halt and puts his hand over his mouth. It's more instinct than nausea but Toddy places a hand on his shoulder and taps it lightly.

'Come away, mate.'

The image of his father fades, leaving behind the soiled corpse of Gareth Whitehouse, the stench of his voided bowels strong in the enclosed space. But the similarities are stark, even the fraying red cord tied to the banister looks the same. In his father's case it had been traced to a sex shop in Attercliffe that sold bondage equipment.

'You read my father's file?'

'Of course I did.'

One of the SOCOs heads towards them and only then does Tyler realise that it's Emma Ridgeway. 'Detectives,' she greets them warmly. 'Don't get too close now, that rope ain't gonna last much longer. We're bringing him down now.'

'Doctor,' Tyler speaks with urgency. 'He didn't hang himself. I know it looks like he did but he didn't.'

Toddy's hand squeezes his shoulder. 'Maybe we should let the doc decide what happened to him, eh?'

'I surely would appreciate that, Detective,' Ridgeway tells them, examining each of them in turn. 'But I reckon Detective Tyler's called this one. There are signs of a struggle and from what I can see I'd say this man was dead when he was strung up.'

'What?' Tyler asks.

'There are marks on the neck that don't match the rope. I'll know more once we get the body down but my guess is he was strangled, at least partially, before they hung him up there.'

'It's not the same as your father, then,' Toddy says, almost sounding relieved.

'He's taunting me,' Tyler tells him.

'Yeah, it's those sort of comments that are the reason Ledbetter wants you nowhere near this.'

'Oh, come on, you can see it, can't you? That's why you called me, isn't it? McKenna's not responsible for this, he's been in custody.'

'He could have got someone else to do it.' But Toddy's face betrays him. He doesn't believe that any more than Tyler does.

'What?' Tyler asks.

Toddy sighs and pulls out an evidence bag with a white piece of paper inside. 'Receipt for paracetamol. On his bedside table next to the empty packets.'

'It's him. The ICER. He wants me to know.'

'Am I missing something here, gentlemen?' Ridgeway asks.

Toddy re-pockets the receipt. 'Okay, let's say you're right. All this has been staged just for you. Why? What can he possibly hope to gain from that, other than to send you bat-shit crazy? Which, by the way, it looks like he's doing a bloody good job of.'

Ridgeway sighs heavily. 'I'd appreciate one of you gentlemen filling me in with whatever this is about?'

'Sorry, doc.'

'It's my father,' Tyler says. 'Richard Tyler. He died in this exact same way. The drugs, the rope, the hanging. You need to look at his autopsy again, see what was missed.'

'Hang on, Tyler—'

'No!' He's waited long enough. 'My father didn't kill himself! Someone fucked up.' He turns back to Ridgeway. 'Probably that useless predecessor of yours, Elliot.'

'You know I'm not Dr Elliot's biggest fan but I can't just go re-examining—'

'Please!' Tyler's not above begging. 'You have to look into it. Stevens covered it up but there must be something Elliot missed or . . .'

'Are you asking me to exhume his body?'

Tyler shakes his head. 'He was cremated.'

Ridgeway exchanges a look with Toddy. 'I'll have to speak to whoever's SIO on this.'

'DI Ledbetter's— Wait, Tyler! Where are you going?'

But Tyler's already outside. Ledbetter's not going to authorise this, which means his only chance is Franklin and he doesn't like those odds. But maybe there is someone she'll listen to. Diane will see he's right about this and maybe she can make Franklin see it too. That will mean more explanations, of course. He'll have to admit to Diane that he and Doggett have been looking into Richard's death all this time without telling her. Maybe Rabbani's right, and it's time to dispense with all the secrets and lies.

*

By the time he gets to the hospital, Tyler's too late. He has a moment of panic when he sees the empty bed but a passing nurse tells him that they've already taken Jordan down for her leg operation. He embraces the guilt like a familiar sore, more painful than the bullet graze on his arm. Once again he wasn't there for her. He pushes away the morbid thought that she might not make it. It's a leg operation, she'll be fine. But without her help, Franklin is going to be a much harder nut to crack.

He checks in on Melanie Darke to see if there's any news and is surprised to find Doggett there. 'I found the girl,' he says by way of explanation.

Through the window Tyler can see Edith Darke, a diminutive skin-headed girl with facial piercings wearing dark clothing and an oversized khaki army jacket. The girl looks up at him and the suspicion in her eyes gives him pause. He smiles at her in what he hopes is a reassuring way but the girl just turns back to her mother.

'How's she doing?'

Doggett chuckles. 'She's a tough little thing. Refused to believe her mother was alive at first. Poor lass. Then she thought I was working with the killer to try and trick her. It took me twenty minutes to talk her out of the house.'

'She saw him then?'

Doggett nods. 'I haven't got much of a description out of her yet but she's agreed to talk to a sketch artist. I couldn't get her to go back to the station without coming here first though and now she won't leave her mum. So

I'm waiting for the artist to come here.' Doggett turns to look at Tyler properly for the first time. 'I take it your lead didn't pan out?'

'Hm?'

'You look like you lost a grand and found your lover in bed with another man.'

'Something like that.'

They move down the corridor to the waiting area and Tyler tells him about Whitehouse and the scene at his home.

Doggett whistles loudly when he's finished, drawing the eye of a passing nurse. He remains silent for a few moments and when he does speak again his voice is unusually quiet. 'It could still be McKenna,' he says.

Tyler closes his eyes.

'I'm not saying this ICER bloke isn't real. I'm just saying that the manner of your dad's death is public record. It doesn't mean it's the same guy. This could all still be McKenna messing with you. Or someone else.'

Tyler has to admit he's right. Worse than that is the fact he hadn't even thought of it. His instincts tell him it *is* the same guy, though. But he knows Doggett and Franklin and everyone else would tell him that just goes to show how blinded he really is.

Edith can't stop staring at Melanie's face. She didn't believe the police detective at first. How could she be alive? Her neck was at that terrible angle, surely no one could survive that.

And yet, here she is, looking no worse than she does on a daily basis, apart from the brace wrapped around her throat and the bruises and cuts to her face.

And to think Edith was about to run away and leave her. She pushes down the terrible thought that a little bit of her was actually looking forward to the freedom. With a dark mind like that she doesn't deserve to have a mother. But it's true that Melanie will need more looking after than ever now. However badly hurt she is, she'll use this as an excuse to do even less.

'Ed–ith?'

'Mum! Mum, you're okay! You're in the hospital.'

Melanie looks up at her, confused. She closes her eyes again.

'Mum, hang on, I'll get the nurse.'

'No.' Melanie grabs her hand. 'Wait!' She opens and closes her mouth. 'Water.'

Edith pours a glass of water from a jug on the bedside table and holds it to Melanie's lips while she drinks. She laps it up gratefully and then chokes when it comes too fast, water spilling out and down her neck, soaking into the soft padding of the brace. Edith pulls the glass away and finds a tissue to mop the spillage from her mother's mouth and chin.

'Better?' she asks.

Melanie nods and winces slightly at the movement.

'Don't move your neck. You had a nasty fall.'

Again Melanie closes her eyes. 'Accident,' she croaks.

Edith sits back in her chair. She doesn't like arguing with Melanie but . . . Maybe she's confused. She can't let her go on thinking the wrong thing though, even if it hurts her.

'Mum, it wasn't an accident. There was a man,' she says. Melanie opens her eyes and Edith can see the fear in them. 'You know that, don't you? You know who it was.'

Melanie twitches slightly. She's trying to shake her head. Edith pulls the photo from her pocket and holds it up in front of her mother's face. 'I saw him, Mum. I saw this man.'

Melanie's eyes swivel towards the window. 'You mustn't . . . Don't tell anyone.'

'Why not? The police need to find him. He's dangerous.'

Melanie squeezes her eyes tightly shut. 'No. He didn't mean it . . . It's not like that.'

'What's it like then, Mum? Tell me.' She's not used to speaking to Melanie like this but she's not going to back down this time. 'Who is he? Is this my father?' She points to the man in the photo with the tattoo. Again Melanie closes her eyes. 'No! Look at him. Look at me! Tell me, Mum. Is that my dad?'

'I don't know,' Melanie says in such a quiet voice Edith's not sure if she heard it correctly. 'One of them is.'

Edith feels those words reverberate around the room. She can see what it has cost Melanie to admit that. 'You don't know.'

'I loved him,' Melanie tells her. 'Jake. I loved him so much.'

'But he wasn't my dad.'

'I wanted him to be.' Tears slip out from the corners of Melanie's eyes and run across her cheeks.

'But it could be this man?' she asks. The Reservoir Man. The man with the hateful eyes.

Melanie doesn't answer and Edith looks at the third face in the photo, the one making her mother laugh. 'It could be any of them?'

Again Melanie doesn't answer but she turns her head away with what Edith assumes is shame.

The door opens and the hairy detective, Jim, looks back down the corridor at someone and says, 'She's awake.'

Melanie wipes her eyes and pushes Edith's hand away. Her intention is obvious: *Hide the photo.* Edith slips the picture back in her pocket.

'I'm tired,' says Melanie, and Edith recognises her poorly voice.

The detective narrows his eyes. 'We need to talk about what happened, Melanie.'

'I don't remember,' she tells him, and the lie feels so huge to Edith that it might as well be another presence in the room.

She stands up. 'I'll wait outside, Mum.' If she can't even listen to her mother lie to the police, how will she lie to them herself?

'Edith, please,' her mother says. Edith stops. 'We'll talk later, yes?'

She's never heard her mother sound so uncertain but Edith

doesn't turn around. She walks on towards the door, the hairy policeman watching her with his beady eyes.

'Edith?'

Edith closes the door on her mother's voice.

Tyler gets out his mobile and calls Rabbani. He listens to the ringing tone with one eye on Doggett as he moves down the corridor. Rabbani answers, just as Doggett shouts back down the corridor at him, 'She's awake.'

'Sorry, Mina, I'll have to call you back.' Tyler hangs up and follows after him. He sees Melanie's daughter walking towards him. Doggett's eyes follow her and he nods at Tyler before turning back to the hospital bed. The inference is clear: *Watch her!*

Edith looks up at him, her eyes wary.

'Hi, Edith. My name's Tyler. I'm a detective, too.'

She looks at him with a puzzled expression. He has to admit, it did sound a particularly stupid thing to announce. But he's not good with kids as a rule and has even less experience when it comes to teenagers.

'Can I get you a Coke?'

She shakes her head and then, as though her manners won't quite allow her to be that sullen, she says, 'No, thank you. I don't drink Coke.'

'Right.' He has no idea what to say next. 'Something else then? Why don't we see if we can find a café? Sit down for a bit while we wait for the sketch artist to arrive.'

She shrugs a little and half smiles.

A nurse gives them directions to a dining room on C-Level and Tyler and Edith begin the long negotiation of lifts and corridors that takes them there. They walk mostly in silence, with Tyler occasionally making unnecessary observations about their journey. It's unlike him. He's never had a problem with so-called uncomfortable silences. Most people in his experience talk too much. So after fetching himself a coffee and Edith an orange juice that she seems indifferent to but not wholly against, he determines not to go out of his way to engage her in idle chitchat. After all, he's not so old he doesn't remember all those excruciating times adults tried to make conversation with him when he was a kid. *How are you getting on at school then?* And *Your dad's in the police, eh, that must be exciting?* And the one he personally loathed most of all: *So, have you got yourself a girlfriend yet?*

For her part, Edith seems as comfortable with *uncomfortable* silences as he is, and sits quietly on her chair displaying very little of the anxiety or tension he might expect from a witness in her position. She doesn't go out of her way to make eye contact, but doesn't avoid it either. Nor does she make much attempt to watch what's going on around her, although he has a sense that she misses very little. The only thing that gives her away is when someone deep in the kitchens drops a tray and the clatter reverberates around the canteen. The noise makes Tyler jump but elicits only the smallest of head tilts from Edith, her eyes instantly alert for danger. She's used to making herself invisible, he realises, keeping her movements small and insignificant.

The tattoos and piercings, and the shaved head, are all part of that, too. She hides in plain sight, makes herself stand out in a way that actually deflects observation. Eyes pass over her, cataloguing her easily – Goth girl – and dismissing her as anything worthy of interest. He was much the same way at her age, uninterested in fitting in or being noticed, happy to go his own way and do his own thing. Until Richard's death changed all that and catapulted him kicking and screaming into the limelight.

Tyler actually begins to find her companionable silence quite comforting and he suspects the two of them might well sit there in silence for hours without any real concern if given the opportunity. But then his phone rings. He sees Rabbani's name on the screen and presses the call cancel button. He can't have a conversation with her about the case in front of Edith. He slips his mobile onto the table between them.

'The man who attacked you and your mum, Edith,' he says without preamble. 'Can you describe him to me?'

She looks at him directly. 'I'm not sure,' she says.

'Could you try?'

'I remember his eyes,' she says.

'What colour were they?'

'No. I don't mean that. I mean . . . I remember they looked like he wanted to hurt me. That's why I ran.'

Tyler realises something. 'You're talking about when you first saw him. At the reservoir?'

Edith hesitates and then nods. So that confirmed one thing at least. Whoever put Jake Baker's body in the boatshed, and presumably shot Stevens, was the same man who came to Edith's house, and attacked Melanie and Rabbani. They had been working on that assumption but now it's confirmed.

'So you don't remember what colour his eyes were?'

Edith looks away and says again, 'I'm not sure.'

Tyler doesn't need to be good with children to know when someone's lying to him. 'You told DI Doggett . . . Jim, that you thought you could describe him.'

'I . . . I think I can but . . . It was all quite fast.' She blushes furiously. She's lying to him and he doesn't know why. She could be scared of course, that would make sense, but why now and not before when she spoke to Doggett?

'Okay, well we're only asking that you do your best. It's important we find this man, Edith, because he's very dangerous.'

Her cheeks turn an even darker shade of red. Why would she want to protect him now and not before? The only thing that's changed is—

Again Tyler's phone rings and Jude's gurning face appears on the table in front of him. The picture he took in the bar the other night. The face that was supposed to represent their reconciliation. Their new start. He should let it go to answerphone but Jude could still be key to all of this.

He glances up at Edith and sees that look on her face again, the one she had when the tray dropped in the kitchen. What's startled her this time? 'I'm sorry, Edith. I just need to take this. It's my brother.'

She smiles and nods but the wary expression remains.

'Hey,' he says as he answers the phone.

'Hey,' says Jude. There's a significant pause that Tyler finds far more uncomfortable than the silence with Edith but in the end it's Jude who picks up the conversation first. 'I didn't like the way we left things.'

'No.'

'I need you to know. I care about you, Adam. I'm sorry I let you down.'

'Does that mean you're ready to talk to me about Jake?' Tyler asks.

There's a heavy sigh down the line. Edith stands up and Tyler throws a questioning frown at her. She points to a directional sign for the toilet up above the nearest door and Tyler nods. He covers the mouthpiece and mouths the words, 'Don't go far,' at her. She nods back at him and again there's that half-smile.

'There's really nothing to tell,' Jude says. 'Mate, don't push this, I'm begging you. None of this is relevant to Jakey's death. The last I saw him he was as alive as you and me.'

'Your friend is dead, Jude. Murdered, then placed inside a freezer for more than a decade. There's a chance you might know the killer. Or at least that you know someone who knows him. How is that not relevant?'

'Bro', please—'

'No, Jude. Either you tell me what happened or . . . I can't protect you if you don't tell me what's going on.'

There's another protracted silence and then Jude speaks in a quiet voice. 'When did it become you looking out for me and not the other way round, eh?'

Tyler wants to say, *when you walked out on me*, but he manages to stop himself. There's no sign of Edith and a nasty thought occurs to him. He gets up and crosses the dining hall towards the door through which she disappeared.

'I've got to go,' Jude says, and there's a finality about the sentence that scares Tyler.

'Look, I don't need to know everything. Just who else you hung around with back then. When you last saw Jake, who else was in his life, what he was like as a person.' There's no sign of Edith in the corridor either. A woman steps out of the toilets. 'Hang on,' he says into the phone. 'Excuse me, did you see a young girl in there? Fifteen, shaved head.' The woman looks at him suspiciously but shakes her head and moves on.

'You still there?'

'Sorry, Jude, I—'

'It's fine. You do what you have to do. I'll see you when I see you, eh?'

'Jude, wait—'

But Tyler's already talking to a dead line. He slips his mobile back into his pocket and knocks on the toilet door. There's no answer. He pushes the door open and glances inside but there's no sign of anyone. He does a quick search of each cubicle; all empty.

Back out in the corridor he starts to worry. He runs along the corridor to the main entrance and checks outside but there's no sign of her anywhere. Maybe she went back to the ward to see her mother. *Shit!* She better had, or Doggett's going to kill him. As he retraces his steps back towards the ward he tries ringing Jude back, three times. Each time it goes straight to voicemail.

Edith walks straight out of the hospital with her head spinning.

She must have been mistaken. She couldn't have seen what she thought she saw . . .

She stumbles to the right along a narrow path, once again her feet moving of their own free will, desperate to get her away from all of this.

When the detective's phone rang she'd looked down automatically and read the name on the screen – *Jude Bollock-head*. The man in the picture was pulling a face but there was something about it that was familiar. And then she'd realised – it was the third man from her mother's photograph.

She stops for a moment, tucking herself up against the wall of the hospital. She pulls out the photo and looks again at the man to the left of Melanie, the one whispering something into her ear and making her laugh. It's him. The same man. Older, of course, but he would be. And the name – Jude. *The three Jays.* She knows one of their names now. Two of them in fact, her mother called the man with the tattoo Jake.

But what does it mean?

She should go back and ask Melanie, force her to finally tell Edith the truth about them – all of them: Jude, the laughing man; Jake, who Melanie fell in love with at the boatshed; and the third J, the Reservoir Man.

But if Jude is the detective's brother how can she trust

400

any of them? They might all be working together with the Reservoir Man, who pushed her mother down the stairs and has eyes that betray him.

She can't trust them, she—

'Excuse me! Please!' There's a woman at the end of the path, at the corner of the building. She's dressed very smartly in an expensive suit and heels. 'Please, can you help me?'

Edith looks around but she's the only person who's near. She begins walking towards the woman instinctively.

'It's my husband. He fell.'

'Should I get help?'

'No!' The woman says, less anxious now. 'I just ... Can you help me get him into the car? I know it's a lot to ask but ...' She gestures around the corner. 'I'm just here.'

Edith moves forward and the tension in the woman's face seems to dissipate a little.

'He's such a pain,' she says, chummier now she's confident of Edith's help. 'He will insist on trying to do everything himself and ... well, since the accident he just can't manage like he used to.'

'I'm sorry,' Edith says.

They move round the corner of the building together, into another section of car park. There are more cars lined up in rows but far fewer people, and Edith can't see anyone lying on the ground.

'Is he—?'

Edith feels something sharp pressing into her back and she freezes.

'Get in the car.' The woman pushes her towards the kerb.

'What are you doing?'

'Get in!' She opens the door and Edith feels herself pitching forwards onto the back seat.

'Wait! Please.' The door closes behind her. Edith manages to get up and reaches for the handle on the opposite side but it fails to open.

The woman gets in the front and throws a bottle of water onto the back seat. 'Take this,' she says, handing her a small white pill.

'What? No! I—'

The woman leans forward and pushes the knife against Edith's thigh. The tip pierces the denim and begins to prick her skin. She cries out and tries to back away but there's nowhere to go.

'Take it!'

Edith takes the tablet from her hand. 'What is it?'

'It won't hurt you. It'll just make you sleepy. But if you don't take it I'll cut you again. I don't want to hurt you but I will if I have to.'

Edith can feel tears welling up behind her eyes but she won't cry. She hesitates and the woman presses the knife deeper.

'Okay, okay.' Edith picks up the bottle and unscrews the cap. She puts the tablet on her tongue, tasting the bitter powdered coating. The woman pushes the knife a little deeper and, with shaking hands, Edith takes a swig from the bottle and swallows.

'Another,' the woman tells her, passing across a tablet.

'Please, I—'

This time the woman raises the knife and holds it in front of Edith's face. She can see her own dark blood glistening on the stainless-steel edge. Edith puts the second tablet in her mouth and uses the water to wash it down.

The woman seems to relax a little and pulls the knife away. 'Put the belt on. That side,' she says, using the knife to gesture to the seat behind the passenger seat. 'Now sit back and relax and everything will be okay. But if you try anything I will hurt you. Do you understand me?'

Edith nods and puts on her seatbelt. As the woman starts the car and pulls away Edith imagines she can already feel the tablets dissolving in her stomach. What has she taken? Who is this woman? Is this really happening?

Her mind scrambles to make sense of it all. She tries to think about what she might do. Wave for help out the window? But how would that help? Even if the person who saw her took her seriously the car would be long gone before they could do anything. What if she grabbed the woman while she was driving? She might be able to force her to crash but she still wouldn't be able to get out of the car and there was the knife to worry about. Her mind races with possibilities but she discards each one almost as soon as it forms.

And then her mind starts to wander in other directions and none of it seems quite as urgent or important anymore. After all, the sunlight reflecting off the side mirror and onto her face is kind of pretty and the gentle whirring of the motor is not all that unpleasant. She closes her eyes and breathes in the sweet smell of the woman's perfume. She feels great. Better than she's ever felt. There's really nothing to worry about . . .

day seven

The ICER Recordings #001

(Archivists' note: This is the earliest file recovered from the hard-drive. There may well be others but from context it seems reasonable to believe this marks the beginning of the so-called ICER's 'career', and as such we have labelled it #001. The assumption is that this is the point at which he decided to begin recording his conversations, presumably in case they might prove useful to him. The voice recorded [labelled Unknown Caller 1] cannot be heard on any of the subsequent recordings recovered but given the reference to 'my organisation', he remains priority #1 in terms of identification [25/04/18])

Call received: 18:24 Sunday 22 Sep 2002

Duration: 5 minutes 42 seconds

Partial Transcript:

ICER   Hello?

UC1   Jackson. Have you had a chance to think about what we discussed?

(recording is silent for 2 seconds)

ICER   Yeah. I've thought about it.

UC1   And?

ICER   I dunno. It's a lot to take in.

UC1   I can fully understand that. You're aware of how generous our offer is? I understand you have a young family to take care of. The fact that you're currently estranged from the mother of your children doesn't mean they won't appreciate the extra income.

ICER   How do you know about them?

UC1   We know about everything, Jackson. Including where to find them. Of course, if you decided not to take us up on our offer, we would be forced to look elsewhere for the requirements we need, and that puts everyone in a difficult position, doesn't it? Us, you. *(pause 1 second)* Your family. But let's not focus on the negatives. My organisation's offering you a once in a lifetime opportunity. A rebirth of sorts. All your past misdemeanours go away.

ICER   Along with my identity.

UC1   Is that truly such an issue for you? We've done our research well and from what I understand you're not exactly burdened with close friends. The mother of your children wants nothing to do with you, and the last woman in your life was, until recently – er … how do we say it in the vernacular? Shacked up with? – your so-called best friend. Until Mr McKenna put paid to him, of course. The only other friend you had has taken himself off to join the army, though I suspect the word 'friend' is a little inapt in that case. I'm sure you'll miss the hero-worship though. It's time to grow up, Jackson. Yes, what we're asking of you leads you down a somewhat lonely path, but you can still have meaningful relationships with people. And the difference is you'll have all the money you could want to enjoy them.

ICER   Why me? What makes you think I want to betray McKenna?

UC1   I see you have a flair for the dramatic, as well. That's not such a bad thing as long as you keep it under control. You mean, other than the fact that he beat your friend to death?

ICER   In case you haven't noticed, people don't just walk away from his employ.

UC1   Simply put, we believe you're the right man for the job. You're ambitious and money-driven. You're not overburdened with scruples, and most importantly, you're intelligent and know a good deal when you see one. You're wasted working for our friend McKenna. And I'm sure you know as well as I do that Mr Baker is unlikely to be the final victim of the man's temper.

ICER   Jake was a fucking idiot! He should have known McKenna would lose his shit after that business at the factory.

UC1   Indeed. However, you're not an idiot, are you, Mr Jackson? With my organisation, you'll have the autonomy to set your own terms. You'll be a partner, near enough. The scalpel we use to cut the rotten core from this city.

ICER   And all I have to do is kill a nosey copper?

UC1   Not all, Mr Jackson, no. Not *all*, by a longshot. But that will be the first part of it. A storage facility has been arranged. An associate of Mr McKenna's has provided a place that, if it were to be discovered, would be easily traced back to him. It seems Mr McKenna's interests and our own are diverging somewhat and we foresee a time when it may be necessary to rein him in. Mr Baker's body has been placed on ice until we need it. An insurance policy, if you will. A warning for him not to talk to any more police officers, no matter how much history he might have with them. As far as Mr McKenna's concerned you will have disappeared, along with your friend, Mr Baker. We will tell him we have taken care of his little *problem*, but that unfortunately you got in the way and had to be dealt with as well.

ICER   And if I say no then the story you tell McKenna gets a little bit closer to reality, is that it?

UC1   As I said, Mr Jackson, you're an intelligent man. That's why we want you. After you've handled the police detective, you'll need to go away for a while and reinvent yourself. We'll give you a new identity somewhere far from here, maybe somewhere near your family on the south coast? You'll be able to reconnect with them if you wish to, but your name change will mean you'll need to maintain a certain distance. You'll be on call then, as and when we need you. Now, how does that sound?

Can I take it we have an agreement?

(*recording is silent for 4 seconds*)

ICER   I guess we do.

UC1   Excellent! Then let's get down to details. The target's name is Detective Inspector Richard Tyler.

ICER   Tyler?

UC1   That won't be a problem, will it? I thought I'd made it clear that your rebirth involves the shedding of all previous ties?

ICER   No. It won't be a problem at all.

UC1   It will need to look like suicide, of course. With your former friend off in the army it should all be easy enough. We have an asset in the department who will arrange to meet with the overly curious detective on . . . shall we say Thursday? Does that give you enough time to prepare?

ICER   Yeah, no problem. But what about the other son?

UC1   He'll be at school. You won't need to worry about him.

ICER   Okay. Fine. Let's do this then.

UC1   My associate will be in touch shortly with all the relevant details. From now on I suggest we talk a little less openly about things over the telephone.

ICER   Will we meet in person then?

UC1   No, we will never meet. You will never even know my name and for my part I will refer to you as . . . well, we'll think up a suitable epithet. In the meantime, I wish you the best of luck, Mr Jackson. May this be the start of a very lucrative relationship for both of us.

ICER   Yeah, let's hope so.

Call ends 18:30

'How could you be so bloody stupid?'

Mina watches Doggett pacing up and down in front of the office window. For someone who was so reluctant to join them up on the sixth floor he certainly seems to have taken to the view.

'She's bloody fifteen years old!'

Tyler's sitting at his desk doing his best to ignore Doggett's tirade. It's not the first salvo, nor does Mina suspect it will be the last.

'She's not bloody Houdini!'

'All right,' Tyler says, snapping. 'Can we let this go now? What's done is done. The important thing now is to find her.'

'What about Melanie Darke?' Mina asks. 'Should we try her again? If she knows her daughter's missing again—'

'Gah!' Doggett's still wearing a hole in the carpet. Mina wonders how much of this rant is down to Tyler and how much is the fact Doggett couldn't get anything out of the mother. A little of both, she suspects. 'Bloody woman's several sultanas short of a fruitcake if you ask me. She's not talking.'

'Not even when her daughter might be in danger?'

'She won't believe it.' Doggett says.

Of course, they didn't know anything for sure. A nurse had raised the alarm at the hospital after seeing a struggle of some kind but had been woefully short on details. She said she thought she saw a woman pushing a young lad into the back of a car but it had been too far away to see properly. She figured it was just a parent with an unruly child but thought she'd better report it just in case. When Doggett and Tyler checked the CCTV footage it showed Edith talking with someone but whoever it was had been off camera. They could find no further trace of her after that so they had to assume she left in a car.

'Kept calling me Taggart and telling me that "I couldn't fool her".'

'You think she knows who attacked her?' *Who attacked us!* Mina touches the bruise on her face.

'I'm bloody sure of it! She's clammed up tight though. Said she couldn't remember anything and then played the sick card.' To hear him tell it, Doggett had been virtually thrown from the hospital by an overly protective matron, although there was something of a glint in his eye when he talked about her that made Mina think he'd be heading back there the first chance he got. 'Anyway,' he says, 'your friend Todd's down there now, taking another look at the CCTV to see if we can narrow down what car she left in. He made it clear enough my services were no longer required so it looks as though Professional Standards has run out of patience with our part in all this. And frankly, who can blame them?' He makes it clear who this last rhetorical question is aimed at by shooting daggers at Tyler again.

Tyler had confessed his little secret to them both when Doggett got back from the hospital. He'd already reported to Franklin that Jude might be a material suspect in the case. Franklin had immediately told him he was off the case pending further instruction and Mina and Doggett had no idea yet whether that included them as well. Mina checks the clock on her monitor. Gone midnight. She supposes they would have heard by now if it was bad news.

Tyler's being unusually quiet, even for him. He's staring at his desk as though trying to decide on something. He's made six phone calls since he got back here – Mina counted – none of which were answered. She's assuming they were to his brother.

She'd been angry with him, of course. Firstly, because he'd managed to palm the photo in the pub without her even noticing – she felt very foolish about that – and secondly, because he was keeping secrets again so soon after they'd agreed to start trusting each other. It hurt. Badly. And her instinct as always was to jump to extreme measures and start considering if she really had a future here in CCRU all over again. But after an hour or so to reflect on matters she was finding it difficult to hold on to her anger. *What would you have done if Ghulam was involved?*

'What about those pictures you got from the pub?' Doggett asks, snapping her out of her thoughts.

Now it's her turn to be on the defensive. 'I've not had

them five minutes! It's gonna take time to catalogue every face, do background checks. That's assuming I can identify all of them and there's no guarantee of that.'

Doggett throws his head back in disgust but must realise even he can't fault her on this excuse.

Tyler stands up suddenly and grabs his car keys.

'Where are you off to?' Doggett demands.

'I'm not just going to sit here. I'm going to find her.'

'You're off the case, remember?'

'Then I'm going home.'

'Yeah, I bet. After you have a good drive around first. I'm coming with you.'

'No, you're not.'

'Try and stop me.'

'Jim, please!' It isn't often Tyler loses his cool but he's highly emotional now. He looks almost on the verge of tears. 'I need to do this on my own.'

They stare at each other for a moment and Mina can't tell who's going to break first. Finally, Doggett backs down. 'You're not on your own,' he says, in a much more measured tone than he's been using up until now. 'You never have been. Don't forget that.'

Tyler nods. He turns to her. 'Mina, have you got that info I asked for?'

'Not yet,' she says. 'I'm working on it.'

'Okay, thank you. Call me when you have it.' And with that he walks out.

Doggett watches him go with a worried expression

etched on his face. Then he realises she's watching him and shakes himself out of it. 'You heard the man, get on with it then!'

Mina smiles to herself. 'Yes, boss.' She turns back to her screen.

There's no sign of Jude at the apartment. Worse than that, his stuff is gone.

It takes Tyler back to that moment in Jude's bedroom all those years ago and all at once he's a kid again. Despite all the promises, Jude's talk of making things right, he's done it again. And Tyler let him. He knew this moment was coming right from the start and he allowed it to happen. He slams the side of his fist against the living room wall; the pain rippling out from his bullet graze is almost comforting. A part of him has been waiting for this moment, this confirmation that he was right. And that's all fine, as long as it doesn't cost a young girl her life. As long as it doesn't mean their father's killer has got away.

He can't focus on that now. Edith's missing, on his watch. She could already be dead. Either way, he *has* to find her.

He's considering where to try next when Mina's call comes.

'You were right,' she says.

'About which bit?'

'All of it. Take your pick – drugs, lock-ins, a far-right group.'

'Okay, send me the details. Just an overview should do. Thanks, Mina.'

'Tyler,' she says, just as he's about to hang up. 'Be careful.'
He promises her he will.

The drive back to the Grapes of Rotherham takes no more
than fifteen minutes at this time of night and the car park is
just as empty. Inside, there are more patrons than there were
earlier in the day but still not many. Some of them are even
the same ones, including the middle-aged woman sitting at
the bar. She smiles at him this time, displaying a row of teeth
that are as in need of repair as the pub itself.

'What now?' Ashworth asks with his usual charm. 'You
after the shirt off me back now, and all?'

'I want you to tell me what you remember about Jake
Baker,' Tyler says.

'I've already told you. I don't.'

'Yes, I thought that's what you'd say. Let's see if I can
jog your memory.' He glances down at the info on his
mobile screen. 'Possession of drugs with intent to supply.
Unauthorised use of premises for illegal gatherings. Lock-
ins. Assault and battery. Three allegations of date-rape
where this venue was cited as the last place the victim
drank. And . . . oh, this is a good one, noise complaint from
a number of neighbours regarding a dog. That's probably
enough to start with although I'm sure there's plenty more.'

'What are you banging on about? I haven't been charged
with any of that crap.'

'No, you haven't. But your old patron, Gareth
Whitehouse, is not going to be able to have a word

with the right people anymore, given that he was found strung up by his neck a few hours ago with his trousers full of shit.'

The snarl on Ashworth's face dissipates and Tyler sees the first signs of doubt creeping in.

'I don't have time to fuck around so I'm not going to. If you don't tell me what I want to know, right now, I'm going to make it my life's work to bring you down, and given the weight of allegations that have already been made about this place over the years it really shouldn't take me very long.

'Added to that, I believe your licence is up for renewal in six months. Have a guess how well that's going to go for you?'

'Fucking cops!' Ashworth grabs a pint from behind the bar and takes a large swig of ale.

'On the other hand, if you tell me what I need to know maybe I'll be too busy dealing with that other stuff to look into this place too deeply.'

'I get the fucking message. What do you want to know?'

'Jake Baker!' Tyler says, slamming his palm down on the bar. 'Who did he hang out with?' McKenna beat Jake up as 'a lesson to the others'. He has a strong suspicion Jude was one of those 'others' but by definition there had to be at least one more.

Ashworth takes his time but Tyler knows he's got him. Eventually, he says, 'There was three of them. Always hanging out together. I'm not saying I know anything about what they got up to but whatever it was, they was probably in it together.' Ashworth stops.

'Names.'

'Haven't got a Scooby.'

Tyler pulls out his phone again and looks around the room. 'Fine,' he says loudly. 'Maybe we'll get a team down here now, shall we? I'll start by having a word with a few of your customers, see if they can help me with these drugs allegations.'

There are a couple of young lads playing pool who glance at each other and avoid his gaze. Tyler turns back to the bar but is satisfied to hear the back door go. He's guessing the lads have decided to abandon their game.

'They called themselves the three Jays,' Ashworth tells him. 'Jake, Jackson and a younger fella. I can't remember his name.'

Tyler finds the photo of Jude stored on his phone and shows it to the landlord.

'Yeah, that's him. He ain't changed much, 'as he? Except for the hairline. But I'm telling you the truth, I haven't got a clue what his name was.'

Tyler pockets his mobile again. 'Fine. Let's talk about Jackson. First name or second.'

'No idea.'

Tyler makes a show of getting his phone out again but Ashworth holds his hands up.

'I swear, I never knew it. So you can do what you want but it ain't gonna help me remember 'cos I don't know.'

Tyler pauses for a moment and then relaxes his body language a little. 'Did they know your friend Whitehouse?'

Ashworth shrugs. 'Everyone knows Mr Whitehouse. There's no crime in that.'

'There is if he asked them to rob his own safe for him.'

'I don't know anything about that.'

'No, of course you don't.'

'I'm telling you, that's all I know. Now you can do what you want. You fuckers always do anyway.'

'What about your regulars? Any of them who might remember something?'

'Doubtful,' Ashworth says, but his eyes flick quickly, once and back, to the woman at the end of the bar.

'Fine. You won't mind if I ask then?'

Ashworth smiles widely. 'Be my guest, *officer*.' The landlord takes himself off out the back. He could be doing anything but if Tyler had money to put on it he'd bet the man was calling for a few mates to back him up. Which means if he wasn't on the clock before he certainly is now.

He smiles at the woman at the end of the bar and makes his way over to her.

'All right, love,' she says. Her words are slurred and she's struggling to focus on his face.

'Don't suppose you overheard any of that?'

'Not my business, love.'

'That's a shame. Because if you knew anything, there'd definitely be a drink in it for you.'

Her eyes take on a new focus. 'How big a drink?'

'Double?'

'Go on then,' she says.

Ashworth reappears at the end of the bar and Tyler calls him over with a flick of his head. The landlord looks away with a scowl and sends the barmaid over in his place.

'Double ... ?'

'Gin, love,' the woman says.

'Double gin for the lady,' he tells the barmaid and the woman titters at his cheek.

'Aren't you joining me?'

'Go on then, make it two,' he calls after the barmaid.

'We'll have the good stuff!' the woman shouts.

He nods his agreement, after all, he doubts the good stuff is all that much more expensive in a place like this. He turns back to his new friend. 'If you're lucky I won't even drink mine.'

The woman raises the remains of her current pint to him in salute.

Tyler fills her in on what he wants, showing her the picture of Jude and a picture of Jake Baker that his mother gave them.

'The three Jays,' he tells her.

'I remember them,' she says. 'Handsome lads. Though none of them was bothered about the likes of me.' She laughs at her own self-deprecation.

'The third man, Jackson,' he asks, as the barmaid returns with his drinks. 'Do you remember his other name?'

'No, love,' she says simply, and Tyler curses himself for being played. But then she goes on. 'I can tell you who they used to hang about with though.'

'Yeah?'

'Yep.' She downs the first gin in one and smacks her lips. He pushes the second glass towards her and she nods a thank you. 'Girl who lived over Oughtibridge way. We was at school together. Darke, her name is. Melanie Darke.'

'You're sure?'

'As sure as I am you're going to buy me another drink.'

He nods.

'The four of them used to be in and out of here all the time for . . . a few months, I reckon. Most of that summer. Till she got herself up the duff. Didn't see her much after that and the others all disappeared an' all.'

'One of them was the father?'

The woman shrugs. 'Could have been any of them, the way I see it. From what I remember, she weren't all that choosy.'

Edith pulls herself up out of the sticky darkness. She opens her eyes and winces at the harsh light shining down on her from above. She raises an arm to shield her face but it responds sluggishly. When she tries to sit up her head hurts but she manages to force herself up, up . . .

'Just stay where you are,' says a voice, a woman's voice.

'Wha—' Edith's mouth won't work properly. It feels like it's full of cotton wool.

'I still have this.' The knife turns in her hand.

Edith shudders and looks away. She tries to take in her surroundings. She's sitting on a black leather couch on one side of the room and the woman from the hospital car park is standing on the other side. There's a desk and a couple of other chairs. It looks like an office of some sort, the harsh strip lighting in the ceiling still hurts her eyes and she has to keep them squinted.

'Who are you?' she manages. 'What did you do to me?'

'Never mind that.' The woman's pacing, back and forth across the room, a mobile phone clutched in one hand, the knife still in the other. She walks gingerly with her high heels making *pok-pok* noises as she crosses the wooden floor. She keeps brushing her red bob back behind her ears, which seems like a colossal waste of time to Edith, given it's not really long enough and instantly falls back into its previous position.

'Why are you doing this?'

'You don't think I want to, do you?' the woman snaps at her. 'I'm sorry, really I am. I put a plaster on your leg. It looks fine.'

Edith looks down at her thigh. 'You gave me something.'

'Just a party drug, don't worry about it. It's already working its way out of your system. I just needed a way of bringing you here quietly. Luckily, I know a man who likes to party with young women and keeps a stash of this stuff around.' She lifts her thumbnail to her mouth and bites on it. 'Or rather, I used to know him.'

'Where's here?'

'Just . . . Stop talking, will you? I'm trying to think.'

Edith decides to hold her tongue for a bit. She stretches her arms and legs, trying to see if they're up for whatever they might have to be up for.

'Whatever you're planning to do, don't!' the woman says, waving the knife at her. But her eyes stray to the door and Edith realises she's scared. She isn't going to use the knife again. If Edith tries anything the woman will just run, no doubt locking the door behind her.

'Please,' Edith says, trying a different approach. 'I think there's been a mistake.'

The woman laughs. 'No mistake. At least, not recently.' Again her eyes flick towards the door and she checks her mobile screen. She's waiting for something. Or someone.

'The Reservoir Man.'

Edith doesn't realise she's said it out loud until the woman looks at her sharply. 'Just be quiet. It won't be long now.'

'You know he's going to kill me, don't you?'

The woman walks back to the desk but doesn't sit down. She doesn't seem to know what to do.

'You said before you don't want to hurt me but you must know he's going to kill me?'

'I don't have a choice!'

'Please, just let me go. I won't tell anyone.'

Again the woman laughs. 'Sure. I totally believe you. But it doesn't make any difference. They'd kill me anyway, long before the police caught up with me. String me up like that pathetic excuse for a man who got me into this mess.'

Edith risks standing up. The woman is instantly alert and moves a little closer to the door. Edith puts her hands up. 'I'm not going to try anything. I just want to explain this to you.'

'Explain? Explain what?'

'That you're being silly.'

'What?' The woman laughs.

'He's going to kill you, too,' Edith says, and she sees by the haunted look in the woman's eyes that this has already occurred to her. 'He wants me because I saw his face. If he's coming here to get me, and if you see him as well, do you really think he's just going to let you go?'

The woman shakes her head. 'You're wrong. I'm one of them. I've been part of this for years, they wouldn't . . .'

'Was he one of them, as well?'

'Who?'

'The pathetic excuse for a man who got you into this mess.'

The woman's lip curls and Edith wonders if she's gone too far. She rushes on. 'That's why he made you get me from the hospital. Because it doesn't matter if anyone saw *your* face. You know the police probably have your car details by now anyway, the car park's full of cameras. He can't afford to let them catch up with you. Which means—'

'Shut up! Just . . . just be quiet.'

'If you call them now, turn yourself in, they can protect you.' The woman says nothing so Edith risks a little more. 'I don't think you want to do this, do you?'

The woman lets go of the knife and it clatters onto the desk. 'My God, I'm going to jail for kidnapping a minor.'

'I'll tell them I came with you.'

'Yeah, right.'

'Prison's better than dead, isn't it?'

'I'm really not sure about that.' The woman sits down at the desk and drops the phone.

Edith wonders if she can make it to the door in time. Maybe. She's fast. Faster than a woman in heels. But she doesn't know if her legs work properly yet and she has no idea if the door is unlocked.

'When's he coming?' Edith asks in a small voice.

'I don't know. Any minute.'

'Do it, please. Call the police! Quickly, before he comes. It's not too late.'

'My name's Harriet,' the woman says, finally.

'Edith.'

'I really am sorry, Edith.'

Tyler can hear Rabbani tapping away on her keyboard down the line. He's pulled up in a layby with the engine still running and every now and then a passing vehicle shakes the car. The hazard lights tick, tick, tick, counting down the seconds.

'Anything?' he asks.

'Bloody hell, give me a chance!'

'Mark Jackson,' he says again, although he knows full well she hasn't forgotten.

'Yes, Doggett texted me after he spoke to you.'

It hadn't taken long to get the man's first name from Melanie Darke after Doggett went back to the hospital. The harder job had been getting in to see her without Professional Standards knowing. He'd managed it by using the excuse of visiting Jordan. Tyler was glad when Doggett had told him she was doing well after her operation.

'You know there's gonna be hundreds though, don't you?' Rabbani asks.

'I doubt that many.'

She tuts. 'You know what I mean. It'll take me hours to go through them all, even siphoning out the ones who are the wrong age and race. And you're assuming he's still going by that name, how do you know he hasn't changed it?'

'I don't, I just . . . We need to find her.' There's a beeping in his ear. 'Hang on,' he says, 'I'm getting another call. It could be Doggett with more info.'

'Great,' Rabbani says, 'I'll call you when I've got something.' And then she hangs up before he can speak.

He puts the other call through. 'Tyler.'

'Detective? It's Harriet Spencer.'

'Ms Spencer?' Tyler's instinct is to brush her off but something about her voice alerts him. 'It's very late.'

'You need to come to the factory.'

'I'm pretty tied up with something right now.'

'She's here. Edith Darke is here.'

'What?'

'There isn't time to explain but . . . the man you're looking for, he's . . . he's on his way here now. Please, you have to help us!'

The hair stands up on Tyler's arms. 'Get up and get out, now. Go to the cab firm and I'll meet you there. If you can't manage that, find a place to hide. Anywhere. I'm two minutes away.'

'Go to the left of reception,' she says. 'My office is—'

The line goes dead.

'Shit!' Tyler pulls out his radio and calls it in. Then he slams the car into gear and speeds out of the layby and onto the road.

There's the sound of a door opening somewhere outside the office and Harriet drops her phone again. 'He's here.'

Edith stands by the leather couch and tries to work out what to do. She can feel her heart hammering so hard it feels like it's going to burst out of her chest. The door to the office swings open and there he is, the Reservoir Man. He looks straight at her and she realises he's older than she thought. If she'd ever got round to completing that sketch they wanted her to do she wonders how much she would have got right. The eyes, she thinks. She would have got those right.

He looks across at the desk and the shaking form of Harriet Spencer.

'I thought you were never going to get here,' she says conversationally. Her voice is light and airy but Edith can hear the tremor in it and she suspects the Reservoir Man can as well.

The two of them stare at each other for a moment, sizing each other up. Then Harriet's phone vibrates with an incoming call and judders across the desk.

'Leave it.' The Reservoir Man's voice is remarkably soft.

There's a split second where neither of them seem sure what's going to happen next and then they both move at once. Harriet dives forward to grab the phone but the Reservoir Man's already there.

'No,' Edith shouts. She watches the two of them grappling with the phone and sees the man bring his elbow down into Harriet's stomach. She doesn't let go.

Then, finally, Edith remembers to run. She's off the starting blocks, her legs wobbling a little, maybe adrenaline again, or possibly it's the drugs that must still be in her system. She's halfway to the door before the Reservoir Man registers her movement. Harriet holds on though and Edith sends her a silent thank you. She sees the woman's face crumple beneath the Reservoir Man's elbow and blood spurts out in a wide arc across the desk.

Edith turns and runs.

The room she emerges into is another office of some kind, a waiting room or reception area, perhaps, but she doesn't have time to take in the details. She only sees two doors, one left, one right, and for no other reason than that the left one is closer she makes her choice. She pushes it open and finds herself in a long, wide corridor with high windows. She runs.

She's less than halfway along when she hears him behind her, his footsteps drumming on the floor in a counterpoint to her own. If she has to stop to open the door at the end, he will have her.

On she runs down the endless corridor. Ahead are a pair of double doors that look as if they swing open. She has no idea if they will but what choice does she have? The cut from the knife on her leg aches and pulses but she has no time to worry about that. And then she senses more than hears him slowing. She feels as though she's pulling ahead of him somehow. Is he giving up? She's nearly at the doors, reaching out for them.

The gunshot cracks down the empty corridor just as Edith reaches the door. She barrels through the doorway and feels a rush of air pass her neck as something slams into the door in front of her, then she's through and running along another narrower corridor. She knows she doesn't have long before he'll have another line of sight on her. She runs faster than she ever has in her life, her feet slamming down hard on the concrete floor. The corridor ends at a twisted metal staircase leading upwards. It will slow her down but again she has no choice and throws herself at them just as she hears the door behind her crash open.

There's another gunshot and a flash at her feet as the bullet hits the stairs. She yelps but her feet are still moving, upwards, two steps at a time. She can't keep going up though, he might be able to see her through the ironwork of the stairs. She peels off at the first landing and along yet another corridor.

The first door on the left is locked but there's a frosted window to the right and then a second door, which opens when she turns the handle. She steps onto a metal gantry that runs around the wall of a large room full of stainless-steel vats and machinery. The walkway leads back the way she came with nothing between her and the corridor she has just run down but the frosted window. There's another door on the far side of the room and a metal staircase leading down into the room itself but to reach them she will have to follow the gantry around the walls. She'll never make it in time.

She's a moving target, she reasons as she runs on, better than standing still and waiting for him to finish the job. She can see his silhouette moving past the window. Edith screams again as the glass cracks. He must have slammed something against it, the gun maybe, but it holds and then she's past it and turning left onto the next walkway.

And now her luck really does run out. The walkway ends a few feet in front of her at a railing. There's a gap of three feet or more and then a separate walkway that leads to the door and the staircase.

From behind her comes the sound of two sharp cracks and the bullets ping off the railing inches from her hands. She turns and freezes. The Reservoir Man has reached the end of the walkway and he walks calmly towards her, along the gantry, the gun held low at his waist but trained on her. Now that she's cornered, he's taking his time.

She looks at him, the demon she's been running from for days now. He's finally found her. He hesitates for a second or two, perhaps not so far gone that he finds it easy to murder a fifteen-year-old girl in cold blood. But then he seems to make his decision. He raises the gun and aims as Edith screams, 'You're my father!'

Tyler screeches to a halt outside the main entrance of Delight!, jumps out of the car and races into the building. The main doors are open, just as the gate had been, with no sign of any receptionists or security guards as there were last time. He supposes Harriet Spencer has arranged to have the place to herself tonight, which suggests she is in on all of this.

In reception he takes the left-hand corridor rather than the right which Spencer and Whitehouse led him down when he was here before. It bends round behind the extravagant waiting room that he and Rabbani were shown into when they first arrived, and opens out into another reception space. The door to the inner office is open.

He finds Harriet Spencer lying face down on the floor near her desk, her mobile just inches from her outstretched hand. He bends down and checks for a pulse in her wrist. He finds it, strong and steady. She groans.

'Harriet. Harriet, wake up.' He has to force himself to be gentle with her. She could have internal injuries. 'Harriet, what happened? Where's Edith?'

Spencer forces herself up onto her knees. One of her shoes has come off and the heel has snapped and is jutting out at an angle. Her nose is red and enflamed and her face covered in blood, her perfect red bob matted with the stuff.

'Harriet!' he says again, drawing her focus as she touches her hand to her nose and winces. 'The girl.'

She shakes her head.

He grabs her by both arms. 'Where is she?'

'I don't know, I don't . . . Honestly, please . . .'

'You're one of them, aren't you? The Circle.'

She doesn't answer but she doesn't have to. It's plain enough that she knows what he's talking about.

'Who did this? The ICER?'

She nods. 'I ... I'll tell you what I know but you need to go after her, now. He was right behind her.'

She's right, he can't waste time on her. He straightens up and heads for the door.

'Left,' she calls after him. 'If you didn't pass them on the way in, they went left.'

He looks back at her once and sees her clutching her stomach. Then he leaves her and turns into the office. Two doors. Was she telling the truth? She must have been or he would have seen them, surely? He can't be that far behind.

Then he hears the gunshots.

Edith opens her eyes. He's watching her but the gun's no longer raised. Her heart is thrumming in her ears. She can see the Reservoir Man thinking about her words.

'How old are you?' he asks.

'Fif–fifteen.'

He cocks his head to one side, examining her like some hunting animal whose prey has suddenly done something wholly unexpected.

'My ... my mum is Melanie. Melanie Darke. I was born in January 2003. She said you were my dad.' It's a lie born of desperation and Edith knows she isn't very good at lying. But it could be true so that doesn't really make it a lie, does it? She hopes she's selling it. 'My mum ... Melanie ...' Maybe naming her again will give him pause, remind him of whatever it was they had in the past. She saw a documentary once about hostage-takers. You were supposed to make them see you as a real human being. She supposes it's worth trying. 'She said you would never hurt us. She said it was an accident what happened at the house. I'm sorry. I'm sorry I ran.'

The Reservoir Man steps closer. 'You can't be mine,' he says.

'Why not? You slept with her, didn't you?'

The man frowns and studies her face, perhaps looking for something that will convince him that what she's saying is true. How can she convince him? She reaches for her pocket and the Reservoir Man twitches the gun.

'I have a photo,' she says, hurriedly. She pulls it out and lifts it up to him. 'See? Here, this is you, isn't it?' She tries to keep her hand over the other man, the man on the right that her mother said she loved, but she can't cover the middle part of the photo, the policeman's brother, without covering her mother as well. And anyway, he was there when the photo was taken, he must remember who else was there.

The man leans forward and studies the photo dispassion- ately. He's so cold, Edith realises. That's what she saw in his eyes at the reservoir. That sliver of ice glinting out at her. For the first time she realises that it may not even matter if he believes her, he might just kill her anyway.

He crouches down and takes the photo from her trembling hand and studies it, moving his finger across the glossy surface. This is her chance, Edith realises, while he's distracted. But what can she do against this man? He could easily overpower her. Maybe she could grab the gun, spin it around, shoot him in the stomach. But she knows she hasn't got the strength and she doubts she could ever pull the trigger anyway.

'Interesting,' he says, and his voice is like a cool breeze over a glacial stream. 'But I don't think so.' He stands up, the photograph still clutched in his hand.

'Wait!' Edith says, but she's run out of arguments.

He raises the gun for the second time.

'Please.'

'You're not my daughter,' he says.

'I could be. How do you know?'

He hesitates one last time, again examining her for a moment. 'You don't have my eyes,' he says, and points the gun at her face.

There are no more gunshots and Tyler doesn't know if that's a good sign or a bad one. He races down another one of the wide corridors with the enormous windows. He doesn't think it's the same one they came along when he was here before but it might as well be. It ends in a set of double doors, the right-hand of which has a fresh hole in the wood. It looks like a bullet hole, but it can't have been the shot he heard. That was farther away, somewhere much deeper in the building.

Behind these doors is another, narrower, more utilitarian corridor leading to a metallic spiral staircase. When he reaches the first floor he has to choose a direction. Did they go up or along? He stops and listens and can hear the faint sound of someone talking. He inches his way carefully along the next corridor, sees the open door to the right and the smashed glass of the frosted window. He steps through the doorway and onto a metallic gantry. This is the room he was shown on his tour. The heart of the operation with its gigantic cake mixers and ovens, all of which currently lie dormant.

He can hear now that it's Edith talking. Clever girl. But he can also hear the fear in her voice. He can't see them yet because of the large vat blocking his view. He treads carefully, inching forward. The back of the ICER – Jackson – comes into view. And then he says something that Tyler can't quite make out and raises his gun.

'Jackson!' Tyler shouts. The man spins and fires and Tyler drops to the metal floor, the bullet smashing straight through the glass behind him. 'Jackson, stop this! We know who you are. There's no way out of this now. Don't make it worse.'

But Tyler's all too aware that he's the one at a major disadvantage. He climbs back to his feet but stays low behind the railing. All Jackson has to do is backtrack a few feet to the corner, and he'd have a clear line of sight. He does just that.

'Detective Tyler,' he says, pointing the gun. 'This is the second time I've had a shot at you. This time I'm not going to miss.'

Tyler hears Edith shout, 'No.'

Jackson pulls the trigger and the gun clicks. He's out of bullets. There's a moment of hesitation and then they're both running, Tyler towards Jackson, Jackson towards Edith. As

Tyler reaches the corner he sees Jackson get hold of the girl. She does her best to struggle but she's so much smaller than he is. He wraps his hands around her body and holds her in front of him, a hand tight around her neck.

'No!' Tyler shouts.

'That's close enough,' Jackson tells him.

Edith's eyes stare at him in horror. Tyler steps forward.

Jackson tightens his grip and tips Edith's head back. 'One more step and I snap her neck.'

Tyler freezes. He doesn't know how easy it is to snap someone's neck but if anyone knows how to, it's this man.

'All right, all right!' Tyler tells him, spreading his hands wide. 'Think about this. We know who you are, Mark. We know who you work for.'

'I doubt that.'

'The Circle, right?'

'You've got no idea who they are.' Jackson adjusts his grip and Edith chokes.

'But you could tell us, couldn't you? You could use that to your advantage. But if you kill that girl in cold blood, in front of me, I promise you, you won't see the light of day again. I'll make sure of that.'

Jackson smiles. Tyler doesn't think he's ever seen anything as cold and emotionless as that smile. This isn't a man who's going to be moved into doing deals. He doesn't care.

'All right,' Tyler says. 'You want us to know, don't you? After all these years don't you want us to know how clever you've been? All the stuff you've achieved. Killing

Whitehouse and Stevens. Setting up McKenna to take the fall for Jake Baker's death.'

Again Jackson laughs, but this time Tyler's managed to touch a nerve. 'McKenna killed him, all right. Beat him to death in front of us all as a warning not to go off doing little jobs of our own.'

'The robbery, here. Whitehouse got you and your mates to steal the cash from his own safe and McKenna wasn't happy about it.'

'My mates,' Jackson says, rolling the phrase around on his tongue as though the concept was new to him. 'No, that was all down to Baker and your doe-eyed brother. Amateur hour. I had enough sense not to get involved.

'But that's what started it. Your old man decided he didn't like the company his eldest son was keeping and spoke to McKenna. McKenna went off the deep end and the Powers That Be decided they needed some leverage over him.'

'So they recruited you to keep Jake's corpse handy in case he ever got out of line again.'

'Chip off the old block, aren't you?'

Tyler's been trying to put off the question. He already knows the answer and he's worried what he'll do if this man says the wrong thing. But he thinks he can maybe hear the distant sound of footsteps somewhere in the building. Doggett's here somewhere, he just needs to stall a bit longer. He tells himself to stay focused on Edith. She's what's important here, nothing else. But he can't help himself, he has to know.

'Did you kill him?'

Jackson smiles that terrible smile again. 'No,' he says. 'He killed himself. Swallowed the tablets, put the noose around his own neck and jumped.'

Tyler's ears are ringing, his vision blurred. 'You're lying.'

'I gave him the choice. Either he could kill himself, with me watching, or I could do it for him. Obviously the former was better for me but I could have worked with the latter.'

Tyler laughs and is surprised by the sound that comes out of his mouth, how mirthless it is. 'Why would he do that?'

'Because of you. You were due home from school at any moment. I told him if he did what I asked I'd let you go. But if he forced me to kill him and ruined my plans, then I'd hang around and finish you off as well. If I couldn't make it look like suicide I would have had to be a bit more creative. A home invasion gone wrong. A family torn apart. So sad.'

A low growl starts up in Tyler's chest and erupts. He takes another step forward and again Jackson tightens his grip and bends Edith's head back. Tyler stops, Edith's face turning red, her eyes bulging, her hands pulling tightly on Jackson's wrist.

'You know,' Jackson says. 'It's haunted me over the years, letting you get away. It just didn't sit right. But somehow I knew this day would come. It's like it was meant to be. Now, let's see just how like your old man you really are, shall we? Jump!'

'What?'

'Jump off this walkway and I'll let her go.'

Tyler hesitates, considering it. 'I don't believe you.'

'No,' Jackson says. 'I didn't think you would.' Then he picks Edith up, one hand still round her neck, the other on the back of her trousers, and hauls her over the railing.

Tyler screams, 'No!'

He runs forward but Jackson already has Edith in the air. She's grabbing at him with her hands, kicking out with her feet. She's over the edge but for some reason Jackson doesn't let go straight away. She manages to get a grip on the railings and only then does he release her. Then he turns, climbs the railing and leaps across the gap to the far gantry. It's only about three feet wide and he makes it easily, crashing against the railing on the opposite side.

But Tyler doesn't have time to watch any further and that's exactly what Jackson must have been banking on. He grabs a handful of Edith's fleece and hauls her up. 'I've got you,' he tells her, but she's squirming and wriggling and can't get her feet to connect with anything. 'Edith!' he says sharply. She stops moving. 'I've got hold of you but you need to climb up. I won't let you fall. I promise.'

She nods her understanding. And then she hauls herself up. It's slow going. Tyler doesn't want to loosen his hold on her to help so she has to do most of the work herself. She doesn't look particularly strong but then she doesn't weigh a great deal either. She's brave though. She doesn't cry out or look down and cling to him. She does what she has to, methodically, calmly. Like she does this sort of thing all the time. Even so, it's a relief when she manages to get her foot on the railing and take some of the weight off his arms. He can't relax though. If she slips, there's only the tight grip his fingers have on her jacket to keep her from falling twenty feet to the concrete below.

Finally she gets her other foot up and he manages to straighten and help her get her leg over the top of the railing. Then she's falling against him, her skinny little arms wrapping themselves tightly round his body.

'Thank you,' she says. 'Thank you.' He can feel her tiny body trembling.

'I'm sorry,' he says. 'He wouldn't have let you go if I'd jumped. You'd seen his face.'

'I know,' she says. 'I know.'

The door on the far gantry swings shut. She lets go of him and must see the direction of his gaze.

'Go,' she says. 'Get him.'

'I can't leave you.'

'I'm fine. Go! *Go!*'

Tyler can hear voices down below. 'Head straight back the way we came. Find DI Doggett. Jim. You remember him?'

She nods, turns and runs.

Tyler climbs up on the railing. This is crazy. It's really not that far to the opposite gantry, though. Or it wouldn't be if the drop wasn't quite so high. He jumps, his body hitting the railing on the far side with a clang. His feet scramble for purchase but his hands have a firm grip. His little finger is bent round and pressed against the mesh but he's safe. He climbs over the railing onto the firm floor of the gantry on the other side.

The door Jackson has taken is the one Spencer opened for him the other day, leading into the old part of the factory. He sees the sign again. *Danger of falling.* He steps through onto another gantry and surveys the room with its giant smelting pot taking centre stage. It would make sense for Jackson to have headed down but there's no sign of him on the emergency staircase where the marked safe path is indicated with green emergency exit signage.

He looks up and just catches a glimpse of movement on one of the gantries above. He's gone up. This staircase has another danger sign and a piece of mesh welded over it to prevent access. He steps over it and begins his ascent.

It's five storeys to the top of the gantry. The walkways on the final level are narrower than the ones below, presumably used for nothing more than occasional maintenance. A few feet above Tyler hangs the ancient glass roof, many of its panels long since shattered and fallen to the ground far below. At least that's letting in enough light pollution from the city so that Tyler can see where he's going. The roof panels that have survived are darkened with dirt and moss and one even has a tree growing down through a gap in the glass.

Parts of the gantry here are red with rust. At one point Tyler stumbles and clutches at the handrail only for a chunk of the metal to break off in his hand. His arms whirlwind in the air as he looks down at the giant rusted cauldron below, before he manages to regain his balance and back away from the edge.

The narrow walkway goes on ahead but there's no sign

of Jackson that way. There's a junction to the right though, that stretches away into the darkness on the other side of the building. Tyler turns right, moving across the centre part of the room, the giant pot lying idle beneath him. No molten steel in its empty black belly but nevertheless, he wouldn't like to fall into it.

There's no sign of Jackson but also no other route he could have taken. Still, Tyler's beginning to worry that maybe he made a mistake. Perhaps the movement he saw was nothing but a pigeon or a rat exploring this abandoned part of the building. But as he gets closer he sees that the gantry ends on the far side next to a skylight in the glass roof. An open skylight.

Surely he can't have gone outside? As if this area wasn't precarious enough, the roof must be deadly. Tyler climbs up a couple of metal stairs and leans out into the night. Now he's here, he can see that there's another gantry on the outside, nothing more than a narrow ledge that goes around the roof, presumably to allow the window cleaners access to an otherwise inaccessible rooftop. Not that these windows have been cleaned for decades. When was the last time someone came this way? Would it even take Jackson's weight?

Tyler's not sure if it's the sound of the air displacing or the shadow that he notices first but whichever it is saves his life. He throws himself left, out of the window and onto the roof, skidding and sliding across the ice-coated glass. The metal bar or whatever it is comes down hard on the sill of the window where he was standing. Tyler feels the vibration run through the metal framework of the building and up through his feet. Jackson's above him, perched on top of the skylight frame, but not for long. He recovers quickly from the shockwave that must have travelled up his arms and is upright again before Tyler can properly find his footing.

Tyler can feel the glass cracking beneath his feet. He dives for the small walkway. It's not even wide enough to walk along without putting one foot in front of the other but he manages to get his body onto it as the glass panel under his feet shatters and falls. He strains with his arms and back to twist his feet up onto the walkway, the wound in his arm ripping open and weakening his left-hand grip. Jackson seems determined to finish him. He's coming at Tyler with the bar raised.

Tyler needs his hands to defend himself but he dare not let go of the walkway. He can feel the bar descending, hear the sound it makes as it splits the air. Tyler twists his whole body and lashes out with his legs, the muscles of his arms straining, trying to hold him in place on the narrow ledge. The bullet wound screams at him but somehow he manages it. Tyler's leg hits Jackson's and the assassin buckles at the knee.

Jackson goes down and Tyler manages to pull himself up into a sitting position. His balance is precarious, the slightest movement to the left will send him through the glass ceiling and down onto the factory floor. The two of them meet in an angry embrace, Tyler managing to catch Jackson's wrists before the metal bar connects. But Jackson follows through with his head, slamming it into Tyler's face. Tyler falls backwards again and the bar comes down across his throat.

He can feel his body sliding, left towards the hole in the glass, head first. He struggles to breathe, the only thing preventing him from choking are his own hands straining against the bar. He takes his right hand off, instantly feeling the increase in pressure on his throat, and slams his elbow into the side of Jackson's head. The assassin jerks sideways and Tyler uses the movement to swivel out from under him. He follows up his first hit with a jab to the man's throat and Jackson drops the bar, falling back towards the hole. Tyler catches hold of his shirt but Jackson tries to fight him off.

'I'm trying to save you, man!' Tyler shouts over the wind.

Jackson looks at him with those stone-cold eyes and Tyler realises the man would rather die than be caught.

'No!' he shouts. He grabs Jackson's arm, and knees him hard in the stomach. From his jacket pocket Tyler pulls out a pair of handcuffs and snaps one end on Jackson's wrist and the other onto the metal framework of the building. The killer collapses onto the walkway in a sitting position, his feet hanging over the edge in mid-air. Tyler smashes him hard in the face with his fist, again and again, using the man's belt to lever him back up onto something resembling firmer ground.

Jackson ends up lying on his back on the walkway with Tyler standing over him panting into the cold night air. He spits blood onto the glass pane at his feet.

'Mark Jackson,' he says, 'I'm arresting you for the murders of Gareth Whitehouse, Roger Stevens and Richard Tyler. You do not have to say anything. But it may harm your defence . . .'

the thaw

When Tyler walks out of the building Doggett is waiting with Edith. Once again, she throws her arm around his waist and buries her head in his chest. He winces slightly; his body feels like one enormous bruise.

Doggett grins. 'Reckon you've got a new fan there. Couldn't stop telling me how brave you are. Weren't sure we were talking about the same fella until just then.' He winks over the girl's head.

'You okay?' Tyler asks Edith.

She looks up at him and nods. Then her expression turns thoughtful.

'What?' he asks.

'Nothing,' she says. 'You have nice eyes.'

'All right,' Doggett says, pulling her away. 'Your mum's been asking for you.' Doggett calls over a young constable to escort Edith back to the hospital.

'Oh, wait,' she says, shrugging her way out of her coat. 'I stole this. Could you get it back to the right owner, please?'

Tyler looks at Doggett, who chuckles.

'Tell you what, you keep it for now. For the cold.'

'Will ... Will I see you again?' Edith asks.

Tyler smiles at her. 'Sure,' he says. 'I'll come by the hospital. There's some things your mum and I need to talk about.'

He watches her walk away through the crowds and only now does he realise what a three-ring circus Doggett has managed to rustle up. 'Did you leave anyone back at the station?' There are detectives and Uniforms gathered together chatting all over the place. Even that new girl from Doncaster – Vaughan? – is rubber-necking, trying to get a better view of proceedings.

'They all wanted ringside seats,' Doggett tells him, pointing up at the roof.

'You saw that, did you?'

'Some of it. What the bloody hell were you thinking?'

Tyler looks up at the roof and shivers as Rabbani and Toddy come out of the building with Mark Jackson cuffed between them. Vaughan jumps forward to open the car door for them. Tyler hears Doggett scoff at her brazen attempt to insert herself into the thick of it. Jackson stares at Tyler all the way to the car and only breaks eye contact when Rabbani puts her hand on his head and folds him into the back seat.

'You got him,' Doggett says.

'Yeah.'

'How tempted were you to let the bastard fall?'

'Never crossed my mind.'

'Sure.'

But it had. Fleetingly. It would have been easy not to help Jackson, to watch him fall to his death knowing he more than deserved it. He'd wanted to do it. For Richard. For his *father*. And that was ultimately what stopped him.

'At least we have a link to the Circle now,' Doggett tells him.

'He won't talk.'

'We'll see about that.'

'There's Harriet Spencer, at least. She'll be easier to break.'

'Assuming we find her.'

Tyler turns to look at Doggett. 'She was here.'

'Not when we arrived, she wasn't.'

'We need to get an All-Ports Warning out for her. Now!'

'All right, all right, calm down. I think you've had enough excitement for one day. Maybe you should get yourself home, eh?'

Tyler considers this. 'You're right. I should. There's still one loose end to tie up.'

He doesn't really expect Jude to be at the apartment when he gets back but he is, sitting on the sofa in his boxers-tee combo as though the place is his home away from home. Tyler's almost disappointed. Half of him had hoped he'd done a runner.

'I thought you'd gone.'

Jude jumps up as he comes in. 'I did. But I came back.'

Tyler punches him hard in the face and Jude goes down onto the sofa again.

'What the fuck?' He sits there, cradling his already swelling nose. 'Jesus!'

'You lied to me.'

'I didn't, I—'

'You were at that factory with Baker, weren't you?'

Jude closes his eyes.

'Were you the one that hit him? Kevin Linville. The security guard. Did you kill that man, Jude?'

Jude cradles his face but he doesn't deny the accusation. 'Kev told me to hit him. He . . . He wanted it to look good, for the police. I didn't mean . . .'

Tyler puts a hand to his head and rubs his eyes.

'I was just a kid, Adam. I didn't know what I was mixed up in . . .'

'Did Dad know?'

'What?'

Tyler shouts it. 'Did Dad know what you did?'

'No! No, he just knew I was mixed up with Jakey and the rest of them, like I told you.'

Tyler turns and heads into the spare room, his brother's voice following him all the way, pleading with him to understand. But Tyler does understand. If Jude hadn't been involved in the factory job then Richard wouldn't have gone to see McKenna. He'd never have heard about the Circle and they would never have sent Jackson to silence him. He knows that nothing is as simple as that, not really, but at the moment he doesn't care.

'Please, mate,' Jude begs, 'don't do this.'

'You asked me the other day if it was your fault.' Tyler picks up his brother's jeans from off the bed and tosses them at him. 'It was. Now put some bloody clothes on. Jude Tyler, I'm arresting you for the murder of Kevin Linville . . .'

Acknowledgements

This book was late. Blame lockdown, blame the creative process, blame whatever you want, just don't blame me. I owe an enormous thank you to Bethan Jones who not only failed to question my 'dog-ate-homework' excuses but also went on to make this book a hundred times better. The team at Simon & Schuster as a whole have been nothing but supportive. Huge thanks in particular to Jess Barratt, Sarah Jeffcoate, Katherine Armstrong, Clare Hey, Hayley McMullan, Harriett Collins and Craig Fraser. Apologies if I've forgotten anyone.

Thanks, as always, to my brilliant agent, Sarah Hornsley. I can't believe we've published three novels! I couldn't have done any of this without you.

An enormous thank you to former DCI David Stopford. David led homicide and kidnap investigations at South Yorkshire Police's Major Crime Unit, and now leads the

Review Team, South Yorkshire's real life CCRU. They review all undetected homicides after 28 days as well as cold cases dating back to the 1960s. Given all the bad press the police have been getting lately, and the fact that a good part of the plot of this book revolves around corruption, I'd like to make it clear that the majority of police officers care very much about what they do, and work hard to get to the truth on behalf of victims and their families. David and his team are solid proof of this. I'm hugely grateful for his help and also for the fact he offers it so cheaply (I definitely owe you a few more pints).

Many, many thanks to Dean Rowbotham, the finest bearded paramedic I know, who talked me through some basic emergency medical care. If I've made any mistakes in this regard, it's undoubtedly his fault.

Thanks to Anne Perry for introducing me to her friend Dr Michael Rathbone who helped sense check some of my ideas and provided lots of gruesome information about bruising, mummification and frozen corpses. Anything I got right is down to him. Anything I got wrong is entirely deliberate on my part and you just haven't understood what I was doing so you should probably read the book again.

And where would we be without friends? Thank you, as always, to Susan Elliot Wright and Marion Dillon for reading pretty much every word I write and telling me which ones are the wrong ones. Thank you to Henna Ahmed for helping me shape Mina's world. To Phillip for marketing advice, sales advice, story advice, romantic advice, and a great deal of advice I never asked for. Thank you to Tony for curling up in a foetal position on my dining room floor to help me work out how to get a body into a freezer. To John Hunter for writing companionship and *kaiju*-vs chats. To Callum and Terry for the occasional use of their kitchen table. And to The Circle, who are far more insidious than their fictional counterparts – you know who you are.

Finally, the biggest thanks of all to the booksellers, the bloggers and the readers. I love hearing from you via my website/Twitter/Instagram, etc. This is what it's all about. Thanks for listening and getting it.